FEB 2013

P9-DOF-023

Hostile Shores

Also by Dewey Lambdin

Hostile Shores

Shores

An Alan Lewrie Naval Adventure

Dewey Lambdin

THOMAS DUNNE BOOKS

ST. MARTIN'S PRESS

NEW YORK

THOMAS DUNNE BOOKS.
An imprint of St. Martin's Press.

HOSTILE SHORES. Copyright © 2013 by Dewey Lambdin. All rights reserved. Printed in the United States of America. For information, address St. Martin's Press, 175 Fifth Avenue, New York, N.Y. 10010.

www.thomasdunnebooks.com
www.stmartins.com

Maps copyright © 2013 by Cameron Macleod Jones

ISBN 978-0-312-59572-2 (hardcover)
ISBN 978-1-250-02883-9 (e-book)

St. Martin's Press books may be purchased for educational, business, or promotional use. For information on bulk purchases, please contact Macmillan Corporate and Premium Sales Department at 1-800-221-7945 extension 5442 or write specialmarkets@macmillan.com.

First Edition: February 2013

10 9 8 7 6 5 4 3 2 1

Once more, to my father,
Dewey W. Lambdin, Lt. Cmdr., USN

Full-Rigged Ship: Starboard (right) side view

1. Mizen Topgallant
2. Mizen Topsail
3. Spanker
4. Main Royal
5. Main Topgallant
6. Mizen T'gallant Staysail
7. Main Topsail
8. Main Course
9. Main T'gallant Staysail
10. Middle Staysail

11. Main Topmast Staysail
12. Fore Royal
13. Fore Topgallant
14. Fore Topsail
15. Fore Course
16. Fore Topmast Staysail
17. Inner Jib
18. Outer Flying Jib
19. Spritsail

A. Taffrail & Lanterns
B. Stern & Quarter-galleries
C. Poop Deck/Great Cabins Under
D. Rudder & Transom Post
E. Quarterdeck
F. Mizen Chains & Stays
G. Main Chains & Stays
H. Boarding Battens/Entry Port
I. Cargo Loading Skids
J. Shrouds & Ratlines
K. Fore Chains & Stays

L. Waist
M. Gripe & Cutwater
N. Figurehead & Beakhead Rails
O. Bow Sprit
P. Jib Boom
Q. Foc's'le & Anchor Cat-heads
R. Cro'jack Yard (no sail fitted)
S. Top Platforms
T. Cross-Trees
U. Spanker Gaff

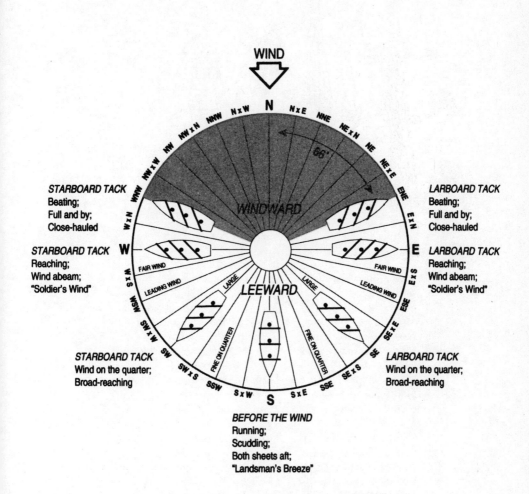

WIND

STARBOARD TACK
Beating;
Full and by;
Close-hauled

STARBOARD TACK
Reaching;
Wind abeam;
"Soldier's Wind"

STARBOARD TACK
Wind on the quarter;
Broad-reaching

LARBOARD TACK
Beating;
Full and by;
Close-hauled

LARBOARD TACK
Reaching;
Wind abeam;
"Soldier's Wind"

LARBOARD TACK
Wind on the quarter;
Broad-reaching

BEFORE THE WIND
Running;
Scudding;
Both sheets aft;
"Landsman's Breeze"

POINTS OF SAIL AND 32-POINT WIND-ROSE

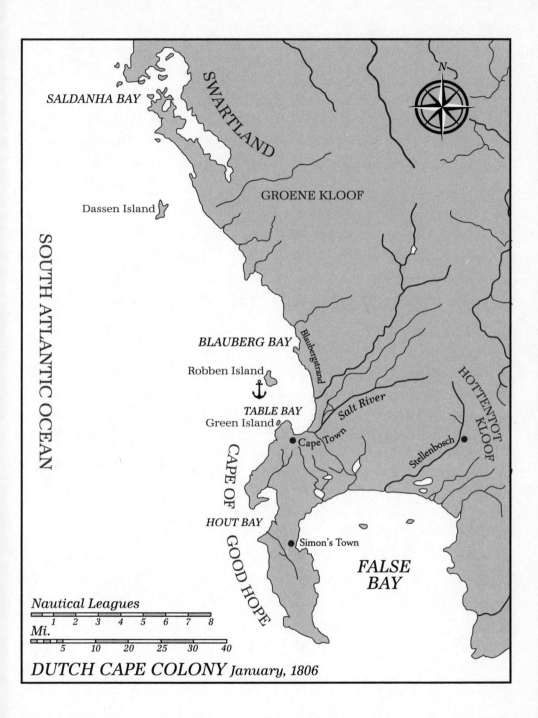

SOUTH ATLANTIC OCEAN

SALDANHA BAY

SWARTLAND

GROENE KLOOF

Dassen Island

BLAUBERG BAY

Blaubergsstrand

Robben Island

Salt River

HOTTENTOT KLOOF

TABLE BAY

Green Island

Cape Town

Stellenbosch

CAPE OF

HOUT BAY

GOOD HOPE

Simon's Town

FALSE BAY

N

Nautical Leagues

1 2 3 4 5 6 7 8

Mi.

5 10 20 25 30 40

DUTCH CAPE COLONY *January, 1806*

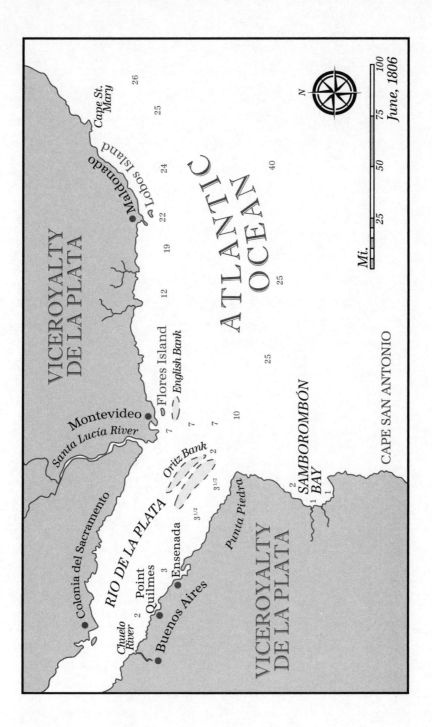

VICEROYALTY
DE LA PLATA

Cape St.
Mary

Maldonado

Lobos Island

26

25

24

22

19

12

ATLANTIC
OCEAN

40

25

Montevideo

Santa Lucía River

Flores Island

English Bank

7

7

7

10

25

25

SAMBOROMBÓN
BAY

2

1   1

CAPE SAN ANTONIO

Colonia del Sacramento

RIO DE LA PLATA

Oritz Bank

2

3½

3½

2

Punta Piedra

VICEROYALTY
DE LA PLATA

Point
Quilmes

Ensenada

3

Chuelo
River

2

Buenos Aires

N

Mi.

25   50   75   100

June, 1806

PROLOGUE

Then should the warlike Harry, like himself,
Assume the port of Mars, and at his heels,
Leash'd in like hounds, should famine, sword, and fire
Crouch for employment.
> -WILLIAM SHAKESPEARE,
> THE LIFE OF KING
> HENRY THE FIFTH,
> PRO., 5-8

CHAPTER ONE

A jaunt ashore would clear his head and provide a brief but welcome diversion from his new responsibility and worry, he was sure of it. It might even result in a dalliance with a young, bored, and attractive "grass widow", he most certainly hoped!

Captain Sir Alan Lewrie, Baronet (a title he still found quite un-believable and un-earned), left his frigate, HMS *Reliant,* round mid-morning to be rowed ashore in one of the twenty-five-foot cutters that had replaced his smaller gig, turned out in his best uniform, less the star and sash of his Knighthood in the Order of The Bath, an honour he also felt un-earned, scrubbed up fresh and sweet-smelling, shaved closely, and with fangs polished and breath freshened with a ginger-flavoured pastille. His ship was safely anchored in West Bay of Nassau Harbour, protected by the shore forts, and the weather appeared fine despite the fact that it was prime hurricane season in the Bahamas.

The man's a fool, Lewrie told himself; *an old "colt's tooth" more int'rested in wealth than in his young wife, so he deserves whatever he gets.*

The husband in question was in his early fifties, rich enough already, but was off for the better part of the month to the salt works on Grand

Turk, far to the South. He was also dull, bland, strict, and abstemious with few social graces, or so Lewrie had found him the two times they'd met at civilian doings ashore.

Captain Alan Lewrie, in contrast, was fourty-two, much slimmer at twelve stone, and had a full head of slightly curly mid-brown hair, bleached lighter at the sides where his hat did not shield it, and was reckoned merrily handsome and trim.

Lewrie had also been a widower for nigh three years, since the summer of 1802, and that fact would set the "chick-a-biddy" matrons to chirping in welcome, in hopes of "buttock-brokering" one of their semi-beautiful daughters off to someone with income and prospects. He was, in short, one reckoned a "catch", a naval hero.

Admittedly, despite the "heroic" part, Lewrie was also reckoned a *tad* infamous; he'd been the darling of Wilberforce, Hannah More, and the Abolitionists dedicated to the elimination of Negro slavery in the British Empire, and had stood trial in King's Bench in London for the liberation (some critics would say criminal theft!) of a dozen Black slaves on Jamaica to man his previous frigate, ravaged by Yellow Jack and dozens of hands short. In point of fact, Lewrie *was* against the enslavement of Negroes, or anyone else, but was not so foolish as to crow it to the rooftops, or turn boresome on the subject. His repute was titillating, but not so sordid or infamous that he did not make a fine house guest.

The lady in question . . . Lewrie recalled that she *seemed* amenable to his previous gallantries, and how she slyly pouted and rolled her eyes when her "lawful blanket" prosed on about something boresome, and how she rewarded Lewrie's teasing jollities, and a double *entendre* or two, with smiles, a twinkle in her eyes, and some languid come-hither flourishes of her fan.

Perhaps this would be the day to see if he would "get the leg over"! Such was becoming most needful, to do the "needful".

Lewrie felt a twinge of conscience (a wee'un) as he thought of Lydia Stangbourne, his . . . dare he call her his lady love? . . . far off in England. But, Lydia was thousands of miles and at least two months away at that moment, and both had agreed that their relationship was still "early days"; no promises had been made by either, no plighting of troths or exchanges of gifts of consequence. On their last night at the George Inn at Portsmouth before he'd taken *Reliant* to sea, she had laughed off the very idea of marrying him, or anyone else, again, after the bestial nature of her first husband, and the scandal which had plagued her after her Bill of Divorcement in Parliament had been made public. To all intents and purposes, Lewrie was a free man with . . . needs.

"*Hmmph,*" his Cox'n, Liam Desmond, grunted, interrupting Lewrie's lascivious musings. "Coulda sworn that brig sailed hours ago, sor . . . th' one with th' big white patch in her fore course? But, there she be, goin' like a coach and four."

"Aye, she did," Lewrie agreed, shifting about on the thwart on which he sat for a better look, and wishing for a telescope. The brig had put out a little after dawn, when Lewrie was on the quarterdeck to take the cool morning air as *Reliant*'s hands had holystoned and mopped the decks. "Did she not go full and by, up the Nor'east Providence Channel? Now, here she is, runnin' 'both sheets aft', bound West."

The weary-looking old trading brig was not two miles off the harbour entrance, and her large new patch of white canvas on her parchment-tan older fore course sail proved her identity.

"Is them *stuns'ls* she's flyin'?" Desmond asked in wonder.

As they watched, a small puff of dirty grey-white gun smoke blossomed on the brig's shoreward side, followed seconds later by the thin *yelp-thump* of a gun's discharge. The many local fishing boats out past the harbour entrance, off Hog Island, saw the shot and they began to put about, too, some headed West as if fleeing to the Berry Islands or Bimini, and some headed back into port in haste.

Oh, mine arse on a band-box, Lewrie thought with a chill in his innards; *It's the bloody French, come at last!*

Mere weeks before, after returning to a hero's welcome from a successful raid on a privateers' lair up the Saint Mary's River in Spanish Florida, disturbing rumours had come from further down the Antilles that a French squadron of several ships of the line under a Frog by name of Missiessy was raiding the West Indies. Even more worrisome was a letter that Lewrie had gotten from his youngest son, Hugh, who was serving as a Midshipman aboard a Third Rate 74 under one of Lewrie's old friends which confirmed the escape of Missiessy's squadron from the British blockade of French ports, and the news that an even larger part of the French Navy, a whole *fleet* under an Admiral Villeneuve, had left European waters, and that Vice-Admiral Lord Horatio Nelson was taking the whole Mediterranean Fleet, of which Hugh's ship was a part, in hot pursuit . . . also bound for the West Indies.

With the former Senior Officer Commanding in the Bahamas and his two-decker 64 accidentally run aground at Antigua, for which the fool was to be court-martialled (and good riddance to bad rubbish as far as Lewrie was concerned), the onus of defending the Bahamas had fallen to Lewrie, since his 38-gunned Fifth Rate frigate was the largest ship on station, and he was the only Post-Captain present on the scene. For that dubious honour, he was allowed to fly the inferior broad pendant, a red burgee that sported a large white ball, and style himself Commodore, even temporarily.

Unfortunately for him, the defence of the Bahamas was a task as gruelling as any of Hercules' Twelve Labours. Nassau and New Providence, the only island of much worth, the only decent-sized town, were lightly garrisoned, fit only to hold the forts which guarded the port, and besides Lewrie's frigate, there were only two or three brig-sloops and a dozen smaller sloops or cutters to patrol the long island chain.

Captain Francis Forrester, the unfortunate former Senior Officer Commanding (the idle, top-lofty, and fubsy gotch-gut swine!), had got it in his head that it would be the Spanish who would be the main threat, but Lewrie had laughed that to scorn, as had any one else with a lick of sense; the Dons were nigh-powerless any longer, with their few warships in the West Indies rotting at their moorings, blockaded by the Royal Navy. But, with the French out at sea, and nearby . . . perhaps storming down the Nor'east Providence Channel that very moment! . . .

Damn my eyes, Lewrie gloomed to himself, after a bleak glance round Nassau Harbour; *We may all be dead by supper time.*

He had precious-little with which to make a fight of it; his frigate, the 12-gun brigantine *Thorn,* but her main battery was made of short-ranged carronades, not long guns, and Lt. Darling would get his ship blown to kindling long before he could get in gun-range. There was Lt. Bury and his little *Lizard,* a two-masted Bermuda sloop that had only eight 6-pounders, and Lt. Lovett's weak *Firefly* in port. The larger brig-sloops, Commander Gilpin's *Delight* and Commander Ritchie's *Fulmar,* were patrolling the Abacos, and Acklins and Crooked Island, respectively.

We'll have to go game, Lewrie thought; *but go we will, even if it's hopeless. At least my will's in order.*

"Back to the ship, Desmond," Lewrie snapped. "Smartly, now!"

⚓

The cutter was not halfway back alongside *Reliant,* the boat's crew straining on the ears, when they almost collided with a fishing boat scuttling into port under lugs'l and jib, crewed by an old Free Black man and two wide-eyed youngsters as crew, all of whom were paying more attention aft than looking where they were going.

"'Vast there, ya blind bashtit!" stroke-oar Patrick Furfy yelled at them. "Sheer off!"

"Ya gon' fight dem Frenchies, sah?" one of the youngsters cried. "Law, dey gon' 'slave us all!"

"You *saw* them?" Lewrie snapped. "You *know* they're the French?"

"Nossah," the older fellow at the tiller shouted back, "but we got told by 'nother feller who got told by dat brig's mastah dat dere was a whole *fleet* o' warships comin' down de Prob'dence Channel, guns run out, an' mo' sails flyin' dan a flock o' gulls! Oh Law, oh Law, what gon' happen t'us'uns?" he further wailed, taking his hands off his tiller to actually wring them in fear.

"Pig-ignorant git," Cox'n Desmond snarled under his breath.

The next fishing boat fleeing astern of the cutter, headed for the shallows of East Bay and the dubious safety of Fort Montagu, told a different story; her crew swore it was the *Spanish* who were coming.

"That'll be the day!" Lewrie scoffed. "Maybe it's the Swedes, or the bloody Russians! It might be one of our—"

There was another boom, much louder and closer this time, for someone on the ramparts of Fort Fincastle, much higher uphill, must have spotted something out to sea, and had fired off an alert gun. At that, church bells began to ring in the town, summoning off-duty soldiers to their duties, and the townspeople to a panic.

Well, perhaps not *one of ours,* Lewrie silently conceded.

Lewrie's quick return to the ship stirred up an ants' hill of bother as he hurriedly clambered up the man-ropes and batten steps from the cutter to the entry-port, making the sketchiest salute to the flag and the quarter-deck as he did so, and waving off the Bosun, Mr. Sprague, and his silver call, and the hurriedly gathered side-party.

"Mister Eldridge," Lewrie directed the first Midshipman of the Harbour Watch he could see, "do you load and fire a nine-pounder as a signal gun, and hoist 'Captains Repair On Board,' along with a recall to our working-parties ashore."

"Aye aye, sir!" the mystified young fellow gawped.

Lieutenants Spendlove and Merriman had been aboard, napping in the wardroom, and were coming up from below in their shirtsleeves. The Marine Officer, Lt. Simcock, followed them, throwing on his red uniform coat, with his batman in trail with his sword and baldric, his hat and gorget to be donned later.

"It may be a rumour, it may be true, but there are reports of un-identified warships coming down the Nor'east Providence Channel, sirs," Lewrie quickly explained. "Just whose, we don't know, but there is good reason to suspect they might be French. Prepare the ship to weigh, and make sail. We'll have a quick palaver with the captains of *Thorn*, *Firefly*, and *Lizard*, and then we shall all sortie . . . God help us. The First Officer is ashore with the Purser?"

"Aye, sir, with the working-party," Lt. Spendlove said with an audible gulp. He was a Commission Sea Officer in His Majesty's Navy, and it was not done for him, or any of them, to show fear before the hands. Nor were they to express doubts, even if all of them thought that putting their little *ad hoc* squadron, chosen months before for shoal-draught work close inshore against lightly armed enemy privateers, would stand no chance against a French squadron, even if that squadron was made up of *corvettes* and lighter-armed frigates. They were facing the grim prospect of certain death, dismemberment, wounding, or capture. Even pride, honour, and glory had a hard time coping with that.

The cutter had been led astern for towing, and the boat's crew had come on deck, and Lewrie turned to face them.

"Desmond, I'd admire did ye and the lads strip my cabins for action, and whistle up my steward, Pettus, so he can see the beasts to the orlop," Lewrie bade. "And, he's to fetch me my everyday sword and a brace o' pistols."

"Aye, sor," Desmond said, though pausing for a bit before obeying the order. "Ya wish th' ship's boats set free for a better turn o' speed, too, sor?" Desmond asked in a softer voice.

"No," Lewrie grimly decided. "We may need them, later."

For the survivors should the ship go down, was left unsaid.

"Clear for action, now, sir?" Lt. Merriman, usually their jolliest, formally intoned.

"Aye, that'd be best," Lewrie told him. "Let's get the gun-deck cleared o' chests, sea bags, and mess-tables, first, but we'll not beat to Quarters 'til we've made our offing," Lewrie ordered as he stripped off his best coat and hat. Fortunately, beguiling young women required his best silk stockings and shirt. Silk was better than linen, cotton, or wool for battle; it could be drawn from wounds much more easily, reducing the risk of sepsis or gangrene.

Bisquit, the perk-eared ship's dog, had been prancing round them for attention and "pets", making wee whines in confusion as to why he was being ignored. The dog could grin quite easily, but he was not now.

Lewrie went to the quarterdeck as Pettus emerged from the door to his great-cabins on the weather deck, followed by the younger cabin-servant, Jessop. Jessop had Lewrie's cats, Toulon and Chalky, in the wicker travel cage, headed for the main ladderway down the hatch for the orlop, the usual place of shelter below the waterline. He gave a whistle and made "Chom'ere" sounds to Bisquit, took him by the collar, and led him below, too.

"Your plain coat, hat, and weapons, sir," Bettus said as he took the finery and handed over the wanted items, helping Lewrie put on his coat, and belting Lewrie's hanger round his waist. The hundred-guinea presentation sword would go below to the orlop, with the cats.

One of the starboard 9-pounders erupted, echoing that first warning gun from Fort Fincastle, and the quarterdeck was briefly fogged with a sour-smelling pall of spent powder smoke. Lewrie looked aloft to see his ordered signals flying two-blocked to the starboard halliards. He turned to look at his frigate's consorts and noted that each had hoisted the same signal in sign that they had seen it and were obeying. Gigs or jolly boats were putting out from all three of the smaller ships, bearing their commanding officers to *Reliant* for a quick conference before they sortied.

And just what'll I order them t'do? Lewrie pondered as *Reliant* thundered to sounds of shoes and horny bare feet as the gun-deck was cleared, as the wardroom was stripped bare, and all the canvas-and-deal partitions which gave a semblance of privacy came down to be piled like unwanted stage scenery and sent below out of the way. From great-cabins aft to the break of the forecastle, the gun-deck would become a single long space, broken only by guns and gun-carriages, the carling posts, and sailors.

The Ship's Purser, Mr. Cadbury, was coming alongside with one of

the thirty-two-foot barges that Lewrie had borrowed from HM Dockyard better than a year before for experimental work in the English Channel and had conveniently forgotten to return. In addition to the barge's
oarsmen, helmsman, and Midshipman Munsell were the hands in the
working-party who would have loaded supplies into it.

"Mister Cadbury!" Lewrie shouted down to the boat even before it
was hooked on to the main chains with a gaff. "Do you release the men of
the working-party, but use the boat's crew to strip the forecastle manger
of beasts, and stow 'em in the barge. We'll tow 'em astern, 'stead o' tossin'
'em overboard."

"Well, aye aye, sir, but . . . ," Cadbury replied, looking stunned.

"There's a fight in the offing, Mister Cadbury, and there's no reason
for the pigs and goats to be shot to pieces, or drown!" Lewrie told him
with hard-summoned false good humour.

"I see, sir," Cadbury said, much sobered and subdued.

"Lieutenant Westcott is coming?" Lewrie asked the Purser.

"I'm sure he is, sir, though . . ." Cadbury shrugged and turned to look
shoreward for the second barge.

Coming! Lewrie told himself with an audible snort; *I'm bound that he*
has, *the once at least.*

Besides himself in his younger days, Lieutenant Geoffrey Westcott
was as mad for strange and lovely "quim" as any man ever he did see, and
after better than two years in active commission, so did every Man Jack
in *Reliant*'s crew! His harsh hatchet face and alarmingly fierce and brief
smiles to the contrary, Westcott always seemed to find himself a bit of
"fresh mutton", was he set down on a desert isle, and the sailors were
right proud of him for it!

Aha! Lewrie told himself as he spotted the second barge setting out
from the town docks; There's *our Lothario!* The set of Westcott's uniform
might be askew, but he was up and dressed, after a fashion, and standing
by Midshipman Rossyngton near the tiller, urging the oarsmen for more
effort.

Lewrie turned his attention closer aboard, to the gigs bearing Lieutenants Darling, Lovett, and Bury to the main-chains. He glanced at their
vessels, satisfied that *Thorn*, *Lizard*, and *Firefly* were being stripped down
for action, as well.

Before his junior officers ascended the man-ropes and battens in order of seniority, Lewrie could spare another glance shorewards to the fine houses at the top of the hill behind the fort and the government buildings, and let out a wistful sigh.

She might've refused me, anyway, he sadly thought.

CHAPTER TWO

*T*here's little I can tell you, gentlemen," Lewrie said to his junior officers as they stood round the dining table in his cabins to hold a quick conference. "There are reports of warships approaching, whose we don't know, or how many so far. We are it as far as a naval defence goes, so . . . we will up-anchor and stand out into the Nor'east Providence Channel. *Reliant* will lead, and draw their initial fire, should it come to that. Lovett, Bury . . . you must pair together with your six-pounders and get *Thorn* into range where her carronades might have some effect. After that, you must stay together as a pair, and double on another target . . . one that looks beat-able."

It was a grim crowd, with pursed lips and dark scowls once he told them that. Lt. Oliver Lovett of *Firefly,* a slim, dark, and piratical-looking fellow, game for anything, usually. Lt. Tristan Bury, their scholar and marine artist, who had surprised them all with his daring and energy, looked pale and stiffly prim. Merry Lt. Peter Darling of *Thorn* slowly nodded his head, his round face flushed.

"Of course, if the foe is come in substantial strength, with large frigates and two-deckers, then all bets are off," Lewrie went on. "Then, discretion may be the better part of valour, and the best we may do will be to return to the harbour entrance and anchor athwart it, delaying their entry to the last of our shot and powder."

"If they do plan to land troops as well, sir," the young but sage Lt. Bury said in cold logic, "might I or Lovett be allowed free rein to cover the shoal waters and beaches West of Fort Fincastle, to take their small boats under fire? *Reliant* and *Thorn* can block the entrance channel with eighteen-pounder long guns and carronades for a goodly time."

"Hmmm . . . ," Lewrie pondered, then shook his head. "I fear that your presence may block the fire from Fort Fincastle's guns, which are already sited to cover those beaches. Best we stick together to the end."

"If they do bring troop ships, sir, why not have a go at 'em?" Lt. Lovett said with a chuckle, and a feral look on his long Cornish face. "If we could get round, or past, the escorts, we could make a *very* bloody *meal* of 'em! What say to that, hey?"

"Damned good idea, Lovett!" Lt. Darling congratulated him, with a hearty thump on the shoulder. "Kick them in their 'nut-megs', while they expect us to box them toe-to-toe!"

"A forlorn hope," Lt. Bury intoned most gravely, as was his wont. "I believe that is what the Army terms such fights. But . . ." For once, Bury smiled, adding, "such battles win undying glory for the participants, and gild their honour forever."

Mad as hatters, the lot of 'em, Lewrie thought, but feeling a pride in their courage.

"Very well," Lewrie instructed. "If there are transports, and I see a chance to get at them, I will hoist the 'General Chase'. If we face ships against which it appears we stand a chance, I will make 'Engage The Enemy More Closely'.

"If, however, we are hopelessly out-matched," he went on with a shrug, "and the best we could do would be to deny them entrance to the harbour, *Reliant* will hoist—"

"How about the 'Church' flag, sir?" Lt. Darling puckishly japed, making them all bray with gallows humour, and amazing Lewrie, again.

" 'Church' it is, then," Lewrie allowed. "Gentlemen, my steward left no glasses, but I do have a decanter of aged American corn whisky. Let's pass it round t'larboard like we do the port, and take a bit of liquid cheer."

"Most welcome, sir!" Lovett roared his approval.

"And, if this is the last time we may stand together in this life," Lewrie concluded, "let me just say that I have never served with a group of officers more energetic, more daring and skillful, and full of courage."

"Hear him, hear him!" Darling crowed.

Lewrie took a gulp from the decanter, savouring the whisky as it burned its way down to his gullet, telling himself that there was no spirit to match aged corn whisky. He liked the look of it in a glass, its smoothness on the palate, even its slightly sweet aroma. He passed the decanter on to Lovett, who glugged down a good measure. Darling was next, and he grimaced when the whisky's bite reached his throat. Bury took the decanter, but paused.

"Gentlemen, recall when first our little squadron was formed, and we first dined together," Bury stiffly said. "I give you the toast we made then. 'Here's to us, none like us, a bold band of English sea-rovers!'"

Bury took his drink then as the rest loudly echoed their agreement with his sentiment.

"Now, let us prepare our ships for sea," Lewrie ordered as he got the decanter back. "Up-anchor and make sail, quick as you can, and follow me out in line-astern."

They shook hands, then departed. Lewrie lingered in the great-cabins for a moment, looking round at how bare it appeared with only the painted black-and-white deck chequer canvas nailed to the planks, and the 18-pounders resting on their carriages, un-manned so far. Even the pillows and padded seats of the transom settee had been sent below for safekeeping, and he wondered if he would ever see his cabins set up properly, again . . . if anyone aboard *Reliant* would.

He took another gulp of whisky, then went on deck, carrying the decanter to the quarterdeck, popping the stopper into place.

"Take it down, sir?" Bosun Sprague asked at the foot of the larboard ladderway.

"Aye, Mister Sprague," Lewrie agreed, and the last deal-and-canvas partitions were taken down, the dining table was collapsed and put to one side, and the great-cabins were now open to the weather deck, just an extension to the rows of guns to either beam.

Lewrie stowed the decanter in the compass binnacle cabinet forward of the double-wheel helm, nodded to the two Quartermasters' Mates already manning the helm, noting their avid interest in where liquour would be if no one noticed them pilfering, and walked over to Lieutenant Westcott.

"All's in order, sir," Westcott crisply reported, raising one hand to knuckle his cocked hat in salute. "Hands are ready for 'Stations To Weigh' and make sail."

"Hands to the capstans, then, Mister Westcott," Lewrie ordered.

"Bosun!" Westcott bellowed. "Pipe hands to weigh anchors!"

"And God help us all," Lt. Westcott muttered to himself.

Even with the best will in the world, getting a ship under way took time; time to nip a messenger line to the thigh-thick anchor cable, wrap the messenger round the capstan, place sailors round it to breast to the capstan bars, and haul in the heavy cable, with more hands to lead the in-board end of the cable down below to the tiers where it would be stowed, where it could drip seawater and spread its accumulated mud and gritty bottom sand, and reek of dead fish and tidal flat miasma. The ship would be hauled in to "short stays", increasing the angle of the cable through the hawsehole, where the strain would be heaviest, and the hands had to dig their toes in and grunt the vessel the last few yards 'til the cable was "up and down". Then came the order for the "heavy haul" to break the anchor's flukes, and its weight, free of the bottom. Up it would come, at last, streaming muck, to be "fished" round a fluke or cross-bar to draw the anchor horizontal, so it could be "rung up" and "catted" to the stout out-jutting timber of the cathead, and the now-empty hawseholes be fitted with "bucklers" to plug the possible in-rush of seawater in heavy seas.

As the cable came "up and down", more sailors, young and spry topmen, would be piped aloft to make sail, to scramble up the shrouds and rat-lines of each mast to the top platforms and beyond to the cross-trees where they would trice up and lay out along the yards, balancing on the precarious, swaying foot-ropes with their arms locked over the yards, where they would remove the harbour gaskets and let the canvas fall. Yards were hoisted off their rests while the topmen were aloft, clews hauled to draw down the bottoms of the sails, and even more men on deck manned the yard braces to angle them to the wind.

In all, it took the better part of an hour for *Reliant* to make sail and begin to ghost across the waters of Nassau Harbour, heading for the entrance channel, with the three smaller warships following in her scant wake.

As the sheets, halliards, jeers, and braces were belayed, then stowed in loops over the pin-rails or fife rails, or coiled on the sail-tending gang-ways, Marine Lieutenant Simcock called for the ship's musicians, his fifer and drummer and a pair of fiddlers, to hoist the men a tune. He did not call for his favourite, "The Bowld Soldier Boy", which accompanied the rum cask on deck when "Clear Decks And Up Spirits" was piped, but "Spanish Ladies", and he requested a rousing lilt.

To watchers ashore who had not yet fled inland or to "Overhill" be-hind the town, to the soldiers and gunners who stood their posts upon Fort Fincastle's ramparts, their little squadron made a brave but desper-ate show. Fresh and bright Union flags fluttered in the wind from every stern gaff or spanker, and larger ones flew from the foremast trucks of the smaller warships, and from *Reliant*'s main mast tip. The long red-white-blue commissioning pendants stood out like slowly curling snakes.

The thin, bracing tune reached shore, almost lost in the rustle of sails and trees along Bay Street. A private gunner who served one of the heavy 32-pounders in a lower embrasure of the fort put his head out the stone port to cock an ear, and savour a faint snatch of cooling breeze. "Gawd 'elp 'em, Corp," he said to his gun captain.

"Aye, them poor bastards ain't got a 'ope in 'Ell," the Corporal sadly agreed, and spat tobacco juice into the swab-water tub.

CHAPTER THREE

*T*he prevailing wind was nearly from the Nor'east, forcing the squadron to stand Nor'west for a time 'til they made a goodly offing, then altered course Sou'east, tacking in succession to larboard tack for a short board to make progress Easterly.

Good Christ! Lewrie thought when he got his first look seaward, clear of Hog Island by two miles or more; *If it ain't a whole fleet, it'll do a fair impression o' one.*

The un-identified ships were almost hull-up above the horizon already, no more than six miles to windward, and even at a leisurely pace under reduced sail could be off the harbour entrance in no more than two hours.

"Time to beat to Quarters, Mister Westcott," Lewrie said as he dug into a side pocket of his coat for the keys to the arms chests. "I will be aloft for a bit."

Lewrie slung a day-glass over his shoulder and climbed atop a gun-carriage to the top of the larboard bulwarks, then up the mizen mast's windward shrouds to as far as the cat-harpings below the fighting top. Looping a steadying arm through the stays, he brought the telescope to his eye and felt even less hope than he had evinced at his quick conference with his officers. From his higher perch, he could make out at least

seven distinct sets of sails, all of them of three masts. The three leading
the line-ahead formation seemed to be one-decked ships, which he judged to
be frigates. Astern, though . . .

Oh, mine arse, he groaned to himself; *Those two aft o' those frigates are*
two-deckers! *Seventy-four-gunned Third Rates? Two more astern o' them,
they look t'be . . . three-masted sloops of war? What the Frogs call* corvettes?

If they were lighter ships, from his own Navy, by this time of the war
they would be two-masted brig-sloops, below the Rates, with fewer
than twenty guns. But French warships below the Rates would be three-
masted, still.

We're going t'get massacred, he mourned as he shoved the tubes of the
telescope shut, re-slung it, and began a slow and cautious descent to the
quarterdeck.

"Deck, there!" a main mast lookout shouted down from the cross-
trees "Th' count is seven sail! Seven sail!"

"Rather a lot," Lt. Westcott softly commented.

"Two of 'em are two-deckers, t'boot," Lewrie muttered to him. "What
looks t'be three frigates in the lead. Hmmm. Unless the pair astern are
transports. *Might* be better odds. But, I don't see how we could get at them
if they are . . . not past three frigates and two Third Rates. Unless . . ."

For pity's sake, think *o' something, ye damned half-wit,* Lewrie chid
himself.

"Ahem, sir," the Sailing Master, Mr. Caldwell, interrupted, "but we
are standing in toward shoal waters, and should come about to starboard
tack to make a long board."

"Aye, Mister Caldwell," Lewrie replied with a jerk of his head, impatient to be interrupted whilst he was scheming for some way to go game
and hurt the foe, even a little. "Mister Munsell?" he called to the Midshipman standing aft with the Afterguard and the signalmen. "Do you hoist
'Tack In Succession.'"

"Aye, sir!"

"Ah!" Lewrie exclaimed as one idea did come to him. "The wind is
more Nor'east by East, Mister Caldwell?"

"Aye, sir, it is," Caldwell agreed.

"And our new course would put us on North by West, beating to
windward, until—" Lewrie hustled over to the binnacle cabinet, where a
chart was pinned to the traverse board for quick reference. "We've bags
of sea-room all the way to Grand Bahama, so . . . do we stand on for a

good while, then come back to larboard tack when the enemy squadron is no more than a mile or two to windward of us, we will cross their hawses at almost right angles, perhaps close enough to serve them one or two broadsides. Bow-rake the *lead* ship, at any rate, before wearing alee, and returning to the starboard tack to do it again, before we are overwhelmed . . . or have to cut and run to block the entrance to the harbour, at last. If we can't fight 'em on equal terms, then at least we can bloody their noses and let 'em know they're in for a hard fight!"

"Maybe we should release the weaker ships now, sir," Wescott suggested in a whisper, leaning his head close to Lewrie's. "We are the only ship that can engage them with our eighteen-pounders, whilst *Lizard*'s and *Firefly*'s six-pounders would have no effect beyond one cable. As for *Thorn*'s carronades, well . . . to get them in close enough to do *any* damage, those lead frigates could just bull on and pass through our line. Simply brush them aside like toy boats."

"I know it's hopeless, but we have to *try*," Lewrie bleakly said in response, hands folded in the small of his back, and his eyes upon the toes of his boots. "Perhaps at two cables' range. That's still cuttin' it *damned* fine, but perhaps they don't know that *Thorn* only has carronades, and will take the blasts as *long* eighteens. Just one good broadside from everyone, and then we'll put about."

"Very good, sir," Lt. Westcott replied, his harsh face fixed in stone. There was nothing else he could say that would not be deemed an expression of cowardice in the face of the enemy, or insubordination to a captain's legal order . . . no matter how suicidal.

"Sorry I ruined your morning's pleasure, Mister Westcott," Alan Lewrie whispered with a faint sketch of a smile. "And, all this."

"Ah, but you didn't, sir," Westcott brightened, his grin flashing a brief show of white teeth. "The alert gun came after the first two main bouts, and only interrupted a second breakfast. One hopes that *you* at least got to grips, as it were—"

"Never even put a foot ashore, no," Lewrie rued. "But then, I do admit that you were always quicker off the mark."

Lucky bloody bastard! Lewrie thought in envy; *He'll go to his Maker, or Hell, much eased, whilst I've been without so long, there's semen squirtin' from my ears do I sneeze!*

⚓

The squadron stood on North by West for a good quarter hour as the strange ships continued up the Northeast Providence Channel, still with no flags flying to identify themselves.

Lewrie paced and fretted, going from the windward bulwarks to the binnacle cabinet and the chart every two or three minutes, guessing how fast that squadron was advancing, and calling for casts of the chip-log to determine his own squadron's pace. At last . . .

"Mister Westcott, prepare to wear about," Lewrie announced. To Midshipman Munsell, who still attended to the signals right aft by the flag lockers and halliards, he ordered, "Hoist a signal to the others for them to 'Wear To Larboard Tack In Succession', new course will be Sou'east. Once we're about, Mister Munsell, you will hoist 'Form Line Of Battle'."

"Aye aye, sir."

Damme, but it's smartly done, at least, Lewrie could proudly tell himself after *Reliant* had swung away off the wind and had rounded up to the wind in a long arc to counter-march down past the rest of the squadron, which was still standing on on the opposite tack. They were one cable apart, as neatly spaced as beads on a string. Lewrie could watch as *Thorn* reached the large disturbed white patch of foam where *Reliant* had begun her wheel-about, and began her wear leeward. A minute later and it was *Lizard* which put about, and *Thorn* was dead-astern of Lewrie's frigate, her up-thrust jib-boom a cable behind *Reliant*'s transom. It was a manoeuvre as well executed as a parade by the Brigade of Guards in London.

The signal halliards had been cleared when the first hoist was struck, the signal for the "Execute" to begin the counter-march. Now, the light blocks squealed as the briefer order for "Form Line Of Battle" was sent soaring up to be two-blocked and lashed securely in place.

"First charges up!" Lt. Spendlove called on the weather deck, summoning ship's boys to come forward from their crouches with their leather or wood cartridge cases. "Load cartridge!" and the rammer-men shoved the flannel powder charges into the opened muzzles of the great-guns and carronades, then rammed them down to the bases of the gun tubes. "Load with shot! Shot your guns!"

Lewrie went to the windward bulwarks, now the larboard side, and raised his telescope, willing himself not to let his hands shake in dread. The ship's people on the quarterdeck were looking to him for steadiness; the sailors on the gangways and the gunners in the waist, the men aloft in the fighting tops who would tend the sails and repair damage to the yards and running rigging, and the Marines in the tops with their swivels and muskets, would all be looking to him.

The frigate seemed to roar as the weather guns were run out to the port-sills, and the gun-ports were lowered to create a chequer down the ship's hull stripe. "Prick cartridge!" Lt. Spendlove was crying, followed by "Prime your guns, and stand ready!"

Damme, I should've waited a bit more! Lewrie chid himself, for his squadron would cross the course of that strange squadron at better than *three* cables, hopelessly beyond the best range for his lighter ships. Only *Reliant* could hit the leading frigate.

"Deck, there!" a main mast lookout screeched. "They're hoistin' *British* colours!"

Has t'be a ruse, damn 'em! Lewrie furiously thought, though he could see the Union flags for himself with his glass.

"The flagship makes her number, sir!" Midshipman Munsell cried from halfway up the weather mizen shrouds. "And, she shows a private signal!"

"Then get *down* from there and look it *up,* young sir!" Lewrie barked, totally befuddled. Munsell scrambled down and dug into one of the flag lockers for the books of private codes that were changed monthly. "Well?" Lewrie prompted again.

"Ah . . . she's the *Athenian,* sixty-four, sir," Munsell hesitantly related, shuffling from one book to the other, "and her private signal is for us to make our number to her!"

"Well, just damn my eyes!" Lewrie snapped, slamming the tubes of his telescope shut with rising anger. "Do so, Mister Munsell."

Each ship of the Royal Navy, from wee one-masted cutters to the towering three-deckers of the First Rate, was assigned a number which would announce her identity, but did not list who commanded her. That would be found in *Steele's Original and Correct List,* and Lewrie did not imagine that Munsell had thought to include *Steele's* in his set of essentials; it was most likely below on the orlop.

"Very well, Mister Munsell," Lewrie grudgingly allowed. "Make our number to her. Mister Spendlove?" Lewrie cried down to the guns. "They appear to be British, so withdraw the priming quills for now, and un-ship the flintlock strikers."

"Aye aye, sir!" Spendlove replied, looking far more relieved by that revelation, as did the gunners, than steely English tars should.

"*Athenian* shows a fresh hoist, sir," Munsell reported. "It is . . . our number, and 'Captain Repair On Board'."

"Very well, Mister Munsell," Lewrie said, beginning to work up a wee "seethe" over how late this new senior officer had left things before showing his true colours. "Strike the hoist for 'Form Line Of Battle', and replace it with . . . the small ships' numbers, and 'Secure From Quarters' . . . followed by . . . 'Will Enter Harbour'. Let's send 'em back to port, before these new'uns get all the good anchorages."

"Aye, sir!"

"Mister Spendlove?" Lewrie shouted down from the hammock nettings at the forward break of the quarterdeck. "Run in your guns, draw shot and charges, and secure."

Lewrie turned to Westcott next, who stood by with a bemused expression on his face, rocking on the balls of his booted feet.

"Once we're Southeast of the squadron's line of sailing, we'll come about to close alee of the first two-decker's larboard side and I'll report aboard her. Have a cutter brought round from being towed astern, and alert Desmond and my boat crew."

"Aye, sir," Westcott said.

"Just damn and *blast* that bastard, whoever he is, for waitin' so late!" Lewrie fumed. "What the Devil did he think he was *playin'* at? Is this his lame idea of a grand *jape*? People could've gotten killed!"

I could've been killed, more to the point! Lewrie seethed to himself.

"I'm going t'give that clown a piece of my mind!" Lewrie declared, tugging his pistols from his coat pockets and looking round for Pettus or Jessop to take charge of them.

"I do note, though, sir," Lt. Westcott cautioned, "that he's flying a broad pendant . . . the senior plain red one."

"At this moment, I don't give a tinker's damn!" Lewrie spat.

CHAPTER FOUR

So, who the Devil's this Lewrie chap, Meadows?" the Commodore of the new-come squadron asked of his Flag-Captain, the officer actually in charge of HMS *Athenian*, as he idly watched the frigate take in her main course to match speeds with his flagship, about fifty yards off the larboard side.

"He's listed in *Steele's* as Sir Alan Lewrie, Baronet, sir," Captain Meadows told the Commodore, Captain Grierson.

"His fam'ly must be poor as church-mice, did they send their eldest to sea, hey?" Grierson scoffed in a lazy drawl. "What is the date of his Post-Captaincy?"

"The Spring of '97, sir," Meadows supplied.

"Ha! Good, then, I've two years' seniority over him, whoever he is," Grierson chortled.

"Beg pardon for the intrusion on a private conversation, sir, but I have some information of him," *Athenian*'s First Lieutenant, one fellow by name of Hayes, spoke up.

It was not as if Grierson's and Meadows's conversation was all that private, anyway, for Captain Grierson always spoke loudly, and Captain

Meadows had been half-deafened by cannonfire since his days as a Lieu-tenant; neither could *hold* a private conversation.

"Indeed, sir?" Grierson snapped, looking down his nose at the inter-loper as if a beggar had tugged at his sleeve for alms.

"Captain Lewrie is known in the Fleet as the 'Ram-Cat', sir," Hayes related as formally as he could; secretly, he did not care for their new Commodore. "For his choice of pets, and his repute for being aggressive. He is also known as 'Black Alan' Lewrie for opposing slavery, and liber-ating slaves from Jamaica to man his ship. He was tried for it, but acquit-ted. Wilberforce and his crowd are mad for him."

"Good God, Wilberforce!" Commodore Grierson spat in disgust, as did a great many of The Quality and men of business. "That *earnest* wee ass! He and his Kill-Joys, pah! They'll be outlawing drink and horse rac-ing, next! Anything else?"

"There *was* some face-to-face bother with Napoleon Bonaparte in Paris in 1802, sir," Hayes went on. "It's said that 'Boney' set some of his agents to kill him, but murdered Captain Lewrie's wife instead, so he's been a widower for some time, and . . . it is also said that he does not have the *most* discriminating taste in women. There was talk of a *divorced* lady. . . ."

"Perhaps his sobriquet of the 'Ram-Cat' is *not* about his pets," Captain Meadows slyly said in jest.

"That'll be enough, Mister Hayes," Commodore Grierson said as he waved a hand in dismissal. "I think I take his measure. And, in any in-stance, he will not be on-station much longer."

"Aye, sir," Lt. Hayes said, doffing his hat and bowing himself away. *Arrogant prick!* Hayes thought.

The Commodore, Captain Grierson, strolled aft to watch a cutter de-part the *Reliant* frigate's starboard main-chains and set out for *Athenian* under oars, steering to cross close under his ship's stern and end up along-side her starboard side, and the starboard entry-port, the port of honour. Grierson thought of requesting a telescope for a look at this Lewrie fel-low, but decided that that would be showing too keen an interest. He would wait 'til he was aboard.

Grierson was certain that he would not like him, already.

"Best coat and hat, sir?" Pettus enquired as Lewrie prepared to board his cutter.

"No, no time for the niceties," Lewrie decided. "A senior officer sends a summons, and it's better to obey instanter."

"I found *Athenian* in *Steele's,* sir," Midshipman Munsell said as Lewrie began to walk over to the starboard ladderway and the beginning of the sail-tending gangway, where the open entry-port and side-party awaited. "She was brought out of Ordinary in October of last year, and her captain is Donald McNaughton."

"Thankee, Mister Munsell," Lewrie told him with a brief grin and nod of confirmation. "A Scot, is he? Perhaps I'll be piped aboard with bagpipes, and be offered a sheep! Carry on."

He doffed his hat to the side-party, the crew, and the flag, and quickly descended to the cutter, where his normal boat crew, hands who had been with him in his retinue for years, waited with vertical oars. Once seated aft by Cox'n Liam Desmond by the tiller, the boat shoved off and began a smart and rapid row to the two-decker.

Lewrie looked up as his boat crossed the *Athenian*'s stern, and he was grudgingly impressed by her transom decoration. Her name board was royal blue, framed in expensive gilded wood scrollings, and wooden letters, also gilded, spelled out her name. To either side, there were representations of Grecian helmets, shields, and spears, also done with gilt paint over bas-relief. Much the same had been applied to all her quarter galleries and stern gallery, where a senior officer could sit with his feet up on the ornate railings in good weather and sip wine, or read in private.

This McNaughton fellow must be rich as Croesus! Lewrie thought.

The bow man hooked his gaff onto the main-chains, the oars were tossed, and Lewrie unsteadily stood and made his way to the gunn'l to reach out to the battens and man-ropes. The climb was a lot longer than on his frigate, though the two-decker's tumblehome was not as steep.

As the upright dog's vane of his cocked hat appeared above the lip of the entry-port, the bosuns' calls began a duet salute, Marines stamped and presented muskets, and sailors' hats were doffed high. Lewrie reached the top step of the entry-port and hauled himself in-board with a characteristic jerk and stamp, well clear of being dunked back overboard should *Athenian* do an unpredictable roll. He doffed his own hat to one and all, to the quarterdeck and flag.

"Welcome aboard, sir," a sun-bronzed and rough-featured Post-Captain said to him. "Allow me to name myself to you. . . . Meadows, the Flag-Captain of *Athenian.*"

"Lewrie, of the *Reliant* frigate, sir, and delighted to make your acquaintance," Lewrie replied with a smile. "Your Captain McNaughton is below, Captain Meadows?"

"Oh sir, I fear your *Steele's* is out of date," Meadows told him with a frown. "Captain McNaughton passed away some weeks back of some fever. Captain Henry Grierson now commands the squadron. If you follow me, sir? He awaits you on the quarterdeck."

That's never a good sign, Lewrie thought as he followed the man aft; *Whatever happened to something "wet" in the great-cabins? Christ, what a fashion-plate!*

Lewrie beheld an officer about one inch taller than his own five feet nine inches, a man whom women might find devilishly and rakishly handsome, but for a long beak of a nose, down which this Grierson peered at the new arrival. Grierson wore his best-dress uniform coat with all the gold lace and twin epaulets and buttons gleaming. Despite the warmth of the day, the coat was doubled over his chest, perhaps to show off the two vertical rows of nine buttons each side, and the expensive width of the lace edgings. There was an expensive and ornate watch fob hung below the waist of the coat, which was cut a bit higher than most. Grierson also wore snow-white breeches of the finest duck, breeches so white that they might never have seen tar, slush, or saltwater washes. The breeches were so snug that it appeared Grierson was *sewed* into them, or greased up beforehand. The shiny black boots were not Hessians like most officers wore, but more like top-boots minus the brown-leather upper band. And Grierson sported a fore-and-aft bicorne hat like a French general!

His neck-stock's starched and ironed, by God! Lewrie took note; *What a fop! Don't he know ye get dirty on ships?*

Conversely, Captain Henry Grierson did not much care for what he saw of Captain Lewrie, either. The plain coat and hat, with gold lace epaulets slowly turning green from exposure to salt airs, the slightly curved and plain-hilted hanger at his hip instead of a small-sword of value, combined with a silk shirt and fresh neck-stock seemed paradoxical. And the old style of that plain hat!

"Alan Lewrie, reporting aboard, sir," Lewrie said, doffing his hat once more, a few feet away from Grierson.

"Sir Alan, I presume," Grierson said in a drawl with one brow up as he doffed his own in carefully studied welcome.

"Only on good days, sir," Lewrie japed and grinned.

Grierson took note of the faint scar on Lewrie's cheek, paler than his dark tan, and wondered where it had come from. This Lewrie fellow, Grierson determined, was a rather handsome and well set up chap, handsome enough to raise his hackles when confronted by one who could be considered a rival in Society. If only this Lewrie would bear himself more gravely! Why, he appeared to be the unlikeliest "Merry Andrew", for all the repute that Lt. Hayes had imparted!

"My word, Captain Lewrie," Grierson said as he put his fore-and-aft bicorne back on, the front so low to his eyes that he just naturally had to cock his head back and look down his nose, "your welcome to the Bahamas was most war-like. One could conjure that you would have crossed my line and raked my leading frigates, ha ha!"

"Until you hoisted British colours, I would have, sir," Lewrie told him with a serious and level expression.

"With a lone frigate and three little cockleshells?" Grierson asked with a loud laugh. "Whatever did you think to accomplish?"

"The rumour was that you were a French squadron," Lewrie said with a shrug. "I was prepared to defend Nassau at all hazards, sir."

"If we *had* been French, you would have been swatted aside in a trice!" Grierson said with another dis-believing laugh, sweeping one arm to encompass his warships, and all their immense firepower.

"Well, we *might've* gotten in a blow or two, sir," Lewrie said in reply, irked at Grierson's dismissive airs, "but, we would have done our duty to the very last. It's what England expects."

Grierson clapped his hands into the small of his back and gave Lewrie a high-nosed glare, as if he'd never heard the like. Out of the corner of his eyes, Lewrie espied a Lieutenant standing nearby who allowed himself an approving nod, and turned to whisper "Ram-Cat" to Captain Meadows.

"Well, at any rate, such neck-or-nothing was not necessary, so all's well," Grierson concluded. "It would appear, Captain Meadows, that my little jest was mis-understood. Ah, well."

"So, sailing in and flying no colours was a jest, sir?" Lewrie asked with a brow up in sour surprise. "I must tell you, then, sir, that you ruined a day's fishing for a great many Free Blacks, and put the wind up the residents of Nassau and New Providence. In point of fact, there were one or two merchantmen who fled you, and sailed on Westerly. It was they who first spread the alarm.

"I'd imagine by now that they're halfway up the Nor'west Providence Channel, fleein' to some American port, with the news that a French invasion force has *taken* Nassau," Lewrie sternly pointed out, and admittedly took some joy in the doing. "Who knows how long before that news reaches our Ambassador in Washington, or the Admiral commanding the North American station at Halifax . . . or London?"

If Lewrie had whipped out a belaying pin and jabbed Grierson in the groin, the fellow could not have *looked* more stricken!

"Captain Lewrie," Grierson intoned after giving that a long thought, and re-gathering his aplomb, "I see that your frigate flies the inferior broad pendant. Did you take it upon yourself to promote yourself in Captain Forrester's absence?"

"I already had independent orders from Admiralty to sail for the Bahamas and form a small squadron in shoal-draught ships to hunt French and Spanish privateers along the coast of Spanish Florida and in neutral American waters, sir," Lewrie patiently explained, resenting Grierson's tone, and the accusation that he had broken out his broad pendant without authorisation. "By the time we returned to New Providence, after clearing out a nest of privateers up the Saint Mary's River, Captain Forrester had already departed, leaving me as the senior officer present. There *was* a promise from Antigua of re-enforcement, but I was not holdin' my breath waitin' for them."

And when are ye goin' t'offer me a glass o' wine, ye top-lofty bastard? Lewrie fumed to himself.

"*Who* made you such an offer?" Grierson demanded.

"That was the word that Commander Gilpin of the *Delight* brig brought me, when he and Commander Ritchie and *Fulmar* returned to the islands from Antigua, sir," Lewrie told him. "And, might I enquire, what has happened with Captain Forrester?"

Somethin' dire, I hope! Lewrie wolfishly thought.

"An old friend of yours, was he?" Grierson said, simpering.

"Not particularly, no, sir," Lewrie baldly admitted, grinning.

"His court-martial found him acquitted of the charge of endangering his vessel," Grierson related, "even though un-bending the cables from the anchors and buckling the hawseholes was thought premature. . . . On the greater charge of abandoning his responsibilities he was found guilty, and has been relieved of his command, with a letter of admonishment. He will be off to England on the next packet."

"Oh, poor fellow!" Lewrie exclaimed, his sarcasm so thick that everyone within earshot, familiar with the case, fought sniggers.

"*Mersey* will be in the dockyard at Antigua for months to patch her bottom, Captain Lewrie," Captain Meadows supplied, "and will then be assigned to another officer."

"And, most likely added to the strength of the Antigua Squadron, in place of *Athenian*," Commodore Grierson announced as if it was so.

"What of the French, then, sir?" Lewrie asked. "We've heard but rumours of Missiessy and Villeneuve."

"Missiessy had but a small squadron," Grierson informed him with a smirk, "and may be on his way back to France. There's been no word of him for weeks. As for Villeneuve and his large fleet, reports say that he made landfall at Martinique and Guadeloupe to land fresh troops for their defence. He's sailed from there, but has made no sign that he would move upon Jamaica or Antigua, or land a force to re-take the Black rebel colony of Haiti. As far as anyone may determine, his fleet has become a Will-o'-the-wisp, a ghost."

"So, it's long odds he might come here?" Lewrie further pressed, wondering why the Admiral commanding at Antigua had stripped himself of ships to defend the Bahamas if he still had cause to worry that his own "patch" might still be in danger.

"Before we were despatched, an *aviso* cutter from Admiral Lord Nelson came in to English Harbour, announcing that he and *his* fleet were near the Windwards in pursuit of Villeneuve," Grierson went on in a blasé manner, "so it may be that the French will pass *near* the Bahamas as they run back to European waters, but will pose no real threat. The French would fear to linger, ha ha!"

"So, you may not stay long?" Lewrie posed.

"Once the threat is well and truly over, I expect I'll have to give up my other sixty-four, and perhaps my frigates, but the Bahamas will be my responsibility 'til Admiralty decides to replace me," the new Commodore replied, rather archly, and nigh purring with pleasure.

Which means I'm redundant, Lewrie told himself; *Will he allow me to keep my wee squadron together? Or, are they all now his?*

"Well, sir, the fresh news which you've discovered to me is most reassuring, as is the presence of your squadron," Lewrie told Captain Grierson, nigh-blushing to "trowel it on", though feeling that he was eating a bowl of steaming turds. "Now that I don't have to sink you or force you to strike, might I take my leave and rejoin my ship?"

"Hmmm . . . well," Commodore Grierson paused as if considering his decision as gravely as a king contemplating a royal decree. "If we have nothing more to discuss at this moment, you may, Lewrie."

"Thank you, sir," Lewrie said, doffing his hat in parting.

"Mind, sir," Grierson added, "you and I must put our heads together later, to inform me of the particulars of the islands and of the other vessels which will be under my command. Once the social niceties have been held ashore, what?"

Christ, no wonder *he is dressed so well!* Lewrie thought; *He was lookin' forward to a hero's welcome and a grand ball!*

"But of course, sir. *Adieu,*" Lewrie said, bowing himself to the gang-way and the entry-port to make his departure.

Commodore Grierson doffed his bicorne briefly as Lewrie went down the battens and man-ropes to his boat, surer in his opinion of not liking him.

I could loathe *him,* Lewrie thought as he entered his boat.

CHAPTER FIVE

*L*et fall the main course and get the ship drivin', Mister Westcott!"
Lewrie called as soon as he got upon his own quarterdeck. "Get us into
port before one o' those new-comes take our anchorage!"

"Drive it will be, sir," Lt. Westcott agreed. "Bosun, set all to the royals! Topmen aloft! Trice up and lay out to make sail! Sheet home the main
course and shake out all reefs!"

"Not that it will do much good, sir," Mr. Caldwell the Sailing Master
laconically said. "Our hull is as weeded as the New Forest."

"What is Commodore McNaughton like, sir?" Westcott asked, once
the crew was at their tasks and sail was spreading.

"Dead as mutton, Mister Westcott," Lewrie said with a wry *moue*.
"His replacement is Captain Henry Grierson." A twitch of a corner of his
mouth spoke volumes to his First Lieutenant. "Does anyone know of
him?"

"The Griersons, sir?" Midshipman The Honourable Entwhistle spoke
up. "I know something of the family."

"Do tell then, Mister Entwhistle," Lewrie bade him.

Entwhistle's father was a Baron, so all of his brothers and sisters ('til
the girls married, of course) were entitled to be called "Honourable" except

for the eldest brother, who would inherit all and become the umpteenth Baron Entwhistle. Of *course* he and his family would know a bit about almost everybody. Entwhistle had entered HMS *Reliant* in April of 1803 a rangy eighteen-year-old, but was now a man grown, and an experienced senior Mid looking forward to standing for the oral examinations before a board of Post-Captains to gain promotion to Lieutenant.

"They are related to Sir Henry Dundas, sir, now Lord Melville," Entwhistle told him, "and I do believe that the Admiral commanding at Antigua is some sort of in-law to the Griersons."

"Damn! Dundas! That murderous fool!" Lewrie groaned.

When the war with France broke out in February of 1793, Sir Henry Dundas had been Prime Minister William Pitt's Secretary of State at War, and Dundas had been brim-full of schemes to fight the French, most of which involving invasions and expeditions to the East Indies to expel France from her last slim grip in India and in the China Trade. In the West Indies, the scheme was to conquer all French colonies that rivalled Great Britain in the lucrative exports from the Sugar Islands, monopolising sugar, molasses, and rum. Both of the Indies were deadly for Europeans, who had to endure Malaria or Yellow Fever during the hot seasons, along with Cholera and Dysentery and God only knew what else the rest of the year. All those hopeful expeditions had resulted in the deaths of over sixty thousand soldiers and sailors who had perished of disease, not battle or glorious conquests.

Dundas had become Henry, Viscount Melville, and had been named First Lord of the Admiralty in 1804, replacing stalwart and honest-to-his-bones Admiral John, Earl Saint Vincent, "Old Jarvy", who had waged a gallant but failed attempt to clean out the greed, venality, corruption, and speculating of Navy suppliers, contractors, the dockyards themselves, and even the Navy Board. Viscount Melville, though, who had been Treasurer of the Navy twice in his political career, knew where the side-profits were, and had come to be sneered at as "Lord Business As Usual" almost from the moment he took office.

Now, even though Viscount Melville's peculations and profits on the sly, and his turning of the blind eye to his fellow plunderers, had finally drawn official notice, resulting in his impeachment and replacement by Admiral Charles, Lord Barham, in this past May, there were too many who continued to hold high offices to sever Melville's influence. Indeed, there were many who wished that the promised trial in the House of Lords might result in an acquittal, and his glorious return!

"Place, patronage, and 'petti-coat' interest," Lewrie commented with a weary, jaded shake of his head. "All damned fine, so long as you're the recipient, of course. Even with Melville impeached, not a thing's changed. Investigators will be reportin' corruption and writin' reform policies 'til the turn of the *next* century!"

"Your pardons, sir," Midshipman Entwhistle said with an adult's firm grasp of reality, "but Old Jarvy's mistake was thinking that refined and educated gentlemen who hold high office are as honest as he is. As if corruption is a high tide that only goes up so far."

"Well said, Mister Entwhistle, damned well said," Lewrie agreed. Turning aft, he called to Midshipman Munsell. "D'ye still have your copy of *Steele's*, young sir?"

"Aye, sir, though it is at least two months out of date," the lad piped up. "Shall I look someone up for you, sir?"

"Aye."

A moment later, Munsell was reading an entry aloud. "'Captain Henry Grierson . . . made Post in June of 1795, Captain of the *Oxford*, seventy-four, May of 1803'."

"A neat trade," Lewrie groused. "Give up a seventy-four-gunned ship of the line for a lesser ship, but a broad pendant!"

He's, what, no older than his mid or late thirties? Lewrie wondered: *That's awfully young t'get a two-decker, 'less he's had a lot o' help up the ladder. Without makin' a name for himself that any of us ever heard of? Hmmm. There's* another *reason for me t'dislike him!*

"Ehm, *Athenian* is making a hoist, sir," Midshipman Munsell said as he put the old copy of *Steele's* back in the flag locker and took notice outboard. "It is . . . 'General' to all ships, and 'Make More Sail'," he deduced after a squint with a telescope and a quick referral to the signals book.

"It appears it'll be a race, Mister Westcott," Lewrie said.

"One we may lose, sir, given the foul condition of our 'quick-work'," Lt. Westcott told him. "Do you wish the stuns'ls rigged?"

Sailing off the wind as *Reliant* was, studding booms could be extended from the course and tops'l yardarms to bare more sail to the following wind, which might gain them a knot or more over the warships of Grierson's squadron, but . . .

"It's not that far to Hog Island and the main channel, Mister West-cott," Lewrie decided, shaking his head No. "We'd barely get 'em rigged and spread before we'd have t'take 'em in for entering port. I'd admire did you remove the larboard hawse buckler and bend a cable to the best bower, instead. Mister Caldwell? How close may we shave inshore of Hog Island?" he asked puckishly. "Closer to the entrance channel than *those* bastards?"

"Oh, I see what you wish, sir," Caldwell replied, spreading a grin on his usually stern face. "Do we alter course a point to larboard now, we should have more than sufficient depth."

Lewrie glanced at the chart which Caldwell showed him, then got his telescope from the binnacle cabinet rack and peered forward. He could see *Firefly,* Lt. Lovett's little 8-gunned sloop, abeam of the wind as she stood in to the entrance channel. Over the trees of Hog Island, he could make out the peaks of *Thorn*'s and *Lizard*'s masts, for they were already in port and rounding up into the wind to ghost to a stop, drop anchors, and pay off sufficient scope as their crews handed the last scraps of sail.

He did not need the glass to look over towards Grierson's leading frigates; they were a cable apart in line-ahead, all driving hard with white mustachios under their forefeet and cutwaters, and creamy wakes curling down their sides. But, the leading frigate was abaft of abeam to *Reliant,* and the second and third were off her starboard quarer. Most importantly, they were now at least two cables or better to *seaward* of his frigate!

Lewrie went to the starboard bulwarks and leaned far out for a look overside. He had to shake his head over the thickness and length of the weed strands that fouled *Reliant*'s bottom and waterline. Some broke off as he watched and swirled astern into the wide bridal train of wake, where sea birds by the hundreds swirled and mewed and dove to snag themselves a bite, or scoop up some of the green slime that flaked off in tasty wee morsels.

"Mister Westcott, when we're near the entrance channel, I wish the ship scandalised . . . Spanish reefs and Irish pendants . . . to take the speed off her. Topmen aloft as we do, to take in courses, royals and t'gallants. Prepare a cable to the kedge anchor, as well. We'll stand in somewhere near our old anchorage, bear up into the wind, then let her fall off Northerly before droppin' the kedge, then ghost on 'til the kedge bites. We'll let go the best bower then, and be abeam to the prevailin' breezes, and won't swing to impede Commodore Grierson's squadron when they enter port."

"And if his lead frigates out-foot us, sir?" Westcott asked with a smirk on his face.

"Then they'll put on a pretty show for the good folk o' Nassau," Lewrie told him. "The main thing about racin' the other fellow is to know when to slow *down*! We'll have the centre of the channel and will be the vessel with the right of way."

"Very well, sir," Lt. Westcott agreed, chuckling in anticipation. "All will be ready when you order us to alter course."

Reliant stood on under full sail, slowly losing the race to the entrance channel to the lead frigate of Grierson's long column of warships. She was two cables abeam of Lewrie's frigate as Hog Island receded and the channel began to spread out alee, revealing the town of Nassau. Almost dead-level and still showed no sign that she would reduce sail! Lewrie could see her captain looking aloft, at the channel as it neared, then astern to the flagship, which had yet to signal any change.

"Enough depth for us to alter course, Mister Caldwell?" Lewrie asked.

"Another minute more would suit, sir," Caldwell told him, busy with his sextant to measure the height of Fort Fincastle and some other prominent sea-marks to judge the distance. "There is nearly the end of Hog Island to larboard, and the channel 'twixt Arawak Cay and Long Cay . . . ah! I would round up now, sir!"

"Mister Westcott, alter course to larboard!" Lewrie snapped.

Round *Reliant* went, her jib-boom and bowsprit sweeping cross the cays and the town in a thunder of canvas as her courses, main and mizen tops'ls, and t'gallants and royals were reduced of a sudden, drawn up in their centres to leave the outer parts bagged and unable to draw the wind in untidy bat wings, leaving the fore tops'l, jibs, spanker, and stays'ls, the fore-and-aft sails, still standing to keep a way on her as she came about, rapidly shedding speed.

The channel led East-Sou'east, close to the prevailing winds before trending Sutherly into the main harbour inside the shelter of the various cays.

"Sheet home the mizen t'gallant once more, Mister Westcott," Lewrie ordered. "Let's keep steerage way on her." The Quartermaster's Mates on the helm were making large swings of the wheel to keep her on course. After the mizen t'gallant gained them a bit more wind, he looked at them again. "Better now, Cottle, Malin?"

"Aye, sir, 'at helped," Cottle replied.

"Lord, he'll miss the channel!" Midshipman Munsell crowed from right aft. Lewrie turned to watch, gloating to see the lead frigate match his tactic of scandalising his ship, but the second and third in line astern of her were forced to alter course to *seawards* to avoid a collision! They would miss the entrance channel altogether, and have to tack about under reduced sail to regain the entrance! Over the top of the low-lying spur of Hog Island, Lewrie could see *Athenian* and her consort, the other two-decker 64, altering course Northerly in succession to avoid being stacked up atop the three frigates!

"I think you might have just made yourself an enemy, sir," Lt. Westcott took a brief moment from his harrying duties to mutter.

"I have the feeling that I had, no matter what I did, Mister Westcott," Lewrie told him, chuckling. "Even did I yield him the entrance first, there's some people there's no living with."

Reliant was anchored by bow and stern, her squares'ls harbour-gasketed and all fore-and-aft canvas handed and stowed, and the Bosun Mr. Sprague and his Mate, Mr. Wheeler, had rowed round the ship to see the yards squared to mathematical perfection before *Athenian* groped a slow way into port behind her frigates.

The *Reliant*'s musicians were playing "The Bowld Soldier Boy" as the gilt-trimmed red rum cask was fetched on deck for a delayed issue. The hands waiting for their grog raised a cheer as the two 64s rounded up to drop anchor. On the quarterdeck, Lewrie was sprawled in his collapsible wood and canvas deck chair, with both of his cats in his lap, and the ship's mascot, Bisquit, dancing on his hind legs and barking a welcome of his own.

Lewrie tipped *Athenian* his cocked hat in salute.

It's the least I can do, Lewrie thought; *and the least is what I* intend t'do! *Along with gettin' my report on Grierson's wee "joke" to Admiralty,* first!

CHAPTER SIX

*L*ewrie had to wait two days before Commodore Grierson thought to summon him for that promised face-to-face meeting to brief the new-come upon the Bahamas, and the vessels and captains Grierson would inherit. The hoist of *Reliant*'s number and "Captain Repair On Board" caught Lewrie in casual clothing, again, in slop-trousers and buckled shoes, a plain coat, and his shirtsleeves as he, the Bosun, the Carpenter, and other petty officers made an inspection of the ship belowdecks. The summons also came after the islands' Governor-General's invitation to a welcoming ball ashore. Grierson had said that they would meet "once the social niceties had been held", so he was obviously wishing to get an oner-ous chore over with before shining at a grand supper dance, at which he hoped to be regaled.

"Welcome aboard, sir," *Athenian*'s First Officer, Lt. Hayes, said at the entry-port, once the salutes had been rendered.

"Good morning Lieutenant . . . ah?" Lewrie responded cheerily; he would not take out his sour mood over meeting with Grierson to extend to others. "I did not get your name, last time I was aboard."

"Hayes, sir," the fellow said, "and may I say that it is an honour to make even your slightest acquaintance, Captain Lewrie."

"I can't imagine *why*, but thankee, anyway, Mister Hayes," Lewrie replied with a dis-arming grin and a laugh. "It was kindly said."

"Why, your repute in the Navy, sir!" Hayes exclaimed. "Your successes."

"Oh, those," Lewrie shrugged off. "Uhm, may I ask why you are turned out in your best-dress? And, why does a Commission Officer be on deck in harbour?"

"Oh, that, sir," Lt. Hayes said, plucking at the snowy lapels of his uniform coat. "It is the Commodore's standing orders that we be dressed properly, else the hands might get Frenchified egalitarian ideas and breach the difference in class and station, sir. As for being on deck at all, the Commodore sent for me soon after his order was sent to you . . . so it would not be a mere Midshipman to meet you."

"Rather hard on the purse, wearin' yer best kit all the time, and what would ye have left for shore calls? The supper ball tonight, for instance. Ye wear yer best even at sea in gale weather?"

"The Commodore will allow us to dress down, are tarpaulins needed, sir," Hayes admitted sheepishly. "And, aye, it is hard for some of us to maintain proper appearances, all the time. The wardroom servants are busy, trying to put us right, and repair smudges and stains for the ball."

"Then I will see you there, Mister Hayes," Lewrie promised. "I must get aft, I suppose. If you will lead the way?"

Athenian, like all 64-gun two-deckers, provided ample room aft for a captain's great-cabins, and more than enough space to accommodate a squadron commodore . . . if the flag-captain didn't mind being turfed out and relegated to smaller quarters. Grierson's great-cabins were as large as Lewrie expected, right under the poop deck, and, without the presence of any upper-deck guns, looked large enough for an indoor tennis court. Not only did Grierson have a lot of "interest" in the Navy; it was obvious that he and his family had a substantial fortune, too, for the dining table would seat twelve round that gleaming cherry wood expanse, and the sideboard groaned under the weight of a palace's worth of sterling silver services. The same went for the day-cabin, which featured a substantial desk, wine cabinet, and seating arrangements, and none of the articles of furniture the usual collapsible and easily stowable type, either.

The door to the stern gallery was open, as were all the transom windows, to catch a morning breeze. Grierson needed one, for he was tricked out in his usual best, right down to silk stockings and soft slipper-type shoes. This morning, Grierson had at least unbuttoned his expensively gold-laced coat against the heat and humidity.

"Thank you, Hayes, you may go," Grierson said in an idle, languid voice. He had been standing in the open doorway to the stern gallery, a wine glass in one hand, and the other tucked in the small of his back as if posing, but turned and raised a brow when he saw Lewrie.

"Prompt, I must say, Sir Alan," Grierson said with a brief hint of a smile as he crossed to his desk and sat himself down in a leather-covered chair. He gestured to another in front of the desk for Lewrie. "Though I do note that you do not think much of dressing properly."

"I was in the cable tiers, the orlop stowage, and the carpenters' walks on an inspection when you signalled, sir," Lewrie told him. "No need for fancy dress there."

"A glass of something, sir?" Grierson offered. "Some Rhenish?"

"Tea for me, sir," Lewrie requested, turning to spot one of the cabin servants. "In a tall glass, with lemon and sugar, and let it set to cool, first, if ye will."

Commodore Grierson gave out a scoffing *harumph* at that request.

"It's my custom t'have a half-gallon brewed up each day and let cool, sir," Lewrie explained. "It's very refreshing in the tropics on warm-ish days. Even better with a sliver of Yankee Doodle ice, when it's available from an ice-house ashore."

"What an odd thing to do with tea," Grierson said, grinning. "Anyway, I suppose that you brought me the outline of the strength of my new squadron, Sir Alan?"

"Of course, sir," Lewrie said. "Though I must admit that some of the smaller sloops, cutters, and luggers are unfamiliar to me. I've never clapped eyes on 'em, nor met their captains, since I've spent so little time in port, and a great many of them are off far down the island chain, as far as the Turks and Caicos."

"Indeed," Grierson drawled with a dis-believing expression, as if to question his diligence during his temporary command of the Bahamas.

"You may not see many of them 'til they return to Nassau for wood and water, either, sir," Lewrie explained. "I can vouch for those I've worked with, but beyond them . . . ?" he ended with a shrug.

The brig-sloops *Delight* and *Fulmar* and their captains he could recommend, as well as the single-master cutter *Squirrel*. And of course, the
three others of his original squadron he could praise highly. The rest of
the vessels were simply names on a list.

"They stay quite busy, down-islands, sir," Lewrie told Grierson. "I do
not know if Captain Forrester put much effort into the enforcement of the
Navigation Acts, since there are so many American merchant ships who
come to trade. American goods are much prized here, and the town
merchants'd be upset did the trade be curtailed. Their goods are just as
well made as British, and cheaper, so . . ." That required one more puzzled shrug. "That will be up to your discretion, sir."

"Quite right it is," Grierson agreed, very sternly.

"And, one must keep an eye out for the wreckers and salvagers, too,
sir," Lewrie went on. "Perhaps, with at least two more of your brig-sloops
and thirty-two-gun frigates on station, they might be able to back up the
authority of your sloops and cutters, down-islands."

"Wreckers and salvagers?" Grierson asked.

"The island soils, and the acreage available, don't support the highest-
paying crops, sir," Lewrie further explained, warming to the subject.
"There's 'red lands' that *seem* fertile, the first season or two, but play out
without fertiliser, and the Bahamas don't have room for pastures, cattle
and sheep, and their dung. The 'white lands' are sandy, and are in need of
fertiliser, too, d'ye see. Now, some get by the Red Indian way, using small
fish planted the same time as the seed, but again, that doesn't support
payin' crops, mostly just subsistence farmin', so the down-islanders need
food imports, and the best way to pay for such is to . . . take advantage of
the odd shipwreck. Many of 'em had kin in the old pirate days, and they
will fall back upon the old ways, when needful.

"When I was here 'tween the wars in the old *Alacrity*, I'd put up bea-
cons and range-marks, and as soon as I'd sailed away, down they came,
the timbers got used t'build houses, and when I returned months later,
there was no sign they'd ever been there, and no one'd give me the time
o' day as to which of 'em did it," Lewrie said in sour reminiscence. "You'll
want t'keep a weather eye on that business, too, sir."

"Good God!" Grierson exclaimed. "Perhaps I should hang one or
two, to dissuade their criminal tendencies."

"Good luck on that, sir," Lewrie said, chuckling. "The courts hereabouts merely wink at cases like that . . . if ye can wake 'em up long

enough t'present one. Then, there's still the problem of French and Spanish privateers, and the coast of Spanish Florida. I've a mind to keep my squadron together and prowl over that way, t'keep the frogs and the Dons honest. And scare any more Americans from aidin' them."

"Well, now I . . . ," Grierson began, but the cabin servant had come with Lewrie's tea, now that it had cooled sufficiently.

"Most refreshin', thankee kindly," Lewrie told the servant after he had taken a sip. He turned back to Grierson. "We destroyed a rather clever cabal, d'ye see. An American company, the Tybee Roads Trading Company, was supplyin' the privateers out of Savannah, Georgia, providin' false registries for their prizes and passage crews t'sail them under American colours to Havana or a French island port, after takin' off a portion of the cargoes for sale in Savannah, or ship North as far as New York or Boston in their own bottoms, and bring back the profits in Tybee Roads ships to give to the privateers, less a substantial commission, of course."

"I am not sure that my brief extends quite *that* far, Sir Alan," Commodore Grierson said with a shake of his head. "You, as you said, held independent orders to conduct such operations, but mine are to defend and administer the Bahamas, what?"

"Well, you might at least send a frigate to prowl up the coast of Spanish Florida, now and again," Lewrie suggested, wishing that he could cross the fingers of his right hand for luck that such searches and intimidation might continue. "Just t'keep 'em lookin' over their shoulders, perhaps send someone to make a port call at Savannah, too, to see if the death of a Mister Edward Treadwell spelled the end of the Tybee Roads Company. Our Consul there, a Mister Hereford, is an ass, but he might know *something* of it."

"The man's dead, do you say?" Grierson asked, sounding bored.

"He was there in the Saint Mary's River, the morning of our raid, sir," Lewrie explained. "Caught red-handed, as it were. We were takin' fire from both sides of the river, the Spanish, and the neutral American . . . musket-fire, mostly . . . and he was fleein' up-river in one of his barges. He took a shot at us with a Pennsylvania rifle and had to stand up to load, and I shot him."

"You . . . with a musket?" Grierson spluttered, un-believing. "At what range?"

"About an hundred and fifty yards, sir. With one of Major Patrick Ferguson's breech-loadin' *rifled* muskets," Lewrie took a secret delight in relating. "A souvenir from the American Revolution that I got from my brothers-in-law who were officers in a Loyalist North Carolina regiment outfitted by their father with Fergusons.

"I hit Treadwell a bit lower than I meant," Lewrie went on with a grin, "just below the waist-band of his trousers 'stead of in his chest, but good enough for 'fatal'. He lived long enough t'tell me what he'd done with the passengers and crews off the prizes before he died . . . horribly."

"Aha, I see," Grierson commented, all but goggling at Lewrie.

"With Treadwell out of the business, there's sure t'be others who might be tempted, sir," Lewrie continued. "It was too profitable a scheme t'let pass. Even a slow cruise outside the Three Mile Limit but close enough t'show British colours might be enough to daunt any who might revive the scheme."

"I will *consider* that," Grierson warily allowed.

"If you do, sir, I cannot recommend Lieutenant Peter Darling of the *Thorn* brigantine, Lieutenant Tristan Bury of the *Lizard* sloop, Lieutenant Oliver Lovett of the *Firefly* sloop highly, enough. All three of 'em are as smart as paint, know the coasts and inlets like the backs of their hands by now, and are as eager t'get at the foe as so many starvin' tigers. During our service together, they've all acquired larger boats for the odd raid into the inlets, and behind the barrier islands. Of course, when we staged our amphibious raids; they had *Reliant*'s Marines to go with them, but their sailors are very familiar with the work, and can pull them off."

"Hmmm . . . I perhaps could spare some smaller vessels, now and again," Grierson uncomfortably allowed, frowning. He called for his servant to fetch him a fresh glass of wine. "Such duties would be a nice change of pace for some of the sloops and cutters relegated so far to drearier chores, down-island."

"Begging your pardon, sir," Lewrie gently tried to object, "but Darling, Bury, and Lovett are used to working together as a team, and a fine one they are. When I was off on diplomatic port calls, they were perfectly capable of playing merry Hell with the Spanish, taking several prizes on their own. It'd be a shame did you break them up and—"

"Did you teach your grandmother to suck eggs, Captain Lewrie?" Grierson snapped of a sudden, glowering up.

"I only knew the one on my mother's side, sir, and she was perfectly capable of sucking eggs with no instructions from me, nor anyone else,"

Lewrie responded, stung by the sudden change in Commodore Grierson's demeanour.

By God, I knew he didn't much care for me, *but he don't much care for advice, either?* Lewrie thought; *No more "Sir Alan" politeness?*

"Sir, you are impertinent!" Grierson gravelled.

"You summoned me to explain the tactical situation and the best use of ships under your command, sir," Lewrie replied, trying not to take umbrage . . . openly, at least. "I mean to lend you my experience in the Bahamas, and what I've learned in my previous time here, along with what has transpired in the last few months. To ignore the risk to shipping by privateers would be remiss. *I* would be remiss, rather."

"You may leave the particulars with me, Lewrie, and I shall take it all under study," Grierson stiffly said, "but, as we both understand, I am now the senior officer in the Bahamas, and every ship comes under *my* command. If I deem your recent actions against enemy privateers successful, then your previous orders, and the necessity of your little squadron, are moot, and I will do with them what I may."

"But of course, sir," Lewrie said, his face set in stone.

"Which means that you and your frigate come under my command, as well, Captain Lewrie," Grierson said, shooting to his feet, ending the meeting, and Lewrie had to rise as well, his hat under his arm.

"Very good, sir," Lewrie said, sketching a wee bow in parting.

"Which means," Grierson continued with a cold smile, still not making a move to see Lewrie to the doors, "that I may do with *you* as I will, and you must haul down that inferior broad pendant of yours."

"I understand that very well, sir," Lewrie replied with a cock of his head, refusing to lose his temper to this . . . arse!

"You may consider yourself dismissed, Captain Lewrie. You may go," Grierson told him in a snooty way, looking down his long nose.

I should've known better than t'try humour on a man like him, Lewrie chid himself as he made his goodbye to Lt. Hayes, who was still on the quarterdeck, and who saw him to the entry-port; *There's some people so "tetchy" 'bout their bloody honour and* prestige *that a gay "good morning" will put 'em in a sour mood!*

Once in his boat and being rowed back to his frigate, Lewrie wondered whether he should "sing small" round Grierson from then on, or do something that would row him beyond all temperance. He could not abide serving under such an arrogant bastard for long, and he knew himself well enough to realise that his own patience was not everlasting. Sooner or later, there would be a blow-up.

Get him so irked, he'd be glad t'see the back o' me, and send me very far away? Lewrie pondered; *There'll be lots o' drink sloshin' at the ball tonight. Maybe that's where t'make a start.*

CHAPTER SEVEN

*D*espite Commodore Grierson's unfortunate little jest that had fright-ened the good citizens of Nassau Town and New Providence Island so badly, they would not have, at that moment, trusted their own arses with a fart, the new Senior Naval Officer Commanding in the Bahamas *had* to be welcomed and regaled with an introductory supper and grand ball, no matter the personal feelings of the aforesaid citizens, who had at last re-gained their accustomed aplomb, and were back to business. The Governor-General, hoping perhaps that the new Commodore had fired the *last* shot from his humour locker, staged the affair at Crown expense, a cost which he would try to get underwritten by the better-off of the aforesaid good citizens, or justify to His Majesty's Government.

Lewrie took pains to sponge off, shave closely, and wait until the very last minute to dress that early evening, so he would not end soaked in perspiration before he combed his hair or left his cabins for the deck. He despised the new style of slipper-like shoes, but he had a good, mostly un-used pair of buckled shoes with coin-silver buckles, into which he stuck his silk-stockinged feet. His breeches were snow-white new, his waist-coat with gilt buttons just as pristine, and his shirt and carefully pressed neck-stock were of silk, as well, stowed at the bottom of one of his sea-chests for such rare occasions. Over the waist-coat, his steward, Pettus, draped the broad blue sash of his knighthood. Lastly, just before departure, Pettus offered him his best-dress uniform coat with the silver and enamelled star of the Order of The Bath pinned to the left breast. Pettus had carefully brushed it earlier, then hung it from a peg driven into one of the overhead deck beams, so the cats, Toulon and Chalky, could not roll on it and mark it with fur. One gold medal hung from a button hole on a ribbon, for his participation in the Battle of Camperdown. Dangling just over the vee of the waist-coat hung another on a pale blue ribbon; that'un was for being at the Battle of Cape St. Vincent.

"You look champion, sir," Pettus told him as he held up a small mirror from the wash-hand stand so Lewrie could preen a bit, and sweep hair back on both sides of his head. At his nape there was a sprig of hair, neatly tied with black ribbon and no more than three inches long.

Styles were changing, and there were many younger officers who eschewed even a hint of sailor's queues, deeming them old-fashioned, or best worn by the common seamen up forward, as a mark of class difference. Lewrie's had been shortened over the years, and he suspected that some-day he might lop his off, too, but not yet.

"Just keep the cats from leapin' on me 'til I'm in the boat," Lewrie told Pettus with a laugh. He donned the offered hat, a cocked one with a wide gold lace band round the outer edges, with the gilded button, loops of gold lace, and the fanned black silk cockade over the left eye, the "dog's vane". "And I hope someone's either leashed our dog out o' the way, or wiped his paws."

"I'll see you to the entry-port and keep a weather eye peeled for Bisquit, sir," Pettus offered.

Thankfully, Bisquit was below with the hands who were just then getting their boiled meat from the galley, hoping for the offer of a nibble or two. Once in the boat, Lewrie sat down on a piece of new, un-sullied canvas to protect the seat of his breeches and coat tails from tar or dirt. "Town piers, Desmond!" he cheerfully ordered.

All the wide double doors and windows of Government House, up Market Street from the piers, were thrown open, and yellow light glowed from within from hundreds of candles. A small batch of liveried musicians were playing light, and somewhat muted, airs to entertain guests as they arrived, were announced, and welcomed inside to stroll and socialise before the supper was announced.

Lewrie took his time to ascend the several flights of stone stairs from one terrace of lawn and garden to the next 'til he was upon the outer gallery. The hike from the docks had all been uphill, and that was asking a lot of a sailor. He stopped to remove his hat, swab the inner band with a handkerchief, and discreetly dab his face and neck. He lingered, savouring the cool sunset breeze, for he could feel a palpable wave of heat coming from inside, from all those candles and so many people crammed into the spacious rooms.

More guests were arriving, by coach, on foot, and some few in sedan chairs borne by liveried slaves. There were officers from the Army garrison and Forts Montagu, Charlotte, and Fincastle in regimental finery, though Lewrie noted that few of them were below the rank of Major, with only a few Captains tossed in. A peek inside revealed the blue of Navy officers, and Lewrie quickly identified a couple of brig-sloop officers, with their Commanders' epaulets on their left shoulders, and an equal number of Lieutenants. All the Lieutenants in command of the sloops and cutters in port were there, but none of the junior officers or Midshipmen. Evidently, the Governor-General was pinching his pennies, and inviting only senior men. His own First Lieutenant, Westcott, had been sent an invitation, but he had begged off, wishing for a night of shore liberty to pursue his own supper, dancing, and . . . other things.

It was cooler without his hat, so Lewrie tucked it under his arm. There were many newly arrived guests who wished to linger in a cooler air, knowing what to expect in a Bahamian summer, and Lewrie chatted them up, accepting and making introductions and chit-chat.

In point of fact, once named to the civilian gentlemen and their ladies, sons, and daughters, Lewrie was pleasingly surprised by how he was praised for his desperate sortie, in some cases almost gushingly, and his face reddened in honest humility (well, he could only play-act humble all *that* long!) and he declared, over and again, that he had only done his duty, no matter the odds.

Medals be-damned, they're callin' me a hero for that!

"You will enter with us, Sir Alan?" one older lady beguiled.

"I do b'lieve I'll wait a tad longer, ma'am," Lewrie told her. "The evening breeze, and the aromas from the flower gardens, are just too delightful."

Yet another coach creaked to a stop at the foot of the hill on Market Street, an open coach which carried Commodore Grierson and his Flag-Captain, Meadows, and Lewrie turned away, wishing to delay *rencontre* with the fellow 'til the last moment. He looked round for a tall planter or bush behind which he could hide.

"Are you avoiding me, Sir Alan?" a lovely voice asked in petulance. He spun about to espy the "grass widow".

"Why, Mistress Frost! Priscilla!" Lewrie exclaimed. "You are invited tonight? Your presence makes the occasion all the more delightful. And, how splendid you look!" he gushed in pleasure as he went to the top of the last flight of steps to offer her an arm after a bow.

Might tonight be the night? Lewrie fervently wished; *After all, I'm nigh the bloody hero of the hour!*

The object of his lust, Mistress Priscilla Frost, would be the desire of any man. She was a wee woman only five feet four inches in height, with a creamy pale complexion, a mass of artfully styled red-auburn hair, and bright green eyes. This night, her filmy sheath gown was of mint green, cut delightfully low, and was almost sheer enough to reveal a slim young body that was promisingly bouncy-looking, with perky breasts that even a modest *bandeau* to press them down could not completely hide. To top all that off, she was a woman of a sinuous, languid, and teasing demeanour.

"It is *too* bad that we shall not be seated close together," she said with a *moue*, and a waft of her fan. "I expect you shall be seated nearer the top of the table, whilst I must languish far down, with the 'chaw-bacons', ha ha!"

"Well, there's the mingling before, and the dancing after," Lewrie said, trying on a leer. "Uhm . . . I note that Mister Frost is not attending with you? He's still down at Grand Turk?"

"An American ship came in with mail, and he sent me a short note," Priscilla told him with another pout. "He's found a market at Cape François, on Haiti, and has sailed there to look into the possibilities, so . . . he will be delayed some more *weeks*."

"Oh, what a pity," Lewrie commiserated.

"Lord only *knows* what dangers he might face among the savage Blacks of that foul place," Priscilla said, not sounding all *that* much concerned for her much older husband's safety.

"They're a blood-thirsty lot," Lewrie told her, looking over her shoulder to see Commodore Grierson mid-way up the flights of stairs. "Be a dear, Mistress Priscilla, and stroll with me into the garden for a bit."

"Why, Sir Alan! Captain Lewrie, will you ruin my repute in Nassau?" She did so with a fetching air of mischief, a merry glint in her eyes, and a tap of her fan against his chin.

"Only with your *complete* permission, dear lady," Lewrie purred in kind, with a flirtatious laugh. "But, I'd rather put off havin' to greet Commodore Grierson 'til later. *Much* later."

"Oh, that fatuous clown!" Priscilla huffed. "But of *course*, I shall aid you in that." She offered her arm to be supported by his and allowed herself to be led towards the gardens. "What a thoroughly thoughtless act! Why, I was so terrified that the French had come to impoverish us all that my maids and I were packing in a perfect *panic*, until it was revealed that his ships were *ours*! *Everyone* is wroth with him . . . 'tis the talk of the town, and none of it *complimentary*, let me tell you! Do I get the chance, I would tell him what I think of him to his face!"

"Then I shall be sure to introduce you," Lewrie assured her. "Do look and see if he's gone in, yet."

"He is just about to enter," Priscilla whispered conspiratorially after a quick peek. "Oh!"

"Oh?" Lewrie asked in dread that Grierson had spotted him.

"Do you enter and be announced *after* him," Priscilla schemed in wicked glee, "you would be *certain* to hear louder approval. You would . . . as the actors say . . . up-stage him?"

"What a clever girl you are!" Lewrie said in open praise. "For that I stand completely in your debt . . . and in complete admiration of you, to boot," he added with another leer.

"Debt *and* admiration, Sir Alan?" she cooed, looking up at him with a lazy and flirtatious smile . . . and an artful hitch of her breath that lifted and swelled her breasts. "Such complete admiration *must* be rewarded. *Amply* rewarded, hmm?"

"Where admiration may turn to worship?" Lewrie dared hint, leering yet again. She slowly batted her lashes and nodded her head to agree.

Huzzah, I'm aboard*!* Lewrie exulted to himself.

"Walk me back to the entrance, Sir Alan," Priscilla said, turning practical, "before people have reason to talk. Make your entrance a bit after me. I shall prepare the ground. A minute or so later?"

Lewrie saw her to the grand entrance doors, bowed her away, then lingered a bit more. Over the mutters of attendees and the musicians, there came a thump of a long cane, and a loud voice announcing the entrance of Captain Henry Grierson, Commodore of the Bahamas Squadron, and his Flag-Captain, Captain George Meadows. Lewrie smiled in delight as the crowd inside paid no particular heed; there was no applause. Indeed, conversations seemed to cease!

Finally, he shot his cuffs, settled his waist-coat and fiddled with his neck-stock, took a deep breath, plastered a benign grin on his phyz, and went inside to check his hat, then name himself to one of the liveried "catch farts", who passed his name on to the major-domo with the long and heavy cane.

"Ladies and gentlemen, Captain Sir Alan Lewrie, Baronet, of His Majesty's Ship *Reliant*!" the old functionary called out.

"Huzzah!" someone called out. "The hero of the hour!"

"Oh, bravely done!" Priscilla ringingly declared, and began to clap her hands, which prompted others to join in.

The fierce scowl on Commodore Grierson's face was priceless, no matter how much bad blood was engendered, and Lewrie secretly delighted in it, even if it cost him later.

Nassau Town was not like London; its Society consisted mostly of commoners, albeit successful ones. A gala gathering such as this supper ball in England would never allow people engaged in "Trade" to attend! Nassauans could not even be described as Squirearchy who owned land and lived off gentlemanly farm incomes, cottagers' rents, and shares in the Three Percent Funds. For the most part, the largest plots of land that Nassau's upper crust owned were the town lots on which their houses sat, where their goods warehouses were situated, or their stores did business.

Lewrie suspected that Commodore Grierson had a low opinion of people engaged in Trade, lumping them in with pie men, knife grinders, or green grocers and store clerks, and could not fathom the conversations over the supper table, the pre-dinner socialising, or at the edges of the dance floor about profit-and-loss, new markets, and opportunities.

He looks damned uncomfortable and mute! Lewrie thought; *They'll give up on him altogether and talk past him in half an hour!*

Lewrie, for his part, simply had a grand time, even if he was seated at least eight people away from the promising Priscilla. There was his rash sortie to be congratulated for. There was his destruction of so many French and Spanish privateers, the very bane of mercantile and maritime *trade,* and his re-capture and return to their owners of several prize vessels.

How had he won his knighthood? Lewrie gave them the Battle of the Chandeleur Islands off Spanish Louisiana in 1803. He had to tell them of his medals, of course, though Lewrie could (modestly!) relate that he had been present at the Battle of the Chesapeake during the American Revolution, had gotten trapped at the siege of Yorktown yet had escaped the night before the surrender, had been at St. Kitts when Admiral Hood had stymied de Grasse, had stumbled into the Glorious Fourth of June in 1794 while being chased by two French frigates and had ended up driven towards the lee of the *French* line of battle, and been with Nelson at the Battle of Cape St. Vincent.

"I was *forced* to go with him!" Lewrie chortled. "I had *Jester* at the time, a sloop below the Rates, near Nelson's ship at the rear of Admiral Sir John Jervis's line, and Nelson swung out of line to wheel about, all by himself. Had I not hauled my own wind, he would have *rammed* me. He shouted over, 'Follow me, Lewrie, we're off for glory!' and so I went. His ship, mine, and one or two others who followed traded fire with the *Santissima Trinidad,* the largest warship in the world, a *four*-decker with one hundred and twenty guns! *Huge* cannon balls went whizzing by, but we weren't hit, and I doubt *we* even marred her paint, but it took 'em five minutes or better to re-load! After that, he went on to win his first honours."

"You *know* the estimable Admiral Nelson, Sir Alan?" an older matron gushed.

"We've met several times, ma'am, it is my honour to say," Lewrie told her. *Even if he is a glory-seekin', press-hungry, temperamental arse!* he thought.

First at Grand Turk Island in 1783, with no mention of how the rashly assembled attempt to oust the French invasion force had failed so miserably; at Toulon, France, at the conference just before the evacuation of Coalition forces; ashore on Corsica just after Nelson had lost the sight of his eye (with no mention of Lewrie's mistress of the time who had dined with them!), then serving under his command along the Genoese and Ligurian coasts when Napoleon Bonaparte had invaded the Italies.

"Last I saw of him was the night before the Battle of Copenhagen," Lewrie reminisced.

"You were there, sir?" a brewer of note asked.

"I was, though there was no 'tin' handed out for Copenhagen," Lewrie replied. "We were not officially at war with the Danes, so . . ."

Lewrie told them of taking HMS *Thermopylae* into the Baltic, all alone, to scout the Swedish and Russian harbours, and the expanse and thickness of the ice that kept their fleets in port (again, with no mention of the Russian noble he carried who tried to murder him over the love of an Irish whore in London!) and of how he found him when he re-joined the fleet on the night before the battle.

"The great-cabins had been stripped for action, but for a brazier, some lanthorns, and Nelson's bed-cot," Lewrie described, sensing a hush round his part of the table as people leaned closer to listen in rapt interest. "It was cold, windy, and raw, just *perishin'* cold in the cabins, and Nelson was tucked into his bed-cot, fully dressed, and with a chequered greatcoat over his uniform, wrapped in blankets, propped up on pillows. His long-time servant, Tom, kept him supplied with hot tea, cocoa, and soup whilst Nelson dictated his orders for the morning. No notes, just from the top of his head, listing each ship under him in order of battle, assigning each which numbered ship in the Danish line to be engaged. It was uncanny! As I left, with my assignment with the frigates under Commodore Riou—a grand man and a fine seaman!—I saw the Midshipmen in the outer cabin, seated on the deck with candles, taking down Nelson's dictation from a Lieutenant, so each ship should have written orders. I was never so awe-struck than that night, for we were anchored just out of gun-range from the Danish line of battle, and I could stand and look at their ships all lit up as they ferried shot, powder, and volunteers from shore . . . like Caesar must have looked upon the campfires of an enemy army, the other side of the battlefield."

Up the table, Commodore Grierson gave him an exasperated squint.

"And did the gallant Admiral really put his telescope to his bad eye, Sir Alan?" a younger woman asked.

"I was not aboard his ship to witness it, ma'am, but I'm sure he did, just as all of us were aghast to see Sir Hyde Parker's signal to 'Discontinue The Action', when we were winning," Lewrie assured her. "We with Commodore Riou had finally forced *our* assigned opponents to strike, and were engaged with the Trekroner Forts. One could look astern to see that we were already victorious."

As for that rumoured French fleet under Villeneuve that sailed for the

West Indies, Lewrie could put them at ease. "I got a letter from my youngest son, Hugh, who is serving aboard a seventy-four under Admiral Nelson, informing me that Nelson and the entire Mediterranean Fleet were setting off in pursuit. Long before the French may achieve any mischief, they will be hotly engaged and utterly defeated, and the Corsican Ogre, Boney, will have lost most of his navy!"

That raised a hearty cheer, and a toast to Nelson, followed by one to the Royal Navy, followed by one waggish proposal for Napoleon to be hanged at Tyburn, and his tiny body hung in a bird cage on London Bridge!

"He's not all *that* tiny," Lewrie japed. "It might take a larger cage . . . much like the ones used to hang pirates on display."

Wonder of wonders, Lewrie had met Bonaparte, face-to-face?

Up-table, Commodore Grierson heaved a silent "Oh, for Christ's sake!"

"The first time, I was his prisoner, temporarily." Lewrie was more than happy to relate how Bonaparte, then a mere general of artillery, had blown up his mortar vessel east of Toulon, and had ridden down to the beach where the survivors had staggered ashore.

"Didn't make a bold picture," Lewrie chortled, "breeches drainin' water and my stockings round my ankles. He came to gloat and call for my parole. I told him I couldn't, for half the crew and gunners were Spanish or French Royalists. I swore the French were from the Channel Islands and really British, so they wouldn't be butchered on the spot, or guillotined later, and I handed him my sword, a rather nice hanger gifted me years before. We'd have been marched off, but for the arrival of a squadron of 'Yellow-Jacket' Spanish cavalry, so I got rescued. He's about four inches shorter than me, is Boney, a dandy fellow with clear skin . . . not the yellow or Arabic brown in the caricatures, with blue-ish eyes. The second time we met, in Paris during the Peace of Amiens, he'd put on a little weight, but . . ."

It did not take any arm-twisting for Lewrie to relate how he and his late wife, Caroline, had taken a second honeymoon to Paris to see the sights—*everyone* was doing it!—and of how he had taken several swords of dead French captains in hopes they could be returned to the families. It was a young, ambitious *chargé d'affaires* from the newly-reopened British Embassy who had managed to arrange an exchange of those swords for his old hanger, from Napoleon's own hands in the Tuileries Palace.

"Didn't go well, at *all*," Lewrie laughed. "Bonaparte showed up in a general's uniform and raved about why we hadn't sent him an Ambassador yet, even if his was in London, why we hadn't evacuated Malta like we promised, and that we had no business tellin' him to get out of Holland and Switzerland, I don't recall what all. To boot, Caroline and I were the only British there, and we got stared at and ogled like a pack o' rabid wolves. Just after that, we got word from another English tourist that Bonaparte had sicced his secret police agents on us, and we'd best flee France instanter."

He told them of fleeing in several sets of disguises, arranged by the other English couple, who had smuggled French aristocrats out to safety from prison or the guillotine, how they had almost gotten to a waiting rowboat on a remote beach near Calais. . . .

"There were cavalry and police on the bluff above," Lewrie said more somberly. "We made a mad dash for the boat, but, just as I was hoisting Caroline in, she was shot. She passed away in the boat, not a minute later."

That drew an aubible gasp and rumble of mutters. Even Grierson was wide-eyed. "Foul murder . . . Bonaparte a criminal, too . . . damn the French, root and branch . . . could be made out, here and there.

"Now, both my sons are in the Navy, Hugh was always to be, but his older brother, Sewallis, was so hot for revenge that I feared that he would enlist as a private soldier, or ship before the mast, did I deny him," Lewrie sadly said. Truth was, Sewallis had *forged* his way to sea as a Midshipman! "My daughter lives with one of my brothers-in-law in a little village, Anglesgreen, in Surrey. Though my father has a small estate there, he's mostly up to London and has little to offer towards a young girl's raising. Too old, now, to tend to a young'un."

No, Sir Hugo St. George Willoughby, damned near a charter member of the old Hell-Fire Club, *liked* young, so long as the girls were over eighteen, and obliging!

"So, when I received orders to *Reliant* in April of '03, I was *more* than ready to sail against the French once more," he concluded.

"A toast! A toast!" a youngish gallant cried, standing, and drawing others to their feet. "To the gallant Captain Lewrie, a man of grand adventures!"

Lewrie sat modestly with his hands in his lap to be honoured, bowing his head to left and right, admittedly with his ears burning.

⚓

Once the supper was over, the ladies excused themselves to the parlours for tea whilst the men gathered higher up the table for port, nuts, and sweet bisquits, and more talk of trade and the war. Lewrie excused himself after a while and went out on the front gallery for a breath of air, and to swab his face of perspiration; it had been nigh a steam bath inside, as he had feared, and the dance would be even worse. There were many supper guests who had the same idea, both men and women. Lewrie envied the fact that the women could cool themselves with their fans, something a gentleman could not.

"Your pahdon, sah, but, are you Captain Lewrie?" a liveried Black servant tentatively asked by his elbow.

"I am."

"Dis note be fo' ya, sah."

Lewrie stepped closer to one of the entrance way lanthorns to peel it open and read it, and his face lit up with a feral smile.

My house. Come by midnight.
    P

Can this evening be even more perfect? he asked himself.

Inside, the musicians struck up the opening strains of formal airs for the minuet, and Lewrie steeled himself for the ordeal to come. He must squire as many ladies present as he could, from the wife of the Governor-General down to the youngest . . . with Mrs. Priscilla Frost in the queue, quite happily . . . without showing any favouritism. It could last for hours, right to the livelier *contre-dances*. He considered bowing out of those after an essay or two; there must be *some* shreds of dignity that a Post-Captain in the Royal Navy should show! Besides . . . the livelier dances would continue beyond midnight.

And he now had someplace else more desirable to go!

CHAPTER EIGHT

*T*hank God you're back aboard, sir," Lt. Geoffrey Westcott said in some urgency once Lewrie had taken the welcoming salute, a quarter-hour past the beginning of the Forenoon at 8 A.M.

"Has a *real* French squadron turned up, then, Mister Westcott?" Lewrie asked, with a brow up in puzzlement that a Commission Officer would be up and stirring, and in full uniform, when it was usually the Mids who stood Harbour Watch. He could not help stifling a yawn, for his night ashore with Priscilla Frost had proven to be a strenuous one.

"No sir, nothing like that," Westcott told him in a confidential mutter.

"Good, for at this moment, a hot kiss or a cold breakfast would most-like put me in my grave . . . and I've had both," Lewrie said with a wry and semi-boastful chuckle.

"It is Commodore Grierson, sir," Westcott went on, drawing from Lewrie a groan of disgust. "*Athenian* has been flying our number and 'Captain Repair On Board' since half past Seven. I sent a Mid over to explain that you spent the night ashore, and despatched the rest of them to hunt you down, but—"

"Didn't know I *was* spendin' the night ashore, 'til after the supper," Lewrie explained, giving Grierson's flagship a bleak glance. "And, 'tis best that you didn't know my, uhm . . . lodgings. The last thing the lady in question needs would be some younker bangin' on her doors and raisin' her neighbours' int'rest in the early hours.

"Nothin' for it, then," Lewrie decided, hitching his shoulders. "Desmond? Back to the boat. I'm summoned to the flag. Carry on, Mister Westcott."

"Aye aye, sir." Westcott said, doffing his hat.

His Cox'n, Liam Desmond; stroke-oar Patrick Furfy; and the hands of his boat crew had barely secured the cutter below the entry-port, and had just gained the deck, before they had to turn right round and descend again without a "wet" at the scuttle-butts, or a chance to go below for a lazy "caulk" with the off-watch hands in their hammocks.

What the Devil does Grierson want o' me this *early in the morning?* Lewrie wondered as he settled himself aft in the boat once more; *Whatever it is, I except I won't enjoy it!*

Commodore Grierson stodd behind his expensive desk in the day-cabin as Lewrie entered, ducking under the overhead beams as he made his way aft to stand before the desk.

"You slept out of your ship, Captain Lewrie?" Grierson began in a frosty tone, as if doing so was a violation of some regulation.

"Aye, I did, sir," Lewrie replied. "To my recall, 'tis only Channel Fleet that requires Captains to sleep aboard, pending an appearance of a French fleet in the middle of the night. At least, that was the case when I was attached to Channel Fleet. Were you thinking of establishing such a rule, might I ask, sir?"

"No, I was *not*," Grierson snapped, furrowing his brows to even deeper wrinkles, as if Lewrie's attempt at "early morning cheery" was putting him off course. "At least your doing so results in your showing up in more suitable uniform, what?"

"Soon changed, as soon as I'm back aboard my ship, sir," Lewrie easily confessed, looking toward an empty chair before the desk as if to prompt Grierson to proper hospitality. Commodore Grierson took no notice of his hint; his eyes were fixed on Lewrie's chest, on the two medals he still wore (the one round his neck admittedly askew!) and on the star and sash of the Order of The Bath.

Damn my eyes, is he jealous? Lewrie was forced to wonder.

"And you enjoyed the supper and ball immensely, I should not wonder," Grierson went on, raising his glare to Lewrie's face, again.

"Oh, quite, sir!" Lewrie said with a laugh. "How do the papers in London put it . . . 'a good time was had by all'?"

"*Hhmmph!*" Grierson sneered. "I found the Society of Antigua and the nearby islands crude and dreary, but that of Nassau! . . . How have you *stood* such a pack of 'Country-Puts' and *tradesmen* but a cut above privateers?"

"I haven't really spent that much time in port t'deal with 'em, sir," Lewrie told him. He doubted if Grierson's complaint was a stab at finding some mutual understanding; the man was just grousing to be grousing!

"They are insulting beyond belief," Grierson went on with his plaint, pacing behind his desk and peering down his nose at the odd corners of his cabins. "One woman even had the nerve to take me to task for the manner of my arrival, sir!"

That'd be Priscilla, most-like, Lewrie happily thought.

"Quite fetching a mort, but for that," Grierson growled. "The *nerve* of the bitch! I *saw* you with her, Lewrie. Did you put her up to it? That Mistress Frost baggage?"

"I most certainly did not, sir," Lewrie vowed.

Aye, I did, did you like it? he thought, his face stony; *And is* that *why ye summoned me, ye petty bastard?*

"She did tell me, though, sir," Lewrie explained, "that there were many locals who were frightened out of their wits 'til they learned the true identity of your ships. Recall, I did warn you that your idea of a jest might turn round and bite you."

Did he expect 'em t'be so relieved they'd cheer him and chair him through the streets? Lewrie asked himself; *What an ass!*

"As I was rowed past your frigate, Captain Lewrie, I noted that she is rather heavily weeded," Commodore Grierson snapped, changing the subject as he whipped round to glare at Lewrie once more. "I saw more green slime than I did coppering or white lead, and I expect you also have so many barnacles that you could not *find* her coppering. How long has it been since your ship was docked and cleaned, sir?"

"Well, since she was taken out of Ordinary in April of 1803, I don't believe we've had time for such, sir," Lewrie informed him. "We spent much of that year in the West Indies and the Gulf of Mexico, then back to

England as escort to a sugar trade, half of 1804 in the Channel, then right back here via Bermuda, since January."

"Then you are more than due," Commodore Grierson said with a satisfied nod of his head, though he didn't even try to plaster on a gladsome smile. "Since I now have three frigates and two more brig-sloops on station, your frigate is redundant to my needs. And, as you say, it is doubtful that the French Admiral, Villeneuve, has designs upon the Bahamas. Those, plus the vessels already assigned here will more than suffice. As slow as your ship is reduced, she would be a hindrance to me."

And . . . and what? Lewrie wondered, waiting for the other shoe to drop as Grierson took his time to walk back to his desk, sit down behind it, and leaf through some correspondence.

"I will send you orders, releasing you from my squadron, sir," Grierson at last said when he folded the correspondence away, folding his hands atop the desk.

"What about the continuing problem with French and Spanish privateers, though, sir? My independent orders from Admir—"

"As Senior Officer on-station, *and* senior to *you,* sir, by nineteen months on the Post-Captains' List, I deem such enemy activities temporarily 'Scotched', and feel that, with my re-enforcements in frigates and brig-sloops, will be more than capable of dealing with any new outbreaks," Grierson cut him off, and simpered at Lewrie.

That *won't last ye six months,* Lewrie sourly thought; *not when the trade route's so busy, and privateerin's so profitable!*

"If you say so, sir," Lewrie said, instead.

"And I do," Grierson gaily rejoined, quite perkily. "As for you and your frigate, Captain Lewrie . . . I will allow you to detach yourself from my command and . . . and sail for England for a proper time in dry dock. Does that prospect not *please* you, sir?"

"Well, aye, it does, sir, but . . . ," Lewrie flummoxed. The prospect *was* pleasing, and he had to admit that *Reliant* was in serious need of a hull cleaning, The loss of his temporary status as a Commodore even of such a small squadron really meant little, either. It was the *way* he was being shooed off that rankled!

"Good, then," Grierson said, smiling at last, though not with the sort of smile one could trust. "That's settled. I will have your orders aboard by the start of the First Dog Watch this very day . . . before I despatch the wee vessels of your former squadron to other duties down-islands. I expect you and their commanding officers will wish a last shore supper together, before you all depart."

Vindictive bastard! Lewrie fumed inside.

"I expect that we shall, sir," Lewrie said, keeping his disgust well-hidden, and thinking that their last shore supper would be a bitch session which Grierson should studiously avoid.

Damn *him for takin' it out on* them*!* he thought.

"Will that be all, sir?" Lewrie asked.

"Uhmm, yes," Grierson said, all a'twinkle by then, rising from his chair to see Lewrie to the doors. "You may return to your ship." Grierson leaned a bit close then away. "Where you may sponge the lady's scent from your clothing."

I wondered *why his cabins smelled like rose water!* Lewrie realised; *Well, they* say *ye can never smell yourself! Priscilla* did *dab it on a* tad *thick.*

"Beg pardon, sir?" Lewrie countered, stiffening his back. Would the fellow prove himself that crude?

"A good ride, was she? Mistress Frost?" Grierson leered.

"I deem it most un-gentlemanly of you to *ask* that question, sir," Lewrie stiffly intoned, glowering at the Commodore. "As for the lady's qualities . . . that's something I very much doubt *you'll* ever know."

Grierson's reaction was a hearty laugh, and another easy and arrogant "we'll see about that" cock-sure leer. "Goodbye, Captain Lewrie. *Bon voyage,* and *bonne chance!*"

Grierson did not go so far as to see him to the deck, so Lewrie had to make his way alone, his ears and the nape of his neck burning, determined to call upon the bouncy Priscilla one more time, if only to tell her what Grierson had in mind, and how low a mind he possessed!

CHAPTER NINE

A day or two later, and HMS *Reliant* was ready to up-anchor and depart. Last-minute rations had been fetched aboard, along with some sheep, pigs, and a bullock for supper on the eve of sailing, and for fresh meat for the first few days on-passage. The officers' wardroom and Lewrie's cabins had been re-stocked with the many needful things that would be unavailable or in short supply on their long voyage to England. For Lewrie, Mister Cadbury the Purser had purchased several one-gallon stone crocks of aged American corn whisky, and an hundred-weight weight of jerked, smoked, or cured meats and hard sausages for his cats and, begrudgingly, for Bisquit, the ship's dog. He might be a playful pest, might still foul the decks, and took to howling whenever Lewrie tried to practice on his penny-whistle, but Lewrie had grown *somewhat* fond of the beast.

"Pettus, wos 'em things in th' quarter-gallery?" young Jessop, the cabin servant, asked the cabin steward as Captain Lewrie finished his pre-sailing breakfast in the forward dining coach, dressed in casual and comfortable old sea clothes, with the finery packed away.

"What things in the quarter-gallery?" Pettus patiently asked as he stowed away spare shirts and trousers, just come back from the shore laundry where they had been washed and rinsed in fresh water, not salt. "You have to be specific."

" 'Em stockin'-lookin' things in 'eir, them wif th' ribbons on 'em," Jessop pressed.

"Those are 'protections', Jessop," Pettus coolly informed him.

"P'rtections f'um wot?" Jessop further asked, puzzled.

"They are cundums," Pettus told the lad in a mutter, not wishing to disturb their captain, who was in a sour-enough mood already. "Things gentlemen wear when they, ah . . . take pleasure with ladies so they don't get them pregnant, or catch the Pox. They are made from sheep gut."

"Wos th' ribbons for, 'en?"

"To tie them on round one's . . . 'nut-megs' . . . so they won't slip off in the middle of things," Pettus said, whispering by then.

" 'At's a lotta work f'r a fook!" Jessop exclaimed, wide-eyed. "Ye kin see right through 'em, anyways. Izzat why the Cap'um needs s'many of 'em?" Jessop scoffed.

"One for each . . . bout," Pettus explained, cryptically grinning.

"Mean t'say 'e topped a mort half a dozen *times* last night?" Jessop gawped aloud. "Or, six *diff'r'nt* doxies?"

"Hush, now!" Pettus cautioned.

Jessop looked forward to watch Lewrie butter a last slab of toast, smother it with sweet local key-lime marmalade, and take a bite. He goggled in outright awe!

Lewrie heard Jessop's later utterances, and looked aft at the lad, smiling and tipping him a cheerful wink.

Not all that bad for a man o' fourty-two, Lewrie congratulated himself quite smugly; *and that don't count the* fellatio, *which I doubt Priscilla's "lawful blanket" is too prudish, or ignorant, t'know about.*

She, like all ladies of worth, kept her fingernails short, but his back felt as if Toulon and Chalky had galloped over him with their claws out.

Poor Mister Frost! Lewrie thought; *He'll never know what he's missin'!*

Priscilla might not have strictly been a proper and virginal bride when she'd wed the old "colt's tooth", but might have been able to play-act a satisfactory sham of inexperience on the wedding night.

Not that her husband knew all that much about pleasuring her, or any woman. Priscilla had told him with sad amusement their first night that the old fellow came to bed in an ankle-length flannel gown, and had hiked it up only far enough to climb atop her, a business as quickly, roughly done to *his* release, before he would roll off and go to the wash-hand stand to sponge off, then fall deeply asleep. He did not find it seemly for her to remove her night gown, so it was possible he had never seen her bounty, which could have given him so much more delight, had he the *slightest* clue! But, Priscilla was his third wife, the first two dying of Child-bed Fever after producing enough males to assure that one would inherit, all now grown with families of their own. Priscilla was less a help-meet, more a house keeper, a hostess at his supper parties, the handy vessel for his rare needs, and a bit of adornment on his arm when invited out, but little else.

Hmm, sounds like most *marriages!* Lewrie had cynically thought.

Priscilla adored baring her body, being outlandishly nude and posing most fetchingly a'sprawl and inciting. Her "lawful blanket" might never worship at her firm and perky breasts, the insides of her thighs, or at "the wee man in the boat", but by God Lewrie had been more than glad to attend "services" there! And the rewards of such ardent adoration had been nigh to Paradise itself!

What a waste of a good woman, Lewrie told himself as he mused over his last cup of coffee; *Wouldn't trust her outta sight, but—*

The Marine sentry at his door stamped boots, banged his musket on the deck, and cried, "First Officer, SAH!"

"Enter," Lewrie replied, dabbing his mouth with a napkin.

Lt. Westcott entered, his hat under his arm. "The ship is in all respects ready for sea, sir. We stand ready to pipe 'Stations To Weigh', whenever you wish."

"Very well, Mister Westcott, I will come to the quarterdeck," Lewrie said, rising and snagging his hat off the sideboard, where it was temporarily safe from his cats, who were still busy at their bowls at the other end of the table. "I am sorry I had to call you back to the ship by midnight."

"Well, sir," Westcott confided with a faint grin, "all that was needed to be said had been said. *Some* tears and lamentations, but I doubt such sentiment will last all that long once we're gone. Dare I enquire of your last night ashore, sir?"

"We're much in the same boat, Mister Westcott," Lewrie said. "I *would* say that I regret parting from the lady's company, but, sooner or later, there'd be her husband t'deal with. At least you have the good sense to get involved with a free lass. Can't imagine *where* my mind went!"

Most of a night on the side portico of her house, in the dark, rowin' just the two of us over t'Hog Island with a basket and a blanket . . . thumpin' about in a closed coach out to East End Point, Lewrie reminisced as they strolled out onto the weather deck and up the starboard ladderway to the quarter-deck; *and last night, for hours and hours?* That's *where my mind, and good sense, went! It's just as well we're sailin' far away, 'fore her husband gets an inklin' and calls me out. Killin' him in a duel—for* her *honour, hah!—would be just too much.*

"Good morning, Mister Caldwell," Lewrie said to the Sailing Master, who was already on deck by the compass binnacle cabinet with all his navigational tools laid out. "Where away the wind?"

"Fresh out of the East-Nor'east, sir, and fair for a beam reach out the channel," Caldwell told him with a satisfied grin. "You will wish to depart up the Nor'west Providence Channel, once we've made our offing, sir?"

"Aye," Lewrie replied, looking up at the commissioning pendant to judge the direction of the wind for himself. "Out into the Florida Straits, reach the Gulf Stream, and shave close enough to the Grand Bahama Bank to keep well off the American coast. With any luck, we'll pick up an East-Sou'easterly breeze that will allow us to avoid the Hatteras Banks, and get well out into the Atlantic." He knocked wood on the binnacle cabinet. "Good morning, gentlemen."

Lieutenants Spendlove and Merriman greeted him with cheery good mornings in return, and a doff of their hats.

"Just as we break the anchor free, I'll have the spanker, the tops'ls, and inner, outer, and flying jibs hoisted," Lewrie decided. "Once we've made our offing into deep water, and hauled off Nor'west, we'll see to the courses and t'gallants."

"Aye, sir,"

"And . . . when the anchor's free, we'll strike the harbour jack *and* my broad pendant," Lewrie further instructed. "I'm sure that that will please our Commodore to no end, hey?"

Sour smiles were shared by all.

"Hands to the capstan, Mister Westcott," Lewrie bade. "Let's have a tune t'spur 'em on."

"Bosun!" Westcott cried to the waist. "Hands to the capstan! Strike up 'Portsmouth Lass'!"

Bisquit the dog dashed round the waist 'til he discovered that he was both ignored and underfoot, and slunk his way up to the quarterdeck to squat behind the cross-deck hammock nettings, looking about for a friendly face and a reassuring pat. He came to sit by Lewrie after a minute or two.

"Short stays!" Midshipman Munsell shouted from the bows.

"Stamp and go for the heavy haul!" Lt. Westcott bellowed.

"Up and down!"

"Bosun Sprague! Pipe the topmen aloft!" Westcott ordered. "Lay aloft, trice out, and man the tops'ls!"

Blocks squealed as the lift lines dragged the tops'l yards up from their rests. Lighter blocks joined the chorus after the harbour gaskets were freed and hands on deck drew down the canvas to the wind.

"Anchor's free!" Munsell cried.

"Hoist away all jibs! Hoist away the spanker!"

HMS *Reliant* began to shuffle uncertainly, heeling a tiny bit to leeward as the canvas aloft began to catch wind, paying off free 'til the fore-and-aft sails were sheeted home. She then started to inch forward, stirring her great weight.

"Steerage way?" Lewrie asked the helmsmen.

"A *bit*, sir!" Quartermaster Baldock tentatively replied as he shifted the spokes of the forward-most of the twin wheels.

"A point up to windward, to get some drive from the jibs," Lewrie ordered, pacing over to peer into the compass bowl, then look aloft at the commissioning pendant and how it was streaming.

Damme, that's the end o' that! he sadly thought as he watched his broad pendant come fluttering down the slackened halliard, that red bit of bunting with the white ball in the centre.

"Way, sir," Baldock reported. "The rudder's got a bite, now."

"Steer for mid-channel, then, with nothing t'leeward," Lewrie told him.

"Mid-channel aye, sir, an' nothing t'leeward!" Baldock echoed.

"Hands to the braces!" Westcott was ordering, now that the topsails were fully spread, half-cupping the breeze. "Haul in the lee braces!"

Reliant was under way, free of the ground, with just enough of a drive to create the faintest bow wave under her forefoot and her cutwater, and Lewrie let out a sigh of relief. Before he would go to the windward rail, where a ship's captain ought to be, he remained in the centre of the quarterdeck, looking shoreward. There were people there, on the piers and along Bay Street, waving goodbye. Some of them were women who waved handkerchiefs. Did some pipe their eyes in sadness?

Just after leaving *Athenian* and his last meeting with Grierson, Lewrie had announced to the crew that they would be sailing for home . . . where their pay chits would be honoured in full, and the shares in their ship's prize-money would be doled out, he had reminded them, to make some of the dis-contented think twice about desertion. He had hoisted the "Easy" pendant and put the ship "Out Of Discipline" for a day and a night to let the whores and temporary "wives" come aboard, and even after full order was restored, he had granted shore liberty to each watch in turn so his sailors could stretch their legs ashore and lounge at their ease in the many taverns, rut in the brothels, and attend the "Dignity Balls" that the Free Blacks would stage. The Mulatto girls, the Quadroons and Octoroons, might be above being shopped by the pimps in the bum-boats like common doxies, but the fancily-dressed "Dignity Ladies", for a *discreet* price, would make young sailormen feel as if they had discovered Fiddler's Green, the sailors' Paradise, where ale and spirits flowed freely, the music never ended, the girls were obliging and eager, and the publicans never called for the reckoning.

"Departing salute to the Governor-General, sir?" Lt. Westcott prompted.

"Aye, Mister Westcott, carry on," Lewrie agreed, pacing over to the windward bulwarks where he belonged, and, as the gun salute boomed out in its slow measure, and the leeward side became wreathed in smoke, Lewrie doffed his hat to the women ashore, one memorable woman in particular whom he, in retrospect, had best never see again!

Once the last gun had been fired, Marine Lieutenant Simcock came to the top of the starboard ladderway. "Beg pardons, sir, but, given our departure for England, I wonder if 'Spanish Ladies' might be welcome."

"A fine idea, Mister Simcock!" Lewrie heartily agreed. "Carry on and put a good pace to it, as you did before."

" 'Fa-are-*well*, and a-dieu, to you *fine* Spanish la-adies, fa-are-well, and adieu, to you *la-dies* of *Spain*! Fo-or *we've* received orders to *sail* for Old England, but we hope very *shortly* to *see* you again! We'll rant and we'll roll, like *true* British sailor-men, we'll rant and we'll roll, all across the salt *seas,* 'til *we* strike Soundings in the *Channel* of Old England, then straight up the Channel to Portsmouth we'll *go!*' "

Reliant's sailors were bound for home. It was a beautiful morning of fresh-washed blue skies and white clouds, and the waters in the channel out to sea were clear enough to see schools of fish darting from the frigate's shadow, the waters shading off to the most brilliant blue-green, bright jade green, and aquamarine. Now that the running rigging was belayed on fife and pin-rails, the excess flaked or flemished down, and the sails drawing well without tending, the crew could find time to sing, belting out the words with the joy of departing.

Older mast-captains and the younger and spryer captains of the tops had gathered in a group atop a hatch grating beneath the cross-deck timbers of the boat-tier beams in the waist, forming an *impromptu* chorus, swinging their arms as if their hands already held home-brewed ale mugs in their favourite old taverns.

" 'No-ow I've been a topman, and *I've* been a gunner's mate, I can dance, I can sing, a-and *walk* the jib-*boom*! I can *han-dle* a cutlass, and *cut* a fine figure, whenever I'm *given* en-nough standing room!

" 'We'll rant and we'll roar, like *true* British sailormen, we'll rant and we'll roar, both *aloft* and be-*low*! 'Til we sight Lizard, on the *coast* of Old England, then straight up the *Chan-nel* to Portsmouth *we'll* go!' " that chorus roared, and the ship's boys, the cabin servants who served as nippers and powder-monkeys, pranced and practiced their horn-pipes round the covered hatchway, and the very youngest raced round and shrieked with delight, with Bisquit in pursuit, or being the chased, it was hard to tell which.

"Let them rant, sir?" Lt. Westcott asked as he joined Lewrie by the windward bulwarks.

"Aye, Mister Westcott," Lewrie replied, a happy grin on his face, and his right hand beating the time on the cap-rails as he sang along now and then. "It'll take half an hour more before we haul off Nor'west. They'll play out long before then."

He looked aft towards the larboard quarter to see Arawak Cay and the eastern tip of Long Cay well clear; off the starboard quarter stood the long spit of Hog Island. And framed between the taffrail lanthorns lay the harbour channel and the town of Nassau, glowing in an infinite variety of pastel paint on the walls, already shrinking away, the green hills of early Spring turning brown and dusty in the glare of late Summer.

"Mind, though," Lewrie said, "does the wind give you an opportunity, I'll have the fore course, main course, and t'gallants filled."

"I don't suppose it matters at this point, sir, what our duty will be once we leave the dockyards," Westcott said with a shrug. "I only hope what-ever we're set to is as successful as our last."

"Even if it ended badly," Lewrie said, sighing and leaving the bulwarks to walk a few paces forward to look down into the waist at his singing and capering crewmen. "Damme, I'm going to miss Darling, Bury, and Lovett. We made a hellish-good team!"

"But, with any luck, sir, we'll find another," Westcott said with a hope-ful tone.

"We'll see," Lewrie said, nodding. "We'll see."

BOOK ONE

KING: Then forth, dear countrymen. Let us deliver
Our puissance into the hand of God,
Putting it straight in expedition.
Cheerly to sea the signs of war advance.
                         —WILLIAM SHAKESPEARE,
                         THE LIFE OF KING
                         HENRY THE FIFTH,
                         ACT II, SCENE II, 189-192

CHAPTER TEN

*C*alling upon the Port Admiral of Portsmouth was always a dicey prop-osition. Admiral Lord Gardner was a lean and sour older fellow, "all seal-ing wax, stay tape, and buckram", it was said of him (as well as his contemporary at Plymouth), who never seemed to have a good day, and God help the fool, or fools, who crossed him, disappointed, discomfitted, or disturbed him, for he never would suffer fools gladly. And this morn-ing, he was looking particularly dys-peptic.

"Lewrie . . . Lewrie . . . ," Lord Gardner mused, working his mouth as if he'd bitten into a rotten lemon, or had dentures made by an itinerant Gypsy tinker. "Aha, sir! I recall you, now. You have not brought in any more of your secret, explosive thing-gummies, have you? Has he, Niles?" Lord Gardner snapped, turning to peer at his long-suffering senior Post-Captain aide. "Come to blow us all to Kingdom Come, has he?"

"Not this time, milord," Captain Niles informed his master with a ge-nial grin. "Our experiments with those infernal engines are done, and good riddance. Complete failures."

"For which I say thank God, my lord," Lewrie stuck in.

"His orders, milord," Captain Niles said, efficiently whipping the single opened sheet of paper out and laying it on the desk before Lord Gardner, who picked it up and peered at it, myopically, his face in a grim and distasteful *moue* as if expecting the worst.

"This Commodore Grierson detaches you from his squadron, with orders for England, for a *re-fit?*" Lord Gardner huffed, waving those orders about. "What an impertinent, jumped-up pop-in-jay he must be, to assume that he may declare authority over His Majesty's Dockyards, and send us whom he will!"

"Well, my lord, not a thorough re-fit, just a hull cleaning," Lewrie offered, hoping that the lesser request would mollify him. "*Reliant* is very weeded, and slow after being brought out of Ordinary in April of 1803, and the bulk of her active commission has been in Bermudan, Bahamian, West Indies, and other tropic waters. The Gulf of Mexico, off Spanish Florida, and the Southern American coast?"

"He also ordered you to strike your broad pendant and sail away?" Lord Gardner gawped. "You are not sent home to face charges at a court-martial, are you, Lewrie? Under some cloud or other?"

"No, sir!" Lewrie quickly assured him. "He came up from Antigua with two sixty-fours, a Fifth Rate and two Sixth Rate frigates, and two more brig-sloops, and deemed my Fifth Rate redundant to his needs. As you will note, too, my lord, he deemed my small squadron's duties against privateers sufficiently done, and that his new-come warships could do a much better job of keepin' an eye on any new outbreak of raiders. And, he wanted the three wee ships under me for other duties down-islands. And, since he's senior to me by nigh two years, there it is, my lord."

"And you just *let* him order you to strike your flag and slink off?" Admiral Lord Gardner spat in astonishment.

"With the threat of privateers reduced, and their bases along the American coast eliminated, there was little I could do to argue the point, my lord," Lewrie told him with a hopeless shrug.

"By God, but he takes a lot upon himself!" Gardner gravelled. "Henry Grierson . . . Henry Grierson. Who the Devil is he, Niles? Have you ever heard of him?"

"Uhm, I do believe that he is distant kin to Lord Melville, my lord," Captain Niles tactfully said.

"Oh, good Lord!" Gardner snarled. "Even is he out of office, it will be some harpy in here, still, some female cousin thrice-removed, waving orders with Melville's seal upon 'em, telling me to build a frigate for her son! The Prime Minister should *never* have dismissed Johnny Jervis from his post as First Lord of Admiralty. What the Devil was he thinking?"

"Given this Grierson's connexions, then, perhaps we should put a new frigate together, for Lewrie here, hey, Niles?" Gardner wheezed.

"Would that a dockyard re-fit be possible, sir," Captain Niles said with a whimsical air.

"Just a hull cleaning, my lord," Lewrie reminded them. "We've weed as long as boarding pikes on our 'quick-work'."

"Recall, milord," Niles said, leaning closer to his superior, "that we spoke with the Commissioner of the Dockyards, Sir Charles Saxton, upon the amount of work he has in hand, and the possible availability of a free graving dock for any vessel coming in damaged? He and his people are completely swamped."

"'Swamped'?" Lord Gardner querulously posed. "What the Devil sort of word is 'swamped'? There are no swamps in England. Ireland, perhaps . . . all those bloody bogs of theirs . . . but not in England!"

"I stand corrected, milord," Niles easily amended, bestowing a congenial look at Lewrie as if to say that Lord Gardner's bark was not as dangerous as his bite, and that such word-play was natural to their working relationship. "Up to his neck in demands and needful work, rather. I fear that it may be weeks 'til what re-fit work and activation of ships now laid up in-Ordinary would admit your frigate the slightest bit of attention, Captain Lewrie. Even with specific, and urgent, orders from Admiralty, there is little we may do for you."

"In the Careenage, Captain Niles? My lord?" Lewrie said, feeling that wheedling might suit. "As I said, we only need a bit of hull cleaning. If not the Careenage, any stretch of beach would do."

"Lord, the beaches!" Captain Niles sadly mused. "I fear that there are now so many private contractors and shipwrights a'building 'back of the beach' that there may not be *room*. So many lost merchantmen to be replaced, new bottoms needed to expand our trade, and many smaller warships being built on speculation, not even under contract with Admiralty . . . I very much doubt there is a single seaport in all England where you might find the space, sir."

Gawd, I've been diddled! Lewrie thought with a cringe; *Sent to "Coventry" like a failure, and stuck there 'til the next Epiphany?*

"What if I went up to London and sought fresh orders, my lord?" Lewrie appealed to Lord Gardner.

"You may try, sir, but even with orders, as Niles said, you do not stand a Chinaman's Chance," Lord Gardner told him, seemingly in sympathy with his plight. He was not snarling or roaring. "Were it me, I'd have stood on my rights, and previous orders, and given this Grierson puppy the back of my hand!"

"Then there *would* have been court-martial charges, my lord," Lewrie croaked, his shoulders slumping in defeat. He puffed out his cheeks in a frustrated sigh, thinking hard.

"Excuse me, my lord, but . . . having just come in, I'm not yet considered part of Channel Fleet," Lewrie schemed. "I *could* leave for London without being faulted for sleeping out of my ship, and see what fresh orders I might . . . wangle?"

"Do *any* of you younger sorts have the ability to speak in plain King's English anymore?" Lord Gardner groused, slapping a fist on his desk top. "'*Wangle*', sir? Learn that word in a *swamp*, did you?"

"I *might've* heard it in Charleston or Savannah, sir," Lewrie said with a shrug, "From the Yankee Doodles."

"Both cities are famous for their surrounding swamps, milord," Niles dared to jape in a mellow purr, tipping Lewrie a wink that the Admiral could not see.

"Aye, Captain Lewrie," Lord Gardner grudgingly allowed, "until someone takes note of a perfectly good frigate lazing at anchor, and snatches you up, you are not under Channel Fleet, strictly speaking. If you imagine that you may discover a solution to your problem up in London, you are surely free to go . . . so long as you do not tarry 'mid the joys of the city."

"Ehm . . . might it be best did we issue Captain Lewrie a document of some kind, milord?" Captain Niles suggested. "An order from you allowing him to seek an audience at Admiralty might not go amiss."

"Fine, fine, scribble him out one, Niles, and I'll sign it, if you think that's best," Lord Gardner said in an irritated growl. His attention had already shifted to a fresh pile of paperwork on the side of his desk. "An excuse for truancy for the headmaster . . . a dispensation for past sins, hey? Carry on, then. Good day to you, Captain Lewrie. Best of luck . . . all that," he muttered, poring over a fresh letter, trying to find the proper "range" at which to read it.

"Good day, my lord, and thank you," Lewrie said in parting as he followed the pleasant Captain Niles to the outer office.

⚓

He had not come ashore with his boat-cloak, and regretted that lack once he left the Port Admiral's office building with his written pass safely stowed away in a dry breast pocket of his uniform coat. A sullen and misty rain had sprung up in the meantime, bringing with it a thin haze. Lewrie strolled back towards the quayside in search of a bum-boat to row him out to *Reliant*. He dodged several timber waggons and goods carts that trundled loudly over the cobblestones of the seaside road 'til he got to the large, mossed, and rain-slick stone blocks of the quayside, and stopped to look round. There weren't any boats to be seen, not within hailing distance.

Dozens of warships lay in the harbour, towering Third Rate 74s and a pair of more powerful Second Rates of at least 98 guns, perhaps the flagships of admirals come in from the blockade, surrounded by frigates, three-masted older sloops of war, and the newer brig-sloops. All were hazed by the rain, those lying further out indistinct. Lewrie looked to his right and left, and peered up toward the inner harbour, and Gosport. All along the hards there were scaffoldings, and ships in the middle of them being constructed. In the stone graving docks, warships were being repaired, temporarily de-commissioned. Even more, stripped to a gantline with all their top hamper above the lower mast trunks struck, and floating high with all their stores and guns landed ashore, lay anchored just off the graving docks, waiting their turns. The soft, misty rain and the wet haze acted like a blanket upon most sounds that morning, but even from this far away, Lewrie could hear the continual din of saws and hammers, and the tinny ringing of metal artificers on anvils and iron fittings. The Admiralty, and the Royal Navy and its supporting infrastructure, was the world's largest commercial and industrial enterprise, and Lewrie felt depressingly awed to think that the bulk of its activities was centred within eye and ear shot of where he stood, that instant. It was far too busy to ever get round to dealing with him!

Pleadin' at Admiralty may not help one tuppenny shit, Lewrie sadly gloomed; *Should I even* try? *Oh, why not? All they can say is no.*

A wryly amusing idea crossed his mind; when his father shoved him into the Navy in 1780, Sir Hugo's old attorney, Mr. Pilchard, had scribbled out a *huge* forgery. When his son Sewallis had finagled his way aboard a warship as a Midshipman in 1803, the lad had forged his father's signature on the introductory letter to an old shipmate that had been meant for his younger son, Hugh—in point of fact, the entire letter had been forged, inserting Sewallis's name for Hugh's. The art of forgery seemed to run in the family, for God's sake! Why not just sit down in some tavern here in Portsmouth with a set of orders done by the First or Second Secretary at Admiralty and write his *own* urgent demand for *Reliant* to be docked? If he waited for the wheels to clack round like a slow-running mantel clock, he'd be twiddling his thumbs 'till next Summer!

"London it is, then, no matter," Lewrie muttered to himself.

At least he could get some shopping done, perhaps look up some old friends for a day or two, once shooed from the infamous Waiting Room at the close of the Admiralty's working day, and . . .

"Oh, shit!" he groaned.

Once in Soundings of the Channel, once the Lizard had been sighted, he had written several letters for instant despatch as soon as *Reliant* was anchored. One, the most important of his personal correspondence, went to Lydia Stangbourne at her family's Grosvenor Street house, in hopes that the Autumn season had drawn her back from their country estates near Reading and Henley. Lydia would never miss the new rounds of plays, operas, symphonies, and art gallery showings.

He had not yet heard back from her, but, if their history together was any judge, it was good odds that she would sling a fortnight's heap of gowns into her coach and come down to Portsmouth, instanter! How wroth might she be to get to Portsmouth to discover that he'd run off to London like the worst sort of cad?

"Meet halfway . . . spot her coach somewhere on the road?" Lewrie said with another groan. "Just damn my eyes!"

CHAPTER ELEVEN

Lewrie considered a fast horse, from which it would be easier to spot Lydia's coach with her family crest on the doors, but in the continual misty rains, a horse just would not do. As quickly as he wished to get to London . . . to get to Lydia's house before she left . . . the roads would simply be too sloppy and muddy, and he would end up looking like one of the urchin Thames-side "mud-lark" boys before he'd gone ten miles, and he had only two uniforms aboard, his daily undress, and his very best, and it was good odds one of them would be ruined. If only he'd kept a civilian suit and top-boots aboard, with a great-coat to protect his trousers with its long, deep skirts, but all his "mufti", as his father called it from his days with the East India Company Army (where he'd made himself an immense pile of "tin" and had come home a full *nabob*!), was still at his father's estate at Anglesgreen. Besides, there was Pettus to think of, and Pettus wasn't skilled enough a horseman to keep up with the pace he planned! Lewrie would take lodgings at the Madeira Club, of course; his father was one of the founders and investors, and Lewrie could count on obtaining a room, at a discount, but he would not trust one of the house staff to "do" for him . . . not if he wished to make a good showing at Admiralty!

Only slightly begrudging the cost, Lewrie hired a four-horse coach for the trip up to the city. With only him and Pettus and their minimal "traps" aboard, he hoped that they would make much better time than buying passage in the diligence or "flying balloon" coaches, with Pettus relegated to a precarious seat on the roof in the foul weather, which would turn him surly for a week or more!

They set off the next morning, just a bit after "first sparrow fart", and *damned* if the lighter coach was still too heavy to breast Portdown Hill, and they had to get down and walk. Pettus did comment that if they had booked seats on the "dilly", they would have had to not only carry their own luggage to the top of the hill, but help with the pushing, too, which was sort of a blessing! The mud covering Lewrie's Hessian boots like heavy plaster casts made Lewrie disagree . . . rather tetchily! And, once back inside and out of the drizzle, there was still the mud and mire and horse, oxen, and mule dung mixed in that was flung up in a fine shower by their coach's spinning wheels that "got up his nose", both figuratively and literally, that had Lewrie swiping his face and his hair in a continual grumble. Every passing equipage that looked expensive enough to be Lydia Stangbourne's *had* to be peered at, did it not?

"It is a good thing that I thought to pack some extra towels, sir," Pettus cheerfully said as he offered Lewrie yet another clean one, then dug into the depths of a woven basket. "Might you care for some of Mister Cooke's pones, with Yeovill's bacon strips, sir? Oh, we have butter, as well!"

"Grrr," was Lewrie's impatient comment to that offer, but he did take two of their Free Black cook's "cat-head" flour bisquits and some bacon, and leaned back inside out of the wet to gnaw at them.

It was a given for travellers, no matter how impatient, that no matter how fast a coach could bowl along, no matter how rapid a pace a mount could be put to, how swiftly one of the new-fangled canal boats could be towed, or how quickly a ship with a fine breeze could sail, if one went a long distance, then it would take a long time to get there.

Making it even worse were the necessary stops every twenty-odd miles to change teams at a posting inn which *had* spare horses beyond the demands of the regularly scheduled diligence coaches. When there, no amount of grumbling and drumming of feet inside the coach would put any "urgent" into their coachman, so there was nothing for it but to clamber out, stretch their legs, head for the "jakes" to relieve themselves, slosh down some indifferently brewed tea, or sample a pint of the local beer, ale, stout, or porter. If they did not, for certain the coachman did, for which Lewrie had to pay to keep him merry and mellow. By the time they actually crossed the bridge into London, the coachman was *so* mellow that he began to bawl out songs in a raspy voice, laughing inanely between verses, and got so lost and befuddled that Lewrie had to mount the box with him to steer him to the corner of Duke Street and Wigmore Street, and the Madeira Club, just around six in the evening.

It was raining for real, by then, of course; just pouring down!

"Good ev'nin' t'ye, fine sir, and I hope ye found th' journey comf'table!" the coachman shouted down as Lewrie and Pettus gathered their belongings. "Ye wish me services for th' return, just ask o'th' publican at th' good ol' Three Nuns for Thom Wheeler, an' I'll come direck t'collec' ye, quick'z ye kin say 'knife'! Huzzah for th' Navy, I say! Gawd bless ye, ye brave tars! 'Rule Britannia, Britannia rules th' waves . . . Bri-tons never never never shall be' . . . someone hold me horses, I gotta get down an' piss like an ox!"

"Should we help him down, sir, before he dashes his brains out?" Pettus fretted.

"After all he's cost me, I don't give a toss," Lewrie said with a laugh. The coachman's drunken bawlings had drawn the attention of the Madeira Club's doorman and desk clerk, who had come out onto the stoop to goggle. "Ah, Lucas!" Lewrie called to the first one he saw and remembered by name. "Captain Alan Lewrie. I will need a room for a couple of nights, and room for my cabin steward!"

"Come in, come in, Captain Lewrie, get out of the rain," Lucas the desk clerk grandly offered, holding the doors open for them. "We do happen to have a vacancy or two, since Major Baird found a bride, and Mister Showalter is away to his home borough, on the hustings for the next by-election."

"What?" Lewrie gawped as he shrugged off his boat-cloak inside. "He ain't elected *yet*? I don't know which is more surprisin', Showalter still standin' for Commons, or Major Baird takin' a wife, at last."

Major Baird had come back from India *years* before a "Chicken *Nabob*" with at least £50,000 in profits, or loot, and had spent that long purportedly searching for a suitable mate . . . when not indulging in "knee-trembler" sex with the orange-selling girls at the theatres, and getting fellated in dark corners with his breeches undone.

"One hopes his new bride is . . . skilled," Lewrie sniggered.

Lucas cryptically grinned, knowing what Lewrie alluded to, but a good enough servant to appear unperturbed.

"There is brandy in the Common Room, Captain Lewrie, Spanish brandy I fear, but quite drinkable, as soon as you are settled in your rooms," Lucas told him as he signalled for a porter to see the luggage abovestairs, "and supper will be served at seven."

Lewrie's rooms were second storey, in the back and away from the continual rumble and skreak of waggon and carriage traffic. There was a coal fire laid in the hearth and crackling nicely, with a brass back-plate hot and radiating both warmth and light into the dank coolness of an un-used room. Lewrie sat down on a short settee near the fireplace and tugged his muddy boots off, which Pettus took away for cleaning and re-blacking for the morrow. He handed Lewrie a pair of buckled shoes which did not quite go with snug white undress trousers, but were pre-sentable enough for the clientele of the Madeira Club, and for a fellow who had no plans to be about the town that evening.

"All is ready for the morrow, sir," Pettus said after brushing the ever-present cat fur from Lewrie's best-dress gilt-laced coat and hat. The coat was hung on a dresser stand, the hat resting atop the round-topped upper spindle, the sash of the Order of The Bath draped round the spindle, and a fresh silk shirt, pressed waist-coat, and new pair of breeches and stock-ings arrayed on the shelves below the coat.

"Dress sword?" Lewrie asked, leaning back with his eyes half-closed. Nigh twelve hours in a swaying, jerking, and rocking coach had wrung him out like a dish-clout.

"Oh Lord," Pettus gasped. "I believe I left it atop your desk, sir, and *meant* to include it, but . . . my *pardons*, sir!"

"So long as we know it's safe," Lewrie wearily allowed, waving a hand. "My ev'ryday hanger'll do. So long as you're *sure* ye left it on the desk."

"Absolutely, sir," Pettus assured him. "I can see it in my mind's eye, and once we were in the coach, I *thought* I had an odd feeling that I was remiss, but . . . it won't happen again, sir!"

"As far as I can recall, Pettus, this is the first time *ever* you've been re-miss, and that's a good record," Lewrie excused. "Don't take yourself t'task over it. You remembered t'pack towels, and a fine basket o' vict-uals, after all."

"Thank you, sir, and I won't let you down again, sir. Now, I've your 'house-wife' laid out on the wash-hand stand, your razor stropped and ready for the morning. Will there be anything else before supper, sir? A pot of tea from belowstairs, or—?"

"No, I think that'll do 'til morning, Pettus," Lewrie said as he hauled out his pocket watch from a waist-coat pocket and peered at it. "Last time I lodged here, the kitchen staff arose round half-past five, so have them stir you, too. I think I'll trust to the staff of the club for the rest of the ev'nin', and you can get settled in with them and enjoy a good supper and some time off."

"Very good, sir, and good night to you," Pettus said, bowing a humble and abashed way out the door.

Most-like, he'll be kickin' himself in the arse the next week, entire, and lookin' at me as cutty-eyed as a whipped hound, Lewrie wryly told himself as he got to his feet. He rinsed his mouth with some water from the wash-hand stand pitcher, brushed his hair into proper order, and went down to the Common Room for some of that brandy.

Lewrie found around two-dozen of the other members of the club gathered by the windows of the Common Room that overlooked the street, whooping and laughing and laying wagers.

"Oh, look, good old Lewrie's back among us!" Mr. Pilkington, a fel-low from the 'Change, and middling in stocks, cried. "Huzzah for the Navy! How d'ye keep, old fellow, and wherever have ye been?"

"Gentlemen," Lewrie said back with a grin, making a half-bow from his waist. "The West Indies, the Bahamas, Spanish Florida, and playin' diplomat with the Americans."

"And none of them scalped you, hah?" Mr. Ludlow, who was big in the leather goods trade, hoorawed. "Come see this, Lewrie. There is a coachee out here, cup-shot."

"Drunk as Davy's Sow, I swear!" Pilkington hooted.

"He's been trying to get back up to his seat, but he's making a rum go of it," another crowed in amusement. "There should be a law for people in charge of coaches and waggons being that drunk."

"All I bought him was ale, beer, and porter," Lewrie said, crowding to the rain-smeared windows for a better look. "He coached me up from Portsmouth, and he *seemed* sober enough."

"Wager you all he's a bottle of rum stashed up there in the box," a younger member cried. "Been nipping on it on the sly, all the way."

"Wager it's more-like 'Blue-Ruin'," one of his fellow clubmen of the sporting sort dis-agreed. "Two shillings on gin, not rum."

"It'll be rum, and make it five shillings!" the first exclaimed with a hearty laugh. "What say you, Captain Lewrie?"

"I say someone'll have t'go out there in the rain to see what he has in the box, if anything," Lewrie rejoined. "Oh, Christ!"

The soused coachman managed to put a booted foot into the spokes of the kerbside front wheel and levered himself up to his seat with the wooden brake lever, but the patient team of horses shifted forward a bit and the coachman made a desperate lunge, arse over tit, almost making it to the driver's bench before falling backwards in a hand-scrabbling heap on the sidewalk. He wore a blissful smile, though, for he now had a blue glass bottle in one hand, at which he sipped deep.

"It's gin! It's gin! That's five shillings you owe me!" the sporting young gentleman cried.

The coachman took off his old-style tricorne hat and swiped at his hair, finally taking note that it was raining, shook water from his hat, and plunked it back on. He leaned an elbow on the coach's metal folding steps, got a clever look on his phyz, and began to crawl to them.

"A glass with you, Captain Lewrie," one of the older members offered, "for you've provided us a rare entertainment this evening! You missed the part where he was singing to his horses and kissing them on the lips!"

"Lord, where's he going now?" Pilkington cried.

The coachman dragged himself up the folding steps, clawed for the door handle, and finally managed to swing it open. Into the coach he went on his hands and knees, amazingly careful not to spill a drop from his gin bottle. The door was pulled closed, and he dropped out of sight for a moment, sprawled on the seats most-like. One moment later, though, up he sat to lower the window glass. He leaned out the door and began to pound on it, bellowing for some phantom coachee to whip up and get a move on, which action raised another gale of laughter in the club's Common Room. They could hear him through the room's windows, imitating the starting horn blown by the big diligence coaches when they rattled out from a posting inn, and the shouts of encouragement to the horse team.

The horse team took his thumping, shouting, and the *tra-tarah* as their cue to breast into their harnesses and begin to shamble forward at a slow walk, with no one tending the reins. The last they saw of the coach, and the drunken coachee, it was meandering East down Wigmore Street towards the cross-traffic of Mandeville Place!

"Gentlemen," the night manager had to call out several times before he drew the members' attention. "Supper is now served!"

Lewrie finished his Spanish brandy, which he had found not too raw after all, and joined the others as they all trooped into the dining room in high spirits, with some of the younger members still willing to wager that the coachman would get his neck broken, after all, if his coach tangled with another in the rain, or whether the coach would make it all the way to Marylebone Lane before the smash-up.

First came fine-shredded chicken in broth soup, followed by individual veal and ham pies, then fillets of grilled turbot accompanied by sweet stewed carrots and peas. The meal was topped off by a monstrous beef roast served with asparagus spears and hollowed-out potatoes with melted cheese and shredded bacon. The white wines with the soup and the turbot were excellent, as usual, as were the Bordeaux with the pies, and the cabernet with the roast beef, and the barge after barge of piping-hot and slightly toasted rolls were individual marvels with a liberal smear of fresh butter. Dessert was a strawberry jam roly-poly sprinkled with confectioner's sugar. Once the tablecloth was whisked away and the remains removed, out came the nuts, cheese, and sweet bisquits, and the club's signature, a rich and fine aged Madeira port, and the wine steward's promise that several casks of the rare "rainwater" port had been discovered at Oporto and were even then sitting in storage for the up-coming holidays.

Lewrie could dab his mouth and lean back in his chair with his port glass in hand, thinking that a meal, a feast, so English, was a topping-fine welcome back to his home shores!

CHAPTER TWELVE

*L*ewrie rose unaccountably early for a fellow so fond of snugly warm and sinfully soft shore beds, scrubbed, shaved, and dressed, then break-fasted on two cups of scalding-hot tea, and buttered rusks which he cadged from the kitchens long before the day's first meal was laid, bolted it all down in a rush, then was off in search of some wheeled transport for Whitehall. The best he found was a two-wheeled dog cart driven by a loquacious Irish pedlar who was willing to abandon his usual spot to hawk his cast-off clothing lines for promise of a shilling.

On the way, the Irishman cheerfully filled him in on the most won-drous event of the previous night. "'Twas a *ghost* coach, Cap'm, sor, rat-tlin' along with a witch at the reins, swear t'God, for how else kin a coach an' four make its way from Wigmore Street t'Oxford Street, turn down Regent Street, an' git t'the Swan an' Edgar, where it drew up nice as any-thin'. Ever'body wot saw it swears they knowed a witch drove it, for they all heard screamin' laughter and evil cacklin', but when the parish 'Char-lies' got to it, there was nary a soul aboard! Fackin' eerie, it wos!"

$\downarrow$

All Lewrie's hurry was for nought, though, for when he got to the Admiralty Office, he discovered an host of others already waiting. He stepped through the archway through the curtain wall, into the wee cobbled courtyard, and found that even the vendor with his tea cart and sticky buns was already there and doing a roaring business with the officers and Mids who had come in hopes of an interview, or the promise of an appointment. There was nothing for it but to go inside, in the process to be cautioned by the surly ancient tiler that "I'd not place much hope innit, Cap'm, sir, for there's a parcel o' unemployed before ya!"

Lewrie left his name with a junior clerk, stressing that he was currently a holder of an active commission, and wished to speak with the First Secretary, Mr. William Marsden, about orders for the cleaning of his ship's hull to make her serviceable for future duties, then looked for a place to sit in the infamous, over-crowded Waiting Room, but all the benches, settees, and chairs were occupied by Commission Sea Officers, the bulk of them Post-Captains with the twin epaulets of men with more than three years' seniority, some newer-minted Captains of less time in command of a Post ship with but one epaulet on their right shoulders, and a rare Commander or three with the epaulet on the left shoulder. Lieutenants with good sense had already surrendered their precious seats and idly, slowly paced about, striving to appear un-worried, among the Midshipmen whom they had turfed out earlier.

For a rare once, Lewrie had pinned on the star and donned the sash of the Order of The Bath, and as he meandered round the Waiting Room, a Commander sprang from his place at the end of a bench to offer it to Lewrie, who thanked him civilly, thinking that now and then the damned knighthood proved useful, even in this desperate place. There were tales of men, and one Midshipman in particular, who had come to Admiralty each working day for three years running to hunt active sea-going employment!

Over the next two hours, names were called out, and the lucky ones ascended the stairs to the Board Room to receive commissions to a new ship, or new orders for the ones they had. They usually came down with smiles. Lewrie began to note that one particular junior clerk was the one who summoned the officers who left pleased, and another clerk who appeared much less often and caused long sighs of disappointment, usually calling out some officer's name and only handing over a folded note; for a future appointment, perhaps, or most-likely a rejection. An aged Rear-Admiral who took a seat next to Lewrie, one who did not have a single hope in Hell of employment this side of the grave, told Lewrie with a cackled whisper that said clerk served the Second Secretary, Mr. John Barrow, upon whom Mr. Marsden usually foisted the chore of delivering the bad news.

By the end of the third hour, Lewrie's arse was numb, he badly needed a visit to the "jakes" to empty his bladder, and he might have gladly killed for a cup of sweetened and creamed tea. He snagged the "happy-making" clerk to inform him that he would be outside for a bit should his name be called, got his hat and boat-cloak from the cheque room, and went out to the courtyard.

Half-past ten of the morning must have been the tea interval for Admiralty drudges, for a great many men in civilian suitings came out to purchase a mug or cup of tea, and something upon which to gnaw, then trotted back inside to more scribbling and copying.

Lewrie got himself a mug with sugar but no cream, and stepped out of the way for the others, quite near two young men who were sipping hurriedly at their teas and sharing a thin Spanish *cigarro*, what some tobacco aficionados demeaned as a *cheroot*. They nodded greetings, hoped he did not mind the drifting smoke, then returned to their conversation, most of which was grousing about their superiors and what tasks to which they were put.

"What about the charts, then, Jemmy?" one of them asked the other. "Dalrymple won't be happy if our office has to pay for them."

Lewrie knew that Mr. Alexander Dalrymple was the Hydrographer of the Navy, for the very good reason that it was to that worthy that Lewrie had mailed the up-dated charts and soundings that Lt. Tristan Bury had made of Bermudan waters, just before Lewrie had dragooned him into his little anti-privateering squadron in the Spring.

"Well, he's in charge of charts and such," the other breezily said between quick puffs on the *cheroot* before handing it over. "Even if Admiralty doesn't print its own. The Board's decided that all the troop transports, and the Lieutenants assigned to each one, must have them . . . the Cape of Good Hope, and the separate charts for Table Bay, and Cape Town, Blaauwburg Bay, Saldanha Bay, even Simon's Bay on the other side of the Cape. If the hired-on transport masters want their own copies, they can buy them, but Admiralty will foot the bill for our people. Now, which office gets the bill, that's the question!"

"We'll be dashing all over London to purchase them, or pay for rush jobs to have them printed," the fellow from the Hydrography Office bemoaned. "Then, we'll have to amend them all with the latest soundings and hazards! By hand! When will Marsden let us know?"

"His Majesty Head Clerk Swami said the Board will tell him by midafternoon . . . just in time to ruin your evening, hah hah!"

"Gentlemen," Lewrie intruded, putting his stern face on. "You may believe that discussing what sounds like a secret expedition to Cape Town is safe, here behind the curtain wall, but you never know who might be listening. The matter is better mentioned safely *inside* the building, if at all."

"Sorry, sir, we didn't—," the young fellow whom Lewrie took to be a junior scribbler in William Marsden's office said with a shocked look.

"Well, I doubt the tea vendor or the newspaper boys are Dutch, so it might be alright," Lewrie allowed, giving them a reprieve, and a grin. "Upon that head, though . . . there *is* an expedition planning to capture Cape Town from the Dutch? I was there several years ago, and took the opportunity to hunt and ride all over the town and its environs, over to Simon's Town on False Bay? When you speak with Mister Marsden, pray do you mention to him that Captain Lewrie of the *Reliant* frigate, who's waiting word for an interview, may prove useful to the endeavour, hmm?"

"Captain Lewrie and the *Reliant* frigate, of course, sir," the young clerk replied, nodding as he committed that to memory. "I shall as soon as I am abovestairs, sir. And, thank you for your caution . . . about the, ahem."

"It always pays t'keep mum about official business outside of work hours," Lewrie congenially agreed, shrugging off the young man's thanks. "His Majesty's Government has an organisation to root out any enemy spies, or people who'd profit by givin' 'em information. You'd be surprised how many they discover."

The two clerks finished their teas, took their last puffs from the *cheroot*, and the one from the Hydrography Office pinched the lit end, stubbed and scrubbed it on the sole of his shoes, and stowed it away in a waistcoat pocket for later. A last "good day" and they went back inside to their scribblings and filings.

Now, let's see if that *gets me invited up to the Board Room,* Lewrie thought, feeling particularly clever for a rare once; *and urgent orders for a hull cleaning!*

Business was suspended for the mid-day meal. Mr. William Marsden trooped down the stairs and breezed out the doors for his dinner with his gaze fixed on the middle distance, acknowledging no one, else some uniformed mendicant on half-pay attempted to catch his eye for a brief word, which would turn into a queue of them. Lewrie followed the herd that left the Waiting Room, to seek his own dinner, but he didn't go far. Only three blocks away, near Charing Cross, there was a chop-house, a cut above the riskier two-penny ordinarys, where the meat on one's plate or wood trencher could be cat, dog, rat, or dead horse—and none of them too fresh, either. No one had died of the chop-house.

For six pence he got a pint of ale, a beef pasty which actually tasted like beef even if it was ground, half of a roast potato, and a glob of currant duff. Quite satisfied, and with no immediate sign of food poisoning, he returned to the Waiting Room a bit earlier than the rest, snagged an upholstered chair near the stairs, and scooped up a discarded copy of *The Times* to while away the rest of the afternoon.

Mr. Marsden returned, again acknowledging no one, and stomped up the stairs to his offices. By two in the afternoon, after another trip to the "necessary" and two more cups of courtyard tea . . .

"Captain Lewrie?" the "happy-making" clerk called out at last. "Captain Alan Lewrie? Is Captain Lewrie present?"

"Here, sir!" Lewrie replied, shooting to his feet.

"If you will follow me, sir?" the clerk bade. Smiling! That Lewrie took for a good sign.

"Ah, good afternoon, Captain Lewrie . . . Sir Alan, rather, I was not aware of your knighthood," Mr. William Marsden said quite genially from behind his desk, waving a hand to steer Lewrie to a chair.

"Good afternoon to you, Mister Marsden," Lewrie replied as he sat down and tugged at the set of his waist-coat. "Thank you very much for seeing me on such short notice."

"Before having you in, I had my clerks look up your latest reports on your Bahamian doings, and the privateering situation which you were despatched to deal with," Marsden said, carefully leafing through a file folder to scan the pertinent reports he'd sent in to Admiralty before leaving for home. "Settled most satisfactorily, it would seem . . . for the short term, at least. One may only hope that Captain Henry Grierson applies himself to the task with a determination equal to yours. It is quite disturbing, however, to read your last despatch in regards to his squadron's arrival, and the panic that ensued. As for him ordering you to strike your flag and surrender the ships of *your* squadron to his command, I am most perplexed as to why he took that action. Do you have an explanation, Sir Alan?"

"He found me impertinent, Mister Marsden," Lewrie baldly said, "for pointing out what a lame jape his arrival was, and insisted that his arrival made my squadron moot. Since he thought me so impertinent, he had enough Post-Captains to form a court, so . . . ," Lewrie said with a weary shrug, then added, "He's distant kin to Lord Melville."

"Ah," Marsden replied with a knowing nod, and a grimace. "At any rate, your initial request for an interview involved a request for dockyard services, I believe?" Marsden went on, referring to a note scribbled on scrap paper by one of his clerks.

"*Reliant* was taken out of Ordinary in April of 1803, sailed in May when the war resumed, and has been in continuous service in West Indies or semi-tropical waters since, sir," Lewrie explained. "She is badly in need of a hull cleaning. We've been able to keep up with the usual wear-and-tear, and rot, *above* the waterline, but she is weeded and slow. By next May, she *should* be due a total docking and re-fit, but . . . with a careening and cleaning, the replacement of any coppering that might have sloughed off, and some fresh white lead, she can still give good service beyond next May."

"Extending your command into her, and your active commission," Marsden sagely nodded, his face stony, giving nothing away.

"I will confess that I do wish to keep her, sir," Lewrie told the sceptical fellow, "to keep my officers and crew together as long as possible. We've done grand things together, discipline is so good that we rarely ever have to resort to the 'cat', and have not had any desertions, even anchored in American harbours. We both know that that is damned rare, and did I have my choice, when the time comes for her to enter the dry dock, I would *love* to see us all turned over into a new ship, entire. My people are that good, sir!"

"The mark of a good captain," Marsden said with another firm nod, then turned to Lewrie's request. "You told one of my junior ink-spillers that you were familiar with Cape Town, Sir Alan?"

"I dare say that I am, sir!" Lewrie quickly assured him.

I do *dare say,* Lewrie told himself; *I'd dare say* anything *to get what I need!*

"A brief breaking of your passage at the 'tavern of the seas'?" Marsden asked with faint good humour.

"I was part of the escort to a 'John Company' trade to China, a few years back, when I had the *Proteus* frigate, sir," Lewrie eagerly laid out in hopes that he could convince Marsden that his experience was vital. "We tangled with a brace of French frigates as we stood off and on Cape Town in the night. We were stern-raked and had our rudder shot away, so we had to put in and try to find a replacement. We were there for more than a month, sir. Landed our badly wounded to a shore sick bay in a rented farmhouse halfway up the Lion's Head, buried some ashore, and took a train of bullock waggons over to the beached wreck of an East Indiaman that mistook False Cape for the real'un in a gale, and hired local divers and artificers t'salvage *her* rudder before the wreckers at Simon's Town got away with it.

"During all that, I got a chance to know the lay-out of Cape Town quite well, too," Lewrie went on, "and hired a local hunter for a guide. We rode up North, into the hills above the lesser bays . . ."

For the life of him, he could not remember the names of all the places that those clerks had tossed out!

". . . got familiar with the land about the town to the East and the South, as well, sir," Lewrie said with a confident but false grin.

"How many forts protect Cape Town, sir?" Marsden shrewdly asked.

"I recall but two, sir," Lewrie replied, "when I was last there, at least. And we had possession of the place. Had no dealings with our Army at the time, d'ye see."

"Which is . . . Fort Knocke?" Marsden enquired, taking a moment to peer at another note on his desk. "However one says that. 'Nok-ah'? 'Ka-nok-ah'? Bloody foreigners!"

"Both are on the seafront, either side of the town, but I do believe that Fort . . . whatyecallit . . . is the one on the Eastern side of Cape Town, closest to the land approaches, sir."

Lewrie tried to make it *sound* as if he knew what he was talking about;

he hadn't a bloody clue if that was right and crossed fingers for luck like the un-prepared student he had been at a succession of schools. The way Mr. Marsden peered at him without comment made him feel as if he'd break out in a funk-sweat.

"I do know that the Dutch had shoved hundreds of guns in both forts, Mister Marsden," Lewrie went on to fill a sudden uncomfortable silence, "both iron and bronze cannon, of heavy and medium calibre, for defence to seaward, and lighter guns against troops. At least, I do recall that they were still there when I was there, long after Lord Keith, Captain Elphinstone then, first took the place."

"Uhmhmm," Mr. Marsden at last said, leaning forward to dip his pen in an ink-well, "where do you lodge when up in London, Sir Alan?"

"The Madeira Club, at the corner of Duke and Wigmore Streets, sir," Lewrie told him, sensing that the interview was over, whether he'd been successful or not.

"I will send you my decision shortly, Sir Alan," Marsden promised, still looking glum and dubious. "We cannot keep you hanging on tenterhooks and idle in town whilst the Fleet is denied the use of your frigate," Marsden said as he finished scribbling the address on a scrap of paper.

"That would be most welcome, sir," Lewrie told him, preparing to rise and depart. "Either way, clean bottom or foul, I am sure that Channel Fleet will soon find *Reliant* useful, unless—"

"Captain Home Riggs Popham may find your ship, and your previous experience, useful as well," Marsden said with a vague-looking smile. "It is he who is to hoist his broad pendant and command the expedition."

Marsden briefly pursed his lips in a wee *moue,* as if the choice of officer commanding had not been his. "The fellow who devised the signal flag code. A *clever* fellow."

That didn't sound like much of a recommendation, either.

"Oh!" Lewrie said, perking up. "I served under him briefly, in the winter of 1804, when we made that attack on the port of Calais with catamaran torpedoes and fireships!"

That was not much of a recommendation on Lewrie's part, either, for the experimental expedition had been a shambles. The few catamaran torpedoes loosed on wind and tide had failed utterly, with only one of them actually exploding, and that nigh *miles* away from anything that could have charitably been called a real target, and the one fireship had swanned about like a hound on a dozen scents at once before blowing up harmlessly. Perhaps the French had enjoyed the show, and their brief respite from utter boredom.

"Yayss, I do now recall that you were seconded to experimental trials with torpedoes," Marsden drawled in sour amusement. "A damned foolish idea, those. And, did you *enjoy* working with Popham?"

"A most inspiriting man, sir," Lewrie replied, "just bung-full of ideas, and energy."

"Oh, yes!" Marsden archly agreed, with a grimace. "Energetic, enterprising, and a most *mercurial* fellow, is Captain Popham. As industrious as an ant hill, just brimming with new ideas. He makes one wonder how he keeps all his balls in the air at the same time, like a juggler at a street fair. A rather un-orthodox man. Who knows *what* he'll pull out of his hat next."

What the Hell have I talked myself into? Lewrie wondered.

"Well, sir," Lewrie said, getting to his feet, "thank you again for seein' me, and I'll be on my way and out of your hair."

"Good day to you, Captain Lewrie," Marsden said with a parting smile, if only to be gracious, "and look for my decision by letter at your lodgings."

Whether he knew that *Reliant* would be seen to or not, whether he would get orders for Cape Town or the utter dullity of the blockade with a foul bottom, Lewrie put a confident grin on his face for the benefit of those still idling in the Waiting Room. He trotted down the stairs to reclaim his hat and cloak with a spry and cocky show of glee and energy. He doubted that Marsden would have a decision to send him by the end of the day, so he might have time to do some brief shopping to supplement his kit and his personal stores.

There was another letter that he was even more eager to recieve. Now, if only Lydia Stangbourne had not yet left for Portsmouth, there was a chance that he might have a supper companion tonight, and perhaps much, much more!

CHAPTER THIRTEEN

*T*hat lascivious hope lasted just long enough for Lewrie to pop into the Madeira Club and ask the desk clerk if there had been a reply to his morning note to Lydia's London residence. There was, indeed, but it was merely a folded-over piece of scrap paper, written in an awkward scrawl in pencil, which stated that Miss Lydia had departed for Portsmouth the previous morning and did not say when she would be returning, signed by someone who claimed to be the family butler, and if it *was* written in English, his name *looked* to be Gullyfart or Cully's Tart. The desk clerk, when consulted, could not make heads or tails of it, either; his best guess was Cuffysdart.

"Is there anything else for me?" Lewrie asked, deflating.

"Just the one, sir," the clerk told him.

That'un was properly wax-sealed and written in an elegant hand, on good bond paper, to boot. Lewrie had sent a note round to his father, Sir Hugo St. George Willoughby, to inform him that he was in town. Not that Lewrie really cared a fig to *see* the old fart, but it was what one did to be sociable, and remain in the will . . . assuming that the old lecher didn't turn dotty in his head and squander all he had on whores and courtesans and race horses.

He was almost (but not quite) disappointed to discover that his father had other plans for the evening with an intriguing lady just new-come to London. Sir Hugo did not propose an alternate time for him to call, unless he was *long* in London, and didn't have to rush back to his ship right away. Sir Hugo was sure he would understand.

I surely do, Lewrie thought in a foul humor; *I can always count on my father . . . he'll let me down every time!*

He slouched into the Common Room and flung himself down into one of the leather wing chairs near the fireplace, wondering what he could do. He ordered American whisky from the steward who came to his side, but there was none available; would Spanish brandy suit, or might he settle for a Scottish whisky? Lewrie stuck with the brandy.

As intently as he'd peered at every passing coach-and-four that had been bound to Portsmouth on the road the day before, he had missed sight of Lydia's equipage. How irked might she be to arrive, after dark and in a nippy drizzle, most-like, to find that no set of rooms had been booked for her at The George Inn, their usual trysting place, for the very good reason that he hadn't gotten confirmation that she would be coming down? How even further irked might Lydia be to send word to *Reliant* and learn that he'd dashed off to London, leaving her to her own devices—without even leaving an explanatory note to mollify her!

It ain't like we're married *or anything like that,* Lewrie told himself, his mood becoming a tad anxious; *I've not even given her "a packet o' pins" as promise for* anything*! By God, though, if she ever speaks t'me after this, I'll get an* ugly *ear full!*

He considered hiring a coach that instant and dashing back to Portsmouth, no matter the perils of a night-time journey, but . . . no. He had to stay in London, bide close to the Madeira Club 'til he got word from Admiralty, whichever way that decision would go.

A damn *good night t'get blind drunk!* he concluded with a sigh, and waved his empty glass at the steward for a top-up.

Needless to say, his next morning was more than a tad blurry. After breakfast, and nigh an entire pot of hot, black coffee, Lewrie spent his time writing letters. Firstly, he penned a grovelling "forgive me" to Lydia to her Grosvenor Street house, explaining as best he was able why he had had to dash off. With no news from Admiralty, he then wrote letters to his sons, Sewallis and Hugh, who were at sea, Sewallis still most-like on the French blockade, and Hugh and his ship, as he'd learned, with Nelson in pursuit of that Frog Admiral Villeneuve and his large French fleet, its location still unknown.

With nothing *else* to do, and admittedly hitting his stride with his scribbling, Lewrie wrote chatty letters to his former brother-in-law Burgess Chiswick and his wife, Theodora, the brother-in-law he liked. He wrote to the other one, Governour, who despised him, and his wife, Millicent, again to be sociable. He wrote a separate letter to his daughter, Charlotte, who resided with Governour and Millicent, though he had no idea if she would even read it, or if Governour would even allow her to see it. Then came his former ward, Sophie de Maubeuge, now Mrs. Anthony Langlie. Sophie and his former First Officer in the *Proteus* frigate were the parents of at least two children by now, and were the most pleasant of his correspondents, were Lewrie given his "d'ruthers".

With *still* no word from Mr. Marsden by noon, and with his appetite stifled by the odd rumbles engendered from the night before, he even went so far as to write to Sir Malcolm Shockley and his wife, the twitter-brained Lucy. Back when Lewrie and she had been teens, he'd been head-over-heels with her, but she *had* been a Beauman, of the Jamaican Beaumans, and nothing good could have ever come from *that* clan.

He paused to wonder if Lucy was still slipping under the sheets with other men and gulling poor, honest, and upright Sir Malcolm into believing her faithfulness!

Lewrie penned shorter notes to Peter Rushton, now Viscount Draywick after inheriting his childless uncle's title; and his younger brother, Harold, who had inherited their father's title of Baron Staughton when Peter had been elevated upwards. Harold, quite unlike his older brother, was level-headed and rather shrewd, when sober at least, and good company when not. Lewrie hadn't seen him in years, but Peter had gotten Harold a well-paying government post under the Secretary of State at War, where he wielded considerable influence. One never knew who might come in handy when it came to patronage and influence! Lewrie even wrote another, shorter, letter to another old school chum, that nefarious "Captain Sharp", Clotworthy Chute, who was rumoured to have turned honest and was now big in the antiques trade. Lewrie carefully stressed that he was in town a little time . . . too short a time for Clotworthy to hit him up for a loan!

By two in the afternoon, and with still no letter for him at the front desk, Lewrie betook himself on a stroll, threading his way through the pedestrian throngs of Wigmore Street, West to Baker Street, then South to the corner of Oxford Street and one of his favourite taverns, the Admiral Boscawen, where he tentatively supped on sliced roast beef, pease pudding, potato hash, and gravy, and was delighted to discover that what *went* down would *stay* down, aided along by two pints of ale.

Not quite as bleary as before, Lewrie returned to the Madeira Club, where he *yet* had no mail, and whiled away the rest of the afternoon by scribbling notes to his old Cox'n, Will Cony, who now owned the Olde Ploughman in Anglesgreen; to his former cabin steward, Aspinall, who was now a published author here in London; and, frankly, got so bored that he even penned letters to his Lewrie cousins at Wheddon Cross in Devonshire, near Exeter.

By the time he had folded, waxed, and sealed the last letter, it was nigh five o'clock, and the club's stewards and servants were circulating to stoke up the fireplaces and light more candles to welcome the club's members back from their days on the town. That passable Spanish brandy appeared on a sideboard.

Pettus made his appearance, yawning and shrugging his clothing into order, looking as if he had used his free time to good purpose whilst Lewrie had spent the day alone, and had caught up on his sleep.

"Will you be dining out on the town tonight, sir?" Pettus asked.

"Hmm . . . think not, Pettus," Lewrie told him after deliberating. Gloster's Chop House and his favourite-of-all *restaurant* in Savoy Street, were both off the Strand, and either were just too far to go at that hour. "I'll dine in here. There's little for you to do for me 'til the morning. Enjoy your idleness," he said with a smile. "I trust they're feedin' ye well, and that your quarters are warm and comfy?"

"Oh, aye, sir, quite pleasant, and they feed extremely well," Pettus told him, "though I do miss Yeovill's way with spices and—"

"Pardons, Captain Lewrie," Lucas, the desk clerk, interrupted, "but a messenger just dropped this off for you, this instant."

"Aha!" Lewrie exclaimed as Lucas handed him a stiff cream bond letter with a large blob of royal blue sealing wax and the imprint of Admiralty. "Wish me luck, Pettus. Thankee, Lucas."

He tore it open impatiently, but, once he had it un-folded, he paused and hitched a deep breath, expecting the worst.

"Uhmhmm, 'directed and required . . . authorised to make such re-pairs His Majesty's Dockyard deems necessary' . . . *Hell*, yes!" he cried, thumping his free left hand on the arm of his chair in triumph.

"Good news, sir?" Pettus asked.

"The best, Pettus, the very *best*!" Lewrie told him, laughing. "We'll be off for Portsmouth at first light. See Lucas to arrange a coach for us . . . *not* that drunken fool who fetched us up! We have orders for our bottom cleaning, and additional orders for the South Atlantic, soon as we can get the ship back on her own bottom and make sail! Hallelujah!"

"I'll see to it, directly, sir!" Pettus assured him.

"Something to drink, sir?" a steward asked.

"I think I'll try the Scottish whisky, this time," Lewrie said. "That Spanish brandy makes me bilious, haw haw!"

Oh Christ, though, Lewrie had to think a moment later; *If I'm off to Portsmouth, I'll miss Lydia* again*!*

CHAPTER FOURTEEN

At such short notice, hiring an elegant coach-and-four for the return to Portsmouth was out of the question, so what Pettus managed to turn up was a weather-beaten and drab coach with cracked or stained glass windows, ratty interior fabrics, and leather bench seats so hard that there might not have been any horse-hair padding left. To make things even worse, the team looked more due the knacker's yard, maybe even over-due. The coachee was rail thin, taciturn, and sour, but swore that he was of the temperance persuasion, and a Methodist Dissenter.

"And here I've thought all this time that Methodists were prone t'leapin' enthusiasm," Lewrie chuckled after they rattled away from the Madeira Club's stoop in the "early-earlies" in a light fog. "It must be the temperance part that makes him as dour as Wilberforce's crowd."

"Does he stick with cider instead of ale, sir, perhaps he will cost you less," Pettus suggested. He was cringing in a corner of the coach's front bench seat, shrunk up in mortification, looking even more abashed than he had when he'd overlooked Lewrie's presentation sword. "And, twenty-odd miles on, there will surely be a better team."

"Assumin' these beasts *live* long enough t'get to the next posting house," Lewrie said with a sigh and a roll of his eyes.

"Sorry, sir," was all that Pettus had to say, in a mutter.

"Oh, worse things happen at sea, I'm told," Lewrie rejoined in slight mirth. "Do you shuffle over to the starboard side, we can both keep watch for Mistress Lydia's coach."

Out in open country beyond London, on the way to Guildford, the traffic thinned out from the nose-to-tail crush of all the waggons and carts and drays bringing goods and produce to town. Even so, a fresh coach came along at least once every two minutes or so. Some were of local origin, light one-horse or two-horse carriages trotting along to carry country folk from one village or hamlet to the next. Every now and then, with a thunder of hooves, the cracking of whips, and the *tara-tara* warnings from the assistant coachees, much larger diligence coaches or regularly scheduled flying "balloon" coaches came dashing toward them with six- or eight-horse teams, swaying and pitching fit to throw passengers and luggage from the cheaper seats on the rooves, barrelling "ram you, damn you" and expecting anyone with the least bit of sense to get right out of their way.

There were young, flashing gentlemen, "all the crack and all the go", driving their two- and three-horse chariots at similar paces as the passenger coaches, dust or mud flying in their wakes, and flashing past their own shabby coach with shouts of glee over how rapidly they could eat the miles, and how daring they were. Lewrie's coach was passed by a pair bound South from behind them, two chariots racing wheel-to-wheel like ancient Romans in the Colosseum, and damning Lewrie's equipage for a "slow-coach" as they careened around them!

Now and then, though rarely, a much grander coach-and-four came trotting toward them, with liveried coachmen in the driver's box and in the bench above the coach's rear boot. Most of those coaches bore no family crests on their doors, and those that did went by so quickly that it was hard for Lewrie and Pettus to discern even the colours or the shapes of the crests, and it was a rare coach with painted heraldry that bore a crest large enough to be recognised.

Lewrie tried to recall how large the Stangbourne crest had been and the colour of the coach they'd shared to Sheerness, the one she had taken the last time she'd come down to Portsmouth, and began to wonder if he would recognise it if it sat right in front of him, at full stop! As rich as

Lydia and her brother Percy were, they might have more than a dozen carriages and coaches for every occasion!

Assuming that Percy hadn't gambled them into debtors' prison in the meantime!

They got to Guildford for a change of horses, and a chance to stretch their legs. The four poor prads were led off to rest and feed, heads hanging low, and as the coachman arranged a fresh team, Lewrie and Pettus had a quick breakfast of bacon strips and cheese on thickly sliced bread with smears of spicy, dark mustard, and pint mugs of ale. When offered, their coachman settled for a hard-boiled egg, toast, and hot tea . . . without sugar or cream.

"Evidently, cream and sugar are too luxurious for 'temperance' people," Lewrie commented in a whispered chuckle. "God only knows what a cinnamon roll'd do . . . one bite, and he'd be found in a gutter with crumbs on his face, clutchin' a bottle o' rum, weepin' for bein' a back-slider!"

Once a slightly more promising team was hitched up, they were off once more, at a slightly better pace this time, for more peering at the passing traffic. They passed the turning for Chiddingfold, the narrow road that led to Anglesgreen and Lewrie's father's estate. He wished that he could spare the time to see his daughter, Charlotte, but . . . no, Lewrie sadly reckoned; that could only turn out stiffly, and badly. He had written her. That would have to be good enough.

A bit North of Liphook, Pettus pulled his head back into the coach to announce, "Here comes another coach-and-four, sir, with liveried coachee and all."

Lewrie stuck his head out of the lowered door window, peering ahead. What he could see of the approaching coachman's livery under his opened black great-coat *looked* like the royal blue and white trim that he remembered, the coach was very *much* like the dark green with discreet gilt trim one that Lydia had used in London, and had used to come down to Portsmouth before, and its wheel rims and spokes *appeared* to be the same jaunty canary yellow.

Lewrie leaned further out, half-standing with head and shoulders out the window, looking to see if the passengers were—!

"Lydia!" he bellowed as he espied a woman seated in the middle of the

front-facing rear bench seat, a woman with loose and curly hair the colour of old honey. "Lydia Stangbourne! It's me, Alan!"

"What the Devil?" the female passenger cried back, mouth agape in
shock as her coach came level with his and whisked by.

"Driver, draw up!" Lewrie bellowed to their coachman, opening the
coach door to hang out and look aft. In his loudest quarterdeck bellow, he
shouted, "Lydia, draw up!"

Sure enough, the other coach was being reined in, and he could see
Lydia leaning out an opened window. It was she!

"Draw up, did you say, sir?" their dour coachman asked.

"Goddamn right I did! Whoa, stop right now!" Lewrie exclaimed as
he kicked the metal folding steps down with a booted foot. Before the
coach could come to a full stop, he was jumping down and running back
up the road. "Hoy, Lydia, it's me!" he cried, waving madly.

He got to her coach in a trice and pulled down the door handle to whip
it open.

"Good God!" Lydia gasped. "Where did *you* spring from?"

"God called away t'London, a bit after I sent you a letter," he said,
knowing that he was grinning like a loon and not caring if he was or not.
He sprang inside her coach, ignoring her goggling maid-servant, and sat
beside her. "I sent a note round your house, and got told you'd already
left, so I was *hopin'* t'run across you like this, *somewhere* on the road, at
any rate . . . comin' or goin', no matter. You look simply . . . wonderful!"

And ain't ye goin' t'gush somethin' back? Lewrie wondered at Lydia's
reticence. She was smiling, but it wasn't the same sort of adoring look
that he remembered. In point of fact, one of her brows was arched, as if
nettled by his sudden appearance. And, she had yet to offer him even one
of her hands, much less a cool peck on a cheek! He put that down to the
presence of the maid-servant. Lydia could be warm, open, and girlishly
animated in private, very quick to smile or laugh out loud. In public,
though, her demeanour was arch and imperious, guarded, cautious, and
aloof. Given that she had been the victim of nearly three years of scandal
and newspaper gossip when she had pled for a Bill of Divorcement in the
House of Commons, with charges and countercharges from her bestial
husband almost a daily thrill for avid readers, it was no wonder that she
had need to armour herself. During the procedure, and even after Parliament had voted her Divorcement and rejected her husband's, Lydia had

become a scorned and rejected woman to all but her closest old friends and her small family.

Lewrie had forgotten that in his eagerness, and silently chid himself for being so boyish.

"I tried to spot your coach on the way to London, but no luck," Lewrie babbled on. "And now you're returning to the city?"

"You were not in Portsmouth," she replied, nigh accusingly.

"Admiralty," Lewrie told her with a shrug. "They summon, I have to go, and I hadn't gotten your reply to my invitation, so I could make no plans for your arrival 'till I knew where we both were, when you were coming down, *if* you would be coming at all."

"The George Inn was full," Lydia said, rustling her skirts in irritation. "I ended up spending the night at some place called the Blue Posts . . . full of Midshipmen and . . . eager young Lieutenants."

Ouch! Lewrie cringed; *Full o' lusty young sprogs, she means, and her the only woman in sight!*

"Sorry for that, Lydia," Lewrie said. "That couldn't have been enjoyable. Er . . . you're not in a *tearin'* rush t'get back to London, are you? Mean t'say, Liphook's but a few miles away, and there's an inn there."

Her expression was stony, and her dark-emerald-coloured eyes bore a leery squint.

"We haven't seen each other in ages, and at the least I could offer you dinner, or just a pot of tea, or . . . ," Lewrie offered, feeling his neck beginning to burn when he realised that he was pleading. "Talk things over? Catch up on the latest news since your last letter got to me in the Bahamas? The last I got was four months ago."

"I would be getting into London a little after dark as it is, Alan," Lydia said, turning her head away in contemplation for a moment. "Even if my coachmen are in Percy's regiment, and go well-armed, he'd have a fit did I expose myself to the risk of highwaymen at night. I fear that I cannot accept your kind offer."

At least she called me by my Christian name, he bemoaned.

"I will take a breath of air, and a stroll whilst we are here," Lydia said to her maid. To Lewrie, with the beginnings of a smile at long last, she said, "If you will be so good as to hand me down, sir?"

Lewrie sprang from the coach to do the footman's job of folding down the metal steps, then offered her a steady arm to support her as she descended. With her left arm atop his right, they began to stroll toward his hired coach. With fewer witnesses, Lydia leaned close to him, pressing her cheek to his shoulder for a second.

"It is so good to see you, too, Alan," Lydia said with evident fondness in her voice, and looking into his face with a grin so wide that her nose did its usual, endearing, crinkle. "I, too, have most anxiously tried to spy you on the road, after I sent a note out to your ship, and your First Officer, Westcott, sent me a reply that you had gone up to London. I dearly wish that I *could* accept your invitation of dinner, or a pot of tea, but . . . I fear you must be back in Portsmouth by dark yourself, must you not?"

"True, I must," Lewrie told her, explaining the sad condition of his ship's bottom, and the urgency of her cleaning before joining Popham's expedition. "The earlier it's started, the earlier it's ended, and we'll be off."

"To the South Atlantic?" Lydia gasped. "So soon?"

"I am so sorry, Lydia," Lewrie said with a long sigh. "Barely back to England, and *whish!*—then God only knows how long we'll be before *Reliant* is de-commissioned and paid off at home, again. Who'd be a sailor, hey? Or . . . someone who waits for one?" he asked as he gently slid his arm round her waist and drew her to face him.

"This is so *cruel*!" Lydia whispered, her eyes going moist. "God, how I've longed for you to return, and not knowing when that would *be*. I thought you were still on the other side of the ocean, then your note arrived saying that you were in Portsmouth, with no hint that you *were* returning! . . ."

"I'd have gotten back before any letter would have arrived, we left so quickly," Lewrie explained. "The mail packet'd still be mid-ocean. Sorry about that."

"How blissfully happy I was to know that you were back safely, and wanted me to come to you," Lydia said, almost in a whimper. "And to dash off like a bloody . . . *fool*! . . . to find you gone, without one *thought* for me. No lodging arranged, not even an explanation left for me 'til I had to *beg* one from your Westcott. Damn you, Lewrie!"

Uh-oh! I'm in the "quag" up t'my neck! Lewrie cringed.

"I didn't *know* you'd be coming down, so how could I . . . ," Lewrie tried to wriggle out, but stopped and peered into her eyes. "I've made you angry, haven't I? Lydia, I am so sorry. Believe me, I wanted to see you just as desperately. If I'd been aboard to get word that you were coming, I'd have strewn the road with rose petals. I did not mean to seem like

I ignored you. Don't be cross with me, Lydia. If we have only a few minutes together here—"

"Yes, you *have* made me angry, Alan," Lydia snapped with an impatient toss of her head. "Angry with you, and angry with myself for being such a bloody *idiot*! Angry for laying myself open to such disappointment. I am angry with you for having to spend a night being gawked at, goggled, and snickered over like a high-priced *whore* at that horrid lodging house. God knows, I should be accustomed to snickers, scorn, and snubs by now, but I find that I am *not,* and I did not care to be reminded of how scandalous people think me!"

Christ, I've opened Pandora's Box! Lewrie quailed; *She's ventin' hot as Vesuvius!*

"Lydia, I didn't mean for that t'happen, I could never—," he tried to say to mollify her, but she was on a righteous tear, by then.

"Now, just because you ran across me on the road, you'd wish me to lodge with you in some ratty country inn, so you can use me for a convenient vessel for your pent-up lust?" she spat.

Thought *of it,* Lewrie qualified to himself; *but I'll not admit that to her, by God!*

"That's *not* what I intended, Lydia," he lied, trying to assure her. "Just an hour or so of your company over tea, or— *Oof!*"

Lydia Stangbourne, daughter of a Viscount, punched him in the stomach with a dainty kid-gloved fist! Lewrie had forgotten that she was stronger than most women, the result of strenuous outdoorsy activities in the country. She hunted and shot and fished, managed horses as good as any groom, and even took secret lessons from a swordmaster.

He stepped back to rub his belly. "Will you strike me, again, m'dear, or should I borrow one of the coachmen's whips?" he asked.

The rant was over, though. Lydia put her hands to her face and lowered her head. When she looked up a moment later, she was weeping, with her face screwed up in misery.

"Oh, Alan!" she cried, and flung her arms round his neck.

"I am so sorry, Lydia," he muttered into her sweet-smelling hair. "We could call it a comedy of errors, 'cept it ain't all that funny. I'm sorry we ended up at cross purposes, missin' each other coming and going, and might not be able t'see each other again for weeks more, if the Navy has their say in it. All I meant was to sit and talk, have a laugh or two, not . . .

Hush now, dear girl," he comforted her by swaying her slowly. "Don't cry, Lydia. Don't cry."

She gave out a loud sniff against his shoulder.

"Have you a pocket handkerchief, Alan?" she softly asked. "I must look a fright, and what any passersby must think of me . . . like a jilted . . . *trull*!"

"A trull, you?" Lewrie tried to cajole. "A fright? No. You're as handsome and fetchin' as ever, Lydia. Remember what I told you the time we all coached down to Sheerness . . . that no one could ever take you for a doxy, or a trull. They'd think you a captain's lady."

She stepped a bit apart to dab at her eyes with the requested handkerchief, blew her nose, then broke out in a shy and embarrassed smile. She handed the handkerchief back, which act made her laugh as she did so. "Sorry about that, now it's so damp."

"Cherish it forever!" Lewrie quipped. "Have it framed—"

Her arms went round his neck again as she silenced him with a long and passionate kiss. Lewrie wrapped his arms round her to lift her off her tiptoes and drape her against him, and coachmen and servants be-damned. Their kisses were urgent, her breath hot and turning musky, and Lewrie felt a rigid awakening in the fork of his trousers.

Lewrie half-heard the clopping of a horse on the road.

"There's rooms to let down the road in Liphook, don't ye know!"

Lewrie broke off their kiss to scowl, discovering an older gentleman in corduroy, tweeds, top-boots, and a curl-brimmed thimble hat as their taunter, obviously a prosperous local landowner, who was in high humour, and sporting a wide leer.

"Sod off!" Lewrie called back, which made the older fellow snap his head about and almost rein in.

"Yes, just . . . sod off!" Lydia added, laughing out loud, then leaning close to Lewrie to whisper, "You must tell me later what 'sod off' means, Alan!" with impish delight.

"Happy to," Lewrie assured her. "You may find it serves usefully in London, when anyone dares snub you."

Both of them had stepped back, though still holding each other's hands. Lydia looked up at him contemplatively. "This bottom-cleaning you speak of. It will occupy you fully? For how long?"

"Assumin' there's a free dock available, better than a week or two,"

Lewrie told her, explaining how his frigate must be emptied of all her guns, stores, and munitions, her upper masts taken down "to a gantline" so she could be heaved over onto her side and stranded high and dry at low tide on one of the hards, or propped up in one of the graving docks. "If there's no dock or stretch of beach available, we might sit and swing at anchor 'til they can get round to us."

"You would have to remain aboard 'til the work begins, then," Lydia said, beginning to look a tad bleaker.

"Aye, but, once it's begun, I wouldn't be captain of anything for at least ten days to a fortnight," Lewrie said, hoping to cheer her up. "We'd have to take shore lodgings, every Man Jack. As soon as that's begun, I'll write you and let you know when to coach back down to Portsmouth, so——"

"No, Alan," Lydia interrupted him, letting go his hands to take another wee step back from him, and crossing her arms. "Even did you find me temporary lodgings in a rented, private residence, I would not feel entirely comfortable with such an arrangement."

"But, Lydia——"

"I fear I would feel much the same dis-comfort at the George Inn as I did at the Blue Posts," she continued, her expression firmly determined.

"The ogling you got? The snickers?" Lewrie asked, worried by this sudden turn.

"That is part of it, I must own," Lydia replied, looking down at her toes as she scuffed a pebble with her shoes, before returning a level gaze at him. "Another part of my dis-comfort is the feeling that I must dash off at a moment's notice to your every beck and call. I would much prefer that you come up to London and call upon *me,* in a—hah!—proper manner," she said with a wryly amused sniff. "I trust that, have you learned to know the least bit about me, you will understand my reasons why."

"So we can scandalise your household staff?" Lewrie posed with a shaky laugh; this was turning serious! Their first night, they had left her brother Percy to gamble in the Long Rooms at the Cocoa-Tree and had coached to her house in Grosvenor Street in the wee hours, and had ended up in a spare bedroom after the house servants had gone to bed. "I suppose we could sit up stiff and proper in your parlour, and swill endless pots of tea."

"There shall be times for such innocent primness," Lydia said with a becoming blush, and another fond smile as she recalled what had passed between them, too. "Though, I was thinking more along the lines of the theatres, the symphonies, dining out—"

"God, not the bloody ballet!" Lewrie cringed.

"No, not the bloody ballet," she reassured him, crinkling her nose in amusement, though she made no move to reach out to him.

"Where Society can point, snicker, and gossip about you?" he asked, perplexed why Lydia would wish more exposure and more risk of snubbing, when that was the very thing she said she had dreaded when in Portsmouth by herself. "Oh!"

"Oh, indeed," she replied, waiting for him to plumb to it.

She wants t'be courted*!* he told himself; *To do things proper!*

"Then we shall do as you wish, Lydia," he promised her, "even if that involves *gallons* of tea. Though, if Willis's Rooms are out, and I lodge at the Madeira Club . . ." Their second night together, she had booked a suite of rooms at Willis's, as a present.

"Lord, how stricken you look, Alan!" she said with a laugh as she came to embrace him, at last, and looked up at him most pleasingly adoring. "Neither of us can pretend that we do not share a powerful mutual . . . desire for intimacy. Trust when I tell you that I have longed for you every moment the Navy takes you away from me, and that this last, long separation has been almost more than I could *bear*! I long for you so much that I would join you this very instant . . . ," she said in a fret, turning her head to look about. "I would let you lead me behind that thicket, yonder, but for the witnesses."

"The thicket ain't *that* far off," Lewrie said with a leer as he took a squint where she had indicated.

"We shall find a way, when you come up to London, Alan," Lydia assured him with a solemn expression. "We may have to be most discreet, but . . . love shall find a way."

Love? Christ, this is gettin' damned *serious!* Lewrie thought.

"I s'pose love will," Lewrie said in a pensive whisper as he pulled her into an embrace, which prompted another long and fervent kiss to which she responded just as eagerly. She stroked his cheek with a shuddery touch, looking as if she would begin to weep, again.

"I must've done somethin' right," Lewrie softly sighed, "for you t'take such a risk to your heart, given all that . . . you know."

"Yes, you have, Alan," Lydia whispered, "you certainly have."

After another long minute of kissing, Lewrie leaned back from her a bit to joke, "Imagine all this, from a chance encounter on the road!"

"A most *fortunate* encounter," Lydia heartily agreed, though she stepped back from him. "Brief it must be, though. I *must* get on to London, just as you must get on to Portsmouth. Someone must be the practical one, after all," she teased, taking his hands at arm's length as if they were dancing.

"Never gave a fig for 'practical'," Lewrie said. "Though I fear you're right." He offered her a polite arm to walk her back to her coach, handed her inside, and folded up the folding steps, then closed the door once she was seated.

He stepped back from the coach, but she leaned out the opened door window to reach out to tousle his hair and stroke his cheek one more time. Lewrie kissed her palm and her wrist.

"I will see you again, soon?" she asked, grinning.

"Count on it," Lewrie promised. "I'll write to let you know as soon as I know when I can get away, and for how long."

"*Adieu,* dear Alan. *Adieu,* dear man."

"'Til the next time, dear girl!" Lewrie replied as her coach began to rattle forward. He waved to her, waited to watch her coach head up the road, then turned and strolled back to his own, shaking his head in be-musement, part wistful, and part disappointed that she would not stay for even a cup of tea, yet . . .

He reached the open door of his coach and turned to look back up the road, and damned if Lydia was still leaning out the window and waving, so he used both arms to return a broad goodbye wave to her with a smile plastered on his phyz that he wasn't sure what it meant.

Now, where did all that *come from?* he asked himself; *I would've thought her so vexed with me that she'd write me off completely, yet . . . hmmm.* Love, *she said? Wary as she was, 'bout love and marriage, and trustin' any man ever again . . . Gawd.*

Did *he* wish to re-marry? he had to ask himself. If he did, he could do a lot worse than Lydia Stangbourne. As far as he knew, she was still worth £2,000 a year, and that much "tin" was nothing to be sneezed at! She was exciting, adventurous, nothing like the properly-mannered hen-heads and chick-a-biddies who populated most of the parlours in the nation!

Shame, though, Lewrie thought; *I'm too "fly" a rake-hell for her. Sooner or later, she'd find me out and go harin' for the hills!*

"On to Portsmouth, coachman," Lewrie said as he mounted the steps into his coach.

"Shouldn't blaspheme, sir," the dour stick grumbled.

"Damn me, did I?" Lewrie quipped as he pulled up the steps and shut the door. "Well, just bugger me! Whip up!"

CHAPTER FIFTEEN

A light and misty October rain was falling, gathering on upper yards, and the rigging, and occasionally massing into larger drops of water that plopped on *Reliant*'s freshly holystoned decks, on the canvas covers of the stowed hammock racks, and Captain Alan Lewrie's hat and epauletted shoulders as he and the First Lieutenant, Mr. Westcott, and the Bosun, Mr. Sprague, made a slow inspection of both the standing and the running rigging, and the set of the top-masts and yards.

Bisquit the dog paced slowly at their heels, on the lookout for attention, or the offer of a nibble of sausage or jerky. When one of the larger drops plopped on his head, he would shy away, then look up to spot whoever it was that was pestering him.

"The cats have more sense, ye know," Lewrie told the dog. "They stay snug and dry below."

"Enjoying their long naps," Lt. Westcott commented with a grin as if he could relish an hour or two of idle snoozing. No one aboard had had much rest since Lewrie returned from London. To prove his sentiment, Westcott fought to stifle a jaw-cracking yawn.

"It appears we're back in business, Mister Sprague," Lewrie allowed once they had reached the bow hawses for a long look at the bowsprit and jib-boom rigging.

"Spick and span clean from keel to truck, again, too, sir," the Bosun pointed out. He was a man who ever strove for order, neatness, and cleanliness, the hallmark of his exacting trade. "She don't smell like a mud-flat any longer."

Despite the orders which Lewrie had waved under everyone's noses, there simply had been no space for them in a graving dock, so the frigate had been hauled over and her bottom cleaned, re-felted, white leaded, and re-coppered in places by a civilian contractor's yard, on a sandy and muddy hard between the tides, and the reek of the beach, and white lead paint had been a long time departing her.

There had been planking in her "quick-work" badly in need of replacing, too. Some were riddled with *teredo* worms, and some gnawed thin from the inside, by rats that had the run of the orlop and bilges.

Once back on her bottom and upright, the contractor had suggested that their rat problem could be solved, at least temporarily, by the introduction of a pack of terriers, as many stray cats as could be had round the yard, and let them have the run of the ship for a few days . . . for which he would be paid, of course, a trifling fee.

"Saw more than one merchant ship and a sloop o' war get sunk by her own vermin, sir," the flinty shipwright had told them. "Starving rats'd eat anything, and usually gnaw through the hull planks down low where you can't tell 'til the water's pouring into the bilges."

The ship's boys had had a field day, following the terriers on their hunts, and collecting keg after keg of dead rats. They had hot been above doing slaughter of their own with hammers and middle mauls.

That vermin-free state would not last; it never would, of course. Ships stores, ration kegs, bales of clothing, and even gunpowder had to be brought back aboard from temporary storage at the warehouses at the naval dockyard, and even more stores sufficient for six months at sea, would bring pests with them, even was the ship anchored out and not right alongside a pier where rats would have easier access.

"How are the new hands fitting in?" Lewrie asked the Bosun.

"Them, God help us, sir?" Sprague said with a weary laugh of dismissal. "Two of the four Landsmen might as well be goony birds and the other two strike me as shifty . . . county Quota Men. The three rated as

Ordinary are passable, but we only could scrape up two Able Seamen, One's alright, but I'm keeping my eye on Shales, and so is the foremast captain. I expect he's a 'sea-lawyer', sir."

"No help for it," Lewrie said with a sigh. The ship's people had had to lodge ashore temporarily, and despite all the cautions that he, his officers, and petty officers had urged, despite all their watchfulness, eleven hands had deserted. Lewrie damned Lord Gardner's office for issuing pay chits *before* the ship was fully back in commission and discipline. It made no sense to him that those eleven men would take "leg bail", obtain a civilian's "long clothing", and run, sacrificing their claims to the substantial amount of prize-money that *Reliant* was due. And all of them had been aboard since May of 1803!

"For that matter, sir," Westcott quipped, "how do you think our new Mid, Mister Shannon, is fitting in?"

"Oh, Lord," Lewrie said, pulling a long face which made all of them chuckle. "No helpin' that, either. He's a young'un, no error."

Midshipman Entwhistle had stood his oral exams before a board of Post-Captains while *Reliant* was on her beam-ends in the mud, and had been rated as Passed. Out of the blue, not a week later, he had been given orders into an 18-gun brig-sloop just fitting out and he, a newly "wetted down" Lieutenant and Commission Sea Officer, was gone, replaced with a twelve-year-old chub. There had been a tit-for-tat made; the Commissioner of the dockyards, Captain Sir Charles Saxton, Bart., had a distant nephew in need of his first posting, and Lewrie had a foul bottom, and no matter his urgent orders for the South Atlantic, things would go more swimmingly should Lewrie welcome the lad aboard.

Lewrie had to give Captain Saxton his due, though; the naval dockyard had stored all his goods without pilferage, and it all had been returned in fine shape, and no condemned casks of salt-meats had been substituted for their own. *Reliant* had gotten all the items that Lewrie had requested, even a more than ample supply of paint for sprucing up the ship! And that in a time when captains would be treated so parsimoniously that more than one had written Admiralty to ask which *side* of his ship he should re-paint!

Midshipman Richard Saxby Shannon, though all puppy-dog earnest and eager, was also all cunny-thumbs, so far, and was as gullible as the day was long, wide open to all of the traditional jokes that Mids played on each other, and even a new one that Lewrie had not heard of before—

they had told him that after six months at sea, even had he yet to experience a girl, he would find himself in desperate need for release, in the form of manual stimulation, or "Boxing the Jesuit" in the dark. They had sent him to the Captain to be issued his Masturbation Papers so he would have official permission!

When Shannon had made his request in Lewrie's day-cabin, with his hat under his arm and his "serious" face on, Lewrie had laughed himself sick, unable to reply, and, wheezing, had just shooed the lad out, and he could not stop laughing for another ten minutes!

"He'll probably not even touch his crotch to change his under-drawers," Lt. Westcott sniggered, smiling wickedly.

"Yes, well," Lewrie said, after another brief laugh, "I think we're ready for sea, as soon as the wind shifts favourably. I will be below. Carry on, Mister Westcott . . . Mister Sprague."

"A cup of good, hot coffee, sir?" Pettus offered after he had hung Lewrie's hat and undress coat up on pegs to dry, out of reach of the cats.

"Most welcome, thankee, Pettus," Lewrie responded as he plucked an older, third-best uniform coat from the back of his desk chair and donned it. He sat down at his desk and went over the muster book once more to see if he fully agreed with the changes made in the assignments of hands to their various stations during the ship's working. Men in each larboard and starboard watch had specific duties to perform when on passage, when hoisting the anchors or coming to anchor, when making sail or reducing them, when top-masts must be struck or hoisted up into place, when boats must be hoisted up and lowered overside or recovered, by day or night. Equally, each man was assigned specific stations and duties when the ship went to Quarters and it was all written down in a series of lists so that every niggling chore was covered and every slot filled by a warm body.

"Turning a bit nippy, this time of year, sir," Pettus commented as he brought the coffee, "and a chilly damp. It will be good we are bound South."

"Aye, with winter comin' on, I'd expect even the heat near the Equator'd be welcome," Lewrie agreed, stirring his mug after adding a large dollop of goat's milk and two spoonfuls of fine white sugar.

"Midshipman Shannon, SAH!" the Marine sentry at the door bawled.

Lewrie looked up over the rim of his mug to see Jessop making a tube of his right hand and pantomiming a jerk-off to Pettus.

"We'll have no dis-respect for any Mid, Jessop," Lewrie said, striving for sternness. "Stop that. Enter!"

"Aye, sir," Jessop answered, still looking a bit too gleeful for Lewrie's liking.

Midshipman Shannon entered and marched to the front of Lewrie's desk at what the lad obviously thought was a properly rapid military pace. "Mister Eldridge's duty, sir, and I am to tell you that there is a boat approaching," he rattled off, chin up, stiff as a soldier at "Guards Mount," and staring over Lewrie's shoulder at the middle distance.

"Very well, Mister Shannon, and thankee," Lewrie replied. "Any idea of its passenger, or passengers?"

"Ehm . . . Mister Eldridge did speculate that it might bear an Admiralty messenger, sir," Shannon answered, looking as if a question had thrown him off-script and nigh clueless in how to respond.

"Fine, we'll soon see. You may go, Mister Shannon," Lewrie bade.

"Aye aye, sir!" Shannon barked, just as loud as the sentry, and all but stamping his boots.

"Just a thought, Mister Shannon," Lewrie said before the lad could stumble through an attempt at an about-face. "In the Navy, there is no need to emulate the Household Foot Guards, or our own Marines, for that matter. All that shouting and stamping about just frightens my cats."

"Ehm . . . I was told . . . ," Shannon gulped, turning red.

"I would not believe *all* that I was told by your fellow Mids," Lewrie cautioned, "recent pranks included, hmm?"

"Very good, sir," Shannon replied, taking on normal posture. With a brief, shy, and much-relieved smile, he saw himself out.

"Lord, what a younker, sir," Pettus said once he was gone.

"Believe it or not, Pettus, I've seen worse," Lewrie laughed.

A few minutes later, after Lewrie had placed cheque marks beside the names of some hands whom he thought too weak, or too dense, to do the tasks assigned them, he could hear the calls of the "Spithead Nightingales" as someone was piped aboard the ship. In expectation of a visitor, he set aside the lists and waited for his Marine sentry to do his duty, which came a moment later. "Messenger t'see th' Cap'um, SAH!"

"Enter," Lewrie bade.

An older Midshipman from the Port Admiral's office entered, with a canvas despatch bag hung over one shoulder. "Orders from the Port Admiral, Captain Lewrie, sir. And, Captain Niles also thought that your latest mail should be delivered aboard, as well," the Mid said.

"Most welcome, and thank you," Lewrie said with a happy smile as he accepted the packet of letters, and his orders. "Do I need to sign for them?" he asked, waving the slim envelope.

"No, sir," the Midshipman said with a grin, and bowed himself out. As soon as he was gone, Lewrie broke the wax seal and opened the brief order. He already had orders from Admiralty to sail as part of Commodore Popham's expedition, "with all despatch" and "making the best of his way", and was just waiting for a favourable slant of wind for departure so he could fulfil Admiralty's parlance for cracking on all sail to the royals and blowing out half his heavy-weather canvas for maximum speed. What could Lord Gardner have to say about it?

"Oh Christ," Lewrie groaned. "Play escort?"

There were, several hired-in merchant vessels also waiting for a change in wind direction which carried a part of Popham's expeditionary force, a troop transport, and a pair of horse transports bound for Madeira, the assembly point in the neutral Portuguese Azores Islands, and carrying two troops of the 34th Light Dragoons.

So much for "with all despatch", Lewrie desponded; *If they can make eight knots in a ragin' gale, I'm a Turk in a turban!*

He cast a longing look at the thick packet of personal mail, but got to his feet and went aft to the windows in the transom. As Lord Gardner had written, those transports were anchored near Southsea Castle . . . but then, so were many other vessels. Through the misty haze and sullen rain he could make out one ship which flew a large, plain blue broad pendant, the sign of the naval officer appointed by the Transport Board to be the Agent Afloat.

Bugger it, Lewrie thought; *I'm goin' t'get wet . . . wetter.*

He asked Pettus for his grogram cloak and worst hat, turned the personal mail over to his clerk, Faulkes, for distribution, and sent Jessop out on deck to pass word for his boat crew to assemble.

"I'll be back later, before Seven Bells, I hope," Lewrie said to Pettus. "Have Yeovill keep my dinner warm. I have to see a man about a horse."

CHAPTER SIXTEEN

$\mathcal{T}$hough he was irked at Lord Gardner's meddling, and the necessity of rowing over in the rain to meet with the masters of the vessels he was to escort, Lewrie was a tad curious. He had dealt with civilian convoys in the past, but had never seen troop ships or the specialised "cavalry" ships.

Before 1794, the Navy Board had done the hiring of ships to bear soldiers, artillery, ammunition, and supplies overseas. In 1794, a six-man Transport Board had been established to handle the task. The Navy Board had been, and most-likely still was, rife with corruption, so it was good odds that the new Transport Board would be no more honest, but somehow the job had to be done on those so-far rare occasions when the small British Army went overseas, mostly to the East or West Indies, or to garrisons in Canada, Gibraltar, and the Mediterranean.

"Arrah, now there's a homey smell," Cox'n Liam Desmond said in appreciation after a deep sniff of the wind. "Horses, barns filled with hay an' straw . . . all that's needin' is a warm peat fire on such a day as this. Ahh!"

"That, an' a pint of stout right under yer nose whilst yer warmin' at that fire, Liam," Patrick Furfy, the stroke-oar, said with a wistful sigh of missed pleasures.

"Make for the one flying the blue pendant," Lewrie bade them.

There were three ships in all, according to Lord Gardner's set of orders: the *Ascot*, the *Marigold*, and the *Sweet Susan*. The one with the blue pendant turned out to be the *Ascot*, the only one named in any connexion with horses or horse races, and she was the troop transport.

Lewrie was *welcomed* aboard her, not piped, by an Navy officer, a much older Lieutenant with a slight limp who named himself as Thatcher.

"You are the Agent Afloat?" Lewrie asked.

"I am, sir," Thatcher glumly told him, "and the only naval officer aboard any of the ships. You are to be our escort, the one named in Lord Gardner's orders? Happy to meet, you, Captain Lewrie. This may take a while, so why don't you call your boat crew up so they can take shelter from the rain, and we can go aft. Look out!"

"What?" Lewrie gawped, just before Thatcher snatched him by the arm, clear of a charge by an angry ram.

"What the bloody Hell's that?" Lewrie snapped.

"The mascot of the Thirty-fourth Light Dragoons, sir," Thatcher spat in a weary tone. "Cornet Allison? Come fetch your bloody . . . beast!"

A lad of sixteen or so, resplendent in the silver-trimmed, blue-cuffed short red coat, dark blue breeches, and high, knee-flapped boots of a cavalry regiment, and with a leather-visored helmet bristling fore and aft with black fur plumes, came to stumble after the ram, take him by the collar and one large curved horn, to lead him away.

"Sorry, Leftenant Thatcher, sir," Cornet Allison added and shifted his grip on the ram so he could raise his right hand and press it palm outward to the visor of his helmet in salute to Lewrie. "I was sure he was tethered, but—"

"Make *sure* he's tethered," Lt. Thatcher insisted. "Else, we'll find what fresh mutton tastes like."

"Yes, sir," Cornet Allison assured him, then pulled a face. "I so wish that we'd voted for a mastiff, or a greyhound, but the Colonel insisted, and so . . . Come on, you," he said to the ram, trotting it to the far side of the deck.

"It has no name, d'ye see, Captain Lewrie," Lt. Thatcher said. "The Colonel of the Thirty-fourth, Colonel Laird, also insists that it is always referred to as the Regimental Ram. Though most of the troopers call it 'that vicious bastard'. 'Cantankerous' is a mild word to describe its temperament, and there's not a soldier aboard that hasn't been rammed when he wasn't expecting it. Will you join me for a coffee, sir?"

"Gladly," Lewrie heartily agreed.

Aft and in the shelter of the ship's master's great-cabins, now divvied up into small cabins with deal-and-canvas partitions, there was a long mess table down the middle. *Ascot*'s master, a gruff older man by name of Settles, stuck his head out of what was left of his formerly spacious quarters just long enough to grunt a gloomy greeting to Lewrie, then shut his door on the lot of them.

The "lot" who shared the approximation of a wardroom aboard a proper warship were the *Ascot*'s First and Second Mates, and officers of the 34th. Lt. Thatcher did the introductions. A Captain Veasey was the senior officer of the regiment, and another Army officer, Captain Chad-field.

"Rarin' t'go and have at the Dutchies, I say!" Captain Veasey hoo-rawed as Lewrie shed his hat and cloak and took a seat at the table. "All this idlin' in the holds are bad for our mounts, and rough on our troopers, too, d'ye see. It's taken two years t'make proper mounts and it'd be a cryin' shame do we lose some on the voyage. Your trained cavalry horse is worth half a dozen regular prads, even blooded hunters. Horridly dear investment."

Captain Veasey was more than happy to prose on, relating that there were two troops of cavalry aboard *Ascot,* one of the four squadrons that made up the regiment, with eighty troopers and horses for each troop, plus Lieutenants, Cornets, non-commissioned Sergeants and Corporals, farriers, blacksmiths, and trumpeters. Naturally, there were more horses aboard *Marigold* and *Sweet Susan,* for no officer of the British Army could go to war without his string of extra mounts; even the junior-most Cornets' parents had bought them at least three. Each transport carried around ninety horses, altogether.

Belowdecks on *Ascot,* Lt. Thatcher stuck in when Veasey ran out of air, there were fewer than 160 troopers, for someone had to feed and tend to the horses and muck out the narrow stalls daily. Detachments of ten troopers under Lieutenants and a Sergeant had been sent to the other ships . . . damned if the merchant sailors would do it!

"A large risk of fire, though, sir," Thatcher cautioned. "The horses are grain-fed, but the bales of hay, and the straw put down in the stalls . . . brr!"

Lewrie got a brief tour of the troopers' quarters belowdecks, a series of cabins where bored and irritable soldiers tried to find ways to amuse themselves. They were issued hammocks to sleep sailor-style, but had to store them in the stanchions and nettings during the day, leaving them little comfort before dark. Many napped under and atop the rough wood mess tables, or on the hard decks.

"They'll tear the partitions down for more room, you wait and see, Captain Lewrie," Lt. Thatcher gloomed once they were back on deck and in much fresher air; un-washed bodies, wet wool, farts, and other un-identifiable reeks had almost made Lewrie gag. Without access to their horses, the troopers would face weeks at sea with nothing to do except dis-mounted weapons drill and "square-bashing" foot drill, and perhaps some five firing at floating targets with their short Paget carbines. Rather neat weapons, Lewrie thought, with their ramrods permanently attached on a chain and swivel so they could not be lost when one tried to re-load on horseback . . . if such was even possible.

Ascot was about 250 tons' burthen, the other two about 200 tons, all of them coppered below the waterline, so all were hired on for nineteen shillings per ton; un-coppered ships were paid from fifteen to seventeen shillings per ton, and contracted for six months' service, though that could be extended. If that became necessary, Lt. Thatcher could issue Transport Board chits to extend the contracts, on his own authority, and risk.

"A rum business, this, Captain Lewrie," Lt. Thatcher sourly said as he pointed up at his blue pendant. "The Board names me Agent Afloat, and gives me the *semblance* of a Commodore, but I'm little more than a baulk of 'live lumber', a mere passenger! I can gather them in, order them when to sail, and to where, but beyond that, I have no say in how any of the ships are run, or handled, and civilian merchant masters are a tetchy lot, and damn the Navy, they'll do things their way and ignore any sugges-tions from me! God forbid I try to give them *orders*!

"You'd not have a sickly officer, would you, Captain Lewrie?" Lt. Thatcher asked, only partly in jest. "But for this bad leg of mine I'd still be aboard a warship. I was Third Officer into a frigate when a gun burst and put a hunk of iron into me. Three months in Haslar Hospital, then a year on half-pay, well . . . wasn't even in action, but at *drill*!"

"All my Lieutenants are very healthy, sorry, Mister Thatcher," Lewrie had to tell him, with genuine sympathy.

"Ah, well then," Thatcher said with a sigh. "Do you still wish to see one of the horse transports?"

"Aye, I do, if it's no imposition," Lewrie said.

True to his promise, Lewrie was back aboard *Reliant* before Noon, just as "Clear Decks And Up Spirits" was being piped and the rum keg was being carried to the forecastle. The welcome ritual was halted for a moment to salute Lewrie back aboard. He lifted his sodden hat from his streaming-wet hair, and made a quick way down the ladderway to the waist, and the door to his great-cabins, shooing off the ship's dog, Bisquit, whose fur was just as wet, and shaking showers of rain from his hair every now and then.

"Good luck with those," Lewrie told Pettus as his cabin-steward took his hat and cloak. "You could get a bowl o' wash water from 'em, do ye let 'em drip long enough. So long as ye don't mind blue water."

"I expect they have bled as much dye as they ever will, sir," Pettus speculated as he hung them up on pegs. "Might you relish a cup of hot tea, sir? I've some on the warming stand."

"Aye, with milk, sugar, and a dollop o' rum," Lewrie decided. "A large dollop."

"Coming right up, sir," Pettus said, pausing to fetch Lewrie a dry towel for his hair and face.

His cats, Toulon and Chalky, had been napping at either end of the starboard-side settee, but came dashing with their tails vertical to greet him. They found his boots intriguing, and sniffed about them, posing their mouths open to savour the aromas like little lions.

"I hate t'ask it of ye, Pettus, but I seem t've trod in horse droppings. Got the most of it off, but . . . ," Lewrie said with a hapless shrug.

"I'll see to them, sir. Jessop? The Captain's boots need a cleaning," Pettus promised, then shared a secret smile with Lewrie as he passed that onus to the cabin boy.

After changing to an older pair of buckled shoes, Lewrie sat at his desk and scribbled out a set of orders for Lt. Thatcher and the masters of the transports, outlining the signal flags he would be hoisting during the day, and the blue-fire rockets he would launch at night when it was necessary to alert them, or keep them in close order. He tried to keep it simple, given his last chaotic experience of escorting a huge "sugar trade" convoy from the West Indies in 1804. Even if Admiralty was *paying* them to sail together and trust their escort, merchant masters were indeed an un-cooperative and tetchy lot.

It was hard going, for Toulon and Chalky always found delight in interfering with people that ignored them when at a chore. First it was his oldest cat, Toulon, who would hop into his lap then atop the desk, there to sniff, swat at the steel-nib pen, and squat on the paper. Just after he was shooed off, it was Chalky's turn to leap up and flop onto one side, then wriggle with his paws in the air for his belly to be tickled.

"Oh, for God's sake, why'd I ever think that cats make good companions," Lewrie growled. "There. Satisfied?" he asked as he rubbed Chalky's belly for a second or two. No, he was not, for he flipped on his side once more and began to snatch at the pen with both paws. Then it was time for Toulon to return and flop and wave for "wubbies". The requested tea showed up, and that required inspection and more sniffs.

"First Off'cer, SAH!" the Marine sentry announced.

"Enter!" Lewrie bawled back, beyond frustrated, by then.

Lt. Geoffrey Westcott came in and approached the desk, a touch warily, taking a cue from Lewrie's tone.

"Rescue me, Mister Westcott," Lewrie demanded. "Take a cat. I can only deal with one at a time."

"Here, Chalky," Westcott said, grinning. "Come nip a finger."

He sat down in a chair before the desk and lifted the younger cat into his lap, which made Chalky flatten his ears, leap down, and run off to the dining coach to sit and furiously groom, insulted beyond all measure.

"How are our brethren in the Army, sir?" Westcott asked.

"Eager t'win their spurs, and gallop through the entire Dutch army," Lewrie said sarcastically. "Cavalry, by God! I met some of the officers, and I swear they're as dense as roundshot. Yoicks, tally-ho. The Thirty-fourth was raised round Shaftesbury—"

"I've friends from Shaftesbury," Westcott said with a knowing nod, and a brief, feral grin, "though none of them are dull enough for cavalry."

"Their Colonel, Laird, raised and paid for them himself," Lewrie went on, "designed their uniforms, armed them with old-style straight Heavy Dragoon swords and Paget carbines, like Viscount Percy did his regiment. But, I doubt there's a professional soldier among 'em, from the horse-coper to the top. Must've made some of his money back from sellin' officers' commissions."

"Well, all we have to do is get them there, and after that, it will be up to whichever General appointed," Westcott said.

"I was in the middle of *tryin'* t'write orders to the transports' masters, but for the cats," Lewrie told his First Officer. "We will up-anchor in the morning, at the start of the Forenoon, and fall down to Saint Helen's Patch. If there's a good wind, we'll stand on, but if there's not, we'll come to anchor and wait for one. Warn the others to arrange their last-minute necessities from shore, and make sure the Purser knows."

"Mister Cadbury believes he has everything in hand, but for one or two bullocks for fresh meat, the first few days at sea, sir," Westcott replied with a shrug. "And the wardroom's needs are met."

"Before I have Faulkes make fair copies, I wonder if you would aid me in draughting the orders . . . see if there's anything I might miss," Lewrie asked, shoving the papers towards Westcott, and brushing Toulon to one side of the desk with his arm. Toulon flopped on top of his arm to weigh him down and began to rumble.

"Happy to oblige, sir," Westcott agreed.

"Tea, with some rum, sir?" Pettus offered.

"Sounds delightful, thank you, Pettus," Westcott perked up.

"And a second cup for me," Lewrie added.

"Hmm," Westcott mused after going over the first two sheets of paper. "I do wonder, sir, if we have to signal changes of course, subject to the weather. It's not as if they'll just plod along astern of us and follow our every move. . . ."

The orders were thrashed out by half-past Noon, and Westcott departed. Faulkes got to copying, and Lewrie's mid-day meal arrived, a hearty chicken and rice soup, a middling-sized grilled beef steak with hashed potatoes and some of the black-eyed peas purchased in Savannah in the Spring, brought to spicy life with Yeovill's stash of sauces, accompanied by brown bread and butter, and a decent claret.

The cats got their own shredded beef, spare rice, and hashed potatoes gravied with dollops of chicken soup in their bowls at the foot of the table, after making a great, adoring fuss over Yeovill when he entered and served out their shares. They came to nuzzle and rub on Lewrie once Pettus cleared his plate, then made for the settee for a long afternoon nap.

Faulkes brought the copies for Lewrie to look over, then folded them and sealed them for one of the Midshipmen to deliver. Whichever one it was, he would be getting wet, for the rain continued, heavier and steadier, and looked as if it would continue all through the afternoon and night.

Lewrie poured himself a fresh cup of tea, minus rum, from the sideboard, and went back to his desk. At last, he could look over his personal mail and respond to some of it. There were some bills from a London shop or two, for which he wrote out notes-of-hand to be redeemed at his solicitor's, Mr. Matthew Mountjoy. There was one from Peter Rushton, an old school friend from his brief stint at Harrow before being expelled for arson . . . not only expelled but banned from the grounds forevermore, upon risk of arrest! That'un would be newsy and chatty!

And, there was one from Lydia.

"Oh, Lord," Lewrie muttered half to himself, feeling wistful and anxious at the same time, turning the sealed letter round in his hands before breaking the wax seal to unfold and read it.

Once *Reliant* had been turned over to the civilian yard, he had gotten a week in London, lodging at the Madeira Club again, coaching to the West End to call upon her. They had *courted*!

Paying suit to Lydia had involved a nightly round of going out, to dine at the fashionable clubs like White's, Boodle's, Almack's, and the Cocoa-Tree, seeing the latest plays in the Covent Garden theatres, and, on a sudden whim, going to Plumb's Comedic Revue in Drury Lane to see the show of that false Sir Pulteney Plumb (only overseas did he claim that title) and his French wife who had been a chorus girl with the Comédie-Française in Paris. It was their quick-change costuming and theatrical talents that had spirited Lewrie and his late wife, Caroline, from Paris to Calais in a variety of wigs, clothes, makeup, and guises, escaping the clutches of Bonaparte's police agents who'd been set to assassinate them. It had not been the Plumbs' fault that Caroline had been shot and slain with a bullet meant for him, and he found that their show, with the clowns and scantily-dressed dancing girls as *entr'actes*, was quite enjoyable and highly amusing.

There were art shows to see at Ranelagh Gardens, subscription balls where anyone could purchase tickets and dance without anyone looking down their noses at Lydia. There were symphonies to attend, and concerts, and music halls where rowdier tunes could be heard.

Eudoxia was down from the country and Lydia's brother Percy was up from his cavalry regiment stationed to guard the coast in Kent, so they attended most events as a foursome. They were almost cloying in their turtledove and open mutual affection; they couldn't keep their hands off each other, and spent a lot of time gazing into each other's eyes and laughing over things that passed between them silently and unknown to anyone else. All in all, they were highly amusing, even when Eudoxia took Percy sweetly to task when they entered the Long Rooms at the clubs to do some light gambling; seeing her watch him like a hawk would a field mouse to dissuade him from wagering too deeply.

They dined in at the Stangbournes' Grosvenor Street house, and entertained themselves at cards or music. From her time as an *ingénue* actress and singer with Daniel Wigmore's Peripatetic Extravaganza, a combination circus-theatrical troupe-menagerie touring group, Eudoxia could sing well, though Lewrie discovered that Lydia could not, despite tutoring by the most accomplished musicians throughout her girlhood. She wasn't all that good at the harpsichord or new-fangled *piano forte*, either. Percy could fiddle away like mad, effortlessly, and Lewrie had fetched along his penny-whistle and had been pronounced "not all that bad", but, poor Lydia . . . she *adored* music, from simple country airs to Haydn, Handel, and Mozart, but was grieved that she would be forever denied the ability to play.

Well, at least she loves t'dance, and does that *well,* Lewrie reminisced. Lydia might wear her bored, languid, and imperious face at the slower, more formal dances, but could turn girlish, bouncing, and almost whoop with delight doing the faster country dances.

Being a foursome, all in all, though, hardly ever just the two of them together, had turned the courting into a guardedly celibate affair. They had embraced, kissed, panted, yearned (Oh, how Lewrie had yearned!), but they had not had those promised nights at Willis's Rooms or any other clandestine lodgings. Riding in the parks, shopping for civilian clothes for him, new books to read on-passage (none of those salacious, for a change, either!), it was all so very *public*!

"Wooing," he muttered. "What a horrid-sounding word. Woo. Woo woo. Woo hoo."

Lewrie hadn't wooed any girl or woman, or couldn't recall doing so since he was breeched! Flirting with a single aim was a different kettle of fish, and he'd been good at that since his father, Sir Hugo, had gifted him with his first dozen cundums, and cited the sage advice of Lord Chesterfield that "pleasure is now, and ought to be your business", a motto that the both of them had followed.

It was not so much the frustration and denial that bothered him, but the sheer *novelty* of a seeming chastity that had him bemused and all-a'mort. Oh, he liked Lydia Stangbourne, and not merely because she had struck him as un-conventional from the first instance, and an obliging lover in the second; not because she came from a wealthy family, either. As he had told her early on, he was comfortable, and didn't have any designs upon her share of the Stangbourne fortune, nor in any need of her standing dowry of £2,000. Stung as she'd been by her first, brutal marriage, and the scandal of Divorcement, she had liked him for *not* trying to win her hand, and Lewrie, in turn, had liked her for how they could play lovers without a *hint* of commitment.

Now, though . . . after a week and a bit of just being together at innocent pursuits . . . he felt . . . what?

Well, just damn my eyes if I ain't growin' fond of her! Lewrie realised with a wrench; *Christ, I do b'lieve I even* miss *her! What* has *the world come to?*

The touch of her hand, the scent of her hair, the merry, adoring glints in her dark emerald-green eyes, the way her nose wrinkled when she laughed at something, or one of his jests. An odd nose, too, a tad too wide front-on, but almost Irish and wee in profile, and the recollection of that made Lewrie smile in pleasant reverie.

My dearest Alan,

I certainly do not wish for you to feel as if our brief Time together in London was to put you on Trial, for that was the farthest thing from my mind.

Words cannot express, however, the utmost Joy your Patience gave me. Your Jests, your Gallantries, your Good Humour in tolerating my Reticence has endeared you to me beyond all Measure, beyond any Fears which I previously held. I have been shamefully out of Temperance over our starcrossed attempts to see each other, and did not intend to behave so stand-offishly, but, with Percy and Eudoxia in Town, I could discover not the slightest Opportunity to show you how warm is my Heart towards you, or how ardent is my Passion, and I beg you to forgive my Foolishness.

How cruel it is, now, that you are bound away on the King's Business
with no Promise of a quick Return, or indeed, a Return at all! As I write
this, my very Soul cries out to be with you, and my Eyes are so aswim with
Tears that I can barely see to . . .

"Well, I'm damned!" Lewrie whispered in considerable awe. She had
lost her dread of trusting her heart to yet another man who would break
it? What was he to make of that? Lydia was a clever and wary grown
woman—did she not see that he was a dissembling rake-hell, sure to dis-
appoint her in future? How to respond?

He opened a drawer in his desk and got out his pen, inkwell, and a
fresh sheet of bond. Such activity bestirred Toulon to pad over to the
desk and meow to announce his presence, and desire. With one leap,
Toulon got into his lap, peered over the top of the desk to see what his
master was doing, then settled down in the shape of a hairy pot roast, the
tip of his tail slowly metronoming, and purring.

"Good old lad," Lewrie praised him, ruffling his fur and stroking his
head and cheeks for a while, then began to write.

October 18th, 1805
Reliant, at Portsmouth

My dearest Lydia,
*   How gratifying it is to receive your latest Letter. Gratifying and Elat-*
ing beyond all Bounds, however, are the Sentiments, the Warmth, and
Ardour in which you say you hold me! Be strongly Assured that my own
Heart swells in wrenching Longing to see your sweet self for just one minute
more, even do we share a parting Kiss, a touch of hands, and nothing more.
Your sudden Openness to Risk quite astounds my soul, and places me in
Dread that I would ever cause you to regret . . .

"Hang it," Lewrie whispered to the cat, who looked up at him. "I
think she's come t'love me, Toulon. And, I think I feel the same!"

BOOK TWO

KING: On, on, you noble English,
    Whose blood is fet from fathers of war-proof,
    Fathers that like so many Alexanders
    Have in these parts from morn till even fought
    And sheathed their swords for lack of argument.
                    -WILLIAM SHAKESPEARE,
                    THE LIFE OF KING
                    HENRY THE FIFTH,
                    ACT III, SCENE I, 17-21

CHAPTER SEVENTEEN

*T*he passage to Madeira was an odd one, quite unlike the last that had taken *Reliant* to Bermuda and the Bahamas in January of 1805. While the prevailing Westerlies in the Bay of Biscay were gusty, they did not vary more than 20 degrees either side of Due West, quite unlike the howling storms and mountainous seas that had raged against their frigate before. The wind direction did not swing capriciously to smack them on the bows and force them to make long boards just to avoid being driven into the rocky angle of the French and Spanish coasts, or force them onto Portuguese shoals. Once out at sea, beyond the Scilly Isles and Cape Ushant, a few days of close-reaching gained them bags of sea-room and hundreds of miles of safety margin from the risk of lee shores. Striding along Sou'-Sou'west or South by West upon a roughly beam wind and a beam sea, even the three clumsy transports could keep up with their escorting frigate, and reel off a satisfactory eight or nine knots from one Noon Sight to the next, making a goodly way.

Those beam seas and winds were rough on the troopers of the 34th aboard *Ascot*, for she would wallow and reel, heeling over to larboard before coming back upright to do it over and over again, as steadily as a clock, sending those lubbers to the lee rails to "cast their accounts to

Neptune" on deck, or into buckets below if they could reach one in time. That gave *Reliant*'s seasoned and strong-stomached tars perverse pleasure, and a cause for jeering following each meal served aboard the *Ascot*.

The horses were another matter.

No matter how narrow the stalls were arranged aboard the horse transports to cut down on room to stagger, the continual rolling and wallowing, and the groaning of the hulls as they worked over the sea, quite un-settled the poor beasts. Some would panic and rear, frightened by the noise and motion, would break their forelegs and have to be put down. As strong and swift as they were, able to live twenty or more years, horses' digestive systems were incredibly touchy, subject to twisted bowels, the strangle, or colic. At least once every two or three days, a horse would die, and be hoisted out of the holds, swayed out overside, and disposed of.

There were, perhaps, no other people on earth more fond of the horse than the English. From the meanest, poorest ship's boy to the officers aft, horses were a part of their lives, for pleasure riding and hunting among the better-off, essential to the livelihood of the cottager farmer, the coachman, the street vendor or waggoner, or the punter at the races. Every loss of a horse turned *Reliant*'s sailors glum and quietly sad. Below over their meals, almost every Man Jack had an idea of how those poor beasts should have been handled, or treated; if *he'd* been over there, they'd not have died, by God!

The other oddity of the voyage to the Azores was the rare empty-ness of the ocean. The Bay of Biscay should have teemed with merchant traffic, with British ships outward bound, neutral American ships headed to Europe, and French and Spanish merchantmen hoping to sneak their way past the Royal Navy's blockade, rare they were, though.

But, except for one trade of two-dozen East Indiamen bound North for English ports under a strong escort, one fast Liverpool slaver that flew past them on the first leg of the infamous Triangle Trade to pick up a cargo of "Black Ivory", and one slow Portuguese ship headed to the Azores which they briefly spoke then left wallowing and plodding far astern, they had the sea to themselves.

Lewrie and his officers were relieved by that lack, though yet a touch uneasy. The Bay of Biscay ports were home to many French privateers which sallied from Brest, Quimper, Quiberon, L'Orient, St. Nazaire, La Rochelle, and the mouth of the Gironde river. And, there was still that large French fleet under Admiral Villeneuve to worry about. Villeneuve

had been the bug-a-bear when *Reliant* was in the Bahamas in the Spring
and Summer, when it had been rumoured to be down South in the Windward or Leeward Islands. That fleet's sailing surely had drawn off the
British blockading squadrons in the Bay of Biscay, as it had Nelson's fleet,
allowing French National Ships, their frigates and *corvettes*, a chance to
put out and prey upon British commerce, too. Yet, there had been no sign
of that threat, either.

So, it was with a great sense of relief when the cloud-shrouded peaks
of the Azores loomed up on the Sou'west horizon, and those peaks became solid as they drew nearer to the island of Madeira. There was even
joy as they rounded the Sou'east cape and could espy the port of Funchal
and its wide, open roadstead, where they could meet up with the rest of
the expedition, and turn their charges over to Commodore Popham, then
come to anchor, and a quiet and peaceful, motionless rest.

"Well, where the Devil are they, then?" Lt. Westcott asked no one in
particular as they beheld the roadstead . . . a very empty roadstead.

"*Senhor?*" the local pilot said, turning his attention from the approaches
to the bay to Westcott. "The English expedition fleet? It has sailed, perhaps a week ago. They did not stay long."

"For where?" Lewrie asked the pilot.

"South, *Senhor Capitáo*, is all I know of them," the pilot said with a
shrug.

"Perhaps we should continue on right away, sir," Westcott suggested
to Lewrie. "If we're a week behind, and they'll be needing our cavalry.
To come all this way, yet miss *out*!"

"Miss out on the action, and the excitement, ye mean," Lewrie replied
with a smile. After three years or so, he knew Westcott's need for any
relief of boredom; combat, *or* women. "No, the beasts aboard the transports are runnin' short on water, oats, hay, and straw, and a good place
t'dump the stable sweepin's. Our compatriots in the Army had planned to
replenish here, counted on it, really. I fear we have no choice. We'll stand
in and anchor, and see t'their needs."

"The stable sweepings, sir?" Westcott posed with a brow up.

"The Azores are rocky. They need all the manure they can get," Lewrie told him, chuckling. "They might consider our arrival a gift from
Heaven."

"Rocky, and dry, *Senhor Teniente*," the pilot chirped up, beaming wide. "Has been a drought for many years, and we do not have the pastures for enough animals. My mother's gardens need more water and fertiliser. One point to starboard, *Senhor* Quartermaster," he added, to the senior rating on the helm.

"Do you happen to know if there is a British Consul in town?" Lewrie asked their pilot.

"Oh, *sí, Senhor Capitáo,*" the perky fellow quickly supplied. "He is *Senhor* Gilberto Gilbao, a big merchant in Funchal."

"Once we're anchored, I'll go ashore to call upon him, then," Lewrie decided aloud. "Perhaps *he* knows where Popham has got to."

"Full fig, sir?" Westcott teased, noting Lewrie's everyday uniform, minus his marks of honour.

"He'll have t'take me as I am," Lewrie scoffed.

"The place I have for you, *Senhor Capitáo,* is close to town and the shore . . . deep water, five fathom, no worries," their hospitable local pilot was quick to assure Lewrie. "You could come ashore with me in my boat, and signal for your own when you have done with *Senhor* Gilbao. I can even show you to his house."

"For that office, *senhor,*" Lewrie responded, striving for the proper difference between the Portuguese and the Spanish for *señor,* "I give you my heartiest thanks. Uhm . . . good dining in Funchal, is there?"

"The finest, *Senhor Capitáo!*"

CHAPTER EIGHTEEN

*O*nce ashore, the pilot gave him a quick tour of Funchal's small down-town features, pointed out a couple of restaurants, an upper-class tavern where music was played nightly for the entertainment of patrons, a laun-dress's house, a vintner and a ship chandler, and a discreet brothel which he swore had the greatest selection of pretty doxies in all Christendom! Lastly, he saw him to a mansion one street up above the town's docks and quays, facing a spacious and shady plaza, where the Gilbao family resided, and did their business.

Lewrie plied the large and ornate door knocker, and the door was opened by a woman in maid's togs, a quite attractive young woman with sloe eyes which belied her prim demeanour, costume, and black hair that was severely pulled back and rolled into a bun at the nape of her neck.

Lewrie almost felt the need to take a second peek at the entry-way, and the plaque which announced the offices of the British Consul in both En-glish and Portuguese; the maid's attractiveness made him wonder if he'd found that forementioned discreet brothel!

He announced himself; she cocked her head over in puzzlement. When he managed to pronounce *Senhor* Gilberto Gilbao, she brightened and summoned him in, steering him to a large parlour, then padded off to seek her master.

It was a huge house, perhaps a century or more old, but well maintained, and full of costly furnishings, musical instruments left on display as if their users were merely taking a break, and artwork hung in profusion on every wall of the grand parlour, or stood upon plinths in the corners. There was a cool and shady atrium beyond a row of pillars and fine sets of glass-paned French doors, with a cool fountain plashing in its centre, surrounded with planted or potted greenery and flowers. Servants crossed the atrium now and then, on cat feet, without a sound. Above, the upper storeys were railed with intricate ironwork, the uppermost shaded with white and yellow canvas awnings. The only sound he could hear was the tinkle of water in the fountain. It was almost uncanny. Costly as all Hell, but uncanny.

"Senhor Capitáo?" a well-dressed youngish fellow enquired, appearing from the opposite side of the wide entry foyer. "My pardons, but Concepcion has no English, and could not manage your name. I am Gilberto Gilbao, *senhor*. I serve as the British Consul for the Azores."

"Captain Sir Alan Lewrie, of the *Reliant* frigate, *Senhor* Gilbao," Lewrie told him with a smile, and a formal bow. "I was expecting to see Commodore Popham and his squadron in port, but missed him. I was told that Madeira was to be the assembly point."

"Ah!" Gilbao said with an open-mouthed and cheerful grin. "Come this way, *senhor*, to my offices. Allow me to offer you refreshments, and I hope that I may fully inform you as to the whereabouts of your . . . incredibly energetic Commodore Popham."

Gilbao's offices were nigh as spacious as the grand parlour on the other side of the foyer, and just as expensively decorated. They took two upholstered chairs to either side of a low tea table, quite informally, rather than Gilbao behind his desk, and Lewrie plunked in front like a supplicant.

"Naturally, *Capitáo* Lewrie, all of Funchal took notice of your arrival in port," Gilbao began as he tinkled a china bell for service. "As for Madeira being the assembly point for Commodore Popham, it was determined that the actual presence of his squadron, and his transport convoy, in harbour *could* be taken as a violation of Portuguese neutrality . . . a violation on our part of our *own* neutrality to the French. For that reason . . . reasons, rather . . . Commodore Popham only cruised close offshore as his transports arrived in dribs and drabs."

"Oh Lord," Lewrie groaned, sitting up straighter. "My bringin' my ships into port could be deemed a violation, too? No one at Admiralty said a single word about that!"

To Lewrie's relief, Gilbao threw back his head and laughed out loud, then looked at him with a merry grin.

"My dear *Capitáo*, could such a generous and hospitable people as we Portuguese deny mariners in need of succour *entrée* to our ports for firewood and water?" Gilbao amusedly posed. "As far as I can see, you have no hostile designs upon Funchal, or the Azores, you do not seem to be acting in any threatening manner to anyone as you convoy ships to somewhere else, which is of no consequence to Portugal, so, just what might the French or her allies have to complain about, or lodge a protest? Funchal is a neutral port, open to all."

"When I called at Charleston, South Carolina, in the Spring, I got chapter and verse in high dudgeon from the French Consul there," Lewrie told him. "Sail out within three days, or else . . . wait weeks before entering *another* American port . . . can't lurk offshore beyond the Three Mile Limit?"

"The French once had a Consular representative here, but when the war began again in 1803, they ceased to pay him, so he resigned the office," Gilbao said. "Ah! Concepcion! Will you have tea, or wine, *senhor*? From Lisbon, I recently received a cask of a splendid wine, very light, a touch sweet, and of a remarkable pale yellow tint. Most refreshing!"

"I will try the wine, upon your recommendation," Lewrie said, secretly ogling the maid, who was casting shy eyes at him as Gilbao ordered wine for both.

"In point of fact, *Capitáo* Lewrie," Gilbao went on as the maid departed to fetch the wine, "the English and the Portuguese people have always enjoyed the most amicable and mutually agreeable relations, in diplomacy, and in trade. We are a small nation, smaller than the British Isles, but have never possessed the large armies such as these of the French, or the Spanish in the old days. Neither did we ever have large fleets, not even approaching those of the Dutch, the Swedes, or the Danes. There is a general assumption that should any other power attempt to seize our colonies, even Brazil, or invade Portugal itself, our good friends the English would side with us, and come to our aid."

"If only to have another good bash at the Frogs and the Dons," Lewrie agreed with a laugh. "I am mortal-certain that did the French try to conquer Portugal, we'd be in it in an instant."

Lewrie had never actually *been* to Portugal, but his father, Sir Hugo, had. Portugal was the only place that British debtors could run before their creditors could nab them and throw them into prison! Lewrie suspected that that was why the wine, port, and spirits trade had arisen in the long-agos; all those bankrupt British scoff-laws on their "skint bottoms" in need of a job, and quick profits! Why, most of the port in the world bore English brand names!

"You enquire about the whereabouts of Commodore Popham and his expedition, *senhor*?" Gilbao said. "He is bound for another Portuguese port on the coast of Africa, San Salvador."

Lewrie had to shrug in ignorance; he'd never heard of it.

"It also is Portuguese," Gilbao said with an airy wave of his hand, as if that was of no matter. "Any chandler in Funchal may sell you charts, including approaches and safe anchorages. It is a minor, out of the *way* place, you see? Of no interest to anyone."

Meanin', no enemy consuls t'spy Popham's presence out, Lewrie told himself; *Out of sight, and out of mind. Put in, load firewood and water, then out again before anyone notices. That's* real *hospitable of the Portuguese!*

While waiting for the promised wine, Gilbao told Lewrie of how his family had settled in the Azores in the 1600s, and of how charming and delightful the climate was. Yes, the house was old, but they had the wealth to keep it up. Several generations lived in it, along with his own wife and growing family, and Lewrie had to compliment him on its grandeur, noting how Greco-Roman or Mediterranean it was.

Concepcion entered the offices, at last, with a silver tray and icing bucket, in which stood the bottle, and two crystal glasses. She set it down between them on the low table and poured.

"Iced!" Lewrie exclaimed in pleasure.

"Sweden is good for something, *Senhor* Lewrie," Gilbao laughed, "though I cannot imagine *living* in such Arctic dullity. Allow me to propose a toast, *senhor.* To the recent epic victory your Navy won off the coast of Spain!"

"Ehm . . . *what* victory?" Lewrie had to ask, his glass held a few inches below his mouth.

"Why, Admiral Nelson's victory over the combined French and Spanish fleets, *senhor*! You do not know of it?" Gilbao exclaimed. He all but slapped his forehead. "But of course, you must have left England before the news could arrive, and have been at sea, out of touch with anyone. My pardons for presuming."

"Tell me of it . . . once we sample this wine," Lewrie urged.

"To victory!" Gilbao responded, allowing them to drink deeply. It was a heavenly white wine, light, flower-scented, and with hints of the slightest sweetness, much like a German Riesling.

"That *is* good," Lewrie agreed, almost smacking his lips.

"The newspapers from Lisbon and Oporto arrived only three days ago," Gilbao informed him, "both in Portuguese, and the mercantile papers printed in English for the many expatriates. I have a copy of the mercantile paper, if you would like to read it. Or, take it with you to your ship."

"You are most gracious, *Senhor* Gilbao, thank you," Lewrie told him with a smile and a seated bow as Gilbao finished his wine, then rose to cross to his desk to shuffle through a neat pile of correspondence to fetch the newspaper.

"I must warn you that not all the news is good, *senhor*," Gilbao said as he returned and handed the paper to Lewrie. "The French and Spanish lost at least twenty ships, but . . . the gallant Admiral Nelson sadly perished."

"Nelson? *Dead?*" Lewrie exclaimed, dropping his hand and the newspaper to his lap in shock.

"Shot down by a French Marine in the fighting tops and taken below to the surgeons, who could do nothing for him," Gilbao said with a sombre tone, shaking his head in sorrow as he sat back down to pour them top-ups.

"The little minikin," Lewrie muttered, shaking his own head. "He always did say, 'Death or Glory' . . . 'Victory or Westminster Abbey'. At Cape Saint Vincent, he ordered me to join him in facing the entire Spanish van, just his sixty-four and my sloop of war. 'Follow me, Lewrie,' he yelled. 'We're bound for glory!' I suppose he's got his spot in Westminster Abbey, at last."

"You *knew* him, *senhor?*" Gilbao marvelled. "You must tell me all of what you know of such a hero."

"I did not know him well, sir," Lewrie said in preface, cautioning Gilbao that he could not relate all that much—quite unlike the supper ball at Nassau—and heaving a small shrug. "We ran across each other several times, but he was always senior to me, and I doubt if I mattered to him. I was not in his intimate circle."

And, I'll not mention Emma Hamilton unless he asks, I won't say a word about how vainglorious he was, or how pettish he could be, either, Lewrie chid himself.

Later that morning, wandering the small town's streets to shop for his personal needs, and have a look-see, Lewrie felt a rare and odd out-of-sorts malaise take him, almost a light-headed separate-ness he could not blame on three glasses of Gilbao's excellent light wine. He stopped in the shade of a row of trees, facing the waterfront to watch bum-boats and barges plying between the shore and the transports with loads of bagged grain and bales of hay, kegs of water, and beer.

There was an iron bench with wooden slats, and he sat himself down. The English-language Portuguese newspaper crinkled as he did so, and he pulled it from his coat side-pocket to re-read the account of the battle. It was a sketchy article, since no news writer had been on the scene, and was likely based on third- or fourth-party word of mouth. If a Royal Navy ship had put into Lisbon or Oporto, one which *had* participated in the battle and was in need of firewood and water, or light repairs, that might explain how twenty enemy ships had been reportedly taken, not some vague number like "dozens" or "many". Not all had been kept, for the winds and seas had gotten up after the hard fight was over, and several prizes had been wrecked on the shore about Cádiz, and some re-taken by their own crews.

Even so, Nelson's victory was a death-blow to French hopes for their long-expected invasion of the British Isles. Without their fleet to cover the crossing of the Channel by their thousands of small craft, or a fleet-in-being and at sea to draw off warships from Channel Fleet, to reduce English resistance, there was no way for Emperor Napoleon Bonaparte to risk the loss of his massive army which he had planned to cram into those small boats. People in England could draw deep breaths and sleep soundly in their beds, after years of dread.

Bonaparte had sent Missiessy and Villeneuve to the West Indies and back to lure the Royal Navy away from the defence of the Channel, and the ruse had failed, thank God. Bonaparte had been too clever for his own good, and he had thrown a significant part of his navy away for nothing.

Thank God Boney's a soldier, Lewrie thought with a snort of derision; *They're not the sharpest wits, and know nothing of the sea.*

Nelson, though . . . dead and gone.

Nelson's gone.

CHAPTER NINETEEN

*N*ews of the grand victory off Cape Trafalgar was heartily welcome aboard *Reliant,* though tempered by a sense of grief that Nelson had been slain. The victory was given three cheers aboard the transports, too, and perhaps some soldiers of the 34th might have felt some sadness over the Admiral's loss, but while Nelson had been a national hero, he had not been an *Army* hero, so it did not affect them as sorely. Now, if they had heard that Jim Belcher, Tom Cribb, or Daniel Mendoza, their favourite champion boxers, had died, they would have mourned.

What really made the Army officers unhappy was Lewrie's estimate that their passage South would be much longer than the first leg from Portsmouth. Once round the same latitude of Cape Verde, they would lose the steady Nor'east Trade winds, and would face winds from the Sou'east, requiring all ships to make many tacks, going "close-hauled to weather", to make ground. They found it hard to fathom that beating to weather would take one hundred and eighty or two hundred and ten miles veering back and forth to make sixty or seventy miles South each day. Making their passage even longer were the currents; there was an Equatorial Current that would be favourable all the way round the Western coast of Africa 'til the Ivory Coast, but then they would meet both the

South Equatorial Current, which would smack them square on their bows, and the counter currents which could swirl them into the Gulf of Guinea, and be foul against them whenever their course had to be seaward, or waft them shoreward and onto the shoals. The quickest course, he told them, would lie closest to shore, emulating the ancient explorers such as Vasco da Gama. Further out to sea lay the Doldrums, the Horse Latitudes, where there were confusing, swirling currents, and no wind for weeks at a time; so named for the complete loss of horses carried by earlier expeditions, when the food and water ran out.

"I wonder what the soldiers will do when we cross the Equator, sir," Lt. Westcott mused as the peaks of Madeira shrank and shortened astern. Westcott looked in merry takings, quite chipper in point of fact. A brief half-day ashore at Funchal, and a visit to that highly recommended brothel, had done him wonders.

"Have a group, ceremonial vomit, I'd imagine," Lewrie chirped back, rocking on the soles of his boots with his hands clapped in the small of his back, and relishing the fresh breezes and the easy motion of their frigate. "Why change routine just because they'll be crossing the line?"

"I was just wondering how they would welcome King Neptune and his Court aboard, sir," Westcott said with a laugh.

"I doubt they'd do anything," Lewrie mused, tickled by an image of riot. "Who'd enforce the rites? The transports are manned at the rate of five sailors and one ship's boy per every hundred tons, plus the master, two mates, and perhaps five or six more petty officers. If *they* tried to initiate the soldiers, I expect they'd end with their throats cut. Speaking of, Mister Westcott . . . you *have* made plain to our 'shellbacks' that they'd best make *their* revels harmless, with no insults against any superiors?"

"I have, sir," Westcott replied with a stern nod.

"Having been 'anointed' once, myself, and a 'shellback' several times over, I intend to stand and watch and enjoy the ceremony. But, Mister Westcott?" Lewrie teased with a leer. "You have not yet said if *you* have ever crossed the Equator. Have you, sir?"

"Ehm . . . I fear that my naval career has taken me no further South than Trinidad, sir," Westcott hesitantly confessed.

"A 'Pollywog' are ye, sir?" Lewrie purred, leaning a tad closer to grin. "Oh, how jolly this will *be*!" Then, to Lt. Westcott's consternation, Lewrie strolled off to the weather rails, his step jaunty, and humming a gay air. Now there was something to look forward to!

The first few days out of Funchal, they still had the Nor'east Trade winds, so the going was good as they sailed past the Spanish Canary Islands with the isles only fifty or sixty miles East of them.

The next few days were also passable as Lewrie led the convoy almost Due South across the Tropic of Cancer, the 20th Latitude, then down the wide strait between the Portuguese Cape Verde Islands and Cape Vert on the shoulder of Africa, where the Equatorial Counter Current, the swirling eddies off that, and the Sou'east Trades began to greet them.

Round the 10th North Latitude, though, the perverse Sou'east Trades forced them to stand Sou'-Sou'west, close-hauled towards eventual shoaling waters, which were badly or sketchily charted, and then all four ships would have to make a heart-breaking turn to the East-Nor'east and sail back towards Africa, losing ground 'til the shore could be seen from the cross-trees, and they would tack and bear off Sou'-Sou'west once more, and safely out to seaward. To make matters worse, it was growing hotter, even though they were well into early December, and the sun, so friendly round Madeira, began to feel brutal, and Surgeon Mr. Mainwaring had little in the way of balms to ease unwary sailors' burns when they worked shirtless.

A little South of the 5th North Latitude, on a shoreward tack, they raised Cape Palmas, the Southwestern limit of the Western bulge of the African continent, and stood away Sou'-Sou'west once more.

At least the next time they had to tack shoreward, there would be hundreds of miles of sea-room before they fetched the coast again, deep into the Gulf of Guinea.

A day or two more and they would cross the Equator, where the Bosun, Mr. Sprague, and his mates and some of the other older, saltier hands would hold court. They were already cackling among themselves and rubbing their hoary palms in glee.

It was then that Pettus, over breakfast, pointed out to Lewrie that Toulon was not acting his normal self.

"Toulon? What's wrong with him?" Lewrie asked. His older cat had been all laps and affection the last week. He looked to the foot of his dining table, where Toulon and Chalky sat by their food bowls.

"He doesn't seem to have much of an appetite, sir. At first, I took no notice, but now?" Pettus said, pointing down-table.

Yeovill had whipped up the last of the eggs purchased at Funchal in an omelet, a third of it laced with dried sausage bits and shreds of bacon just for the cats. Chalky was nibbling away at his bowl, but Toulon was just hunkered down over his, paying no heed to the welcoming aromas, and just staring off into the middle distance, eyes half-slit as if he was napping. And, when Chalky had polished off his own bowl and nudged Toulon aside to wolf down his as well, Toulon paid no heed. He had never been the assertive cat, but allowing himself to be robbed?

Lewrie left his plate, and his chair, to go to the other end of the table and stroke Toulon. "What's wrong, littl'un? What's put you off your victuals? Are ye feelin' ill?"

Toulon looked up at him, made a meek little *Mrr,* and licked at Lewrie's hand. Lewrie pulled out the chair at that end of the table and sat down to gather Toulon into his arms, where the cat went willingly, starting to purr.

"My Lord, he's light as a feather!" Lewrie exclaimed. "Ye can feel his ribs, and his backbone. Here, Toulon, have a wee bite or two. Come on, now." Lewrie dug into the food bowl for a tiny morsel of sausage and put it under Toulon's nose, but he would have none of it.

Jessop had come to the end of the table to watch.

"'E's been pissin' a lot, too, sir," Jessop informed him, "an' 'ardly ever in their sand box. Seems all 'e warnts t'do is sleep, an' drink water. Won't play like 'e usedta."

"Whenever you're on deck, sir, he's most likely to be found in the starboard quarter gallery," Pettus contributed, "napping atop the crates and chests, so he's level, with the windows. I thought that he was just watching sea birds."

Lewrie cradled Toulon, stroking his cheeks and chops with one finger, and Toulon tilted his head to look up and meet Lewrie eye-to-eye, slowly and solemnly blinking. He might be softly purring, but his tail tip did not move.

Lewrie sat him back on the table right over his food bowl, now all but empty after Chalky's raid, got to his feet, and went for the door to the ship's waist. Coatless and bareheaded, he mounted to the quarterdeck. Lt. Spendlove, the officer of the watch, began to move leeward to cede the weather rails to his captain, but Lewrie stopped him with a question. "Have you seen the Surgeon, Mister Spendlove?"

"At breakfast, sir," Spendlove replied, knuckling the brim of his hat in salute. "I believe he is forrud, holding the morning sick call. Shall I pass word for him, sir?"

"No, I'll go forrud," Lewrie told him, and went back to the deck to make his way to the forecastle. Bisquit the ship's dog darted out of his cobbled-together shelter under the starboard ladderway and came bouncing to join him, prancing for attention, Lewrie took time to give Bisquit some pets and "wubbies" before reaching the forecastle.

HMS *Reliant* was a modern ship. Her sick-bay was not below in the foetid miasmas of the orlop, but right forward, where the warmth from the galley fires could keep patients comfortable in cold weather, and still provide fresher air during their recovery. In battle, surgeries and the treatment of wounded men would still take place on the orlop, in the Midshipmen's cockpit, but after as many wounded as could be accommodated under the forecastle would be moved there.

"Good morning, Mister Mainwaring," Lewrie began.

"Ah, good morning, Captain," Mr. Mainwaring cheerfully replied. He was a burly, dark-haired, and swarthy-complexioned man, with hands and fingers more suited to a blacksmith or butcher, but he had turned out to be a skilled and able surgeon for all that.

"How are things this morning?" Lewrie asked.

"Tolerable, sir," Mainwaring told him, "I've one bad tooth that needs pulling, some saltwater boils to lance, and more men with sunburn. Collins, yonder, I've put on light duties for three days, after he pulled some muscles at pulley-hauley."

"Fetchin' up fresh water casks, was it, Collins?" Lewrie asked.

"Aye, sir, it was," the young fellow shyly admitted, grinning.

"Enjoy it while you can, Collins," Lewrie said, then turned to the Ship's Surgeon. "When you're done here, Mister Mainwaring, I'd admire did you attend me in my cabins."

"Shouldn't be more than an hour, sir, then I am at your complete disposal," Mainwaring agreed, turning back to the bare buttocks of one sailor bent over a rough wood table, waiting for the jab of a lancet.

"Wonder if t' Cap'um's askin' f'r t' Mercury Cure," one sailor whispered in jest once Lewrie was gone. "Mad as 'e is over quim, it's a wonder 'e ain't been Poxed yet. Has the lucky *cess*, 'e does."

"Now, we'll have none of that, Harper," Mr. Mainwaring chid him. "There's *your* boils to be seen to, next, hmm?"

"It'd be Mister Westcott, more in need than Cap'um Lewrie," one of the others snickered.

"Now, now," Mainwaring cautioned again, trying to appear stern; though his mouth did curl up in the corners in secret amusement.

CHAPTER TWENTY

"Ship's Surgeon, Mister Mainwaring, SAH!" the Marine sentry at Lewrie's doors cried, stamping his boots and musket butt on the deck.

"Enter," Lewrie called back. "All went well, sir?" he asked as Mainwaring stepped inside and approached the desk in the day-cabin.

"Quite well, sir," the Surgeon replied. "What may I do for you, Captain Lewrie? Some malady that ails you?"

"It is a rather odd request, but I wonder if you might be able to use your general knowledge of anatomy to aid me."

"Indeed, sir?" Mainwaring said, a bit perplexed.

"A glass of wine, sir?" Lewrie said, pointing to a chair before his desk in invitation.

"Ehm . . . I've been told by the others in our mess that your cool tea is quite refreshing, Captain," Mainwaring said with a hopeful grin. "I would prefer to sample that, have you any brewed."

"Always," Lewrie said with his own grin. "Pettus, a glass of tea for the both of us." Once the Surgeon was seated, Lewrie went on. "It is not my health that is in question, Mister Mainwaring. It's my cat."

Mainwaring pulled a dubious face, mugging in surprise. He had been a

Navy Surgeon long enough to know that most ship's captains were possessed of *some* eccentricities, and some of them daft as bats.

"Bless me, Captain . . . your cat, did you say?" Mainwaring said. "I fear that I know next to nothing of dogs or cats. I doubt if anyone does, really. What symptoms does it present?"

Lewrie laid out the moroseness, the sudden lack of appetite and the sudden weight loss, the incontinence, and thirst. Mainwaring sat and *hmmed*, nodding sagely here and there.

"And how old is it, sir?" Mainwaring at last enquired.

"Over eleven," Lewrie told him. "I got him as a kitten in the Fall of '94, just as we were evacuating Toulon during the First Coalition. That's how he got his name. That, and him, were calamities."

"Well, off-hand, I'd say that it is suffering renal failure," Mainwaring supposed, "a malady which comes to man and beast in their dotage. The kidneys stop working, for one reason or another, and the sufferer wastes away, becoming enfeebled. There's little that I may do for it, sir . . . little that even a skilled, university-trained physician may do for a *man* in such a situation."

"I see," Lewrie said, crestfallen. "He's dyin', d'ye mean. I'd hoped . . ."

Lewrie got to his feet and went to the starboard quarter gallery and brought Toulon back from his solitary roost. He sat him down on the desk between them, and stroked him to calmness as Toulon curled up into a pot roast; paws tucked under his chest and his tail round his hind legs. Toulon had not seen Mainwaring that much but for rare supper invitations with other officers, but he made no move to curry attention, nor did he shrink away as a "scaredy-cat" might. He just sat and blinked, eyes half-slit.

Mainwaring took a deep, pleasing sip of his cool tea, smiled in delight, then leaned forward to touch Toulon, giving him a closer examination. At last, he leaned back into his chair.

"Renal failure, of a certainty, Captain," Mr. Mainwaring said. "The dullness of the eyes, the lack of body fat, and perhaps of some of his musculature? When one is starved, for whatever reason, fat is the first to go, before the body begins to use up the last source of nourishment, which are the muscles. Note that when I lifted a pinch of his skin, that it did not fall back into place at once, but stayed erect before slowing receding? No matter how much water it drinks, it is of no avail, for the kidneys no longer function."

"If there was some way to *force* water into him . . . ?" Lewrie asked with a fretful frown, stroking Toulon with one hand.

"Perhaps with a clyster up its rectum, sir," Mr. Mainwaring speculated with his large head laid over to one side, "directly into the small intestines, where the water would be absorbed more quickly, but . . . that would only delay the matter, sorry to say."

"Perhaps if he's only running a temperature," Lewrie said, with an eye on Mainwaring's leather kit, which he'd brought with him.

"I am certain that it is, sir," Mainwaring countered, "but, do cats or dogs have the same temperature as people? I could listen to his heart rate, but what *is* the normal pulse of a cat? How often to the minute is its rate of respiration? I am sure that there are game-keepers who know something of dogs, horse copers and grooms who know how to fleam a sick horse, what feed to provide, or aid the birth of a colt . . . or calf, or lamb, or whatever, but . . . it's all beyond my experience, sir."

"Is renal failure, and the wasting away, painful, d'ye think?" Lewrie asked, despairing. "He's been a fine old cat, and I'd not let him suffer."

"It *could* be," Mr. Mainwaring said with an uncertain shrug. "Or, it could be that it will fall into a deep torpor and just pass away. I *do* recall barn cats in my childhood that limped off or just went off on their own, and the next we saw them, they'd died of old age or some disease. Perhaps you should just let him expire, on his own."

"Or, find some way to help him along, painlessly, and without terrorising him," Lewrie wished aloud. "I can't put a pistol to his head. The crack of the priming'd frighten him."

"Well, there's smothering, or a quick wring of its neck, as one does fowl, or, tied up in a bread bag and dropped over—"

"All of which are violent, Mister Mainwaring," Lewrie snapped. "Sudden, violent, and frightening. From the time he took hold of my coat sleeve and clambered up to my shoulder, Toulon's known nothing but fun, play, affection, and trust, and to put him down as you suggest would be . . . he would die in fear, feeling betrayed. No! There must be another way."

"Well, sir . . . ," Mainwaring said with a shrug.

"Sorry, Mister Mainwaring, but . . . I know I must seem overly sentimental," Lewrie went on in a softer voice. "Toulon's just a poor cat, after all, but he and Chalky yonder are great comforts, and companions. They're all the . . . friends I may allow myself from out of the whole ship's company. Losing one, or both, is a wrench. I must think that the crew would feel the same if Bisquit died."

"I shall look into the matter, sir, and get back to you should I find a painless solution," the Surgeon promised. "Thank you for the cool tea, Captain. It really is remarkably refreshing."

"Carry on, Mister Mainwaring," Lewrie said in dismissal as the Ship's Surgeon departed. Once Mainwaring was gone, Toulon got to his feet and slowly padded over to the edge of the desk to Lewrie's thigh and rested in his lap, to be gently stroked and petted. He stayed only a minute or two, then cautiously hopped down to the deck and went to his water bowl under the wash-hand stand for a lap or two, then he slowly stalked off for the starboard quarter gallery once more to take up his post atop the wooden crates and sea-chests.

Whatever shall I do with ye, poor thing? Lewrie mourned.

"Perhaps it would be best, sir, did we stand on on this tack at least 'til Noon, and make more Southing before we come about East-Nor'east," the Sailing Master, Mr. Caldwell, advised as he, Lewrie, and the First Officer, Mr. Westcott, convened in Lewrie's chart space. "Do we close the shore, making a long board, we *should* fetch the coast *below* San Salvador, and enter port with the Sou'east Trades large upon our starboard quarters."

"Which would beat fetching *North* of the port all hollow, aye," Lewrie agreed. "We'd end up short-tacking off-and-on most of the day, else, just t'get level with the bloody place."

"Sou'-Sou'west it will be, then, all through today and tonight, and 'til Noon Sights tomorrow," Lt. Westcott said with a pleased nod. "Lieutenant Spendlove and I will be standing the Evening and Middle Watches, and thought to let the Mids of the watches have more responsibility . . . without any radical alterations of course, or the need to pipe 'All Hands'. Loaf aft by the flag lockers? Let them run the ship on their own?"

"Just so long as the weather allows," Lewrie cautioned. "Might you wish to borrow my penny-whistle? Or a book to read by the light of the taffrail lanthorns?"

"Don't know about Spendlove, but I could do some sketchings," Westcott said with a small laugh.

"Sounds like a good idea," Lewrie told Westcott. "Do so. And I, on my part, will stay below as much as possible, t'give 'em a sense that they're really runnin' their watches. A good idea on your part, as well, Mister Caldwell, and we shall stand on 'til tomorrow's Noon Sights before altering course. As shallow as the coast of Africa is, I'd not wish t'thrash about in short tacks t'fetch harbour. Is that all we have to discuss at the moment, gentlemen? Very well. We will stand on as we are, and I will have a wee nap, you poor, over-worked fellows."

"Very good, sir," Westcott said with a brief, savage grin.

Lewrie lingered in the small chart space after the others had left the great-cabins, puzzling over his copy of the chart of San Salvador which he'd purchased at Funchal, noting how far out one would have to anchor off most of the African shore in the Gulf of Guinea. He had seen woodcuts and paintings of the work of slavers who came for "Black Ivory"; but for the trading forts and barracoons which held the captive Africans established at the mouths of the great rivers, most of those infamous ships, even the middling-sized ones, anchored far out, and sent their boats in several miles. The local Africans had low-sided canoes for fishing, which barely drew a foot of water. Low tide produced beaches and flats nigh a half-mile deep, and one could wade another whole mile before the sea got up to one's thighs! When the weather got up, the rollers and breakers were tremendous, flooding inward over those wide, shallow shoals.

San Salvador was on a minor river, its bay barely large enough to anchor the hundred-or-so ships under Popham's command. Why would he choose the place to get firewood and water? Lewrie speculated; *he* would have avoided San Salvador like the plague!

Leaving the chart space, Lewrie headed aft towards his sleeping space, a wide-enough-for-two hanging bed-cot slung from the over-head deck beams. The bed-cot was a wooden box with stout heavy-weather canvas bottom and lining, a rigid hammock with a thin mattress of cotton batt. It looked very inviting, for the oppressive heat of the sun as they closed upon the Equator created a torpor that Lewrie could gladly sleep right through. Before throwing a leg over the edge and rolling in, though, he went aft to the starboard quarter gallery once more to check on Toulon.

The old black-and-white tom was on his right side, as if he was looking out at the horizon as it gently heaved and rolled. When Lewrie stroked his side, he didn't even move, but just gave out a weary *Mrr*, a complaint that he had been sleeping and did not appreciate being wakened. Lewrie leaned down to kiss him on the top of his head, stroking Toulon's chops and cheeks.

"I always loved you, ye clumsy old thing," Lewrie whispered, recalling his cat's kittenhood, and his adjustment to life at sea. Once, Toulon had hopped atop a table, a freshly polished one, upon which a sheet of paper rested, and he could not quite understand why or how he had slid off when he was sitting perfectly still on top of it. *That* had driven him under the starboard-side settee, abashed, where Toulon could commune with his cat gods and live down his shame! Or, when in the North Sea in late 1801, Lewrie's previous frigate, HMS *Thermopylae,* had been rolling just hideously, and Lewrie had been trying to shave, and Toulon had tried to get up to the water bowl on the wash-hand stand and had ended up with a tumble to the deck, and a face covered with soap foam! Once again, the dark under the settee had been a refuge.

Lewrie gave him a last stroke or two, then let Toulon be, with a faint and guilty hope that, did he check on him round suppertime, he might discover that Toulon had passed over peacefully.

He sat on the transom settee and pulled off his boots, took off his waist-coat and un-did his neck-stock, then rolled up his sleeves before rolling into his bed-cot atop the embroidered coverlet. He was almost asleep in moments, but was stirred awake by Chalky's arrival. The younger white-and-grey cat hopped up and padded to Lewrie's chest, to peer at him, nose-to-nose.

"Right, then," Lewrie said with a sigh, rewarding Chalky with strokes down his back, ruffles of his chest fur, and "wubbies" on his cheeks and chops. Chalky flopped onto his side, extended his paws, and began to wriggle, eager for belly-tickling play. That could be a dangerous game for the unwary, for Chalky would nip and catch fingers between his paws, claws out.

"Must I?" Lewrie asked. "Oh, very well. I should find a pair o' thick leather gloves t'play with *you!*"

It took a quarter-hour to wear Chalky out. Lewrie closed his eyes and tried to return to his nap, but no . . . Chalky got his wind back, hopped down, and returned with a ragged old knitted wool mouse.

"You really are a pest," Lewrie muttered, rolling out of bed and giving up on his nap. At least he still had one cat who needed to be amused.

CHAPTER TWENTY-ONE

San Salvador looked to be a pestilential place, a sprawl of low native huts and the reek of cow dung, sweat, and human ordure, commanded by a separate European quarter of tile-rooved stone buildings and barracks, and a small fort which overlooked a series of long and low-slung barracoons with iron-bound doors and a few barred windows, where captured Africans were held 'til a slave ship put in for human cargo. The river mouth ran the colour of red clay, splaying its dubious freshness far out in a delta-like fan off the coast, between gritty stone and sand beaches. The lush greenness of "deepest, darkest Africa" began almost half a mile further inland, beyond fields of millet and mealies, corrals of livestock, and paddocks for the unfortunate Portuguese who did business there. There was a three-masted slave ship anchored in the river mouth . . . but there was no fleet of British warships and transports.

Lewrie ordered a signal hoisted to his three charges for them to stand-off-and-on while *Reliant* closed the shore. As soon as the frigate altered course to stand in, a very shallow, crude boat put out for them, paddled by a crew of Africans wearing little more than sandals and what looked to be Red Indian–style breechclouts, with one European seated in the stern-sheets. The boat came close aboard as Lewrie ordered his ship rounded up into the wind to fetch-to, so he could speak to the White fellow, a rumpled-looking man in off-white cotton canvas trousers and coat, with a wide straw hat on his head.

"*Senhor*, you weesh to enter the reever?" the man asked.

"I wish to know where the British fleet has gone, *senhor*, and how long ago was it that they sailed?" Lewrie shouted back to him.

"Three, four day ago, *senhor*," the fellow said, scratching at his bearded cheek, and flicking ash from a crooked *cigarro* that he held between his teeth. "They take on wood, water, and meal, and go South. We have cattle and peegs, *senhor*," the fellow tempted. "You weesh fresh meat? You trade us rum and brandy, yes?"

"No need, sorry," Lewrie called back. "We have all we need at present. We are bound South to catch them up."

"Ah, well," the unkempt fellow said with a sigh and a slump of his shoulders in disappointment. "Go weeth God, *senhor*."

"Get way on her if you please, Mister Westcott," Lewrie ordered as he stepped back from the bulwarks. "Shape course out to our charges and we'll speak 'em t'see if they've enough supplies to last 'til Cape Town. It's only a few hundred miles, now, God willing."

"Aye aye, sir," Westcott replied, his face screwed up. "Lord, what a reek! Is all Africa this foul-smelling?"

"Cape Town wasn't, as I recall," Lewrie told him. "No worse than a small town in the country, back home. It's the heat and rot in the jungles round this latitude, the smell of long-settled native villages, and the foul reek of the slave pens. Did you ever get close aboard a 'blackbirder', Mister Westcott? Once you do, you never can forget the odour of human misery. God knows how many in the barracoons will perish before the next slaver puts in . . . nor how many of the healthy chosen from that lot live t'see a vendue house in the Americas. Just get me away from all this . . . foulness, sir!"

Reliant closed *Ascot* close enough for Lewrie to converse with Lt. Thatcher with a brass speaking-trumpet and enquire about his dwindling supplies.

"I reckon that Cape Town is nigh twelve-hundred or more miles off, sir!" Lt. Thatcher shouted over. "After victualling at Funchal, we *should* have sufficient water and rations for another two months! The Army would wish to put in to get their mounts ashore and exercise them on dry land. Captain Veasey fears that by the time we join the other transports at Cape Town, his horses won't be able to *stand*!"

"And how might they land them ashore?" Lewrie replied with the trumpet to his mouth. "Hoist 'em out over the side and swim them in, through shark-infested waters, and crocodile-infested river? We would have to anchor at least a mile out, and God only knows how many horses would get eaten, or drown."

Lewrie could see Captains Veasey and Chadfield bristling with concern, a few feet away from Lt. Thatcher. The troopers of the 34th Light Dragoons aboard *Ascot* were more vociferous in their disappointment that *they* would hot be allowed off the ship for a day or two of ease, either, cat-calling and booing Lewrie's decision.

What did they expect o' San Salvador? Lewrie wondered; *Black whores, rum, and roast beef? And the whores for* free*?*

"We will crack on South, Mister Thatcher!" Lewrie shouted to him. "Steer Sou'-Sou'west, and follow me!"

"Very good, Captain Lewrie!" Thatcher replied, sounding a bit disappointed, himself.

Lewrie left the bulwarks and stowed the speaking-trumpet in the compass binnacle cabinet, then went to the windward side to take proper station as *Reliant* hauled up close to the winds to begin her seemingly endless beat to weather in chase of their perpetual Will-o'-the-wisp, Commodore Popham and his phantom invasion fleet. It was an hour later before the Trade wind whisked away the reek of San Salvador that seemed to cling to every fibre of the ship.

"I'll be below," Lewrie told the officer of the watch.

Once in his cabins, Lewrie tore off his neck-stock and drank a full tumbler of water, then asked Pettus for one of cool tea, sugared and lemoned. While that was being poured and mixed for him, he went in search of Toulon, but he was not in the starboard quarter gallery, nor on the bed's coverlet, or the transom settee cushions.

"Here, Toulon. Here, lad," Lewrie called out.

" 'E's unner th' settee, sir," Jessop told him. " 'E come outta th' quarter gallery f'r some water, an' tried t'jump inta yer bed, but 'e couldn't manage it, poor thing. 'E's sulkin' unner there, an' won't come out f'r nothin' nor nobody."

Lewrie knelt down by the collapsible settee which was lashed to the cabin's interior planking. Sure enough, Toulon was there, curled up with his tail under his chin, and his paws tucked under his chest, nodding as if unwilling to sleep, but totally spent.

"Here, Toulon," Lewrie softly coaxed. "Come on out to me. No? It's alright, little man. Come on out."

Toulon opened his eyes to weary slits, uttered an un-characteristic wee *mew*, then went back to drowsing. Damning his dignity, Lewrie got down on his stomach on the Turkey carpet and chequered canvas deck cover to reach in and stroke a finger under Toulon's chin and along his jaws. The cat seemed to enjoy the attention, but made no move to come out. Lewrie reached in and took him by the scruff of the neck to drag him out, cradle him in his arm, and got to his feet. Lewrie sat down on the settee and held Toulon close with both arms, slowly petting and cooing to him, and his cat at last shifted to press closer to Lewrie's chest and begin a faint, ragged purr.

"Ship's Surgeon, Mister Mainwaring, SAH!" the Marine sentry at the door shouted, stamping boots and slamming his musket butt.

Burly Mr. Mainwaring bustled in at Lewrie's order to enter, carrying his leather kit-bag. With him was one of the Surgeon's Mates, Durbin.

"Your pardons if I do not rise, sirs," Lewrie apologised, still cradling Toulon. "Sit, please. Cool tea, Mister Mainwaring?"

"Yes, thank you, Captain," Mainwaring said, taking one of the collapsible chairs and indicating that Durbin should take the other. "I've a mind to purchase the makings and serve it out to the men on light duties or in sick-bay . . . does the Navy Board allow me the funds.

"As to the matter you mentioned the other day, sir, about your cat," Mainwaring went on as Pettus fetched tea, "Durbin here, Lloyd and I, put our heads together as to how one might painlessly ease a cat from life and end its suffering, and Durbin came up with a solution. Pray do explain it to the Captain, Durbin."

"Ehm, yes, sir," the younger Surgeon's Mate began, shifting in his chair and swiping a mop of dark hair back from his forehead, shyly cutty-eyed to be speaking with a senior officer. "Before I came away to join the Navy, Captain, I was studying to be a surgeon, in London. I apprenticed to an older fellow, worked with him and others at some of the poors' hospitals . . . and, to make ends meet, I also assisted a 'Pox' doctor." He looked shamed by that confession.

"Pricking with Cowpox against the Smallpox?" Lewrie asked. He had been inoculated long ago, himself, and wondered why Durbin would be shy about that good work. There were some pox doctors who made more than £50,000 a year!

"Not *that* sort of Pox, Captain," Durbin said, blushing. "He and I administered the Mercury Cure for the *venereal* Pox. In his offices, at the better brothels?"

"Ah. Yes?" Lewrie replied, hiding a wince. The idea of having a metal clyster shoved up his penis for an injection of mercury, or a narrow rasp shoved up and jerked out to break the pustules—! Lewrie all but crossed his legs to avert even the thought of such! "But, what would that have to do with Toulon, here?"

"Well, sir," Durbin hesitantly continued, "it was more the use of the clyster for *other* things, do you see. That, and laudanum."

"Hmm?"

"The juice of the opium poppy, distilled if you will, into the drug laudanum, Captain, is quite addictive," Mr. Mainwaring stuck in, "and, taken beyond moderation, so depresses the rate and depth of respiration and the beat of the heart that death will eventually result in those unfortunates who abuse it."

"I've been administered small doses of laudanum to ease pain, after being wounded," Lewrie slowly said, still without a clue as to where the men were going. "It tastes vile, even when mixed into brandy with sugar, or a dram of honey. You'd force laudanum down his throat with a clyster?"

"Ehm . . . not his throat, sir," Durbin said in a small voice. "Up his anus, rather. That's where the brothels come in, Captain, sir. While on the premises to inspect for, and treat, venereal Pox, the man I worked with would, ehm . . . help the ladies, and rather a great many of their clients, get drunk and woozy all the faster, with a mixture of laudanum and ardent spirits . . . gin, mostly . . . up their anuses and into the lower intestines, where the bulk of digestion takes place—"

"And, where the nutritional benefits of digestion reach the body and the blood stream more readily, sir," Mainwaring supplied, to bring their discussion back to a less sordid tone. "To imbibe gin and laudanum the normal way by liquid ingestion, the effect desired might not become apparent for some time, but . . . injected into the lower intestines, the alcoholic spirits and laudanum take effect within minutes."

"I've seen one . . . courtesan at one of the better houses in Panton Street, who weighed ten or eleven stone, take two drams of gin and a dram of laudanum, together, and become half-seas-over within five minutes, Captain," Durbin promised. "With small glasses of brandy and champagne throughout the night, she could take on any number of clients. And, when she wished to sleep the night's work off, my old patron would increase the laudanum a bit more, and she'd sleep 'til noon of the next day. A lot of the girls would do that . . . to get started and tolerate the work, and to sleep soundly after.

"After a time, I was allowed to service one house whilst my old patron would handle another, for more fees," Durbin went on. "We'd make the rounds each night . . . 'til he got too fond of the drug and took too large a dose and died."

"So, the dose necessary to addle a woman of considerable weight would surely put your cat to sleep, painlessly and humanely, Captain," Mainwaring assured him. "A moment or two of surprise, as the clyster is inserted, and then perhaps a state of inebriation which may be pleasureable to even a cat, followed by a . . . fatal lethargy."

"But, you're not sure," Lewrie sceptically asked. "No one ever tried this. The brandy or gin might turn him rabid, ravin' mad before the laudanum takes effect. I don't know. . . ." Lewrie looked down as he stroked Toulon, who was looking up at him with wide eyes, as if he was aware that his demise was being plotted. Toulon was not struggling to escape, though. But, he had stopped purring, and the tip of his tail no longer slowly flicked. Lewrie felt a lump of grief in his chest.

"Well, sir . . . perhaps the laudanum only," Mainwaring allowed. "If I may examine it, Captain?"

"Him," Lewrie corrected. "Toulon."

"Of course, Captain," Mainwaring replied, pausing for a moment to be chided, then fell upon his best bedside manner. He checked the dullness of the cat's eyes, listened to the heart and respiration with a long horn, felt the temperature of Toulon's nose, then sat back down in his chair and took a sip of cool tea. "I fear that . . . he . . . does not display any sign of improvement, Captain. He has been sleeping most of the day and night? Apart from everyone? A bad sign. Do you wish to wait 'til he is even more lethargic, we may, though I do not know if his fatal condition pains him now, and may get worse the longer we delay. As I said, no one I am aware of knows the first thing about the physiology of cats and dogs."

No longer being pawed at by Mainwaring's large hands, Toulon stopped fretting and snuggled down, eyes shut and his head nodding as if he would fall asleep right there in Lewrie's arms. His breath was faint.

"Perhaps . . . perhaps, it would be best did we proceed, Mister Main-waring," Lewrie sadly, slowly agreed.

"A towel, sir," Durbin softly suggested, getting to his feet. "Something to swaddle him during the procedure?"

"A restraining towel, yes," Mainwaring agreed, finishing his cool tea before rising, himself. "Perhaps at your dining table, sir?"

"Dram and a half, sir?" Durbin asked his superior.

"Hmm, best make it a full two," Mainwaring proposed. "Prepare the clyster."

Pettus fetched a used towel and laid it on the dining table. Lewrie carried Toulon to the table and gently sat him down on it, then folded the towel round him, petting and softly cooing affection to keep the cat calm. Pettus and Jessop came close to witness, with Jessop holding Chalky in his arms to keep him from interfering.

Surgeon's Mate Durbin produced the clyster, a metal cylinder about six inches long with a plunger at one end, and a long, narrow, and hollow metal tube, no wider than a goose quill, at the other. He withdrew the plunger and laid it aside, put a finger over the end of the tube, and presented it to Surgeon Mainwaring, who carefully measured out 120 minims, or two fluid drams, into a graduated glass tube, then poured the laudanum into the clyster. Durbin re-inserted the plunger for him, still holding a finger over the needle's opening to prevent spillage.

"I will take it now, Durbin," Mainwaring said, placing his own finger over the needle's aperture, allowing a drop or two to dribble out. "Even the tiniest *bolus* of air would impede the efficacious administering of the dose, do you see, Captain."

"Umhum," Lewrie replied, his heart in his throat.

"If you will hold him firmly, now, Captain, I will begin," the Surgeon said, leaning down over the end of the table.

Toulon emitted a loud, outraged *yeowl* as the needle went up his anus and its contents were injected with a push of the plunger, and it was all Lewrie could do to hold him still in the folds of the towel.

"You tell him, Toulon," Lewrie cooed, his eyes turning hot and moist as he tried to calm his cat. "I'd be at his throat with claws out if someone did that t'me, too! Hush, now. Hush, little man, it's done. If God's just, there's a Fiddler's Green for you, too, with all the mice and birds ye wish t'chase, milk pools, and all the fish and sausages ye'd ever want. Other cats t'play with . . . perhaps even old Pitt. Ye might get on with him.

Hush, now. Go t'sleep, and dream a happy cat's dreams. I always loved
ye, d'ye know that, Toulon?"

"'Is fav'rite people, too, sir," Jessop said in an awed whisper, "an' 'im
be there a'waitin' on yer when ye goes t'Heaven yerself."

"I pray so, Jessop," Lewrie managed to choke out, "I surely do pray
so."

Toulon did calm down, muttering a bit and going limp after a minute
or so. His front paws twitched as if he was having a chase dream, and his
jaws chittered silently as he did when seeing a bird.

They all waited for a full five minutes, in silence. Toulon seemed completely asleep, with no response when Lewrie folded back the towel and
gently stroked and caressed his fur. Chalky was having no part of it,
mrring and wriggling out of Jessop's grasp to run aft and fuss and groom.

"If I may, Captain," Mainwaring said, at last. He bent down to press
an ear to Toulon, gently rolling him onto one side. He used his amplify-
ing horn device, a stethoscope he termed it, to listen even more carefully
for a full minute more before leaning back and digging into his bag for a
small mirror and a lancet.

"There is no sign of respiration, Captain," Mainwaring said as he
looked at the mirror. "I can no longer discern a heart beat, nor a bit of fog
on the mirror."

Lewrie thought it rather gruesome, but Mainwaring lifted a paw to
expose the sensitive pads and made a first light jab with the lancet, then a
stronger second. Lastly, he pricked Toulon on his nose, with no response.

"I believe I may state in perfect conviction that he is gone, sir," Mainwaring said with a slight nod of satisfaction. "I am sorry for your loss. He
was dear to you, and a great companion."

"Thank you, Mister Mainwaring," Lewrie managed to say, with a curt
nod. "Pettus, will you go pass word for the Master Gunner and the Bosun? I will need a nine-pounder roundshot and a baize bag."

"Yes, sir," Pettus muttered, wiping his eyes as he left.

The towel was sacrificed for a winding cloth, the requested baize bag,
quickly sewn together out of the red baize usually used to hold a defaulter's
"cat-o'-nine-tails", was three times normal size, as if Bosun Sprague knew
its purpose beforehand, and Jessop added one of Toulon's favourite old
woven wool toys before Lewrie drew and tied the bag shut, and went out

on deck to the waist, then up the ladderway to the quarterdeck. He threaded his way aft through the Afterguard and watchstanders, surprised by the presence of not only the men of the watch but most of the hands who were at that hour off watch on deck and along the sail-tending gangways. Officers, Mids, and petty officers doffed their hats as he passed. It was impossible to keep secrets from any ship's company; they all knew of the Surgeon's speculations and the fact that the Captain had requested his help to ease his pet's passing.

Lewrie got to the taffrails right aft and took off his own hat, laid it down atop the flag lockers, and stood bareheaded with the bag cradled in both arms.

"I'm sorry, Toulon," he whispered, "but it had to be done, and I meant for you t'go easy. I loved you from the first sight of you, and always will." A captain's stern dignity be-damned, Lewrie lifted the bag to bestow a last kiss on the baize, then extended his arms over the stern. "Goodbye, littl'un. See you in Heaven."

He let go of the bag and watched it drop into the white trail of the frigate's wake, where it made a small splash before sinking to the deeps.

The ship's fiddler and the Marine flutist began "Johnny Faa"!

They tryin' *t'break my heart?* Lewrie thought, unable to turn to face forward without showing his sudden tears. He had not heard "Johnny Faa" since he had given his old Cox'n, Matthew Andrews, a sea burial after conquering the French frigate, *L'Uranie,* ages before, and the sadness of that tune always made him brokenly mournful.

At last, Lewrie pulled a handkerchief from a coat pocket, blew his nose, and dabbed his eyes before shoving it back away and clapping his hat on his head to turn away from the taffrails and face his crew.

He got to the forward edge of the quarterdeck, and was amazed to see all hands standing with their hats off. No one had ordered it, but they had done it. Doffing his hat to them, he called out, "Thank you, lads. Thank you," then made a slow way down to the waist and to the doors to his great-cabins, nodded to his Marine sentry, and went inside.

Lewrie stayed aft and below the rest of the afternoon, going to the quarterdeck for a breath of fresher and cooler air round the middle of the Second Dog Watch. Though there was no point in doing so, he did go aft to the taffrails for a while, looking far astern. Bisquit, now allowed the liberty of the quarterdeck, joined him and sat down atop the flag lockers, nuzzling for attention and pets, and Lewrie rewarded him before returning to his cabins for a silent and bleak supper. There was only one feeding bowl at the foot of the dining table for Chalky, who seemed oblivious that his long-time friend was no longer present. Once fed, the younger cat came to be petted, arching under Lewrie's hands and rubbing his cheeks on his fingers before flopping on his side to play.

And that night, long after Lights Out when Lewrie was in bed, sleeping atop the coverlet in his underdrawers for coolness, he came awake. The hanging bed-cot was swaying gently to the roll of the ship, a motion which always calmed him and lulled him to deep sleep, but . . . he felt as if Chalky had leapt from the deck to the bed, and was walking and brushing up his legs and chest. Lewrie opened one eye and reached out to stroke Chalky, but there was no cat there.

He sat up on an elbow and looked round in the deep gloom of the cabins. There was Chalky, curled up at the foot of the bed with his head resting across Lewrie's ankle! He lay back down on the pillows and was almost drifted off once more, but, there was the feeling of a cat padding up behind his back, this time, and he sat up once more in a start. Chalky woke, still draped over his ankle, yawned widely, and sat up to give out a low, challenging *Mrrr!* with tail thrashing. In the faintest light of pre-dawn, Chalky's eerie green chatoyant eyes were fixed intently on nothing, just to the starboard side of the bed, then to the overhead, as if fearfully watching something that drifted away!

Chalky finally hopped over Lewrie's legs and came to Lewrie's face, nuzzling for a hand and looking over his shoulder to larboard.

"Don't *you* go dyin' on me, now, Chalky," Lewrie whispered as he stroked and calmed him. "I wouldn't know what t'do with both you *and* Toulon hauntin' my cabins."

CHAPTER TWENTY-TWO

*I*t was almost Christmas Eve before *Reliant*'s little convoy finally caught sight of tops'ls and t'gallants on the Southern horizon, a wide smear of weathered tan or ecru canvas that spread from three points off the larboard bows to three points off the starboard. When the cry of "Sail Ho!" came, Lewrie was in the middle of shaving, and he dashed to the quarter-deck with a towel still round his neck and the thin foam of shaving soap still on his face.

"It would appear that there are at least seventy ships, sir," Lt. Spend-love, the officer of the Forenoon Watch, eagerly reported. "I *believe* I can make out their fores'ls . . . fore topmast stays'ls . . . lying to the right, so they must be making the long board Sou'-Sou'west, the same as us, sir!"

"Hmm, that'll make for a long stern-chase, then," Lewrie speculated aloud. "As we close with them, we'll fall into their wind shadow and be blanketed. They're hull-down under the horizon, so we're about twelve or more miles alee of 'em, but it may be dusk before we come to hailing distance. Mast-head!" he shouted aloft. "Any signals yet?"

"Just now, sir!" Midshipman Munsell cried down. "It is 'Query'!"

"Very well. Mister Spendlove, have our number hoisted, and in this month's private signals book, add 'Come To Join'."

"Aye aye, sir," Spendlove said, turning aft to relay the order to Midshipman Rossyngton at the taffrails, flag lockers, and signals halliards.

"Caught them up at last, sir?" Lt. Westcott asked as he mounted to the quarterdeck, with Lt. Merriman right behind him, and both of them as hastily half-dressed as Lewrie.

"It appears so, Mister Westcott," Lewrie told him with a grin.

"Do we know which ships Commodore Popham commands, sir?" Lt. Merriman asked, with his own telescope glued to one eye.

"I think I recall that he has the *Diadem*, sixty-four," Lewrie said, off-handedly stroking a raspy cheek in thought and finding that his fingers came away soapy. "He's the *Raisonnable* and *Belliqueux* as well, also sixty-fours. There's sure t'be frigates and such, but at the moment the names escape me. Oh, there's the *Diomede*, one of the old two-decker fifty-gunners. *Diadem, Diomede?* Easy to get them confused."

"As a trooper, sir?" Lt. Merriman further asked.

"As far as I know, *Diomede*'s still rated as a warship," Lewrie said with a shrug. Fifty-gunned two-deckers had been a failed experiment, much cheaper to build, crew, and maintain than 64s or 74s, but unable to match weight of metal with larger ships even in their brief hey-day. There weren't more than a dozen 50s left, and most of them had been converted to troop transports, and the few remaining in the Navy as ships of war were found only in the farthest corners and backwaters of the world, where the stoutest opposition they might meet would be frigates, sloops of war, or brigs and light privateer vessels.

"Pity the poor fellow who has charge of *her*!" Lt. Merriman said with a snicker of derision.

"Oh, I don't know," Lewrie, laughed. "One could be worse off. One could be appointed an Agent Afloat with the Transport Board!" After the others had had a slight laugh, Lewrie ordered, "Carry on, Mister Spendlove. I will be below, finishing my shave."

"A close, Sunday Divisions shave, sir," Westcott teased. "You will be reporting aboard Commodore Popham's flagship by supper time."

"And, after this long on-passage, sir," Lt. Merriman, their wag, posed, "you might have to fetch them rabbits and quail for the *entrée*, else the Commodore serves you salt-meat junk!"

"Like a housewarming supper?" Lewrie laughed. "Signal my host t'see if I can bring anything before I boat over? Hah! Carry on, gentlemen."

⚓

By five of the afternoon, in the middle of the First Dog Watch, *Reliant* gladly shedded her three charges, and *Ascot, Marigold,* and the *Sweet Susan* swanned off into the larger convoy's gaggle in search of the ships bearing the rest of the 34th Light Dragoons. Lewrie had the frigate steered over to join the rest of the escorting warships, and hoisted the very welcome signal "Have Mail", which elicited an invitation from HMS *Diadem* to send a boat at once, followed shortly after by a second invitation for *Reliant*'s captain to dine aboard Commodore Popham's flagship at half-past 6 P.M.

Lewrie found that almost bearable. For many long weeks, he had dressed any-old-how in his oldest, plainest coat, loosely tied neck-stock, and roomy slop trousers. Now, he would have to dress in snug breeches, silk shirt and ironed stock, snow-white waist-coat, and his finest uniform coat with the sash and star of the Order of The Bath. At least the supper would be held after sundown, so the present latitude's oppressive heat would not be as bad as a mid-day dinner, and on the long board on larboard tack which the fleet held, the humidity of the African coast was far away, and there was a fresh-enough breeze off the sea.

Once the salutations had been rendered, one of *Diadem*'s officers showed Lewrie aft to the Commodore's great-cabins, where he was announced.

"Lewrie! My Lord, you're a sight for sore eyes!" Commodore Sir Home Riggs Popham happily exclaimed as a cabin servant took his hat and sword. "You didn't bring along any of those damned torpedoes, did you? Good riddance to bad rubbish, hah hah! Those infernal engines, I mean, not Lewrie! Come, sir! Have a glass of Rhenish, and allow me to name to you the others."

Sir Home Riggs Popham was ebullience itself, but of course, in Lewrie's brief experience with him, he always was the epitome of good cheer even in adversity. Popham was considered dashingly handsome by many, with a high, intelligent brow, pleasant eyes, good cheekbones, and a firm, clefted chin, and was possessed of a slim but solid build. In the latest mode, Popham wore his thick blond hair without even a sprig of an old-time sailors' queue, and long sideburns below the lobes of his ears. Perhaps his only mar was a long and pointed nose with an up-tilt. Popham was garbed in his best, and costly, uniform coat which also bore the star of the Order of The Bath.

The others of whom Popham spoke were senior Army officers in command of the five thousand or so soldiers sent to take the Cape of Good Hope, a General Sir David Baird, and his second-in-command, Brigadier-General Sir William Beresford. Baird seemed a gruff and capable sort to Lewrie, though Beresford struck him as overly mild. Beresford had thick hair brushed back over his ears on the sides of his head, but was as bald as an egg above, and the fellow almost had pop-eyes.

There were some aides-de-camp with them, to whom Lewrie was named but they made little impression; he was sure that he would not have much to do with them once the army was set ashore.

"Besides the most welcome mail from home, what else did you bring us, Lewrie?" Commodore Popham asked.

"Two troops of the Thirty-fourth Light Dragoons, sir," Lewrie told him, dreading the coming announcement. He brought the newspaper he had gotten at Madeira from a side pocket of his coat.

"Oh Lord, Colonel Laird!" General Baird said with a sniff. "One *does* hope he's pleased, at long last."

"I obtained these papers at Funchal, sir," Lewrie said, holding them out for Popham to take. "I don't know if you've had word of the battle off Cádiz, and Cape Trafalgar, yet. Nelson—"

"Caught up with Villeneuve at last, did he?" Popham exclaimed, beaming with pleasure and anticipation.

"He did, sir, the combined French and Spanish fleets," Lewrie went on. "The foe were utterly defeated, and upwards of twenty ships were taken as prize, but . . . Admiral Lord Nelson was slain, sir. So soon after, and by word of mouth to Lisbon and Oporto, I expect the details are half rumour, half wild speculation, but—"

"Good God! Nelson, dead?" Popham yelped, taken all aback and suddenly "in-irons" at the news. "That is simply impossible to imagine! Why, even credible *London* papers had Nelson meeting Villeneuve half a dozen times, and all of the accounts pure fantasy. How much faith may be put in Portuguese scribblers?" he scoffed.

"The English language paper from Oporto tells the same story, sir," Lewrie pointed out, "as did our Consul at Funchal, Gilbao? At any rate, it appears there *was* a battle, and a victory."

"If true, such a victory would be England's salvation from the fear of French invasion, at last," General Beresford hesitantly said, "though at much too high a cost. What joyous celebrations our nation will hold would be tempered by the sense of loss, and grief."

"Doubt there will ever be another quite like him," General Baird gruffly said.

"Oh, I don't know about that, Sir David," Popham said with a brief smile, almost a sly look. "Nelson was a product of our Navy, and our Fleet will produce a worthy replacement, eventually. The nation may grieve for a time, but . . . when they hear of our success at Cape Town? And a success it will be, hey? New heroes will arise."

"I thought it best to inform you at once, sir," Lewrie said, "and allow you to decide whether the news should be passed on to our sailors right off, or you wish to wait 'til there is solid confirmation."

"Quite right, Lewrie, aye," Popham said, nodding. "It might be best to pass the word that Nelson smashed the Frogs and Dons, but hold off on the details 'til we truly *do* have confirmation. *That'll* put a fire in their bellies, and make them eager to succeed. Well, sirs, shall we dine?"

At least I didn't have t' fetch him a chicken, Lewrie wryly told himself; *I don't think* admirals *live this well at sea!*

Sir Home Riggs Popham's great-cabins fair-screamed money, and extreme good taste, worlds beyond the bare-bones spartan quarters the Navy approved of from its officers, no matter how senior, or wealthy. Lewrie's own tastes, and comforts, had been sniffed at by dis-approving seniors in the past, deemed almost sybaritic, but his could not hold a candle to Popham's. Atop the usual black-and-white chequered canvas deck cloth which emulated tilework, the figured carpets were thick enough to trip over, or sink into at each step. Polished brass or coin-silver lanthorns hung from the painted or polished overhead deck beams in profusion, the chairs, settees, wine-cabinets, the wash-hand stand, and Popham's desk gleamed, and the aroma of bees' wax polish was everywhere. Popham's sleeping space, chart cubby, and the dining coach were partitioned off with half-louvred panels made from polished oak, not the usual deal-and-canvas temporary walls. In the dining coach there was a table which could seat twelve, covered with a glaringly clean and white tablecloth, with pitchers, bowls and candelabras down the centre all in shining coin-silver, with even more pieces resting atop the magnificent sideboard. Once inside and seated, the partitions were chair-railed and wainscotted below, the upper parts painted light canary yellow, picked out with white trim.

I'd heard *he'd deliberately married for money,* Lewrie scoffed to himself; *and it appears he gained a* barge-load *of "tin" from the bargain! There's enough candles lit t'light a bloody ballroom!*

The soup course was "portable", the usual boiled dry and pressed into cakes vegetable soup so beloved of the Navy Victualling Board, though made more palatable with shredded bacon bits and tangy spices, served with white-bread baked rolls, globs of "fresh-ish" butter, and a sprightly German Riesling.

"Do you believe the accounts, Captain Lewrie?" General Beresford gloomily enquired after a slurp or two.

"I fear that I do, sir," Lewrie admitted. "Lord Nelson pursued Villeneuve so hotly, there is no way that he would *not* bring him to battle, once Villeneuve returned to Europe from his jaunt to the West Indies. If the French put into Cádiz, as is reported, and sailed out with his Spanish ally, Nelson would have been there, right off shore, and *thirsting* for a fight. My main fear is for my youngest son, Hugh, who is aboard the *Pegasus* seventy-four, under an old friend of mine, Captain Thomas Charlton."

"Charlton!" Popham cried in delight. "A damned good man, is Thom Charlton, and a fine sailor. Straight as a die, and as smart as paint. You chose well for your son's first captain. Where did you serve with him?"

"He commanded a small squadron in the Adriatic, sir, about the time of Napoleon's first invasion of Italy, and I had *Jester,* a French *corvette* that we took just after the evacuation of Toulon," Lewrie gladly told him. "Aye, salt of the earth is Charlton, though never the life of the party."

General Sir David Baird then spoke highly of the soup, sharing an account of how Napoleon fed his armies fresh soup and gravies, put up in magnum-sized champagne bottles and carefully sealed to remain fresh and edible for months on end. "Naturally, Horse Guards will *not* follow suit," Baird grumbled. "The French thought of it first."

"If our Army won't, then I most certainly shall!" Commodore Popham declared. "If only for my own use. How dearly a *consommé* or a broth, or a good, thick gravy, is desired at sea!"

The soup was followed by individual bantam chickens, and Lewrie could boast of his fast-growing quail and rabbits kept in his frigate's forecastle manger, and Popham swore that when dined aboard *Reliant* off Calais, before their failed expedition with torpedoes and fireships at the tail-end of 1804, Lewrie had been his own inspiration for the keeping of bantams.

"I found a whole new flock of bantams when we put into San Salvador," Popham told them. "Pigeons and doves are also toothsome, and reproduce in sufficient abundance. When I dined with the Prime Minister in London before receiving this appointment, the high point of our supper, beyond the excellence of the beef roast, was a pigeon pie, hah hah! A pity, though, that, one good omelet is the destruction of one's pigeon flock for the next six months!"

Just how well-connected is he? I wonder, Lewrie asked himself, noticing the faintest pauses and disguised sniffs from the Army officers. It appeared that Baird and Beresford had heard Popham's casual mentions of his ties to the high-placed and powerful men in the government once *too* often. Then, during the next course, a roast pork loin gone "shares" with *Diadem*'s captain and officers' wardroom, when Popham spoke of his connexions to the former First Lord of the Admiralty, Henry, Lord Melville, even Lewrie had to hide a snort, for Lord Melville had been turfed out in disgrace for being so corrupt that even the other crooks had noticed.

The rest of the repast passed pleasantly, right through to the nuts, cheese, and port, with sweet bisquits, and innocuous topics of conversation.

"Well now, Captain Lewrie," Popham said, peering down the table at him rather sharply, "what brings you to become part of our little expedition?"

"When up to London, sir, I mentioned to the First Secretary that I had spent some time round Cape Town several years ago," Lewrie told him. "I had no choice, really . . . a French frigate sneaked up on me in the dark and shot my rudder to bits, had to be towed in, and spent some weeks scrounging up a replacement and getting it fitted. During that time, I hired a local hunter as guide and rode or hunted all over the countryside. Mister Marsden deemed that experience might prove of use to you, sir."

"And well it might," General Baird pronounced, thumping a fist on the table top. "Just where, exactly, Captain Lewrie?"

"Aye, let's bring out the chart one more time," Popham called out. "Supper is officially over, so there's no harm discussing 'shop'. And I'll request the port decanter, if you will, General Beresford."

A large chart, more a land map than a sea-chart, was fetched and spread out atop the dining table, the corners weighted down with the cheese plate, the bisquit barge, the nut bowl, and the port decanter.

"We anchored here, sirs, under the guns of the seaward fort, near the town quays," Lewrie sketched out, pointing his movements during his forced stay. "Our sick and wounded, we placed in a rented cottage a little way up the Lion's Rump, South of town, where there was a fresh-water well and cool and fresh sea breezes. When it came to the rudder, we put together a train of bullock carts, with native drivers, and trekked down to Simon's Bay, where an Indiaman had mistaken False Cape for the proper one, and ripped her hull open on the rocks. Fortunately, she was able to beach herself, and there was little loss of life. The locals at Simonstown were scavenging her for her timbers and metal fittings, but they hadn't gotten round to her rudder, yet. We camped there several days, living off game meat we shot, sleeping rough under canvas, and playing ball in the late afternoons. After we got the rudder replaced, I did ride out as far as the Salt River, to the Nor'east, and North round the shore of Table Bay."

"As far as Blaauwberg or Saldanha Bays, sir?" General Baird enquired.

"Not quite that far, no, sir," Lewrie replied. "Once my ship was seaworthy, a small home-bound 'John Company' convoy had come in, and its Commodore requested additional escorts, what with so many Frog raiders working out of the Indian Ocean as far North up the Western coasts of Africa as the Equator. I *might've* gone as far as the South end of the beaches of Blaauwberg Bay, but it was only a day ride, and we didn't find the type of antelope or whatever that my guide, Piet Retief, promised. Some of my sailors, four or five of my Black hands, had run off with a circus's hunting party, and some had come back badly mauled, so I also had that on my plate to deal——"

"A circus!" General Baird gawped.

"Mister Daniel Wigmore's Peripatetic Extravaganza, sir. They were after strange, new beasts for their menagerie," Lewrie explained. "*They* hired the biggest fool in all of Africa for *their* guide, and it was a total disaster. Does a Jan van der Merwe offer you his services, sir, shoot him and run like Hell. He thought that the Cape buffalo would be a good replacement for domestic oxen, and that hyenas could be tamed as guard dogs, and God only *knows* what other foolishness. Baboons as nannies, I expect!"

"Yes, your famous Black sailors," Popham said with a simpering drawl. "Lewrie was tried and acquitted, don't you know, sirs, for liberating a round dozen Black slaves on Jamaica, and signing them aboard his ship as free volunteers. 'Black Alan' Lewrie? Or, 'Saint Alan, the Liberator'?"

"Oh yes, I recall hearing of that," General Beresford said, nodding.

"That must have made William Wilberforce and his Abolitionist crowd perfectly giddy."

"They were, for a *time*, my patrons, sir," Lewrie had to admit. "Once I was acquitted, though, they found a new'un."

"That must have been miserable," General Baird grumbled. "All that tea-slurping and hymn-singing, and deadly-dull earnestness. The lesser races may be taught to make good servants, perhaps even sailors in your case, Captain Lewrie, but, without the firm, guiding hand from a civilised race, they will never amount to much. Pray God that after we take the Cape from the Dutch, we keep it and make it part of our empire forever. Then, you'll see how much more we English may make of the place than ever the complacent Dutch could."

"Hear hear!" Commodore Popham enthused.

"Now, with these two forts commanding Table Bay, there is no way to land our force directly upon Cape Town," General Baird went on, returning his attention to the map. "Commodore Popham, Beresford, and I have thought it best to go ashore in either Saldanha or Blaauwberg Bay, which, or so Commodore Popham and his officers assure me, are open to the sea, and relatively free of any rocky shoals or reefs. Behind either, there is a chain of hills which must be surmounted, but there are passes through which we must march, before descending the Eastern slopes to what is reputed to be a decent road which leads all the way down round the shore of Table Bay to Cape Town.

"It is our intention to flank wide round Fort Knocke, here, at the East end of Cape Town," Baird went on, "and, should it prove necessary to assault the town proper, it should be done from the South and East, out of the range of Fort Knocke's heavy artillery, up through the outskirts and street-to-street. I would much prefer, though, for the Dutch to meet us in the open long before, so we may bloody their noses and reduce their numbers *before* we fall upon the town, eliminating the risk of laying siege."

"I don't remember either fort mounting all that many pieces of artillery facing landward, sir," Lewrie offered, "though I suppose they could shift some guns from the seaward side. There *were* openings in the ramparts for such. But, once your troops get into the houses on the South side of town, would the Dutch really fire at their own town? They don't strike me as ruthless enough to risk killing their own people."

"It's all profit and loss for the Dutch, yes, Lewrie," Popham said with a laugh. "They are ever a *mercantile* lot!"

"What is there, Lewrie . . . on the Southern outskirts?" Baird asked him directly.

"As I recall, sir, it's all truck gardens and vineyards, cottagers with some livestock, and some native African workers' housing," Lewrie said, tilting his head to one side to summon the images from his memory of the time he'd ridden the area, back when he and Eudoxia Durschenko had flirted with each other . . . before she'd discovered he was married. "Cape Town's not all *that* large a city, sirs. The farms and such just get larger the further one goes outside the commercial centre, warehouses, and docks. Larger pastures, more livestock, more space between dwellings 'til one's in open country, where the native people still have a few *kraals*. They lost their own pasturage to the Dutch a long time ago. And the Dutch brought in slaves from the East Indies t'make up the numbers of farm workers. It just straggles off. There aren't many free natives or East Indians, and those who are are gathered together in little, separate quarters. Unless they tear down the rich, White part of town for fortifications and dig trenches, the town's wide open, as is the countryside."

"No impediments," Brigadier General Beresford said, sounding like a man with his fingers crossed.

"Not unless one calls wood fences impediments, sir," Lewrie assured them all.

"At any rate, our sudden appearance just out of range of their heavy guns will give them no time to prepare against us," Commodore Popham idly dismissed. "We bring the fleet to anchor . . . well, here," he said, tapping a finger just West of Robben Island at the Nor'west end of Table Bay, "sort ourselves out, and begin landing the cavalry and the regiments of the Light Brigade of Foot in either Saldanha or Blaauwberg Bay a day or two later, the winds and surf allowing, we'll be at their throats before they know it! Forewarned even a week, the Dutch would still have too little time to prepare fortifications for a siege of Cape Town."

"Their key defences are the two fortresses, though, Commodore Popham," Beresford hesitantly pointed out. "Is the officer in command of their forces the cautious sort, he may not wish to stray too far from their reach."

"Then he will be lost," Baird countered, scoffing. "Where we face the worst peril is upon the beaches, or just behind them in the hills. Counter us there, and he could delay our advance to a crawl, and a series of head-on assaults from one advantageous point of terrain to the next, especially did he deny us a crossing of the Salt River. No, Beresford, I still say *their* general, whoever he is, will and *must* meet us in the open. The Cape Colony is too large an area to be defended by infantry alone. I expect that the Dutch will have more horse than we may field, so he will possess the advantages of rapid mobility, and only a pluperfect *fool* would throw that edge away."

Christ, a soldier with a brain in his head! Lewrie thought with admiration for Baird; *Now* there's *a rare bird!*

"And, what part will *Reliant* and I play, sir?" Lewrie asked of Popham.

"Admiral Villeneuve and *his* huge fleet may be destroyed, do we believe your news, Captain Lewrie," Popham quickly told him, with a grin, "but the French still have more than enough ships in the Indian Ocean, prowling *this* side of the Cape of Good Hope. 'Til we have established a firm lodgement ashore, we must keep one eye peeled seaward against their interference. Your *Reliant, Leda,* and *Narcissus,* I will keep mobile, cruising close ashore, perhaps to provide some fire support against any Dutch batteries, but still able to sortie should any French warships turn up . . . to protect the transports."

"'Til we may shift them deeper into Table Bay, sir? But, what should I be doing after that?" Lewrie pressed. "If I was sent along to share my experiences ashore—"

"There is that, Commodore Popham," General Baird said. "If there is a threat from the French, your larger ships would be more than a match to any of their frigates, hmm? Captain Lewrie here might prove to be useful and informative ashore."

"It'll be Navy boats that get your troops to the beaches, sir, and to sort out the cavalry, artillery, and supplies," Lewrie quickly suggested. "I could bring along my Marines, and an equal number of armed sailors, say . . . eighty or so, in all. If the French show up, my First Officer is more than capable of fighting my ship for me."

"And, your own Flag-Captain, Captain Downman, you have already assigned the role of supervising naval co-ordination of the landing, sir," Baird added. "Indeed, let's bring Lewrie ashore with us."

"It will be as you say, Sir David," Popham consented. "Well, gentlemen. Now that's settled, let us have a 'stirrup cup', as it were, to bid Captain Lewrie a safe return to his ship!"

CHAPTER TWENTY-THREE

*C*hristmas came and went, with raisin duffs for each eight-man mess, and a "Splicing of The Main-Brace" issue of grog, to celebrate, minus the wilder rites of civilians, and no Lord of Mis-Rule leading a ravening pack of carolers to barge into houses and demand dinner and drink from their betters. Very quietly the next morning, Boxing Day was observed, with minor gifts for stewards and servants in the Midshipmens' and officers' messes, and in Lewrie's great-cabins.

The great-cabins were also the site of the New Year's Eve supper for the officers, with as grand a repast as could be concocted after several months on-passage, livened by music and song, and a flowing bowl of punch which had to be refilled twice over.

The First of January of 1806 the next morning was welcomed with yet another "Splice The Main-Brace" and a day of "Make And Mend" idleness for all hands, beyond necessary ship's work. With *Reliant* and the invasion convoy now below the 30th Meridian, and hundreds of miles out to sea from the shores of Africa, the temperatures were once more bearable, as was the glare of the sun. Many sailors went bare-chested and hatless as they sewed to repair or alter their clothes, wrote letters or had them written by more literate mates, read books or months-old newspapers, worked small-stuff twine to fashion rings, bracelets, and lanyards for their personal knives, or more complicated brooches that they hoped to have sewn on distant loves' gowns, someday. Some carved rock-hard salt-meat into snuff boxes, or combs. And, many "caulked", seizing the rare opportunity to sleep without disturbance beyond their few hours off-watch in their hammocks below.

"It is now official," Sailing Master Caldwell declared after he lowered his sextant and scribbled his sums on a scrap of paper. "May I now wish you all a Happy New Year, sirs."

"Ehm . . . would the new year actually have started at Eight Bells of the Night Watch, sir?" Midshipman Shannon piped up.

"For landlubbers, aye, Mister Shannon," Caldwell grudgingly allowed. "For them, the last stroke of midnight would do, along with all the church bells, but . . . the *ship's* day begins at Noon Sights. Happy New Year, Captain Lewrie."

"And the same to you, Mister Caldwell," Lewrie answered, admittedly a trifle blearily. His supper party the evening before had polished off a round dozen bottles of various wines, two massive bowls of punch heavily laced with rum, gin, some precious champagne, and great sloshes of his personal store of aged American bourbon whisky, and it had taken a hard look and a long try to rouse himself when wakened at 4 A.M. at the change of watch. There were some bohemian types and young sprogs of the sporting set who wore coloured glasses, and today Lewrie wished that he had a pair, for the bright and lovely day was painful on his eyes, and enflamed the dull headache that throbbed behind them.

I do b'lieve a passionate kiss, or a cold breakfast, might kill *me,* he told himself in moody misery, stifling yet another belch from his dicey stomach. All he wished was a *very* quiet few hours below in the relative silence, and dimness, of his cabins 'til sundown.

"I reckon us to be here, sirs," Caldwell happily babbled on, "and am most pleased that *most* of the younkers' reckonings agree with me." He cast a chary eye upon Shannon. "We are actually a bit Sou'west of the Cape of Good Hope, and still on larboard tack. Almost in the latitudes of the prevailing Westerlies, hmm."

"Do any of you young fellows have an explanation why Commodore Popham would lead us so broad?" Lt. Westcott posed to the Mids.

"Well, sir, sailing this far South, perhaps he *intends* to fetch the North-most fringes of the Westerlies," Midshipman Eldridge said. "In that way, we could approach the Cape below it, then alter course and sail up to Cape Town and Table Bay on the Sou'east winds, from a quarter which the Dutch would not expect."

"The Commodore is a very clever fellow," Midshipman Rossyngton quickly agreed. "Why, the Dutch might even take us for a large French trade making its way to Europe from their Indian Ocean possessions!"

"Did we continue our slow approach from the North, they would spot us and be on the alert for days, else," Midshipman Munsell speculated. "But, coming from the South, we'd be on the Cape, and along the shore, as quick as one could say 'Knife'! Right into Table Bay in the middle of their dinners! Catch them with their breeches down!"

"Not into Table Bay itself, no," Lewrie grumbled. "Can anyone tell me why? No? Pray do refer to the other chart."

Once rolled out and pinned to the traverse board, Lewrie jabbed a finger at several features depicted, saying nothing, and leaving it for the Mids to figure out.

"Ehm . . . there are those two forts," Midshipman Grainger shyly said. "Fortresses, really, especially this one on the West side of Cape Town, guarding the seaward approaches."

"And here, and here?" Lewrie prompted, pointing to the mountains South of the town and the bay. "First, there are the Twelve Apostles along the shore. Above them on the West side of town are the Lion's Head and the slightly lower Lion's Rump. South of town is the Tafelberg . . . 'Table Mountain' . . . *and,* the lesser mounts of Signal Hill by Green Point, and the Devil's Peak below Table Mountain's foot. Any of them are tall enough for any watchers to see twenty miles or more out to sea on a good day, so there's little chance of catching them with their breeches down. An approach from the South, as it appears that Commodore Popham prefers, *might* give the Dutch a day less to get ready to resist us, but I doubt they'd take us for a French commercial trade. And why is that, young sirs?"

"That they no longer have any, sir?" Munsell guessed.

"Spot on," Lt. Westcott said with a laugh. "The French lost all their trade from China and India in the first months of the first war in 1793, and never could revive it, even during the Peace of Amiens. They've been driven from their few footholds in India, and only hold naval bases in the middle of the Indian Ocean. The Dutch might expect to see one or two frigates or large privateers coming round the Cape to put into Table Bay for provisions, but not a fleet such as ours."

"So, even coming from the South, on favourable winds, there's no chance of surprise," Midshipman Warburton concluded.

"Well, *some* surprise, but not a *total* surprise," Mr. Caldwell said with a grunt of satisfaction.

"If the fortress on the West of Cape Town commands the way into the Bay, where are we to land the Army, then, sir?" Midshipman Shannon hesitantly asked, his head laid over to one side in puzzlement.

"North of Robben Island, on the Nor'west side of Table Bay, Commodore Popham favours either Saldanha or Blaauwberg Bay. Blaauwberg lies much closer to our objective," Lewrie told them. "Depending on the wind, weather, and the surf conditions, of course. That's where we will land General Sir David Baird's soldiers, God help 'em."

"They're rather open to the sea, really," Grainger pointed out.

"So's Table Bay, when ye get right down to it," Lewrie said. "I spent weeks anchored there repairin' *Proteus,* and when the winds got up, we *did* drag a little, even with both bowers and kedge anchor down. And us with no rudder! *That'll* keep one up at night!"

"Once Cape Town is taken, sir, might there be a chance for us to go ashore?" Rossyngton asked. "I'd imagine that every Man Jack'd be keen to see the sights."

"Go for a ride on an ostrich?" Lewrie suggested.

"Oh, surely, sir!" Eldridge hooted, leery of such an implausible notion. Even gullible little Shannon pulled a wary face.

"I've seen it done," Lewrie declared. "S'truth! Not that I did so. But, there's lashings of fresh water, fresh fruits and vegetables, vineyards everywhere ye look, and the Dutch've managed t'produce very good wines . . . whites, mostly. Their red wines are fine if drunk here, but they don't travel well. And, bein' Dutch and all, their beers are hellish-good. Aye, Mister Rossyngton, I'd imagine that once the Army is successful, we'll be here awhile, and can land liberty parties for a whole day or so . . . once the working-parties' chores are done, mind."

"Long enough to go hunting and riding, sir? Long enough to see elephants and lions and such?" Shannon enquired, so eager that he seemed to bounce from one foot to the other.

"Well, one'd have t'ride rather far abroad t'see the wildlife," Lewrie told him. "and I don't think we could spare you that long. The Dutch have been here for centuries, and have driven most of the lions and all far away from their farms. That'd be like tryin' t'find bears and stags roamin' Islington, these days. Elands, kudus, and gnus are still near the settled lands, and you must have at least *one* meal when ashore. The game meat's marvellous! I had a chance to shoot a few, when I was here last, and even bagged a rare crocodile. Still have its teeth back home in England. Some say that crocodile tail-meat is as good as chicken, but I found it rather tough."

"Lord, how *many* odd creatures' flesh is compared to chicken!" Lt. Merriman exclaimed. "Snakes and I don't know what-all. Why can't we just stick with good old barnyard chicken and have done?"

"One might hope that there is more for us to do than landing the Army and then just waiting round 'til they take the Cape Colony, sir," Lt. Westcott, ever in search of glory, honour, action, and favourable notice at Admiralty, groused. "Some way to take an active part?"

"And be among the first to encounter any fetching blond-haired Dutch maidens, do you mean, Mister Westcott?" Lt. Merriman teased.

"Well, there is that," Westcott rejoined with a shrug and one of his brief, almost feral tooth-bearing grins. "Perhaps, sir, when you next meet with the Commodore," Westcott said to Lewrie, "the offer of our services ashore might be deemed . . . welcome?"

"Get into some action alongside the Army?" Lt. Simcock, their Marine officer, stuck in with an eager look. He had been drowsing on his feet, drawn to the quarterdeck for the daily Noon Sights for lack of something better to do, but came awake at the prospect of gunfire.

"I will, of course, suggest such to the Commodore, but he and General Baird may think their five thousand men sufficient," Lewrie told them. "I wouldn't mind a chance t'do more than sit and twiddle my thumbs, either. Aye, we'll see, Mister Westcott, Mister Simcock. The Day Watch is set, Mister Merriman? Very good. Carry on with the 'Make And Mend' 'til the First Dog. I will be below."

Payin' for the sin of inebriation, Lewrie thought, wincing at the twinkling glare of the sun off the wavetops, and wondering if the "hair of the dog" was a legitimate treatment for hangover.

He made it down the windward ladderway to the ship's waist and tarried to pay attention to Bisquit, who was proud to show off his new collar, which was of red leather with ornate sennet work all round it. The dog put his front paws on Lewrie's waist and whined for petting, his tail whipping like a pendant in a gale as Lewrie obliged him with head rubs, ear rubs, and soft words of praise.

Two loud thuds erupted from somewhere, taking Lewrie, and his attention, back to the quarterdeck.

"'General Signal' with two guns from *Diadem*, sir!" Midshipman Eldridge was calling out to Lt. Merriman, the Officer of the Watch, with a long telescope to one eye. "It is . . . 'Fleet . . . Will . . . Alter . . . Course'. Due East!"

"Bosun Sprague?" Merriman shouted down to the waist. "Do you pipe 'All Hands', Mister Sprague. 'Stations for Wearing About'!" Then he looked to Lewrie, excitement all over his usually jovial countenance. "Huzzah, sir! It is beginning, at last!"

"Indeed it is, Mister Merriman," Lewrie replied, remembering to play-act stern and stoic, and clasping his hands in the small of his back, and looking up the long line of warships. "I would expect the next order will be to 'Wear in Succession'. Carry on, sir."

"Aye aye!"

CHAPTER TWENTY-FOUR

Ships' Masters sailing from Europe to the West Indies fell down to the latitude of Dominica before turning Due West to ride the Trades, for the towering height of Dominica's mountains could be seen over sixty miles out to sea on good days, a sure sea-mark, and a merchant captain, even one less-skilled at navigation, could count on spotting them and adjusting his course after determining his position.

So it was with the fleet's first sight of Table Mountain, and the welcome cries of Land Ho on the 3rd of January 1806. It was much closer to the sea than Dominica's peaks, and nearly 3,600 feet high, a massive, looming blotch on the horizon which first could be mistaken for the thunderheads of a black-hearted and murdering storm. But, as the ships of the expeditionary force slogged on Nor'easterly with the prevailing Trades abeam, its solidity became apparent, dark blue-grey and streaked with wisps of clouds streaming past its tops. From that point on, even the most in-experienced helmsman on the wheel, or the cox'n at the tiller of a small boat, could steer for it and be sure of an eventual safe landfall.

An hour or two after Table Mountain had been deemed solid and not an apparition, the signal for "Captain(s) Repair On Board" went up HMS

Diadem's halliards, summoning all naval captains to a conference with Commodore Popham aboard his flagship.

"Ah, welcome back aboard! Will you take a glass, Lewrie?" the ebullient Popham gaily offered as the other officers gathered. Cabin servants were circulating with coin-silver trays of glasses and white wine, and Popham was turned out in his very best uniform, complete with the sash and star of the Order of The Bath, and he gave Lewrie a quizzical look to note that Lewrie's everyday uniform coat was bare.

"No matter," Popham poo-pooed. "You remember Sir David Baird, and Brigadier Beresford and their aides? Uhm, good! Allow me to name to you your fellows . . . gentlemen, I give you Captain Sir Alan Lewrie of the *Reliant* frigate. Sir Alan, this is my Flag-Captain, Downman. Josias Rowley, of *Raisonnable* . . . George Byng, of *Belliqueux;* Captain Honyman who has the *Leda* frigate; Ross Donnelly, of the *Narcissus* . . . Commander Joseph Edmonds, Acting-Captain of the old *Diomede* . . . and Lieutenants William King and James Talbot, of the *Espoir* and the *Encounter,* respectively."

A burble of "Happy to make your acquaintance", some nods, and the lifting of glasses in welcome followed Popham's introductions.

"Stout, canny, and adventurous souls, all, I vow," Popham said in praise, "and each that eager to be at the Dutch and conquer, ha ha! You will all have taken note of the various charts laid out upon my dining table? Let us gather round it and make our plans."

Happy as a boy with a jam jar! Lewrie thought, noting Popham's almost playful demeanour, and eager, forceful motions.

"Here, gentlemen, is Robben Island," Popham said, using a ruler as a pointer. "Though some charts name it Penguin Island. It is not all that high out of the sea, but protects Table Bay from the worst of most blows. Fairly flat, too. Once we are a few miles offshore, it is my intention that the fleet come to anchor West of Robben Island. Not *too* close ashore, for the Dutch may have mounted batteries there, and garrisoned it."

"It's a prison, sir," Lewrie told him. "When I was here before, the Dutch, and we, used it as a prison . . . for criminals and rebellious sorts, mostly. The many sharks in the strait 'twixt the island and the mainland prevent escape attempts. The prisoners are put at hard labour, making gravel out of big rocks. The guards ain't soldiers."

"Hmm, well, in any instance, we shall anchor far off the shoals and rocks," Popham said with amusement, "which would put us out of the range of any light artillery the Dutch may have . . . or showers of rocks flung at us in pique, hey, gentlemen?"

After faint chuckles had faded, Popham went on. "Then, sirs, I intend to make an inspection of Blaauwberg Bay, our primary choice for where we land the army. Lieutenant King, I would much appreciate did you do me and Sir David the honour of taking us aboard your *Espoir* for a reconnoiter of the bay for the most suitable beach? Capital! Most kind of you. Now, sirs—"

Popham slid another chart atop the first, one that showed Cape Town and Table Bay in greater detail.

"Sir David and Brigadier Beresford have suggested that we make a demonstration to confuse the Dutch and lure their army far enough away from Blaauwberg Bay so our landing may face lesser opposition. On that head, Sir David has allocated the Twenty-fourth Regiment of Foot. Captain Honyman, I wish you and your *Leda* to escort the transports carrying the Twenty-fourth. As soon as we are come to anchor off Robben Island, do you acquaint yourself to the masters of the transports in question, and prepare them to sail down . . . here . . . as soon as the order for execution is hoisted to you. Feint a landing on Green Island, as if we intend to go right at the town. Bombard, if you wish, without putting troops ashore, in fact."

"Most happy to oblige, sir, and it will be done as you wish!" Captain Honyman replied with a perky grin, as if he had just been given the most important duty, not a feint.

"Once a suitable stretch of beach has been selected in the bay, I will expect all our men o' war to lend their largest ships' boats to supplement the transports' boats, so we may establish the strongest lodgement, as quickly as possible, ashore," Commodore Popham went on, looking up from his charts to peer at each of his captains, in turn. "Launches, cutters, even your own gigs . . . though I think we may leave the little jolly boats to your Bosuns so they may row about to see if your yards are squared, ha!"

"If I may, sir?" *Diadem's* Flag-Captain, Downman, a pleasant and inoffensive-looking fellow, interrupted. "I was wondering about the order of anchoring, both off Robben Island, and in Blaauwberg Bay. Which group of transports, bearing which regiments, should be closest to the chosen beach to form the initial lodgement, and which units might Sir David deem to be of lesser importance, which could be anchored behind those at first, landing their troops, artillery, or cavalry, later? It would seem to me that do we establish the order of landing now, we could reverse the order of anchoring off Robben Island, placing the most important furthest out from the island, but first to sail, when the order is given to land the army."

Commodore Popham twitched his mouth as if irked by the suggestion, but quickly recovered his aplomb and leaned back from the table and charts to beam at Downman. "An excellent suggestion, Downman! We do wish to pull this off with the neatest sort of efficiency, hey? It will be up to Sir David, of course, as to which regiment he chooses to land first."

"Well, actually, I was of a mind, to put *two* regiments ashore at once, Sir Home," General Baird said to Commodore Popham. "Not knowing how quickly, or in how much force, my Dutch opponent might respond, it would be best to get the Thirty-eighth Foot and the Ninety-third Highlanders ashore. Do you concur, Beresford?"

"Hmm, well," Brigadier Beresford pondered, "two regiments would be best, though perhaps one might substitute the Seventy-first Highlanders for the Thirty-eight Foot. They're better-drilled than the Thirty-eighth, and the Twenty-fourth, for that matter."

"And two regiments of Scots would naturally be competitive with each other," General Baird agreed with a small laugh. "God help the Dutch. Yes, I agree, Beresford. You take the Thirty-eighth for your brigade, along with the cavalry and artillery, and we will land the Heavy Brigade first, with your Light Brigade to follow."

"With that settled," Commodore Popham said, "and with the names of their transports known, we may write instructions as to the order of anchoring, and the subsequent sailing into Blaauwberg Bay. I trust you to organise all that, Downman."

"Of course, sir," Captain Downman replied, almost in a whisper, as if having such a task thrust upon him was nothing new since sailing under Popham.

"And, whilst we're all here, do you determine how many boats we possess, and of which size, to lend to the army for the landings," the Commodore added.

Did Downman wince? Lewrie wondered; *Is he that put-upon? What's a Flag-Captain for, if not to be the serf for his lord and master.*

"I've two cutters and two barges, Captain Downman," Lewrie volunteered. "I had need of 'em in the Channel, the summer of '04, and the dockyards never *really* asked for 'em back, so——"

"They'll be most welcome, Captain Lewrie," Downman promised him with a brief, shy grin.

"You use a barge fit for a full Admiral for your gig, do you, Captain Lewrie?" Popham teased, with a faint sniff.

"Just an humble cutter, sir," Lewrie replied, tongue-in-cheek. "Ev'ryone knows I'm the modest sort. Ehm . . . might I ask what we will be doing during the landing, sir? Do we anchor far out, or sail in close to lend support with gunfire?"

"*Diomede* and the other two-deckers I wish to stand off-and-on, under way," Popham told him. "Though we've seen no sign that the Dutch have their own warships at the Cape, there is always the odd chance. In like wise, we have not seen any French warships lurking in the vicinity, either, but there's always a risk of their turning up at the worst time.

"A pity, do they not," Popham went on in a whimsical manner. "How glorious it would be to gain a victory over a combined squadron of enemy vessels, *and* pull off the conquest of the Cape Colony, both! Ah, well."

He shrugged off that hopeful fantasy, tossed them all a boyish smile, and continued. "*Diomede* and the sixty-four-gunners will stand guard against just that possibility, slim as the odds for that may be. It would be best did our frigates and lighter vessels close the shore and anchor near the first transports which bear the regiments for the initial landings."

"If the wind is up and there's a heavy surf running, sir, then we might help form a breakwater," Captain Donnelly of the *Narcissus* frigate posed. "We, and the transports together . . . hey?"

"But, should Dutch artillery appear upon the hills behind the landing beach," Commodore Popham countered, "you will consider yourself free to close to gun-range and engage with what fire you are able to deliver. Can't let the Army do it all by themselves, what?"

"Of course, sir," Donnelly said, seemingly satisfied with the Commodore's reply.

Lewrie thought that Popham's response to Donnelly's query was just a tad "tetchy". For all his charm and *bonhomie*, he might not care for doubtful questions from his subordinates, nor for suggestions on details which he had not yet fully considered, either.

"Once all the troops are landed, though," Popham went on with a grin on his face, "we cannot let our compatriots in the Army have all the *fun*, either. I intend that we combine all our Marines, and such parties of armed sailors as we may spare, to go ashore and lend a hand."

"Well, sir," General Sir David Baird said, after a long pause and a tug at one earlobe, "that is a generous gesture, though hardly a necessary one, Sir Home. I fear your Marines and sailors would feel wasted guarding the beach, and the supply train."

"Does the Navy do the guarding, Sir David, that spares your men from doing so," Popham told him. "We determined earlier that the foe might possess more cavalry than infantry, given the vast size of the Cape Colony. Do the Dutch think to emulate the exploits of mounted partisan militias, like the Americans during their Revolution, or the irregular tactics of Red Indians, well! *Your* cavalry might be best-employed harassing *them*!"

Lewrie relished the sound of that, and was quick to volunteer.

"God yes!" he piped up. "I can land fourty Marines and an equal number of sailors under arms without diminishing *Reliant*'s ability to fight, or provide fire! Put me down for it! After all," he added in jest, "I know the country, and all the poisonous snakes, scorpions, centipedes, spiders, and bugs!"

"By name, sir . . . personally?" Captain Byng of the *Belliqueux* said with a snicker. "*All* of them?"

"Once we take Cape Town, I also know all the good taverns and eateries," Lewrie quickly rejoined in equal humour. "That's surely worth something. And all the scorpions answer to Jan van der Merwe!"

"A moot point, for the nonce, gentlemen," Popham told them, after he and the rest had had a good laugh. "But, once the bulk of the army and their supplies are ashore, we shall see about forming a Naval Brigade. First things first, hey? It may be that Sir David overwhelms the Dutch so quickly that our services might not be necessary, and we may go ashore at our leisure, after. Then, Captain Lewrie may give us a nature tour, ha ha! That may be as much as we may expect to contribute, more's the pity."

I don't believe a word *of it!* Lewrie scoffed to himself; *He's nigh-droolin' t'take an active part! If he can't have a victory at sea as grand as Nelson at Trafalgar, I'd lay guineas that he's cravin' his name featured prominently in the papers back home! Didn't he already say the Navy'd give the nation a* new *Nelson . . . and that he's the best candidate for that . . . in so many words?*

Lewrie accepted a fresh refill of wine and took a slow sip or two, looking round at the other officers in *Diadem*'s great-cabins with an eye for other candidates to inherit the title of National Hero. It was circumstances that caused that, being at the right place at the right time, and being lucky enough, stubborn enough, or talented enough to succeed, to win. He found it nigh-impossible for a man to *arrange* success, and acclaim. *All* Navy officers were aspiring, for promotion, command, and for honour and glory, though it usually was the rare one in an hundred who gained such fame.

Lewrie had had his short stint at being well-known and even famous . . . or infamous, depending on how you looked at stealing those dozen slaves to man his ship at Jamaica, becoming the darling of the Abolitionists and Wilberforce and his crowd, then being acquitted at his trial for it. Stout and prosperous London businessmen *still* gave him the evil eye, the ones who saw nothing wrong with the slave trade and the wealth that came from it!

Aye, and look where all that's *got me!* he scoffed; *But . . . it* might *be nice t'be mentioned in despatches, now and again. Hmm. Me, the new Nelson? Oh, bosh!*

The conference ended about half an hour later, after the last niggling details had been threshed out, and Lewrie went back to the upper deck, and the sunshine, waiting his turn to depart in order of seniority, the junior-most first, and the senior-most last, into their boats. While chatting with the others, he became even more convinced that there *would* be a Naval Brigade formed, whether it was needed or not . . . with Popham at its head, most likely!

He determined that as soon as he was back aboard his ship, he'd see to his personal weapons, oil them and clean them, and fit fresh flints in the dog's jaws of their locks. He'd take his pair of double-barrelled Manton pistols, and his pair of single-barrelled pocket pistols, too, the ones made by Henry Nock. Of course, he'd take his Ferguson breech-loading rifled musket, which could shoot accurately almost three times as far as any Tower musket, and fetching along the longer fusilier musket wouldn't go amiss, either. And, for hunting game, the Girandoni air-rifle, which was almost silent.

Game! Fresh game meat, roasted over a campfire on a spit. His mouth began to water at the thought, and if Popham didn't send a Naval Brigade ashore, then By God he'd find a way to land with the Army, and Devil take the hind-most!

CHAPTER TWENTY-FIVE

A pretty day for it, I must say, sir," Mr. Caldwell the Sailing Master commented as Lewrie paced the quarterdeck near him, in passing.

"Pretty, aye, but a windy one," Lewrie responded after a long squint aloft to the stiffly fluttering commissioning pendant and the thrumming and clattering of running rigging and blocks. HMS *Reliant* lay almost beam-on to weather, rolling alee, then upright, and snubbing at her anchor cables. "Yesterday was calmer. Better for it."

The fleet had come to anchor just West of Robben Island on the night of the 4th. Yesterday, on the 5th, the demonstration towards Green Island had been made. Now this morning, the 6th of January, was the day selected by Commodore Popham to land the army.

At the moment, that prospect didn't look all that promising to Lewrie, for though the skies were clear blue and the high-piled clouds were as white as fleece, there were strong winds from offshore, which had stirred up a heavy surf, combining to make a landing very risky.

Lewrie fetched a longer, more powerful telescope from the binnacle cabinet forward of the double-wheel helm and went to the bulwarks on the lee side to extend the tubes and raise it to one eye to peer deep into Blaauwberg Bay.

"Christ on a crutch," he muttered in dour appreciation.

The bay was chopped with white-caps and white horses right to the shallows, and streaked with long, white curling waves mostly parallel to the shore where they began to break, rank upon rank of them marching onwards to crash and expend themselves upon the shingle and sand, each a little more than one hundred yards apart. Were heavily loaded boats sent in under oars, they would be hobby-horsing up and over each wave, bows-high first, then stern-high as they passed over the steep crests, and burrowing their bows in. Their final dashes to the beach would be nigh un-manageable, riding the crests if they were lucky, but it was good odds that many would broach beam-on to those waves, and be rolled over and under!

"Still no signal from *Diadem*?" Lewrie asked over his shoulder.

"None yet, sir," Lt. Westcott told him.

"It might be best were the landings put off 'til tomorrow," Lewrie said as he lowered the long day-glass, collapsed the tubes, and turned away from the rails, with a frown on his face.

"Perhaps conditions may be better in Saldanha Bay, sir," Lieutenant Merriman hopefully suggested. "It is a *bit* more sheltered."

"But, only the slightest bit, Mister Merriman," Lewrie pointed out as he pulled out his pocket-watch to see how much of the morning had been wasted. "From Saldanha Bay, it's more than a day's march to Cape Town. That'd give the Dutch bags of time to mount a counter move. Daylight's wasting. If we don't move soon, we might as—"

The blustery morning was broken by the report of two guns, the announcement of a general signal to all ships. Two sour and yellowish-white puffs of powder smoke sprouted from the flagship, HMS *Diadem*. A long moment later, strings of brightly-coloured signal flags went soaring up her halliards.

"It is . . . 'To Weigh . . . In Order of Sailing'," Lt. Westcott slowly interpreted. "The last is spelled out letter-by-letter, sir. It is . . . 'Saldanha'!"

"Very well, Saldanha Bay it is," Lewrie said with a quick nod of his head, puffing out his cheeks in a disappointed sigh. "And God help poor soldiers. Hands to 'Stations To Weigh', Mister Westcott."

"Aye aye, sir!"

Once every warship and transport had hoisted their own 'Affirmative' signals to acknowledge receipt and understanding of the orders, *Diadem* struck her string of signals, which was the 'Execute'. On each vessel, messenger lines were fleeted to capstans, the messengers nippered to the much stouter anchor cables, capstan bars fitted to the tops of the drums, and sailors breasted to the bars and began the heaves to reel in the hawsers. Most ships were anchored fore-and-aft by best bowers and kedges, so bow hawsers had to be eased and the aft hawsers taken in to break the kedges free; then, the process had to be repeated to bring the bow hawsers to "Up And Down", just shy of breaking the bowers from the bottom. Sail began to appear on every ship, mostly jibs, stays'ls, and spankers to begin with, to gain some control and keep them from sagging alee onto the shoals round Robben Island, and to put a bit of forward drive on.

Altogether, all those evolutions took the better part of an hour, before the first transports bearing the 38th Regiment of Foot, the bulk of the cavalry, and the artillery led out ahead of the rest on course for Saldanha Bay, up the coast.

"Hmm," Lt. Westcott said, looking aloft. "We may need to let the tops'ls fall to the next reef point, sir. I think the winds are moderating."

Lewrie, who had been standing by the windward side of the quarter-deck, on the larboard side, first looked seaward to determine if another column of ships was stealing their wind, then turned to face his First Officer. "Damned if it ain't, Mister Westcott. Do you bare more canvas, aye." He took another long moment to judge how his ship moved underneath his feet, then exclaimed, "And, damned if the sea's not as lively, either. Think I'll take another peek ashore."

Back to the compass binnacle cabinet he went to fetch out that powerful telescope, went to the lee, starboard, bulwarks, and looked shoreward. Blaauwberg Bay was off the fleet's starboard quarters, by then, and the approaches to Saldanha Bay were off the starboard bows, still miles away, and Blaauwberg Bay was . . . calming!

The confused chop had ebbed in a single hour with the dropping of the offshore wind, and the clashing large white horses seemed to have dissolved, leaving only scattered white-caps and cat's paws on the sea. The strong sets of rollers and breaking waves no longer crashed on the beaches, but merely gushed ashore in sheets of foam, and were much reduced in height.

"Signal from *Diadem,* sir!" Midshipman Eldridge sang out. "Two guns, general to all ships, and it is . . . 'Columns Wear South In Order

Of Succession' . . . and 'Leading Columns First'! 'Land . . . Army' . . . she's spelling out *B* . . . *L* . . . 'Blaauwberg'!"

"Now *this* is goin' t'be a rat-scramble!" Lewrie hooted in sour amusement. "Recall our bloody 'sugar trade' two years ago, Mister Westcott? And what a cock-up that was when America-bound ships tried t'leave the convoy?"

"Sadly I do, sir," Lt. Westcott agreed, snickering.

There had been over an hundred merchantmen to herd and guard from the "rondy" at Jamaica to England, but no one had given a thought to the ships bound for Savannah, Charleston, the Chesapeake, and ports in New England. They'd been scattered throughout the convoy like raisins in a pudding, and when they'd altered course to thread their ways through the long columns of ships, perfect panic had resulted, and it had taken the better part of a whole day to sort the convoy back into proper order again, with the America-bound ships posted down the lee side, so they could leave without frightening the wits from everyone!

"Well, here it comes again!" Lewrie said, laughing out loud. "I expect the Commodore will wear out two sets of signal flags before he's done . . . and he's the one who invented the code system!"

The fleet was sorted out in order of importance, with the merchantmen and transports bearing the intial landing force in the lead, and the secondary waves astern of them. Now, the lead group must go about, one at a time, to reverse their order of sailing, and steer for Blaauwberg Bay, whilst the rest would have to stand out to sea to give them room, then wear about to reverse *their* order and fall astern of those ships carrying the first regiments.

Hmm, I don't recall the Popham Code includin' stock curses, Lewrie told himself; *I s'pose we'll have t'spell 'em out. Takes all the spontaneity, and the fun, from 'em!*

And, indeed it was far past mid-day by the time all ships had managed to come about and sail into Blaauwberg Bay in their proper order, close the shore, and come to anchor in ragged, dis-ordered ranks parallel to the beaches, about one mile to seaward. It helped that the winds were still from offshore, instead of the typical Sou'east Trade winds, so they could wear about from one beam-reach to another, not butt their way in a series of short tacks *into* the Trades!

"Signal, sir!" Midshipman Grainger, who had taken Eldridge's place at the change of watch, crisply reported. "It is . . . 'Send Boats', and . . . 'Commence'!"

"Very well," Lewrie said. "Hoist the 'Affirmative', then take your place in charge of the second cutter, Mister Grainger. Mister Westcott? See to haulin' our boats from towin' astern to the entry-ports, and muster the boat crews."

"Aye, sir!"

The sailors told off to man the boats left their watch-standing duties and gathered round the four most-experienced Midshipmen assigned to lead them, along with the tarry coxswains specially selected to the tricky and risky work of conning the boats through the surf and foamy breakers to safe groundings on the beach, land their soldiers, then get the cutters and barges safely off and back to the transports for a second load; as many runs as it would take in concert with the transports' boats to get a full regiment ashore.

Lewrie left the quarterdeck and descended to the waist before the ship's boats reached the entry-ports. Bisquit, the ship's dog, was already out of his shelter beneath the starboard quarterdeck ladderway, prancing about and through the groups of men, curious to see what this unusual activity was about.

"Lads!" Lewrie called out. "The surf's subsided considerably, and conditions have improved, but . . . the Army's trustin' to us to see 'em safe ashore. It might be a temptation t'rush things, but this'll best be like 'church work' . . . slow and steady. You cox'ns . . . ," he said, looking the chosen men in the face directly, his own boat's Cox'n, Liam Desmond, too. "Every man's life'll be in your skilled hands. That's why you were picked for it. And you young gentlemen," he said to the eager-looking Midshipmen, "you trust to your cox'ns' skill and experience, the closer ye get to shore. It *won't* be an occasion for sky-larkin', and with the late start you'll probably be at it 'til sundown, and might have t'finish the work to-morrow mornin', too, so give your hands a rest when ye can, and breaks for water.

"As to the second rum issue, lads," he added with a grin. "It will be doled out late, once you're back aboard."

That raised a cheer.

"Away ye go, then, do your best, and show our redcoats, and the idle lubbers aboard the transports, what the Navy, and Reliants, can do!"

Lewrie concluded, doffing his hat to them. "And, as the Spanish say, 'Go with God', and I fully expect t'see all your smilin' faces when you return!"

He returned to the quarterdeck as the boat crews began to go down the battens to the waiting boats, to stand amidships of the cross-deck stanchions and hammock nettings to see them off. Poor Bisquit dashed about, yipping and whining as if all his friends and playmates were abandoning him. As the last hands left the deck, he sat down and looked left and right, ears perked in puzzlement.

"Bisquit," Lewrie called to him, and the dog bounded up the ladderway to the quarterdeck to press against Lewrie's leg for reassurance. Lewrie leaned down to pet him and ruffle his fur.

"No need t'fret, ye silly beast," Lewrie cosseted in a soft voice. "They'll all be back aboard by supper time. Even if they won't have time t'hunt ye up a nice, fresh bone or two."

Well, at least I hope *they will,* he grimly thought.

CHAPTER TWENTY-SIX

Lewrie hosted a supper for his officers and the four Midshipmen who had led the boats, and his cook, Yeovill, had done his best with what little variety was left in his personal stores after the long passage South from Madeira. There was reconstituted vegetable soup, no chance for a fresh salad, a roast duck from the forecastle manger, and yellowfin tuna steaks from a smallish fish which Yeovill had gotten once they'd come to anchor, eked out with shrivelled baked potato halves smothered in the least-mouldy cheeses and shredded bacon, and a bowl of boiled green snap beans purchased at Funchal. Lashings of wine more than made up for the lack of anything special, or fresh.

"Well, it wasn't all *that* bad a day, after all," Lt. Merriman commented. "We managed to get most of the infantry regiments ashore."

"And, half the cavalry," Lt. Arthur Simcock, their Marine officer, crowed.

"And, some of the artillery, too!" Westcott pointed out. "The Army won't be over-run during the night, God willing, and we'll have the rest ashore by tomorrow, mid-day."

"Too bad about the poor Scotties from the Ninety-third, though," Lewrie said from the head of the table.

Several boats bearing one of the Highlander regiments had been over-set as they had hobby-horsed over the breakers, and thirty-five soldiers, heavily laden with muskets, packs, cartridge boxes, hangers and bayo-nets and bed-rolls, had been drowned despite efforts to save them.

"I thought it canny of *Diadem*'s captain, Captain Downman, to run that wee old transport onto a shoal to make a breakwater, and a lee for the landings after that," Westcott said as he topped up his glass of port and passed the decanter along, larboardly. "He saved more than a few lives."

"She drew what . . . only six or eight feet?" Lt. Merriman said with a sneer. "Who in their right minds would send a ship so small and shoal-draught to sea on such a long voyage, as a transport worthy of carrying soldiers?"

"Our Transport Board, and a venal owner, most-like," Lewrie carped. "Now, does the sea get up before they work her off that shoal, she'll be a total loss, and her owner'll collect her full value in insurance from Lloyd's. *Then*, at least, the Transport Board won't risk any more lives to such a scow."

"Is there much left to do in the morning, for us I mean, sir?" Lt. Sim-cock asked, between bites of a ginger snap.

"Mister Warburton?" Lewrie prompted.

"Well, sir," their senior-most Mid spoke up, "we got the light com-pany, the grenadier company, and five of the eight line companies from the regiment ashore by sundown. That leaves three more to go, and if the weather holds, I expect that, between our boats and the transport's boats, we *could* be done by the start of tomorrow's Forenoon Watch."

"If we begin just before sunrise," Midshipman Grainger said in weari-ness, stifling a yawn. "But, most-like it'll take 'til Noon, with three round-trips, if today's confusion is anything to go by."

"Dis-organised, was it?" Lewrie asked, reaching for the pewter barge which held the sweet bisquits and choosing an oatmeal one.

"Well, sir," Midshipman Eldridge, who was usually too shy to voice an opinion, hesitantly contributed, "it struck me that the Army types were more concerned with *getting* here in one piece, and fit to go on shore, but didn't give the actual landing a single thought, leaving it up to the Navy, or Fate. Look at how they got their cavalry and artillery horses ashore. Goose 'em over the side into the sea, rope them, and lead them behind boats! The Lord only knows how many they lost, poor things."

"Aye, I expect some sharks fed well today," Lt. Westcott said.

"I'm not sure that ship's boats are the best choice for landing troops, or horses," Lewrie said, mulling things over. "When we were in the Channel, playin' with those damned torpedoes, you and Merriman had all sorts of ideas for improvin' 'em, and designing boats that could sail themselves in with fused explosives, 'stead of just driftin' on the tide, Mister Westcott. Perhaps you and Merriman could put your minds together, again, and draw up something."

"Hmm . . . I suppose such a study could be productive," Westcott said with his head laid to one side in thought. "And, dull as things are so far, sir, it would keep us all from keeling over in boredom!"

That raised a laugh, and a call for the port decanter to make another round.

"Well, speak for yourself, sir," Lewrie countered, grinning, "for I doubt our *Mids* thought the day boresome."

"God, no, sir!" Grainger said with a mock shudder. "It was . . . not terrifying at times. Let me say . . . adventurous!"

That opinion was loudly seconded by his fellows.

"There may be a way to relieve your boredom, Mister Westcott," Lewrie went on once the laughs died down. "The last time I spoke with Commodore Popham, he mentioned his desire to form a Naval Brigade for service ashore, alongside the Army. Hmm?"

"Huzzah!" cried their Marine Lieutenant. "At last!"

"I must lead it, sir!" Lt. Westcott almost begged.

"So you shall," Lewrie quickly assured him. "*If* the brigade is formed. Generals Baird and Beresford didn't sound too keen on the idea. Probably worried how they'd *feed* 'em from their stores. How *would* you expect to victual your Marines, were you ordered ashore, Mister Simcock? How would you go about it, and what would you take along?"

"Hmm," was Lt. Simcock's answer as he leaned back in his chair, stared at the overhead deck beams, and crossed his arms in thought. "Beyond our weapons, packs, and bedding, spare ammunition and such . . . well, sir, one would likely assume that the *Army* would supply us. Barring that, I'm not really *sure*."

"Then let us assume that the brigade is assembled, and that we must fend for ourselves," Lewrie said, hunching forward on the table. "Fourty private Marines, two Corporals, one Sergeant, and you, sir, that's fourty-four. An equal number of armed sailors, the Bosun's Mate and a Ship's Corporal for enforcing discipline, two Mids, and an officer, that's fourty-five. I think the ship may spare that many and still be able to fight, should the French turn up, hey?"

"Sounds about right, sir," Westcott quickly agreed, his eyes lit up with pending delight.

"Muskets, bayonets, and cutlasses should it come to close quarters," Lewrie sketched on, "hammocks for ground cloths and a blanket for each man, cartridge boxes, spare flints, spare cartridges, and if any weapon needs repair, we *might* be able to prevail upon some regimental armourers. Rations, though?"

"The hands each have their knives, sir, and forks and spoons," Lt. Merriman offered. "They've pewter or china mugs, but . . . what sort of dishes? As easily broken as they are, our people *prefer* to eat off china plates; I doubt I've seen the old square wood trenchers since I was a Mid. 'Three square meals a day', what?" he said with a quick grin. "I suppose that the Purser could provide pewter plates."

"Ah, but what do we *put* on those plates, sir?" Lt. Westcott asked them all. "And, who does the cooking if we *do* have rations? We would have to lug along kegs of salt-meats, full bags of ship's bisquit, and some vessels to serve as steep-tubs to rinse off the salt from the meat, and others to boil it. Ladles, meat forks, mesh mess bags—"

"Rum, sir," Midshipman Warburton suggested. "Our hands expect two issues a day. How much would that be for, say, a week away from the ship?"

"*Water,* sir," Midshipman Eldridge gloomily contributed.

"Don't your Marines have water bottles of some kind, Mister Simcock?" Lewrie asked him.

"Somewhere deep in the hold, sir, we've two wood crates, with four dozen wooden canteens, of quart volume . . . or so I may recall from my inventory," Lt. Simcock told them all, shrugging. "As to what our sailors might use, I haven't a clue. It will be thirsty work, to march several miles a day, ascend the mountains behind the beach, and fight. Hellish thirsty work! Even do we simply ferry Army supplies ashore and guard them, our people will be parched in the extreme."

"Our sailors aren't known for long, hard marching," Merriman said. "All but the 'Idlers' are young, fit, and spry, and used to hard work and 'pulley-hauley', but they'll be gasping after a few hours."

"We'd best fetch along one of the Surgeon's Mates and his kit, should we *do* fight, and suffer casualties," Lt. Westcott suggested.

"Beginnin' t'sound daft, don't it," Lewrie summed up, grumpy with disappointment over the mounting impossibility of the Commodore's airy plan. "To carry all we need ashore with us, we'd need carts of some kind, and there's no way t'make 'em, no harness, no draught animals, and no bloody *wheels*! The Army does, but none t'spare for *us*."

He looked to the sideboard, hoping that Yeovill or Pettus had set out a bottle of brandy, or American whisky, for he felt a strong desire for something to lift his spirits. There were empty bottles of wine, and a full bottle of port, just in case the decanter ran dry.

"Hmm," Lewrie said, rising just enough to reach over to the sideboard and fetch an empty bottle that had contained the Rhenish that had accompanied the fish course. "As for water, we could issue wine bottles. Most of 'em are *near* a quart in volume, or thereabout. Rinse 'em out, fill 'em just before we leave the ship, and slap the corks back in, and there you are."

"But, how would the men carry them, sir?" Lt. Westcott asked. "Army canteens have slings for wearing over one shoulder down to the opposite hip. They'd drop or break them in the first two hours!"

"Cartridge bags?" Midshipman Grainger piped up in the deep, pondering silence.

"What?" Lewrie asked.

"Well, sir, a serge cartridge bag for the quarterdeck nine-pounders is about the same diameter of your average wine bottle," Grainger slowly explained. "Using that as a pattern, the Sailmaker and his Mate, and the Master Gunner and Yeoman of The Powder, could sew up some snug bags from spare canvas, *and* sew on a canvas shoulder strap. In the magazine, there is a wooden form for making new powder bags, one for each calibre of ordnance aboard, really."

"That might be *one* problem solved, sir!" Lt. Westcott was quick to agree, eager to forward the plan, and get his idle arse ashore and in some sort of action.

"Where would we get nigh fifty empty bottles, though?" Merriman said with a sigh.

"That might depend on how many you can drink 'twixt now and then, Mister Merriman," Lewrie said, laughing.

"Lord, sir!" Merriman gawped. "We consume nothing *near* a civilian gentleman's usual half-dozen. Why, the wardroom's practically *abstemious*! I doubt we down a half-dozen a day between all of us!"

"Drink up, then, sailors," Lewrie merrily urged.

"Ehm . . . it's the *better* wines that come in bottles, sir," Lt. Simcock objected. "The poorer ones come in stone crocks, barricoes, and pipes. Our entire mess stores would have to be—"

"We need four-dozen," Lewrie said. "Two cases from the officers' wardroom, and two cases from my personal stock."

Merriman and Simcock looked as if they might whimper or moan.

"Aye, Mister Westcott, that *is* one problem solved. Though one of many," Lewrie declared. "Hopefully, Commodore Popham will be able to prevail upon our redcoat compatriots for at least *one* cart for all we'll need to take ashore. He's a way of getting what he wants, and getting his way, no matter."

One bell was struck at the forecastle belfry; the first after the change of watch at 8 P.M.; it was half-past, and almost time for all glims and lights to be doused at 9 P.M.

"Heel-taps, gentlemen," Lewrie announced, "a last glass of port before we retire . . . before the Master-At-Arms comes round and glares at me, hey? I apologise for the poor meal, but the company at-table this evening is always delightful. Allow me to propose a toast . . . to success on the morrow, and confusion to the foe!"

"Success and confusion!" they all shouted once the glasses had been poured full, then tossed their ports back to the last drop.

Once his dinner company was gone, Lewrie requested a glass of American bourbon whisky from Pettus. Yeovill gathered up the scraps and leftovers—damned few of those!—into his brass barge, and slipped a few shreds of duck to Chalky, who had hopped atop the table in eager search for more tucker, as if he hadn't eaten his food bowl empty, and was simply famished.

Jessop helped Pettus clear the sideboard and the last plates; Pettus had paid attention during their after-supper discussions, and put the corks back into the empties, setting them aside for rinsing out later.

"Anything else, sir?" Yeovill asked, ready to depart.

"Don't think so, Yeovill," Lewrie told him. "You can turn in, and thank you for a toothsome meal on such short notice."

"Evening, sir," Yeovill replied, always happy to prepare a big spread for guests, and pleased with his handiwork.

Lewrie went to sprawl on the starboard-side settee, feet up on the low brass Hindoo tray table, and sipped on his whisky. With no more treats in the offing, Chalky jumped down from the table and ambled over to hop onto the settee, pad onto Lewrie's lap, and nuzzle him, nose-to-nose for strokes and pets. After a few minutes of that, Chalky turned about, made a circle, and slung himself against Lewrie's hip, making faint purring rumbles.

Now, how the Devil do we get all we need ashore? Lewrie wondered to himself; *If we're ordered ashore. Put wheels under a cutter and* drag *the damned thing with* ropes?

No matter how daunting the whole thing seemed, though, Lewrie more than half-way hoped that Popham *would* get his way. It would have to be fourty-*six* empty wine bottles, for he would need one, himself!

BOOK THREE

Therefore, great king,
We yield our town and lives to thy soft mercy.
Enter our gates, dispose of us and ours,
For we no longer are defensible.

                        -WILLIAM SHAKESPEARE,
                        THE LIFE OF KING
                        HENRY THE FIFTH,
                        ACT III, SCENE III, 47-50

CHAPTER TWENTY-SEVEN

*T*he 7th was a let-down. *Reliant*'s larger-than-normal cutters and barges were assigned the task of ferrying the remaining troops of the infantry regiments, and the dis-assembled artillery pieces, their carriages, caissons, and limbers, ashore as the army slowly gathered on the beaches amid piles of stores, and the *Leda* frigate, along with the *Encounter* brig and the newly-arrived gunboat *Protector*, were sent near the shore to engage Dutch batteries on Blaauwberg Mountain with fire.

Other than those few Dutch guns on the heights, there was little sign of enemy resistance, so far. Some thought it odd, and ominous; others considered their absence providential. The bulk of the British field force might be onshore, but looked to be very vulnerable to any spoiling attack. The cavalry mounts and artillery team horses would be weak after weeks at sea, and getting over sea-sickness and barely getting their shore legs back, and every trooper or infantryman would be in much the same condition. With little of the artillery landed, and that portion still being re-assembled, an attack by the Dutch in force could be disastrous, with their backs to the sea already.

"Lucky bastards," Lt. Westcott groused as the last of their cutters came alongside the larboard entry-port, and its weary crew began to clamber up to the deck, their onerous task completed at last.

"Who, the oarsmen?" Lewrie asked.

"The *Leda* and the others, I meant, sir," Westcott explained. "At least they got to fire at *something*."

"We earned our day's pay, even so, Mister Westcott," Lewrie told him. "Princely as *that* is, hey? And, there's still hope for an order to form the Naval Brigade."

"Pray God, sir," Westcott said with little enthusiasm.

"Now our army's all ashore, I expect General Baird will march them off inland, tomorrow morning," Lewrie told him, rising from his sinfully idle wood-and-canvas deck chair. He went to the bulwarks to peer shore-wards with a telescope. "Hmm . . . perhaps by noon tomorrow. Christ, what a mob they make. *Several* mobs, in point of fact. About as organised as a horde o' cockroaches."

What he beheld were groupings of soldiery by regiment and by squadron or battery. Tents were pitched in seemingly well-ordered lines, horses were tethered in groups of teams or cavalry troops, and field guns were parked wheel-to-wheel. Soldiers, though, milled about in their shirtsleeves, sat under canvas and smoked or chewed out of the heat of the sun, or snored in their tents. Only a few were posted as pickets under arms and in full kit. Officers and messengers were the only ones mounted and riding about, and none with any sense of urgency.

"It appears the landing was so strenuous that our soldiers are in need of a 'Make And Mend' day, Mister Westcott," Lewrie said with a sneer. "I swear, I doubt there's an ounce o' 'quick' in the whole lot. Napoleon, now . . . he may be a whole *clan* o' bastards, but when he puts an army in the field, they tramp along at the 'double-quick'!"

"Our army is better going backward, sir," Westcott said with a sour laugh. "Like they did in the Dutch expedition in '98?"

Before Napoleon Bonaparte had wooed, or bewitched, the insane Tsar Paul of Russia in 1801, Russia and Great Britain had briefly been allies, and had launched an invasion of the Lowlands, which had turned into a shameful embarrassment. The first time that the British Army had met the terrifying and seemingly invincible French Army in battle, it had been British redcoats that had been routed.

"Mister Munsell? Is the chore done at last?" Lewrie called down to the ship's waist.

"It is, sir!" Munsell replied, doffing his hat. "The army now has the last of their stores ashore."

"Went well, did it?" Lewrie asked.

"Very well, sir, The wind and surf are very calm today," the Midshipman reported. "It is too bad that we did not begin the landings today, instead of yesterday."

"Very well. Carry on, Mister Munsell, and well done," Lewrie said in dismissal. "There's a fresh-water butt on deck. Drink your fill, you and your men."

"Aye, sir."

Two muffled gunshots broke the day.

"*Diadem*, sir," Midshipman Rossyngton announced. "The signal is . . . 'Send Boats', and . . . 'Have Mail'!"

"Pick a fresh boat crew, Mister Westcott, and you might as well let Rossyngton command it . . . he's fresh," Lewrie directed, beaming in expectant pleasure that he would soon have letters from home and his sons, and Lydia, after months without. And, was he allowed to share copies of the London papers, he could find out what the rest of the world had been up to, to boot!

I could pace and fret 'til it arrives, or . . . , Lewrie thought.

"I will be below, Mister Westcott," he decided, instead. "Do inform me when the mail arrives."

Half an hour later, and he had a tidy stack of correspondence on his desk in the day-cabin. He quickly sorted out the lot, fresh newspapers on the bottom, personal letters atop them, and the official bumf the first to be opened. Long before, he had been bent over a gun and caned, "kissing the gunner's daughter", for ignoring that rule.

Paramount to all the letters from Admiralty was a folded note from Commodore Popham. With a tall glass of his trademark cool tea near to hand—though it was January, it was summer in the Southern Hemisphere—he broke the wax seal and spread it out. It could be an invitation to supper aboard the flagship, congratulations for the efficient landing of the army, or an order sending *Reliant* far away on a new duty, but—

"Aha!" he read with satisfaction. "Pettus, open two bottles of Rhenish, set out glasses for five, then pass word for the officers to attend me."

"Yes, sir," Pettus said, headed for the wine cabinet.

"The Commodore *will* be forming the Naval Brigade," Lewrie told Pettus and Jessop with some glee. "All those preparations we talked about . . . see that all's ready t'go by dawn."

"Very good, sir," Pettus replied, pausing before pulling the first cork. "And . . . might you need my services ashore, sir?"

"Hmm . . . I thought I'd take my boat crew, Furfy, and my Cox'n as part of the naval party, so they could do for me . . . unless you're volunteering?" Lewrie replied.

"Be nice to go ashore and see Africa, sir," Pettus told him. with a wistful grin. "Do something . . . active, for a change?"

"Well . . . see you have a stout pair o' shoes, then," Lewrie said. "Draw a musket, cutlass, and a pistol when we unlock the arms chests in the morning."

"Careful ye don't stab yerself, Mister Pettus," Jessop teased.

"Fetch out the glasses, you, and make sure they're clean!" the cabin steward snapped, pulling a cork with a loud *thock!*

Lewrie had time to go through the rest of his correspondence from Admiralty, most of it of little import. There were changes to be made to charts, where one of His Majesty's vessels had discovered an unknown rock or shoal, or fresh soundings; quarterly promotions lists; directives Fleetwide about excessive purchases and the need to conserve, etc. That left the personal letters, and the very first one atop the pile was from Lydia Stangbourne. The next one beside it was from Hugh, who had surely been at the battle of Trafalgar, as part of Nelson's fleet, and sure sign that he was still *alive*, but—

The Marine sentry was pounding, his musket butt on the deck and bawling the arrival of his officers.

"Enter!" Lewrie bade them, getting to his feet to stand before the desk.

"Reporting as ordered, sir," Lt. Westcott said for all.

There was one extra; the Purser, Mr. Cadbury, had come along. Pettus took quick note, and slunk over to the sideboard to put out an extra glass.

"It's on, gentlemen!" Lewrie crowed. "First light, tomorrow, and we'll be off!"

"Huzzah, sir! Huzzah, I say!" Marine Lieutenant Simcock cried.

"You've your lists of all the items our people will need ashore, I take it?" Lewrie asked. "Good! Commodore Popham assures me that the army will provide us with at least one four-wheeled waggon, and two horses, and one waggoner from the Quartermaster's. He cautions that the waggon will have only limited space, since the horse team's needs for water and feed will be aboard, in addition to all of our gear, so we will have to carry as much as our men can on their backs, and all hands will be on 'shank's ponies'. There will be no mounts or saddlery to spare for officers or Mids. As I told Pettus, be sure ye have your best shoes or boots on."

"Who will go, sir?" Lt. Merriman eagerly enquired as the wine was poured for them.

"I promised Mister Westcott that he would go," Lewrie said with a grin. "Does he not, there'd be a one-man mutiny! Since I've been at the Cape before, I will go ashore, myself. Sorry, sirs. But, someone more than capable must remain aboard to command the ship in my absence, and you and Mister Spendlove are more than able to fight the ship, do the French, or a Dutch squadron, turn up. The Bosun's Mate, Mister Wheeler, and two Mids . . . I'm thinking Mister Warburton, and Mister Rossyngton, to keep the men in the naval half in good discipline.

"Now, how are we doing with the water bottles, their slings, and the canvas haversacks?" he asked, taking a sip of wine.

"The Sailmaker, Master Gunner, and their mates have all but a few to finish, sir, and every man will be equipped with them by the end of the First Dog, tonight," Lt. Westcott reported.

"Good! Ammunition, Mister Simcock?" Lewrie continued.

"Thirty paper cartridges per man and musket, initially, sir," Simcock happily informed him, "and sixty more rounds on hand, to be carted in the waggon for each man after. Do we begin now, sir, the Armourer can put fresh edges on cutlasses, hangers, and bayonets, if you will open the arms chests."

"I will give you the keys once we're done here," Lewrie promised. "Rations, Mister Cadbury?"

"Four kegs of salt-meat, sir, two each of beef, two of pork, and a whole box of portable soup portions," Cadbury piped up. "Three bags of bisquit, and two five-gallon barricoes of rum. I may spare you my assistant to keep track of issuing victuals. The Ship's Cook has set aside spare utensils and pots, but, he and his helpers must stay with the ship to do for the rest of the crew, so I don't know—"

"I've spoken to my cook, Yeovill, and he thinks he can cook for us whilst we're away," Lewrie said, "though he's none too keen on the task. Nothing t'do but *boil* stuff, he said, with no real call for his culinary skills!"

"Unless we shoot some game meat, sir," Westcott said in hope.

"Let's hope that our army, or the Dutch army, haven't driven all the tasty beasts away," Lewrie said. "The overall command of the brigade is given to Captain Byng of the *Belliqueux*, assisted by Captain Hardinge and his officers. He was sent out with us to take command of a ship in India, and is available.

"*They*, I am informed, will be busy with landing the *heavy* artillery, the presence of which I just learned. And here I thought we were done with ferryin'."

"Our transports must be like the Horn of Capricorn, sir," Lt. Merriman said with a snicker, "filled with infinite plenty! What'll they trot out next? Hindoo war elephants?"

"You will be taking your Ferguson along, sir?" Lt. Westcott asked, after he'd gotten a re-fill of his wine glass from Pettus.

"And my Girandoni air-rifle, should there be any game," Lewrie said with an agreeing nod. "Assumin' the bloody thing still holds a charge of air. Damn all leather washers and seals in this weather."

"Then I wonder if I might borrow your fusil musket, sir," Lt. Westcott requested. "A fusil's longer barrel makes it more accurate than a Brown Bess musket, even if it is a smooth-bore."

"Of course ye can, sir!" Lewrie gladly told him. "And, does it come to a fight, I pray you make good practice with it!"

"Mister Spendlove, sir," Lt. Simcock spoke up. "I've a man, Private Radley, who is a keen shot. I wonder if I might borrow your splendid Pennsylvania rifle for him to use. I promise to bring it back in good condition, and he's the very man I'd trust for any long-range shooting . . . a sight better than me, in truth."

"I would be more than happy to oblige you, sir," Lt. Spendlove replied. He sounded gracious, but a tad glum that his rifle would go and he would not.

"Mister Westcott and I have come up with a list of our sailors we deem suitable for the duty ashore," Lewrie told the gathering. "If there are any objections or substitutions you gentlemen wish to make, look it over."

Lewrie got the list from his desk, and handed it to the First Officer, who gathered the rest round the dining table to put their heads together. A few names were substituted, but in all, the list was found acceptable.

"Most of these lads gained experience ashore last year in Spanish Florida," Lt. Merriman took note. "They'll do handsomely."

"Though they never had to march far inland under a soldier's heavy kit, or did much skirmishing with the Dons or the Indians," Lt. Spend-love said with a hopeful shrug.

"And that encounter with the Seminoli up near Amelia Island put the wind up 'em," Lewrie said with a laugh.

"Or with the rattlesnakes, coral snakes, and alligator," Lt. Simcock hooted. "That was a draw, at best!"

"I thought the alligator won," Lewrie added. "Good trainin', that was, for all the beasties that Africa has t'offer. Can anyone think of anything else we haven't considered? Medical care? Clean spare stockings? Very well, then. Inform the Mids and hands chosen for the expedition, Mister Westcott, and allow them to make their preparations." He went to his desk and fetched out the precious, closely guarded keys to the locks on the arms chests. "Take these, Mister Simcock, and see to the sharpening, then lock everything back up 'til we issue weapons at dawn. It will take at least three round-trips to land all our men and supplies, so let's be sure that all's in hand to start before dawn, at Two Bells of the Middle Watch. Re-fills, please, Pettus," he ordered. "And, allow me to propose a toast."

Denied the choice opportunity of serving ashore or not, with a precious shot at making their names known and "gazetted" or not, all expectantly stood with their full glasses ready.

"To us, sirs," Lewrie intoned with due solemnity, "and to our success, and victory!"

"Us, success, and *victory*!" they roared, tossing their wine back to "heel-taps".

Once the last of his supper guests had bowed their way out, Lewrie wheeled about and almost dashed to his day-cabin desk, fetching along a short candelabra from the sideboard for more light, so he might read his personal letters, at last. Lydia's, or Hugh's? That decision took but an instant, and he broke the wax seal of the one from his younger son.

It is Victory, complete and Glorious, and our good ship Pegasus, *your old friend Capt. Charlton, and, dare I say my own humble Efforts in our perilous Endeavour, contributed to the Triumph of Arms!*

Hugh had been posted on the upper gun-deck, he wrote, and had a better view than some of his fellow Midshipmen below on the lower gun-deck.

He described how grey, gloomy, and overcast was the day, and how scant the wind, and how slowly the action had been joined, with some ships in the two long columns of warships, sailing bows-on at right angles to the horizon-spread combined French and Spanish fleet, struggling to maintain steerage way.

HMS *Pegasus* had been near the rear of the right-hand column led by the massive *Royal Sovereign,* close to *Swiftsure, Dreadnought,* and *Defiance,* spared the drubbing that the lead vessels suffered as the miles-long French and Spanish line had opened fire, unable to reply for what seemed hours of punishment, sure to be shot to pieces long before the British Navy could come to grips, but . . . !

Hugh described his awe and joy as the two columns speared through the enemy line and let loose with both batteries, sailing into that massive, impenetrable fogbank of powder smoke! The enemy's ships had been isolated, lost in their own fogs, in singletons, pairs, and trios upon which Nelson's fleet had fallen, "doubling" two-on-one to either beam to pound them and shatter them at "close pistol shot," and it had been the Frogs and Dons who had been shot to pieces!

We came upon a lone French 74, crossed her stern to deliver a devastating Rake which brought down her mizen, came along her stabd. side at close range, & traded shot for nigh an hour before lashing to her & boarding. We'd never seen our gallant Capt. Charlton, usually the most phlegmatic of men, get so lively & excited! Despite the volume of musketry, which took my hat, and the Capt.'s hat and one of his epaulets, we boarded her, my brave gunners among the first to gain her gangway, cheering & shouting like Billy-Oh, which spurred my courage to be ever in front. Thank you and Grandfather for the pair of Pistols you gave me, which, along with a cutlass and my dirk, I put to good Practice. The carnage aboard was unbelievable. We cut our way to the quarterdeck before her Capt. called for Quarter, lowered her Colours, and she was ours!

"Good God, I've raised a real scraper!" Lewrie whooped with delight.

Hugh had gotten a scratch or two, though his ship had paid a steep price in killed and wounded. And, by dark that evening, the weather had gotten up, so fiercely that they had had to cut the tow, and had lost their prize. Theirs, and many of the already-damaged prizes, had been cast ashore on the Spanish rocks, reefs, and shoals.

And, there was the death of Admiral Lord Nelson, which Hugh had learned of hours later. The rumour was that the Nelson had been dressed in his finest, with all his foreign decorations, and some French Marines in one of the fighting tops had shot him down.

Hugh closed by reckoning that he had acquitted himself main-well in his first true action, if he did say so himself, and that *Pegasus* was off to Gibraltar to make repairs and re-victual, and that he would write more, later.

"Thank God," Lewrie whispered, faintly smiling as he laid the letter aside. "He's safe, he's blooded, and he *did* do damned well . . . but Lord, what a way t'learn t'fight!"

Lewrie wondered if he'd even recognise Hugh the next time they met, whenever that might be. He'd seen him off by the King's Stairs in Portsmouth as an active, lark-happy thirteen year old in 1803. Though only sixteen now, he sounded as adult as any "scaly fish" in his twenties! He'd crossed swords with men out to kill him, fired his pistols, stabbed with his dirk, and had slain men in furious, face-to-face battle! Sixteen or not, he was a man, now.

Lewrie turned to Lydia's letter, and it was certainly not the plaintive expressions of longing that he had expected! It had been written and sent before news of Trafalgar had reached England, for she made no mention of it. No, *her* news was of her brother Percy's wedding to Eudoxia Durschenko, at long last!

They'd *planned* to marry last summer, when Lewrie was still in the Bahamas, and he'd doubted they'd ever go through with it, but here it was, daft as it sounded.

Lydia had been enjoying late summer in the country at their estates near Reading and Henley-On-Thames, riding daily over their acreage (which consisted of miles and bloody miles of land), dining *al fresco* with childhood friends, relatives, and neighbours, when she'd gotten an invitation from Hawkinge in Kent, where Percy's self-raised cavalry regiment was posted to guard against the threat of invasion by the French. Just before the annual London Season, when Parliament re-convened, she and several others had coached down in a gay train of equipages, lodging together each night at the same posting houses, and having a quick round of shopping in London to look their best, when the time came, and the trips each way had been the jolliest.

The church at Hawkinge, near Folkstone, had not been all that grand, but the officers of the regimental mess had decorated it and turned the "happy occasion" into a grand military affair. A troop of horse had escorted Eudoxia's carriage to the churchyard, another troop had brought the groom. Trumpets had blown fanfares, the band had been boisterous, accompanied by some new-fangled tinkly bell-draped thing called a "Jingling Johnny", and they had made an arch of swords as the newly-weds left the church, and the wedding breakfast had been held close by under canvas pavilions, all to the delight of the locals.

Eudoxia's father, Arslan Artimovich, that vicious, sneering, eye-patched old bird, had turned out in new suitings, rather grandly, Lydia wrote, with no muttered curses in Russian, and no sign of his wicked daggers.

The old fart saved his curses for me, *whenever he saw me and Eudoxia together,* Lewrie told himself; *He likes Percy's horses too much t'curse* him*! Arslan Artimovich might still despise aristocracy, but Percy comes with too much "tin" attached.*

Lydia wrote that the affair had become "soggier" and more exuberant than most weddings, and that Arslan Artimovich had gotten as drunk as only a Russian can, and had tried to teach the subalterns how to do a wild dance, which involved whirling about, turning Saint Catherine's Wheels, and squatting with arms crossed and kicking legs straight out in turn, to the further delight of local witnesses, before the "happy couple" had coached off.

Despite her initial reservations, Lydia expressed that she had come to like Eudoxia, her *outré* past aside. Eudoxia had become a good influence on Percy and his penchant for gambling deep, finding her a level-headed, sensible, and clever young woman, and, with her sunny and amiably amusing disposition, she kept Percy distracted enough to submit to her wishes.

After that, Lydia had returned to London to stay at their house in Grosvenor Street for a few days, eschewing most of the public events where she would feel uncomfortable, but had attended some symphonies and new plays, done some shopping to see the new fashions, but expressed how relieved she would be to return to the country and take joy in the Autumn and the holidays to come. Percy, Eudoxia, and the regiment would march back to Reading and their permanent station once the winter weather precluded any attempt by Napoleon to cross the Channel, and be home for the harvest festivals and Christmas.

The rest of her letter expressed fondness, longing for his return, and concern for his safety so far away, at whatever it was that required him to be months away and thousands of miles off. Perhaps it might transpire, she wrote, that they could pick up where they had left off, and see what their relationship could be, in future?

"What a scandalous set *we'd* be!" Lewrie muttered to himself in wry humour. "Lydia and her un-warranted bad repute as a divorcé . . . Percy and his mad-cap ways, married to a foreigner who'd been a trick shooter, bareback rider, and actress with Dan Wigmore's Peripatetic Extravaganza, her lion-tamer papa t'boot! Christ, scandalous little me would fit right in!"

There was a discreet rapping on the great-cabin door. Pettus went to see to it. "Master-At-Arms, sir," he announced.

"Right, then," Lewrie said with a groan. "Tell Mister Appleby I'm just retiring, and all the lights will be extinguished in five minutes . . . if he'll give me that long, that is."

"Aye, sir," Pettus replied with a grin.

Lewrie put the letters away in his desk drawer, and rose to begin undressing, reminding himself to write replies, soonest, and one to Thom Charlton to congratulate him, too, once he was back aboard.

Once in his hanging bed-cot and under the covers, in the dark, Lewrie did feel a faint prickle of worry. As grand and adventurous as he and his officers anticipated their jaunt ashore would be, there was always the risk that he'd never get to *write* those letters.

He could drown if his boat was overset in the surf upon landing, for he, like many British tars, could not swim a stroke. He could put a foot wrong and meet up with all manner of venomous puff adders and mambas and cobras, rest under the wrong tree and be bitten by the slim green *boomslang*, be swarmed by scorpions in his sleep, and God only knew what-all. If the Dutch put up a fierce resistance, he could get his fool head shot off!

They don't pay me half *enough t'do what I do,* he told himself; *They really don't.*

CHAPTER TWENTY-EIGHT

Reliant's Marines in the barges, and all the supplies in one of the slightly smaller cutters, were landed first. By the time the Navy complement had been put ashore on the crowded beach, it was half-past six in the morning. Blaauwberg Mountain cast the beach, the towering and widespread piles of supplies, and the army encampment in shadow from the rising sun, and it was still pleasantly cool. The air was sour with the smells of burning wood in the many campfires, manure in the horse lines, and un-washed soldiery and their sweated wool coats.

Lewrie strode over the sand and shingle of the beach to higher ground, and the stubbly wild grasses and rock; careful where his boots landed, for there was a fair amount of manure right down to the back of the beach. He took a deep sniff, but it didn't smell like the Africa he remembered!

"What a pot-mess our army's made," he commented to Lt. Simcock, who was amusing himself with his sheathed sword to flip a crab over and over, and herding it to prevent its escape.

"The horses and draught animals aren't the worst of it, sir," Simcock said with a faint smile. "They should've dug sinks for their own wastes, but it doesn't smell like it. I have yet to see the waggon they promised us."

"Well, keep a good guard over our stores 'til we do," Lewrie told him.

"Do soldiers think there's un-guarded rum about, they'll fight us for it. Ah, good morning, Mister Westcott! Have you ever seen the like?"

"Perhaps only at a Wapping hiring fair, sir," Westcott replied. "It appears we've landed far South of the main beach, and the rest of the brigade." He pointed North up the beach to where some large oared barges were struggling to fetch long and heavy siege guns ashore with one piece amidships of each. "Shouldn't we be up there, sir?"

"Hmm . . . do you *really* wish to spend all day helpin' 'em do that? Looks t'be warm work, to me," Lewrie said, chuckling. "No, I'm more of a mind t'find ourselves a waggon, load up, and march inland with the regiments, or just a bit astern of 'em. Commodore Popham offered us as guards to the baggage train, and there's sure t'be lots of ammunition and such close behind the leading regiments . . . more valuable than casks o' salt-meat. Does that sound more palatable, sir?"

The army encampment's sleepy breakfast came to an end with the blaring of bugle calls, the rumble of drummers playing the Long Roll, and the reedy shrieks of Highland bagpipes. In a twinkling, what had been somnolent dis-order turned to roaring chaos!

All of a sudden, the hundreds of tents were being struck and rolled up, mounts were being bridled and saddled, mules and horse teams were being harnessed, and thousands of soldiers rose to gather up their bedding, wash out their mess kits, stow bundles on the pack mules, and load waggons. Mules brayed in resistance, horses neighed and snorted, and got led to their places at the trot, raising great clouds of dry African dust that mingled with the steam and smoke as campfires and cookfires were doused.

Officers shouted orders to Sergeants, and those Sergeants bellowed sharp orders to Corporals and Privates, who raised their own voices to spur themselves along as they packed up. The bands of the various regiments began tuning up and were starting to play competing martial airs. The pipers and drummers of the Highland regiments seemed likely to win that contest. As to who could curse and scream invective the loudest, that was still un-decided!

"Here comes a waggon, sir!" Lt. Simcock pointed up the beach.

"Mister Rossyngton, see that'un? Go see if it's empty, and seize it for us," Lewrie ordered, and the Midshipman sprinted away. He back-pedalled near the right-side front wheel and got the waggoner to draw his team to a halt, conversed a bit, then dashed back.

"He says he doesn't know what we're talking about, sir, and he has orders to go forward and load up the officers' personal goods from one of the infantry regiments, but he doesn't yet know which. He was told to hitch up and wait for orders," Rossyngton reported.

"Isn't that just bloody typical," Lewrie said, sneering and shaking his head. "It's empty, then."

"So far, sir, aye," Rossyngton replied.

"Then it's ours," Lewrie snapped, and strode over to the waggon with his orders from Popham in his hand. "You, there! Yes, I mean you, Private! Stand fast!"

"Sir?" the soldier said with a gulp at the sight of *some* kind of officer tramping up at speed and bellowing at him.

Lewrie got to the right-hand wheel and laid hold of the box.

"I am Captain Sir Alan Lewrie of His Majesty's Frigate *Reliant*. Part of the Naval Brigade?" Lewrie said with his stern face on.

Comes in handy, my damned knighthood! he told himself; *If I can impress somebody with it when I need something!*

"General Baird promised Commodore Popham that the parties off the various ships would each be supplied with a waggon and team, and I must get my stores loaded so we may go forward," Lewrie spun on in a more conversational tone; he could save threats and roaring for a later time, if conversational did not suit! "Your waggon is empty . . . Private whom?"

"P-Private Dodd, sir," the waggoner hesitantly said.

"Very good, Private Dodd, if you'll be so good as to wheel over to yon pile of stores, my sailors and Marines can begin loading," Lewrie said with a brief smile.

"But, Ah *cain't*, sir!" the soldier wheedled. "Me Sergeant'll have me back lashed *open* do Ah not wait here for orders, an' he comes an' tells me *which* regiment Ah'm t'go to! Ah cain't let ye have it, sir."

"So the brandy and wine, the silk sheets and silver tableware, of an officers' mess is more important than ammunition, food, and rum? Tosh, Private Dodd!" Lewrie snapped. "The Dutch're waitin' up there, entrenched most-like, and there's sure t'be a fight before the day's out." He jabbed his arm to point at the summit of the Blaauwberg. "I ask ye, will the officers of whichever regiment your sergeant had in mind *need* any of their luxuries before dark?"

"Ah jus' cain't, sir," Dodd wavered, looking up to the summit then back down, miserably torn. "The lashin'd half kill me."

"If General Baird promised us a waggon, then he must've had one to spare, Private Dodd," Lewrie went on, trying reason. "If he does, then he surely has one extra for that regimental mess. Just a matter of whistling up the spare for *them*! Besides," Lewrie cajoled, turning mellow and friendly—it *might* work!—"if your officers or your Sergeant try t'give ye any grief, they'll have me t'contend with, and a Post-Captain in the Royal Navy outranks 'em by a long chalk! And, they'll have t'*find* ye first, and you'll be with my sailors and Marines, sharin' our rations, and our rum. The Navy issues *twice* a day, ye know . . . half past eleven of the morning and another in the evening."

"Eh, ya do, sir?" Dodd perked up at that prospect, but then as quickly slumped in dread and indecision. "Ah don't know, sir. I've me orders, an' all. Yet—!"

"Just wheel over yonder and we'll begin loading," Lewrie prompted. "There's a good lad."

"Well, sir . . . iff'n they's waggons enough for your lot, *and* that regiment's mess, Ah s'pose they's no harm," Dodd surrendered, at last. "You've a heavy load, sir?"

"Salt-meat casks, large cooking pots . . . ," Lewrie began to tick off.

"Best they go 'tween the axles, then, sir," Dodd said. "That'd be easier on the team, with the road up the mountain steep-lookin'."

He clucked to his horses, shook the reins, and got the waggon turning round to clatter and rattle over to the shore party.

"Huzzah!" Lt. Westcott shouted. "Heave it up, lads, and hoist it in!"

"You can really protect him from his officers' wrath, sir?" Midshipman Rossyngton asked in a soft voice once the waggoner was out of ear shot.

"If I have t'convince the poor fellow t'volunteer as a sailor or Marine, sir!" Lewrie told him with a happy bark of laughter.

More bugle calls sounded as the waggon was loaded and the load roped down against shifting, then covered with a large scrap of spare canvas. The army encampment was packed up, and the soldiers were now donning coats, shakoes, hangers and cartridge boxes, bayonets and the cumbersome and heavy chest-strapped packs. At another series of calls, and more shouts and curses, thousands of men in the infantry took their muskets from stands and scurried into ranks and files, forming columns four-abreast. Cavalrymen swung up into their saddles and chivvied their mounts into similar order. Artillerymen with the light field pieces assembled atop the limbers and caissons, or astride the lead horses in their teams. King's Colours and regimental Colours were un-cased and allowed to stream in the light wind, just as the sun rose high enough to banish the dawn's shadows and spread warm light over the now-assembled army, and polished cross-belt plates, regimental shako plates, and weapons glistened brightly.

"I had lead soldiers when I was a boy," Lt. Westcott mused at the sight, "but the real thing is grander by far."

"Mister Simcock," Lewrie said, turning to the Marine officer. "You and your men *somewhat* resemble redcoats, so it might be best if you march ahead of the waggon, and Mister Westcott and our sailors bring up the rear. I'll come with you, at the head of our column."

"Pity we don't have Colours of our own, sir," Simcock said. "If we'd thought to bring a Harbour Jack or boat Jack? Ah, well."

"Perhaps we can steal one from another ship's shore party," Lewrie suggested, laughing. "The same way we stole our waggon. Let's get our little company movin' forward, Mister Simcock. Up close to the head of the baggage train, like we really are guardin' it."

He looked down the short length of his column.

We haven't got bugles, so——? he thought; *Might we need to pilfer one o' those, too? Well, there's Mister Wheeler.*

"Mister Wheeler?" Lewrie called to the Bosun's Mate. "Do you have a call t'get this shambles movin'?"

"Ehm . . . ," Wheeler replied, scratching his head for a moment. "How about 'Stations To Weigh', sir?" he said, lifting his silver bosun's call.

"Aye, that'll do. Tootle away!" Lewrie agreed, laughing.

Christ, what does the Army say? Lewrie asked himself, stumped.

"Forward . . . march!" he extemporised, waving his arm as the bosun's call *fweeped.*

"For'd march!" Lt. Simcock shouted, calling the step for a bit to his Marines, since they had left their fifer and drummer aboard the ship. Lewrie stood beside to admire them, thinking that his Marines were as smart as any of the Army soldiers. The waggon came up level with him, and Private Dodd gave him a shy smile and nod. Then came his sailors, and they were a different proposition. Westcott, the Midshipmen, the Bo-sun's Mate . . . *they* looked "martial" enough.

Their Purser, Mr. Cadbury, had long ago kitted the men out in red-and-white chequered gingham shirts from the same baled lot, and blue neckerchiefs for all. All hands wore the waist-length, opened jackets with bright brass buttons and white-taped seams of the nautical trade, and white slop-trousers. All had been issued stiff and flat-brimmed, low-crowned tarred hats, and every hand had opted for a bright blue ribbon band to trail off the backs of their hats, with HMS RELIANT block-painted in white.

It was just that no one had ever taught them how to march in step! The captain who tried might have created a mutiny, for "square-bashing" drill was the stuff of "soldiers", a much inferior lot!

They *shambled* in four ragged lines, swaying out of order like a weaving worm, their muskets not held at Trail or Shoulder Arms, but over their shoulders any-old-how, like oars or gaffs. There was his cabin-steward, Pettus, without a single clue how to handle a weapon; his personal cook, Yeovill, sporting a red waist-coat and a longer blue coat, with a black civilian hat on his head, and his attempt at a sailor's queue as bristly as a fox tail, and about as gingerish. His Cox'n, Liam Desmond, and his long-time mate, Patrick Furfy, were near the tail of the column, peering all about wide-eyed, with their hats on the backs of their heads.

No one'll ever believe we're supposed *t'be here!* Lewrie told himself; *We look more like a parcel o' drunken revellers!*

With a long sigh, he hitched the sling of his Ferguson higher up on his shoulder and stomped back to rejoin Lt. Simcock.

There was a sudden fanfare of bugle calls, more shouts, and the army lurched into motion, five thousand men in all in both the Heavy Brigade and the Light Brigade of Foot, and the drums began to thunder out the pace for smartly-drilled soldiers to advance at the one hundred steps a minute. Cavalry moved out at the Walk, and the dust clouds rose again as thousands of boots and hooves struck the ground. Artillery batteries clattered and lumbered, and the waggons of the baggage train began their slow groaning forward movement.

"We can't wedge ourselves into the baggage train, sir," Lt. Simcock observed as they reached the head of the first waggons. "It might be better did we swing out to the right flank of it, and try to stay level with the leading columns."

"Sounds right, Mister Simcock," Lewrie agreed. "Uhm . . . how does one order that, in Army parlance? You're the closest thing we have to a proper soldier."

"Column Half-Right!" Simcock bellowed, turning to march backwards and pointing in the right direction. *"Tah!"*

" 'Tah'?" Lewrie whispered to him as the Marines altered course.

"That is what my drill-masters shouted when I was learning, and what they used as a word of execution," Simcock explained in a lower voice, baring a sly smile. "Some prefer 'Har!' Makes no bloody sense at all, really. Battalion, Attention, comes out as ''Talion, 'Shun!' for example; Arms in any movement of muskets is said 'Hahms!'; and so on. It's all up to the Sergeants' preference, really. Isn't that right, Sarn't Trickett?"

"Whatever the Leftenant says, sir!" Sgt. Trickett barked back.

Their swaying little column angled out from the baggage train, and its cloud of dust, about one hundred yards before Simcock ordered Column Half-Left, with a requisite *Tah!* to bring them back on their original course, parallel with the waggon train.

The march, or the shambling, continued up the slightly rising slope from the sea towards the Blaauwberg, through a dusty brown haze raised by the regiments ahead of them. The land was deceptively green, at least in the middle distance, though the ground they marched over seemed half-parched by a Southern Hemisphere summer, with most of the grasses only ankle high and sere, and rare patches of taller clumps of reeds and greyish-green bushes here and there. What thickets of trees they encountered were thin and spaced far apart from each other, most of them spiked with long thorns. The denser, greener, and more succulent groves lay ahead near the foot of the Blaauwberg, but even those were widely scattered, and formed no impediment to the skirmishers of regimental light companies or cavalry videttes that rode through them. As they got closer, the Blaauwberg did not look as steep as it had at first, but it was treeless and stony, thinly furred with short green grasses between scattered outcrops of bare rock, appearing at that distance as if the green was a thin covering of moss, or a green mould on a stale loaf of bread.

About an hour into the march, which was beginning to be sweaty and arduous, the drums ceased to beat and bugles blew. Loud and deep voices ahead shouted a chorus of " ''Talion . . . Halt!"

"Column . . . Halt!" Lt. Simcock called out.

"Thank th' saints!" Seaman Furfy could be heard saying at the rear of the sailors' party, raising a weary laugh.

"The foe?" Lewrie asked aloud, pulling a shorter telescope from a coat pocket and looking up to the top of the Blaauwberg.

"A five-minutes' rest, most likely, sir," Lt. Simcock speculated. "Though it's very likely that the Dutch have had time to entrench above the beaches, and are ready for us . . . somewhere up there. Time for some water. If you do not mind, sir, I think it a caution did we send some pickets out to our right, about fifty yards or so, just in case, whilst the rest get off their feet for a bit."

"Good idea," Lewrie said, turning to walk back behind their waggon to see Lt. Westcott and have him send out some scouts.

"Five minutes' rest, and water, Mister Westcott, and I'd be much obliged did you send about ten hands out to the right, about fifty or sixty yards, to be lookouts once they've had a 'wet'."

"Aye, sir," Westcott replied as he mopped his face with a handkerchief, then passed the chore to Midshipman Warburton. "Bless me, but I doubt I've walked this far since our ship was commissioned. Even in Spanish Florida we did not venture so far inland."

"That's the trouble with seeking after adventure, sir," Lewrie said with a snicker. "But, we'll be all the fitter for it, when we do run into it."

"I'd more expect dead-tired, sir," Westcott drolly replied. He pulled the sling of his improvised canteen up, un-corked the wine bottle, and took a long pull of water.

Lewrie looked all about the landscape, then went to the waggon to clamber up the spokes of the rear wheel and into the bed, sitting down on a keg and pulling out his telescope once more for a closer inspection of the land to their right.

I could see more if I stood up, but damned if I'm goin' to, he thought. The muscles in his thighs and calves were complaining about the long, and rare, expenditure of effort. Three or four turns from the taffrails to the forecastle, or hours spent on his feet pacing the quarterdeck, had not prepared him for this trek. To make things worse, his well-made Hessian boots, fashionable and snug-fitting, now felt two sizes too small, and his thick cotton stockings had turned two sizes too loose, clumping in the worst possible places!

It felt rather pleasant, sitting on a keg of small beer, but, he stood with a stifled groan, raised his pocket telescope once more, and gave the terrain a very close look-over.

Damme, are those springboks? he wondered, noting some white-and-tawny-coated things deep in a thorn tree thicket; *Thought the clatter from the army would've scared them off!*

They were nigh a cable's distance off, he estimated, but there might be a chance to stalk them, pot one, field-dress it for supper . . .

"No," he muttered. "It'd rot before we camp for the night, and the rest period's too damned short, anyway."

He sat back down, raised his magnum champagne bottle canteen, and took a deep drink.

"You, there! What detachment is this, and how do you come to be here?" someone was calling at them in one of those arrogant, and plummy, voices that simply got up Lewrie's nose.

He stood and looked left, to see an elegantly uniformed young officer on a fine blooded horse pacing up to them. The officer wore a fore-and-aft bicorne trimmed with gold lace, and plumed with white egret feathers. It was tipped so low on his forehead that he had to look down his nose at them—or was that his usual demeanour when dealing with common soldiers and social inferiors?

"Good morning," Lewrie called to him. "We are part of the Naval Brigade, sent ashore to land the siege artillery, and guard your baggage train. Captain Sir Alan Lewrie, Baronet, of the *Reliant* frigate."

The bloody knighthood looks like it'll prove useful, again, he thought.

"Good God above, sir!" the officer yelped in indignation, after taking a quick and dismissive look at Lewrie's men. "You are *drinking,* sir? You allow your men *spirits?* Scandalous!"

"It's water, sir," Lewrie told him, feeling the urge to raise his bottle to his mouth for another guzzle. "My Marines are the only ones with proper canteens, so we had to improvise."

At least he *hoped* that his men had only water! He had learned long ago how devious sailors could be when it came to getting and hiding stashes of rum or brandy, in the most unlikely places. His party might not be able to pass a close inspection, no matter how carefully their bottles had been checked before being filled. In point of fact, he had two pint flasks of spirits in his own bed-roll!

The officer, a Captain of Foot who had yet to introduce himself, unbuttoned his elegant tunic and clawed out a sheaf of papers from an inside breast pocket. "Look here, Captain . . . Lewis, was it? I find no mention of *any* naval parties serving ashore, and certainly no mention of your party in our order of march."

"It's Lewrie, not Lewis, and my orders come from Commodore Popham *and* General Sir David Baird," Lewrie countered, producing his own papers. "And, strictly speakin', we are not listed in the order of march, but are out on the *flank* of the baggage train, doin' what we are ordered t'do . . . guarding it."

"Humph! I see here that the so-called Naval Brigade's *first* duty is to land the siege artillery, and guard the stores still piled above the beaches," the Army officer said, looking up from the offered papers with a raised, dubious brow and handing them back. "I very much doubt that even the broadest interpretation of your orders may justify your presence anywhere near *here*, sir! Besides," he huffed, and made a snide little grin, "the baggage train is already guarded by a battalion of Foot, as one may clearly see from here."

"Your battalion's spaced out in company lots, on both flanks, and at the rear, sir, right next to the waggons and pack animals, and eatin' so much dust, they can't see their hands in front of their faces. Have they any idea there're impalas in the thorn trees? Or warthogs rootin' round out in the open, not a quarter-mile off?" Lewrie pointed out, becoming irked at the man's high-handedness. "Now, do those impalas spook, it's good odds that it could be Dutch cavalry, sneakin' up on the waggons. Do they break cover East or West, it's *something* t'be concerned about. Do they run off South, then it's our noises that does it. That's why we're out here, sir, where we can see any threat, and why I've pickets out beyond us."

Which is what yer battalion should *be doin'*, Lewrie left to the soldier's imagination—if he had one; *And yes, I* am *teachin' your granny how to suck eggs!*

"I would strongly advise that you and your party return to the beach, Captain Lewrie," the Army officer said, stiffening in umbrage to be told his trade. "Your men are not trained soldiers, and are an impediment to the Army's movements. Too weak a force, more in *need* of protection than anything else!"

"I think I'll obey my orders as written, sir," Lewrie objected, "and we stand warned."

"I will report this to General Baird," the Army Captain threatened, glowering.

"When you do, sir, please extend my warmest regards to Sir David," Lewrie replied with a perky version of his best "shit-eating" grin, and doffed his hat. "Good day to you. Hoy, Mister Simcock! Hoy, Mister West-cott! Call in the pickets, and form ranks!"

Lewrie hopped down from the bed of the waggon and went to join the Marines at the head of the column, leaving the Army officer to fume, jerk reins, and canter off in search of someone to complain to.

"You have been making friends with our compatriots in the Army, sir?" Lt. Simcock said from the corner of his mouth.

"Makin' friends *wherever* I go, Mister Simcock," Lewrie beamed back. "Will you just look at that, sir!"

That mounted officer had ridden to the infantry companies down the right flank of the baggage train, and was chivvying them to take positions further out.

"He may come back and tell us to bugger off for good and all," Lewrie speculated to the Marine officer, "now that those soldiers are out far enough t'do a proper job."

"Back to the beach, then, sir?" Simcock asked.

"No, sir," Lewrie countered. "We'll just amble on up with the regiments and see what we can see. Carry on, Mister Simcock."

"Detachment, 'Shun! Shoulder, Hahms! For-ward, March!"

CHAPTER TWENTY-NINE

A drift and un-wanted, their little column shuffled its way out further to the right, beyond the head of the baggage train and up to the rear of an infantry battalion, taking their own half-hour break for water as the heads of the Army columns began their ascents up towards the Blaauwberg. Up close, the Blaauwberg looked to be merely a pimple compared to the rocky heights beyond, and its slope looked to be even easier, even for field artillery or supply waggons.

"Simply lovely," Lt. Westcott commented. "The Cape Colony has the grand landscape of Scotland beat all hollow. As impressive as any paint-ing I've ever seen of the Alps!"

"Aye, it is dramatic. Starkly so," Lewrie agreed as he took a slug of stale ship's water from his magnum bottle. "Once we're at the top of this hill, I expect one could see for fifty miles on a clear day."

"As soon as we clear the Dutch off it," Westcott said with a chuckle. "If they're there, that is. They might have decided to fort up nearer Cape Town and make their stand there."

"They had batteries at the head of the bay when the other ships took them under fire, yesterday," Lewrie cautioned. "No reason for them t'be

run off by a few broadsides. Oh, look, Mister Westcott! Here comes the
Thirty-fourth Dragoons!"

The infantry columns had halted for a rest and water break, but the
Light Dragoons had been ordered forward to screen. By fours, the squadrons and troops cantered past, raising more dust. Lewrie waved to Captains Veasey and Chadfield, whom he had met, and to the youngster,
Cornet Allison, when he rode past. Cornet Allison heaved off a great,
rueful shrug, for he seemed to be saddled with the care of the Regimental
Ram, which he was leading by a long rope. The Regimental Ram looked
as if someone had washed it recently, combed it, and picked "dilberry"
shit balls from its arse. To make the Regimental Ram even surlier than
normal, it wore a gilt-trimmed royal blue saddle blanket with the 34th's
crest bravely embroidered on it.

"Bleatin', buckin', and sure t'attack somebody," Lewrie joked. "You'd
not catch Bisquit puttin' up with such."

"The Dragoons appear to be going ahead of the infantry columns,
sir," Lt. Westcott said, flashing one of his brief, savage grins. "We could
get up even closer, with them. At least out to the flank of the lead battal-
ions. See, sir? The soldiers are taking off their packs. Preparing to advance!"

"Aye, they are, Mister Westcott," Lewrie took note, exchanging his
water bottle for his pocket telescope. "And changing from columns of
fours to line! Yes, let's go up there, out to the right. It will be a good spot
t'watch the show! Mister Simcock? Let's get 'em up and moving!"

"When they go in, sir, could we go in with them?" Lt. Westcott asked,
sounding as if he was begging.

"Don't know if *that's* in our brief, Mister Westcott," Lewrie mused
aloud, considering the risks. "If the leading regiments *are* to go in, that
snotty Army Captain was right. We'd just be in the way of their attack.
But, nobody's tellin' us we can't be spectators!"

Up ahead, the regiments were forming two ranks deep, arrayed across a
wide front with their grenadier companies on the right, the traditional
point of honour, the eight battalion companies to the left of them, and the
light companies on the extreme left. Their Colours and commanding officers were in the centre, and their bands, who would also serve as aides to
the surgeons, were in the rear. Behind each leading regiment, another thin
line of a second regiment was forming. Field pieces were being ordered up
to place artillery between, and cavalry took position to either flank.

All this was, of course, accompanied by bugles, drums, and the barks and shouted orders from officers and Sergeants-Major. In all of that stirring and din, Lewrie and his party could amble up alongside the right-most troop of the 34th Light Dragoons, with no one in authority taking any notice of them, at all, or making any objections to their presence, until they reached a small rise, a knob, just a bit ahead of the right-most troop of Horse, and about twenty feet higher than the cavalry, a splendid spot from which to see it all.

"Private Dodd? Keep your waggon a bit further back," Lewrie ordered. "Mister Simcock? Mister Westcott? I think it's time for us to load weapons. Load, but do not prime, just in case."

"Aye, sir!"

"Once we've done that, we'll all move atop the knob, and rest easy," Lewrie added, swinging his Ferguson rifled-musket off his now-sore shoulder and digging out a paper cartridge from his slung box. One at a time, he did the same for his four pistols, then stowed them in coat pockets or thrust them behind his sword belt.

Someone must have tutored his cabin-steward, Pettus, in the handling of firearms, for Pettus had torn a cartridge open with his teeth, poured the powder down the muzzle of his Tower musket, rammed it down, added the ball and wad, rammed them home, and replaced the ramrod into the rings under the barrel. He did it slowly and carefully, but he got it right, and got a congratulating nod from Lewrie.

"Right then," Lewrie called. "Up on the knob, and take your ease." As much as he sorely desired to sit down and get off of his feet, too, he strolled up near the head of the cavalry troop.

"Captain Lewrie?" Captain Veasey exclaimed, goggling. "What the Devil brings *you* up here? 'Tis a long way from salt water, don't ye know, haw haw!"

"Idle curiosity, Captain Veasey," Lewrie said back, grinning, and explaining for the umpteenth time about the forming of the Naval Brigade. "We *were* guarding the baggage train 'til some staff officer shooed us off, so I thought we'd come up and see the battle. If there is to be a battle, that is."

"Oh, there will be, mark my words, sir!" Veasey chortled with impending glee. "The Dutch are at the top, in some force. You can see 'em, plain as day."

Lewrie pulled out his pocket telescope and had a squint. The Dutch *were* there! Shakoed heads, bayonet-tipped muskets, and a hint of epau-letted shoulders and the tops of white cross-belts could be seen along the crest. He looked for the muzzles of artillery pieces, but wasn't sure if there were any. He did a long and careful sweep of the entire crest, from the far North end to the South end above their position. There was an-other slight rise at the South end, before the land fell off, and there was some movement there, which he—

"Ah, Leftenant Strickland," Captain Veasey said as a mounted officer came up to join him. "Captain Lewrie, have ye met Leftenant Strickland? O' course ye didn't. Strickland was on the transport with the horses, not the troops. Allow me t'name him to ye. Captain Lewrie, Leftenant Strick-land. Leftenant, Captain Lewrie commanded the frigate that saw us here."

"Happy t'make your acquaintance, Mister Strickland," Lewrie said, dis-tracted from his inspection of the crest. He doffed his hat, whilst Strickland raised his right hand in salute, palm outward, to the brim of his helmet vi-sor. "Glad to make your acquaintance, as well, sir." Though he didn't sound glad, which made Lewrie recall the brief conversation he'd had with Veasey before the voyage had begun. He had been dismissive of the unfor-tunate junior officers placed aboard the horse transports, with all the filth and stinks that that had been, and had sneered over the fate of one officer in particular who did not possess the wealth needed to purchase a full string of mounts, when most other officers had four or five.

This Lt. Strickland was a tall and well-knit fellow with a swarthy com-plexion, and a scar on one cheek, and gave the general impression of someone who had soldiered before.

"Where'd ye get that, sir?" Lewrie genially asked, sketching a slash at his own cheek.

"India, Captain Lewrie, with Gordon's Light Bengali Horse," Strick-land replied, squaring his shoulders as if expecting a slur. Soldiering with "John Company", or with the few British units shipped out there, was not considered "proper" soldiering in most Army messes.

"I was out there, 'tween the wars in the '80s," Lewrie told him with a smile. "And my father was, too, in Calcutta, when he had the Nine-teenth Native Infantry. Were you there for the campaigns against the Tippoo Sultan?"

"Yes, sir!" Strickland said, perking up. "Your father, you say?"

"Then Colonel Sir Hugo Willoughby," Lewrie replied, pulling a face. "I expect you *heard* of him, at least."

"I did indeed, sir," Strickland replied, shifting in his saddle and grinning slightly.

"Aye," Lewrie said with a knowing nod. "*Hamare gali ana, acha din,* hey?"

"Let us say, his reputation preceded him, sir," Strickland replied, laughing, for Lewrie had quoted the traditional greetings of Calcutta's whores; "Hello, won't you come into our street."

"Oh God!" Veasey groaned. "*Two* who can sling Hindoo! Much of a piece with Dog-Latin, or crow squawks, t'my ears! Why *can't* the whole bloody world learn English, and have done?"

"I was noticing some movement out yonder, sirs," Lewrie said, returning to his inspection of the crest with his telescope, "on that knob. But, I don't think it's the Dutch. Can't quite make out—"

"Irregulars?" Veasey wondered aloud, his own attention drawn. "Brown or grey uniforms? There's someone there, as you say, Lewrie."

"Not like any soldiers I've seen," Lt. Strickland agreed.

"Baboons!" Lewrie exclaimed. "They're baboons, a whole troop of 'em! Ugly red-arsed beasts. They wouldn't be there if the Dutch had men near them. The last Dutch unit on their left would be over . . . there," Lewrie guessed, pointing to a spot closer to the centre of the crest. "So, what happens now? Will you charge 'em?"

"Not very likely!" Captain Veasey said with a barking laugh. "Not into the teeth of an entrenched foe, with no clue as to what's on the back slope, waitin' for us. No, the artillery may have first go, before the infantry is ordered forward."

"Guns'd be wasted," Lewrie told him. "Firin' uphill at a thin target is useless. The shot'd strike short, clip the crest, and ricochet off, or sail right over and land half a mile beyond. It'd be like shootin' at a ribbon. Howitzers at high angle might do some good, but mortars would be best. Might you happen t'know if the Army brought any along, Captain Veasey? Perhaps some of the infantry regiments still have some old Coehorn mortars." They both looked puzzled; evidently, cavalry didn't bother with such in-elegant things. "Coehorn mortars are light, short, and fat, fixed to wood blocks and man-carried instead of carriage-mounted," he had to explain, "like a *prouviette* that tests the strength of gunpowder?" He was still speaking Greek to them.

"I s'pose that you, sir, bein' in the Navy and all, must know miles more about artillery and such," Veasey said with a guffaw as he shook his head.

"Cavalry has no need of howitzers or mortars, or any knowledge of 'em. We stick to our last, hey?"

"Perhaps if our gunners have Colonel Shrapnel's bursting shot, they could work good practice on the Dutch, sir," Lt. Strickland said to Veasey, though looking at Lewrie and winking. "They are fused, and explode in the air right over enemy formations, flinging chunks of the roundshot in all directions."

"Now, that I'd like t'see!" Veasey enthused, oblivious.

"Might General Baird be delaying his assault because he has no idea what's on the back side of the crest, sir?" Strickland continued. "Perhaps a reconnoitre from that knob which Captain Lewrie pointed out might be in order. It appears high enough to offer a good view right down the entire length of the Dutch positions, and what lies on the reverse slope, as well. A small party could make it up there with ease," Strickland suggested, pointing to indícate a path. "From where the sailors are, there's a saddle that runs to the base of the knob. A small party could go a bit below the crest of the saddle, out of sight, hopefully, and get about halfway round the knob, where the way up does not look all that bad a climb, sir. Once there, a runner could return with a report."

"There's only baboons up there, now," Lewrie stuck in. "Else, the Dutch would've run 'em off. Small party, my eye, sirs! One could put a whole dis-mounted troop up yonder, along with my sailors and my Marines, and threaten the Dutch left flank!"

"Yes, what say you to that, sir?" Strickland eagerly asked.

"Our Colonel'd never allow it," Veasey countered, shaking his head again. "He'd wish t'keep the regiment intact, ready to exploit any breakthrough by the infantry . . . t'harass and ride down the Dutch when they flee. No, no, we'll let the Heavy Brigade go in."

"Half a troop, sir," Strickland pressed. "Fourty men."

"Along with mine," Lewrie insisted.

"And how far off might the closest Dutch soldiers be, once ye get up there, Strickland?" Veasey snapped. "An hundred yards or more? Our short-barrelled Paget carbines couldn't hit the side of a *palace* at that range, much less a man-sized target! I *pressed* the Colonel for the Elliot-pattern carbines, you will recall, but no!"

"The *Dutch* don't know you have Paget carbines, sir," Lewrie said quickly. "If we do open upon them, all they'll hear is lots of gunfire, see a lot of powder smoke, and have shot throwin' up dirt round their feet . . .

and all my men have Tower muskets. Good 'Brown Bess'! Along with one Pennsylvania, rifle, a fusil musket, and this rifled Ferguson of mine."

"Half a troop, sir, and I will bear all the responsibility for it!" Strickland swore.

"And, do remember two old military adages, Captain Veasey," Lewrie said with a quick laugh. "One, it's easier t'beg forgiveness than ask permission, and Two, success will always trump anything else!"

"Colonel Laird won't miss half a *troop*, sir," Strickland added. "Even if the regiment's loosed to hack through the whole Dutch Army! Let me go!"

Veasey's reddish-complexioned face looked even ruddier, and he twisted his features and groaned as if in great physical pain to make such a rash decision.

"Oh, very well, Strickland," he gruffed a long moment later, "but on your head be it, hear me?"

"Thank you, sir!" Strickland cried, wheeling his mount about to trot back down the line of their troop. "The two right files . . . prepare to dismount! Dis-mount! Horse holders, Sarn't Strode! Bring sabres and carbines, and follow me!"

"Up, Mister Westcott! Up, Mister Simcock!" Lewrie was yelling to his men at the same time as he sprinted back to them. "We've work t'do, up yonder on that knob t'the right."

"We're to get into a fight, sir?" Lt. Westcott asked, springing up from lolling on the grass.

"We are. The Dragoons're sendin' fourty men up to see what's waitin' for the infantry, and we're t'back 'em up," Lewrie cheerfully told him, as eager as a teen-ager at the prospect of action. "Choose two relatively sober hands . . . along with Pettus and Yeovill, to stay with the waggon and keep the cavalry troopers out of our goods whilst we're gone. Drop bed-rolls and packs in the waggon, bring nothing but water, weapons, and ammunition!"

Lt. Strickland and his fourty troopers were already moving past Lewrie's party before Lt. Simcock got his Marines sorted out into two files, and Lt. Westcott got the sailors into a somewhat organised herd. Strickland and his troopers looked oddly comical afoot, with sabres in one hand and their carbines in the other, and their tall knee-boots looked wholly un-suitable for dis-mounted work, especially so as they moved at the trot, half bent over as if that might hide them from the Dutch above.

"Double time," Lt. Simcock ordered, "and hang the step! Sling your muskets to keep your hands free."

Strickland led at the head of their re-enforced column, down below the crest of the saddle which lay between the first knob and the one at the end of the ridge. Lewrie looked up at their objective as he trotted along. The baboons had grazed their way a bit down the slope above them, still peacefully rooting for grubs, insects, and succulents. One or two of them took notice of their approach and stood on all four feet, heads swaying to right and left, and baring their long teeth in warning as they made tentative chuffing barks to alert the rest.

Hope that ain't an omen*!* Lewrie told himself; *Hope they don't alert the Dutch. Lousy, flea-ridden bastards!*

The first of Strickland's cavalrymen reached the base of the rise, halfway round from the line of the Blaauwberg's crest, and out of sight of any Dutch sentries at long last, and began to ascend, going much slower. Some had to drop halfway to their knees to use their hands to make the climb.

More baboons were barking warnings, the big males dashing a few feet forward, then back, as if they would fight for their hill.

BOOM! BOO-BOO-BOOM!

The British artillery had at last opened fire, and the roars from their muzzles were echoed seconds later by lesser but sharper cracks from air-bursting shrapnel shells above the Dutch positions.

"Come on, lads! No need for stealth, now! Go, go, go!" Lieutenant Strickland was shouting, echoed by Simcock to urge his Marines up and along behind the cavalrymen.

Now, all the baboons were barking and hooting shrill yells.

They ain't cheerin' us, that's for sure, Lewrie thought.

CHAPTER THIRTY

*B*y the time that Lewrie got to the top, Lt. Strickland had ordered his soldiers into two ranks, with their sheathed sabres at their feet, and loading and priming their carbines. He was in consultation with Lt. Simcock, who was nodding and agreeing with him.

"Ah, here we all are, sir!" Strickland gaily said. "I've suggested that Leftenant Simcock should place his Marines in two ranks on the right, and let your sailors fill the gap between, if you have no objections to that, Captain Lewrie."

"Sounds fine to me, sir," Lewrie allowed, after he'd worked up some saliva in his cottony-dry mouth; the ascent had been much steeper than it had first looked.

"I've also cautioned him that the Dutch have what looks to be a troop of Horse on the reverse slope, un-tended so far," Strickland went on. "Their riders must be dragoons like us, able to dis-mount and fight on foot. The slope from here to there is slight, but not too wide, thank the Lord, so if they mount up and charge us, they'll come on a narrow front."

"I see," Lewrie said, with half an ear for Strickland, and all his attention upon the view from his pocket telescope.

"If they do, best we shoot the horses, right off," Strickland suggested.

"If they get close enough to use their swords, tell your men to jab their mounts in the nose, the lips, and the eyes with bayonets or swords. That will always make them stop and rear, and then you can get at the riders."

"I'll see to instructing our people, sir," Lt. Westcott said, between deep breaths. "Don't believe we've met. I'm Westcott, First Lieutenant."

"Strickland, of the Thirty-fourth," the cavalry officer replied, offering his hand. "Your men are loaded and primed?"

"Loaded, not yet primed," Westcott told him, "which I'll also see to, this minute. Christ, there's rather a lot of them, aren't there?"

"At least a battalion," Strickland estimated, looking North along the ridge, "with a four-gun battery of artillery. Duck!"

Several shrapnel shells burst over the Dutch troops in yellow-white blossoms of smoke and fire, one of them near the left end of the lines, and almost uncomfortably close to the knob!

"I don't know if we can fire as efficiently as a well-drilled infantry battalion can," Strickland went on, after rising from a half-crouch, "but we might pull it off. My first rank will fire first, and then *your* first rank, sir," he said to Lewrie, "followed by Simcock's Marines. My first rank will be re-loading whilst my rear rank fires, and so on down our line, like the rolling and continuous platoon fire our infantry practices. I do not wish to sound as if I try to supplant your authority as the senior officer present, Captain Lewrie, but—"

"I'll take good suggestions from the more experienced, every time, Mister Strickland, and we'll try it your way," Lewrie assured him with a dis-arming smile. "You'd wish the front ranks kneeling, I take it, and the rear ranks crouching, rising to fire when ordered?"

"That would work, sir," Strickland agreed as another salvo of shells burst down the Dutch line.

Lewrie walked over to stand behind his sailors, who were passing horns of fine-mealed priming powder between them, drawing their firelocks to half-cock and opening the frizzens to expose the pans. After their first shots, they would tear their paper cartridges open with their teeth and sprinkle powder from the cartridges before pouring the rest down their muzzles.

Lewrie knelt and pulled his own copper priming flask round from being slung on his right hip, and did the same for all of his weapons, stuck all his pistols back into his sword belt or pockets, and rose to use his telescope once more.

Christ, there are *a lot of 'em!* he thought, wondering if he'd bitten off more than he could chew; wondering also what he had been thinking to bring his men right up to the "tip of the spear". There were four horse-drawn artillery pieces spaced down the Dutch lines, and an effort had been made to partially protect them with wood barriers under the barrels and down each side. That might have been good shelter from British guns firing uphill with roundshot, but nothing could hide from the shrapnel shells. So far in this war, Britain was the only nation that had them, and the French, or any of their allies, had yet to encounter their use. The gun teams . . . half their horses were down, already, and the gunners were cowering beneath the carriages and their own gun barrels! The poor infantry had dug some shallow trenches from which to shoot, but they were having a rough time of it, too!

"I think they'll break if we open upon them!" Lewrie shouted to Strickland, who nodded agreement. "Let's do! Ready, lads! Ready, Mister Simcock?"

"Front rank . . . *fire!*" Lt. Strickland cried.

"Front rank . . . fire!" Westcott ordered.

"Front rank . . . fire!" Lt. Simcock yelled, waving his sword.

Lewrie brought the Ferguson to his shoulder and looked for an officer. *There*—an older fellow with gilt epaulets and a bicorne hat! Lewrie took aim, a foot or so above the man's head, and pulled the trigger. A second or so later, the officer clutched his left side, looked down astonished, then crumpled up and sprawled flat on the ground. Lewrie quickly re-loaded, hunting for another even as his hands did the re-loading almost by rote. He saw a tall officer with bright blond hair and beard, waving a sword and shouting orders to his men, but that fellow's head exploded, and, over the crackling of their gunfire he heard a loud whoop down the line among the Marines, turned, and saw Simcock's sharpshooter pumping the borrowed Pennsylvania rifle in the air in triumph.

"Rear rank, fire!" from Simcock, then "Rear rank, fire!" from Strickland, and the ragged rolling platoon fire continued. At that range, well over one hundred yards, hits with smooth-bore muskets were nigh impossible, but some Dutch soldiers were down, and their bullets were kicking up puffs of dust or quick bursts of sparks when they hit the nearest artillery piece's barrel.

More shrapnel shells exploded over the Dutch, then the noise of battle was increased by the eerie skirling of Highland pipes and the rattle of drums as the 93rd Regiment stepped off. Beside them, the 38th began to march forward with their muskets poised as if for a full-out charge, and their bandsmen and drummers launched into their own march music.

"I think they've noticed us, sir!" Lt. Westcott shouted, his face twisted into a savage grin of joy. "We'll be having company in a minute or so!"

At least a company of Dutch infantry were leaving their lines, clambering out of the nearest trench where they had been sheltering, and began to form up in the open, three ranks deep. Lewrie put his Ferguson up to his eye, again, sought what he took to be their officer, held high, and fired. As the smoke from his lock and muzzle cleared, he could see that his shot had struck the fellow square in the chest, dropping him as if pole-axed, and spread like an X on the ground. It took the Dutch a gawping few seconds before that company's junior officer got them to move forward. Lewrie shot down a soldier in the front rank, who stumbled backwards into his rear-rank mates, slowing them a bit more.

Dutch cavalrymen who had been re-enforcing the lines scrambled out of the waist-deep trenches for their horses in the rear, on the reverse slope.

They'll saddle up and keep on goin', if they've any sense, he thought as he reloaded yet again; *But, no . . . they'll come up here!*

The Marine sharpshooter hit the officer at the head of their column as his horse reared and he waved his sword over his head to rally his men, and he reeled out of the saddle with one boot caught in the right-hand stirrup, to be dragged by his panicked mount down hill several yards before flopping free. The horse kept on going. Again, another junior officer took charge and urged the Dutch horsemen on, up the slope towards the centre of the British line, right at Lewrie's sailors. The crest of the ridge *was* narrow as it rose to their knob, so no more than seven or eight riders could attack them, pressed together knee-to-knee.

"Front rank, ready!" Lewrie shouted, dropping his Ferguson and pacing over to stand by the front rank of sailors. "Everyone, fix bayonets and remember t'stab the horses if they get close!"

Lewrie drew the first of his double-barrelled Manton pistols and cocked the right-hand lock, then drew his hanger to prepare for the onslaught.

"Hold fire 'til I order!" Westcott sternly cautioned. "Hold fire 'til we can see their *teeth,* then *skin* the bastards!"

"A pity, arrah, sor," Patrick Furfy said with a shake of his head, "I've always liked horses."

"You're worth more t'me and your shipmates than *ten* blooded hunters, Furfy!" Lewrie cried, laughing. "So be sure you kill them, no matter! That goes for all you lads! We'll show these Dutch sons of bitches they've messed with the wrong crew!"

A bugle was blown, and the Dutch horsemen launched into their charge, right off, with no trotting first to approach nearer. Their surviving officers must have wagered that they would suffer less if they closed quickly, with no messing about. Sabres were levelled with the points down and the cutting edges up, stiff-armed. Spurs were cruelly thrust upon their mounts to goad them into a full gallop, and harsh, howling cries came from the enemy troopers' throats.

"Steady . . . steady!" Westcott shouted.

The first rank was eight abreast, a wall of flesh and thundering hooves! Closer . . . closer . . . within fifty yards . . .

"First rank . . . fire!" Lewrie cried, thinking that he might have left it too late, and that dead horses might stumble onto his front-rank men, crushing them and opening everyone to being hacked to pieces.

No! Those first eight horses were down, kicking their legs in the air, flailing in their death throes and screaming! Half their riders were down, as well, shot and flung off, pinned under their dying horses' great weight with shattered legs or hips, or left helpless if they had managed to leap free of their saddles. The nearest dead horse was only six yards off, but that pile of downed horses made a sudden barrier to the next rank of eight. Their horses tripped over the ones which had preceded them, making an even bigger pile-up! The charge came to a sudden halt, with Dutch troopers savagely sawing their reins to keep from tumbling into the mess!

Gunfire from Simcock's Marines, and from Lt. Strickland's men, had not stopped, either, tearing at the Dutch cavalrymen from either flank and killing horses and men who rode behind the leaders.

"Second rank . . . fire!" Westcott shouted, and the Dutchmen who sat at the halt were hit and daunted, some shot from their saddles and others slumped low over their horses' necks, trying to turn about and go back down the slope. A bugle rang out and the rest wheeled round to retreat, still under fire, and did not stop 'til they were out of what they thought was musket-range, leaving at least two-dozen of their fellows behind.

There was a reef, a shoal, of dead horses in front of Lewrie's position, which he hoped would end any thoughts of a second try. There was still that company of infantry to deal with, though, coming up to within one hundred yards and almost in decent shooting range.

They're lookin' over their shoulders, though, Lewrie told himself as he dropped his spent Manton and went back to re-load his Ferguson. Sure enough, the British regiments were advancing smartly and almost within their own musket-range of the shallow Dutch trenches. The Dutch were firing at them, their artillerymen coming out of their dubious shelter and aiming their guns, readying with grapeshot loads or wicked canister. One artillery piece roared and rocked back on its trail, then another. From their knob above it all, Lewrie indeed had a grand view as the British infantry broke into a rapid uphill charge, their bayonets glittering, and hundreds of wild and feral cries, with the pipers of the 93rd breaking into what sounded as urgent as a reel, a demonic war cry all of its own.

"They're breaking!" Lt. Strickland shouted, standing fully erect and waving his sabre over his head in glee. "They're running!"

The Dutch cavalry troop gave the situation a quick look, and wheeled about by fours to clatter away, downhill for the plain below with hardly a backward glance.

"Huzzah! Huzzah!" the men on the knob were shouting as the British charge reached the trenches, and the Colours were carried forward. The Dutch infantry would not be as lucky as their cavalry, for they could not retreat as fast. They melted away, abandoning the trenches and turning their backs in flight. Those unable to scramble out, the laggards and the slowest, got swarmed over by British red and bayonetted. Some knelt in surrender, holding their muskets in the air or planting them muzzle down in front of them, and others just abandoned their weapons and ran like skittered deer. British blood was up, though, and the attacking troops had taken casualties and lost mates. Not all those Dutch who surrendered were taken prisoner; it would be a minute or so before sanity was restored.

The Dutch company that had tried to come up the hill to attack them were now trapped between Lewrie's position and the British infantry who were now rampaging down the line of shallow trenches, looking for someone to shoot or bayonet. That company was now a herd of terrified men looking in all directions and looking for escape, which was now cut off. Their own retreating cavalry had delayed them too long.

"You, down there!" Lewrie shouted in his best quarterdeck roar. "Surrender to us!" He pumped both arms up several times. "Surrender! Bloody Hell, Mister Westcott. How did our old Master Gunner, Rahl, say it in German? That's *close* t'Dutch, ain't it?"

"Haven't a single clue, really, sir," Westcott said, shrugging.

"*Soldaten!*" Lt. Strickland yelled, raising his own arms as if giving up. "*Haende hoch! Kapitulation! Hinlegen deine waffen!*"

The Dutch soldiers dropped their muskets as if they were red-hot fireplace pokers, and littered the ground round them with shakoes, cartridge boxes, hangers, and equipment belts, and knelt with their hands high over their heads in a twinkling.

"What was all that, after *soldaten*?" Lewrie asked him.

"Told them to put their hands up, surrender, and drop their weapons," Strickland said with a grin. "I had a German nanny," he further explained, "and she was a right bitch."

"Whatever, it worked," Lewrie said. "D'ye think our own soldiers've lost their 'mad', or should we stay up here awhile more? I'd not like my men shot 'cause they're not wearin' red."

"Oh, I think it's safe enough now, Captain Lewrie," Strickland allowed. "The rest of the Heavy Brigade is coming up in march order."

Sure enough, the two attacking regiments had rushed on past the Dutch trenches and were moving down the East side of the Blaauwberg in skirmish order, their light companies firing at the fleeing Dutch survivors now and then. The other regiments of the Heavy Brigade were coming up towards the crest in columns-of-fours with their drums rattling the pace. Bandsmen and surgeons from the 38th and 93rd were busy picking among the few British casualties, or pilfering from the Dutch dead and wounded, on the sly.

"Canteens, sir." Lt. Westcott pointed downhill to their prisoners. "We should go take possession of some, whilst we see to our own wounded."

"Get them down so the Army surgeons can see to 'em, aye," Lewrie agreed. "How many, Mister Westcott?"

"One hand dead, sir, two wounded," Lt. Westcott told him as he took a deep drink from his wine bottle canteen. "Those two not badly, thank God. We've lost one Marine dead, and one wounded, as well. Durbin is tending them, but he will need assistance from the Army."

Lewrie looked down-slope for a way to leave their knob. Horses and dead Dutch cavalrymen blocked the easiest way, many of the horses still screaming and thrashing.

"First off, Mister Westcott, have the lads shoot those poor horses, and see that all our muskets are empty," Lewrie ordered. "If the Dragoons will . . . Ah, Mister Strickland!" he gladly said, spotting him. "If you'd be so good as to take charge of our prisoners, whilst we clear the way for our wounded? Good. Were any of your men hurt or killed?"

"No dead, sir, and only two lightly wounded. We came off rather easily, altogether," Strickland reported, "though it seems that your men took the brunt of it, holding the centre of our line."

"Once down with the nearest regiment, please direct their surgeon in our direction, sir, and we'll try to move our wounded to them," Lewrie requested. Strickland saluted and set off.

"Mister Rossyngton?" Lewrie called over his shoulder.

"Aye, sir?" the Midshipman replied.

"You've young and sturdy legs," Lewrie said. "Do you run down to our waggon and order it up."

"At once, sir!" Rossyngton said, doffing his hat and setting off at trots and bounds.

I just hope no one takes him for Dutch in his blue coat, and shoots him! Lewrie thought.

He went to where their Surgeon's Mate, Durbin, was binding up his men's wounds, and knelt and spoke words of assurance and thanks to them.

"Beg pardon, sir," Durbin said, "but, do we take the blankets from the dead Dutchies' bed-rolls, we can fashion ways to bear our men down the hill."

"Aye, see to it," Lewrie agreed.

That scavenging, and the slow procession of bearing both dead and wounded off the knob, was a gruesome ordeal. There were nearly fifteen or so dead horses which had to be bridged, and dead Dutchmen to be stepped and stumbled over, with here and there some few cruelly wounded, some still pinned under their dead mounts, who reached out with weak, bloodied hands, crying *"Hilfe!"* and *"Wasser!"* Sailors who were not carrying their mates bent down to give them a drink, a pat on the shoulder, but there was little they could do for them, not 'til all the British wounded had been seen to. That was the necessary triage following combat. Lewrie looked up to the morning sky and grimaced at the sight of hideous vultures already circling, and daring to swoop near the corpses round the Dutch trenches. The warm, coppery reek of spilled blood was almost as strong as the stink of voided men's bowels and un-ravelled horse intestines.

At last, they got past the last of the Dutch casualties, and reached the South end of the Dutch trenches, where Army bandsmen were already carrying dead soldiers, British to one trench and Dutch to another, for a quick burial.

Lewrie stood and watched as Durbin had his two dead borne to the appropriate trench, and began to compose some final words in his head to see them off. He had left his Book of Common Prayer aboard ship, and would have to depend on an Army chaplain for the bulk of it. He was interrupted, though, by loud shouts, and turned about.

"You, there! You, sir!" a senior officer of cavalry shouted, coming on astride a glossy horse with a long riding crop in a gauntletted hand. "Come here at once, do you hear me? I've a *bone* t'pick with you!"

Damned if I ain't gettin' tired o' bein' shouted at! Lewrie fumed inside; *From the Thirty-fourth? Their Colonel? Serve him sweetness and light, old son . . . sweetness and light.* He put a faint smile on his face and raised a brow as if hailed by an old school chum.

"Good morning, sir!" Lewrie perkily said, doffing his hat. "I take it that you are Colonel Laird of the Thirty-fourth Light Dragoons? Sorry we have not yet made acquaintance. I am Captain Sir Alan Lewrie, Baronet, of the *Reliant* frigate, which escorted part of your regiment."

"I *know* who you are, sir, and I am indeed Colonel of the Thirty-fourth Dragoons!" the livid fellow barked. "Those fools, Veasey and Strickland, have already informed me of your high-handed actions which instigated this idiocy!" he roared, sweeping a hand towards the carnage on the knob. "How dare you! Who gave you the right to order my officers about, deprive me of half a troop, and lead them into un-necessary peril, sir? Damme, had we gotten orders to charge this position, I would have been under-strength!"

"Captain Veasey, Leftenant Strickland, and I considered it a reconnaisance in force, since the knob was un-occupied, sir, so we came up to discover the enemy's forces," Lewrie replied as congenial and casually conversational as he could and still smile. "It worked, as you see."

"Damn your *eyes*, sir!" Colonel Laird exploded, frightening his horse into shivers, circles, and flat-eared, eye-blared dread. "I'll not have a

bloody *sailor,* who knows nothing of proper military tactics, play 'tin soldiers' with *my* regiment! And, just what the Hell are you doing up *here* in
the first place?"

"We're part of the Naval Brigade that Commodore Popham offered
to General Baird, sir, under the command of Captain Byng of the *Belliqueux,*" Lewrie sweetly answered, shifting the sling of his rifled musket on his shoulder. "We were landed to get the siege guns ashore, and
re-enforce the guard on the baggage train. We came up alongside the
train, sir."

"The bloody baggage train is still far down bloody *there!*" Colonel
Laird howled, pointing downhill to the West, where the regiments of the
Light Brigade were now tramping up the slope to the crest of the Blaauw-
berg. "Damme if I do not settle you, this instant, Lewrie, for here comes
General Sir David Baird. I will see you brought before a *court!* I will see
you *sacked!*"

Colonel Laird snatched the reins of his horse and sped away at a brisk
gait towards a clutch of senior officers at the head of the first regiment of
the Light Brigade.

"Ehm . . . our waggon is coming up, sir," a cautious Midshipman
Warburton announced, daring a grimace of worry. "Should I see our
wounded into it when it arrives, sir?"

"Do so, Mister Warburton," Lewrie told him, "and break out the spare
scuttle-butt. Our people will have need of replenishing their water bottles when the waggon's up."

"Warm work, indeed, sir," Warburton commented, then went to his
work.

"Mister Westcott, let's see to collecting those canteens from the Dutch
prisoners," Lewrie ordered.

"Aye, sir," his First Officer replied.

Minutes later, and Westcott was back, to whisper, "Trouble's coming,
sir," as General Baird, Brigadier Beresford, and their staff came over.
Lewrie tried not to wince, for that supercilious officer they'd met by the
baggage train was with them, as was Colonel Laird.

He set his shoulders, un-slung his champagne bottle canteen, and took
a sip to moisten his suddenly dry mouth, wondering if he really *was* "in
the quag" up to his neck, this time.

"He's *drunk,* by God!" Colonel Laird exclaimed. "*That* explains his actions, Sir David! Just as Mortimer here saw earlier. They *all* are! See those wine bottles, sir?"

"Good morning, sir," Lewrie said, ignoring that rant, doffing his hat to the senior officers with more deference. "I would offer you some of our water, General Baird, but I fear it comes from our butts aboard *Reliant*, and is rather stale, by now," and went to explain again how they had had to improvise before coming ashore.

General Baird took the offered bottle just long enough for a quick sniff, wrinkling his nose. "Well, I do remember how foul water becomes, after a few months in cask, Captain Lewrie," he said in a rather kindly way. "What happened up here? Colonel Laird seems to think that you have acted rashly with some of his troops."

"In point of fact, sir, it was a co-operative endeavour that could not have succeeded without the participation of the Thirty-fourth, and the skill and experience of Leftenant Strickland and his half-troop," Lewrie replied.

Out of the corner of his eye, Lewrie saw disaster looming, of a sudden, and he tried not to quail. His sailors had approached the Dutch prisoners and had gotten their wood canteens, here and there in exchange, but mostly by appropriation by the victors. Patrick Furfy and a few others were looking just *too* damned sly-boots as they took sips, sniffed with sudden delight, and tipped the canteens back for deeper quaffs. It wasn't just British soldiers and sailors who were mad for drink, any sort of alcoholic guzzle; the Dutch soldiers were just as guilty, and had filled their canteens with rum, brandy, or the national "treasure", gin!

Trust Furfy t'find it, and get howlin' drunk! Lewrie winced.

Ignoring that, while twitching the fingers of his left hand to Westcott to see to the problem, he genially laid out the situation, the possibilities, and what actions they had taken.

"Just as the shrapnel shells began to burst over 'em, sir," he related, "we opened upon 'em. They had about five or six hundred men in all, and they pulled one infantry company out of line, and a troop of dis-mounted cavalry, t'deal with us, weakening the line. You can see the results, sir."

"So, you did not play too high a hand, Captain Lewrie?" Baird asked, nodding his head in appreciation.

"Captain Veasey let Leftenant Strickland take half a troop, sir, and it was he who led the way and set us in our defensive positions, and instructed us both in how to receive cavalry and in how to deliver rolling volley fire, sir. In point of fact, it was more my lending him my men to his command than t'other way round."

"Well, he is to be commended, then," General Baird decided, "as is your regiment, Colonel Laird."

"But, Sir David—!" Laird spluttered, red in the face, nigh *puce* with indignation.

General Baird grimaced at Laird's overly-familiar use of his Christian name. "Sir Alan is to be commended, as well, Laird," he said, stiffening his back, and making it quite clear that Laird was over-reaching. "Rest assured that your regiment, your junior officers, and Sir Alan will be mentioned favourably in my reports to Horse Guards, and Admiralty," he added, with a brief grin and nod in Lewrie's direction. "Will that be all, Laird?"

"Uhm, well . . . ," the deflated, frustrated Colonel managed to gravel out.

"Then do you take your regiment forward of the Heavy Brigade and scout by troops for the main Dutch force, sir," General Baird ordered. "Find them, and report back, leaving a screen."

"Yes, sir, at once," Laird said, his chin tucked hard into his stiff collars, and spurred away.

"Just what *are* you doing so far forward, Captain Lewrie?" the General enquired once Laird was gone.

"Guarding the baggage train, sir, and getting shoved out of the line of march," Lewrie explained with a shrug, "and made our own way."

"Then do you wait 'til the baggage train is over the Blaauwberg and fall in with it," Baird directed. "It may be best did you remain with it, the rest of the way, you know. I expect a hard battle with the Dutch before the day is out, and your wee lot would be of little help. You were lucky once," Baird said, with a brow up.

"Once is quite enough, thankee, sir," Lewrie replied, feeling sheepish.

Baird and his party wheeled away and clopped off, over the crest and downhill to the East, leaving Lewrie to finally let out a long-pent whoosh of relief.

Hah! Cheated Death, and Ruin, again! he told himself.

"Furfy!" he called out. "You men with him? The First Officer will be smellin' those canteens ye pilfered. If there's spirits in 'em, best pour it out, now. The Bosun's Mate brought a 'cat' ashore with him, don't ye know."

"Breakin' me heart, arrah," Furfy muttered, sorrowfully turning his new Dutch canteen bung-down and spilling its contents on the dust of Africa.

"When the waggon's up, we'll re-fill with water," Lewrie told them all, "but, we'll also break open the cask of small beer."

"Huzzah!"

CHAPTER THIRTY-ONE

*H*oy, the boat!" Midshipman Munsell hailed the barge as it approached.

"*Reliant*!" Cox'n Liam Desmond shouted back from the bows and showed four fingers to indicate the size of the side-party required to receive the frigate's commanding officer back aboard. Sailors scrambled to toe the line of deck planks, and Bosun Sprague piped a long call as the barge came alongside and Captain Lewrie ascended the boarding battens to the entry-port, still laden with weapons. Once at the top and in-board on the starboard gangway, Lewrie doffed his hat to one and all, beaming fit to bust. Lt. Spendlove was his usual rather serious self, but could not hide a grin. Lt. Merriman, of a more cheerful nature, was almost chortling.

"Welcome back aboard, sir," Spendlove intoned. "And, might I enquire how things went ashore, sir?"

"Just topping bloody *capital*, Mister Spendlove!" Lewrie said in high spirits. "Mister Merriman? Did things go well aboard? I see the French didn't turn up. Well, hallo, Bisquit!" he cried, kneeling down as the ship's dog pranced about in tail-wagging glee. "Here, I brought ye a *fine* new bone, and some *biltong*, to boot! It's a stout impala bone, and the *biltong*'s hartebeest. Ain't that tasty? Aye! No fear, there's two hundredweight comin' aboard."

He got back to his feet and began to shed his Ferguson and the Girandoni air-rifle, and his pistols, piling all that ironmongery on the binnacle cabinet.

"Things went very well, sir," Lt. Spendlove reported. "We've been anchored here in Table Bay two days now, ever since word came of the Dutch surrender. I saw to our old water butts getting emptied and scrubbed out, and fresh shore water taken aboard."

"Very good, sir," Lewrie said with a glad nod. "We were told of *one* Dutch warship, over in False Bay. What of her?"

"The *Bato*, sir, sixty-eight," Lt. Merriman said. "Commodore Popham sent one of the other frigates round to see to her, but the Dutch burned her to the waterline before she could be made prize. We *heard* there was a battle, but so far no one's told us anything. May we prevail upon you—?"

"Over supper tonight, once Pettus and Yeovill get me set back up," Lewrie promised. "Aye, there was, and the Army went through the Dutch like a dose o' salts. We had a grand view of it. And, a grand time ashore, too. Now Cape Town's ours, and the Army garrisons it, I have hopes our people will be allowed shore liberty for a rare once. No risk of 'em takin' 'leg bail' in a foreign country, hey?"

"Welcome back aboard, Mister Westcott . . . Mister Simcock," Lt. Spendlove said in greeting as the other two officers gained the deck. "I gather we missed a grand adventure?"

"Didn't you just!" Westcott hooted in glee. "Camping out in the open, sleeping rough, getting in some grand hunting and shooting? Campfires, roast game meat by the *pound*, as much as a man could cram down every night, and not an ounce of salt-meat junk boiled once we set foot ashore! Washed down with small beer or *rooibos* each night!"

"It's a native bush the Khoikhoi . . . what people call the Hottentots nowadays . . . brew up," Lewrie supplied, "and it makes a grand substitute for tea."

"There will be several pounds of it coming aboard, so you may try it," Westcott assured them. "With sugar, it's delicious."

"We even had a chance t'have our laundry done, as will you all once you get ashore," Lewrie told them. "And hot fresh water to bathe in, too."

"And are the Dutch laundresses handsome, Mister Wescott?" Merriman teased.

"Handsome, sturdy, blond, and *most* obliging," their ever-randy First Officer said with a devilish grin.

The second barge was coming alongside with half of the Marines aboard. Pettus and Yeovill had accompanied Lewrie in the first, and Lewrie felt that he could quit the deck and retire to his cabins.

"Warn Mister Cooke that there will be lashin's of fresh game meat comin' aboard later for the hands' supper for him to roast," Lewrie said to Spendlove. "Onions, fresh fruits, potatoes, God knows what-all. I will be below."

Once Lewrie was in his great-cabins, Chalky sprang off the bed and ran to him, tail high and meowing loudly in complaint. Lewrie scooped him up and carried him to the desk in the day-cabin to give him all the "wubbies" the cat demanded, at least 'til all the greetings had been made, and Chalky began to nip and swat at his fingers in lively play.

"Has Chalky behaved himself, Jessop?" Lewrie asked his cabin servant. "More to the point, have you been behaving yourself?"

"He missed ya somethin' fierce, sir, slinkin' about lookin' for ya," Jessop replied, "an' meowin' right pitiful. An' aye, sir. I behaved. Might ya care for somethin' t'drink, sir?"

"A Rhenish'd be welcome," Lewrie said, going to the settee on the starboard side to put up his booted feet and slouch into the cushions. "Aah!" he said with pleasure to have something soft under his backside, at long last, and to rest his tortured feet.

"Lord, who'd be a soldier," he said with a long sigh, after a first deep sip of his wine, and laid his head back and closed his eyes.

With their dead interred alongside the few slain from the two attacking regiments of the Heavy Brigade, Lewrie led his party and the trundling waggon down from the Blaauwberg to the interior, following a long, snaking column of infantry, cavalry, and the field artillery, and the dust clouds which all those booted feet, hooves, and wheels roiled up. That journey was like an ant descending the inside of a gigantic punch bowl, for, once past the coastal mountain chain, they caught sight of even more rugged, taller, and more impressive mountains and buttes that seemed to ring the plains on every hand.

The plains themselves rolled gently, sprinkled with knobs or *kloofs* of up-thrusting bare rock. On those plains they encountered their first farmsteads, with houses and barns and outbuildings made of stone and stuccoed stark white, surrounded by orchards and grain fields, paddocks and pastures filled with reddish cattle, all miles apart from each other, and too far away from the line of march for any foraging for fruit or the odd chicken.

At least they were at the head of the baggage train, half of which had yet to descend the Blaauwberg, and close up with the trundling gun-carriages, limbers, and caissons. They even had time to stop and dole out the first rum ration of the day at half-past Eleven of the morning before being overtaken.

An hour or two later, urgent bugle calls stopped the columns and shook both brigades out into lines, and the artillery left them almost at the gallop. Lewrie spotted a low rise off to their left and directed his men to go there.

He would not press his luck a second time; he and his sailors and Marines would be mere witnesses. And, once settled at their ease on the rise, what a grand view they had! It *was* like lead soldiers on the children's room carpet as five thousand British soldiers formed long lines, with the drums rolling and the regimental bands playing, the bright colours waving, and the elegantly uniformed cavalry trotting or cantering to either flank.

They had found the Dutch, and they would make a fight of it, at last. Everyone with a pocket telescope stood and fidgeted with anxiety and excitement, and the Midshipmen counted the Dutch artillery and made estimates of enemy strength.

Five thousand Dutch soldiers, at least a third to a half of them cavalry or dis-mounted dragoons, or mounted infantry, and there were at least twenty Dutch field pieces, arrayed in line of battle the equal of British strength, but that made no difference. Bugles, drums, martial airs, and skirling bagpipes blared, the British guns barked, bucked, and roared, and Col. Shrapnel's deadly bursting shot decimated the Dutch as both British brigades marched up to the range of musketry and began the continuous rolling volleys at three rounds a minute from each man. The British Army was the only one in Europe to practice regular live-fire musketry, and that steady hail of lead melted the Dutch away. Then the bright winks of sun on steel could be seen as the regiments fixed bayonets, the roars from the throats of five thousand men could be heard as the regiments were loosed at the charge, and it was over. The Dutch broke, turned their backs to their foe, scrambled for their horses, abandoned most of their guns, and ran, or surrendered in place!

Once their cheers had died down, and the last hat recovered after being flung aloft in triumph, Lewrie led his party forward, eager for loot and souvenirs . . . and some spare Dutch horses to ride. They found plenty of all their wants: shakoes and hats, brass plaques from enemy cross-belts, more wood canteens, spare wool and cotton stockings from spilled and abandoned packs, extra blankets and groundcloths for bedding, and farm lads from the crew managed to round up and calm enough horses for all officers and Midshipmen to ride. Even so, Lewrie and his men were pikers when it came to looting compared to the soldiers of the British Army, and their appalled officers' attempts to quell the looting of the Dutch baggage train and stores of wine and spirits let Lewrie and his men make their pickings without notice.

The Army camped on the near banks of the Salt River for the night to await the arrival of the siege artillery, and Lewrie laid out their own separate camp, cautioned his men to take sticks and beat the ground from the centre outwards to drive away any snakes, saw firewood gathered and Yeovill put to work with a cookfire before he, Lt. Simcock, and Lt. West-cott rode out to do some hunting. They came back with three native antelopes, grysboks, and a bushbuck, had them butchered, the hides and offal thrown into the river so predators would not raid their camp at night, and spitted them on frames made from Dutch muskets and barrels. With cheese, ship's bisquit, small beer or *rooibos* tea, everyone deemed it a feast, and every man rolled into his bedding round the campfires that night feeling stuffed and sated, most of them who were *not* poachers back home in England tasting their very first game meat!

The rest had been anti-climactic, a stroll through a parkland. The siege guns came up, the army marched on Cape Town, and word came that the Dutch governor of the Cape, Van Prophelow, would negotiate. In sign of that, he allowed Fort Knocke to be occupied, and Lewrie's party could boil up salt rations in the shelter of the fort's courtyard, marvelling at the number and great calibres of the guns mounted there. On the morning of the 10th of January, Van Prophelow formally surrendered, and the enemy general they had defeated, Jannsens, who had retreated with the remnants of his army to Holland's Hottentot Kloof, surrendered as well.

They were idle all the next day, but took part in the victory parade into

Cape Town itself on the 12th, found that all the taverns and eateries that Lewrie fondly remembered were open for business, and that Dutch beers flowed freely at the cost of only a few pence.

Lt. Westcott did ask if Lewrie also knew the locations of the best brothels, but that knowledge was ten years out of date, and he would have to fend for himself!

If there was anything to mar their merry jaunt, it was a confrontation with Captain Byng of *Belliqueux,* who was irked that he'd been counting on *all* landed sailors and Marines to help get the siege guns and carriages ashore, and Lewrie had run off on his own to play a game of soldiers, *very* loosely mis-interpreting his orders!

"You've a *name* for scraping, Lewrie, so I can understand *why* you dashed off for more derring-do, but you can't have fun *all* the time," Byng had chid him, and that not all that sternly, "now and then, you *must* join in at the onerous pulley-hauley with the rest of us!"

That reverie made Lewrie smile, and Chalky's arrival in his lap, then onto his chest, made him open his eyes. He took another sip of wine, and then it was back to routine. Yeovill was announced and given leave to enter the cabins to make the arrangements for the supper for all officers and Mids not on Harbour Watch that evening. Guinea fowl from shore would be one course, ham for another, some fresh-caught yellowtail would be the fish course, and beef steaks would complete it. There would be baked rolls, boiled maize and garden peas, snap beans and sauteed onions, and dessert would be strawberries and cream over pound cake.

"Am I allowed ashore with the Purser tomorrow, sir, I can have a wider selection," Yeovill boasted, as if his best efforts would not be up to his standards that evening. "What little I saw in the local markets today, well! What a selection of East Indian spices, and the sauces the Malays and Hindoos who live hereabouts make!"

"Aye, it appears that Cape Town ain't just the 'tavern of the seas', but the pantry as well," Lewrie agreed. "Carry on, Yeovill, and surprise me tomorrow night."

"Do my best, sir!" he promised.

A Marine sentry guarded his cabin door again, and that worthy stamped boots, slammed his musket on the deck, and shouted, "First Officer, SAH!"

"Enter," Lewrie called out, sitting up a bit more.

Lt. Westcott entered, looking natty and clean in his freshly-laundered clothing, but with his inevitable sheaf of paperwork.

"A glass of something for you, Mister Westcott?" Lewrie asked.

"A Rhenish, if you'd be so kind, sir," Westcott said, baring one of his brief, savage grins. Lewrie waved him to a seat by the settee. "I have made a tentative change or two to the muster book, sir, to compensate for the men Discharged, Dead. Our wounded are at present being tended ashore by the Army surgeons, but look fair to heal up and return to us . . . if only on light duties for a week or so afterwards. Mister Mainwaring will surely request a chance to go ashore and see to them."

"He'll also wish t'palaver with strange, new 'saw-bones'," Lewrie said with a snicker. "Must be a lonely lot, a surgeon on a warship, with no contact with others in his trade for months and months on end. And, I'm certain that Mainwaring will also wish to re-stock his dispensary ashore. He'll be free to take a boat with the Purser, any time he wishes, tell him."

"Aye, sir," Westcott said, nodding as he ticked off one item of his report. "Ehm . . . once we've re-stocked the ship, there will be the matter of liberty. Will it be shore liberty, or should we put the ship Out Of Discipline for a day or two, and let the doxies and bum-boatmen aboard, sir?"

"I'll speak with Commodore Popham tomorrow on that subject," Lewrie promised. "As I said earlier, now we own the Cape Colony, and our troops garrison and patrol the town, shore liberty should be of as little risk of desertion as any island port."

He stifled a sudden yawn, a real jaw-cracker.

I might not stay awake *long enough t'dine my guests in!* Lewrie thought; *Go face-down in the soup if I do? The last few days've been a lot more strenuous than I thought. Damme, am I gettin' . . . old? A nap 'twixt now and then is definitely in order!*

"All the hands have settled back in, sir," Westcott told him, "though the people left aboard are jealous. There's quite a trade in looted items for cash, or promised shares in the rum ration."

"No one managed t'smuggle any new pets aboard, did they? No bush-babies, mongooses?" Lewrie asked.

"Mongeese, sir?" Westcott said with a smirk. "No, sir, we saw to that. We'll have to keep a sharp eye, though, when the bum-boatmen traders come out to the ship . . . with or without the whores. In the markets we saw, there were quite a lot of colourful caged birds. Do we allow the men shore liberty, they'll surely try to come back with something amusing."

"Well, caged birds maybe, but I draw the line at monkeys," Lewrie said, laughing, welcoming Pettus as he came with the wine bottle to top them both up. "Shore liberty'd be best, all round, I believe, and I'll argue for it. The men who stayed aboard will be sullen if they're not allowed a chance t'see all that our landing party did. Have enough hot water for decent baths, and their clothes laundered in something besides salt water?"

"Lastly, sir, there's our . . . stowaway, Private Dodd," the First Officer said in a softer voice, as if some Army officer was listening. "We will have to make arrangements with his unit."

Their "shanghaied" waggoner, Private Dodd, had found the issue of rum *twice* a day, with a gallon of small beer allowed for every man per day as well, just too enticing. He had been trained with the musket, and had "square-bashed" before being shuffled off into a transport company, and had shyly offered his services to Lt. Simcock as a replacement in the Marine complement.

"They'll stop his pay and tell his kinfolk that he deserted or went missing in battle if we don't, sir," Westcott said, with a brow up.

"I know, I know," Lewrie groused. "That'll be one more task for me t'deal with. I'll go ashore tomorrow and speak with his commanding officer. I *hope* they'll let him go. If not, perhaps we could trade one of our worst lubbers for him. Anyone in mind, right off?" he asked Westcott.

"What, sir?" Lt. Westcott hooted in mirth. "Take a perfectly good sailor and hand him over to the misery of being a redcoat? Perish the thought, sir!"

"Well, I made them *all* into redcoats, for a few days," Lewrie said, laughing along with him.

"Aye, sir, and I won't be the same man 'til I've had a new pair of boots made, or my old ones re-soled," Westcott said, shaking his head. "Who'd be a soldier, hey, sir?"

"Who'd be a soldier, indeed, Mister Westcott," Lewrie agreed.

"I think that is all for today, sir," Westcott told him. "I believe the biggest concerns for the next few days will be the victualling and watering to Mister Cadbury's content." He shuffled his papers one last time as if looking for a topic he'd forgotten, then got to his feet. "I will take my leave, sir."

"See you at supper, the middle of the Second Dog," Lewrie told him, rising to see him out.

"Anything else, sir?" Pettus asked.

"Lay the table, set out the wines on the sideboard, and have an eye towards my best-dress uniform for the morning, with all of the frippery attached," Lewrie instructed with a slight sneer. "Commodore Popham don't like me showin' up without 'em, as if I'm a pauper. Make sure Chalky doesn't get at it before I put it on, though. Commodore Popham most-like doesn't care for cat hair, either."

"Aye, sir," Pettus said with a smile.

He sure as Hell didn't care for my appearance when he met me ashore, Lewrie thought; *He didn't even like my borrowed horse!*

As soon as Fort Knocke had been surrendered and taken over by General Baird's troops, and the eastern end of Cape Town was safely in British hands, the Commodore had come ashore to take part in the negotiations for the Cape Colony's complete surrender, natty in a dress uniform complete with sash and star of his own knighthood, his boots blackened and polished to a high gleam, with a fore-and-aft bicorne hat adrip with gold lace. A Dutch senior officer's horse had been provided him at once, a glossy blooded hunter, and he had ridden the bounds of the fort and nearby environs with Baird and his staff as grandly as King George taking the air in Hyde Park.

Then he met Lewrie—he whose boots were still filthy, with begrimed breeches, stained with saddle leather, dust, spent gunpowder smoke, and the juices of roast game meat, whose shirt collars and neck-stock were sweat-stained and loose, whose waist-coat also bore the mark of rough feeding, and whose older-style cocked hat had turned tannish with African dust, and lacked its "dog's vane" cockade, which had been shot off. At the moment, Lewrie was in need of a shave, to boot.

"Good God, sir!" Popham had grimaced. "You must send to your ship for better uniform at once, Lewrie. What will the Dutch think of us to see our officers so . . . scruffy?"

To which Lewrie had replied, "They'll be studyin' the toes of their shoes, sir, in shame of their defeat, rather than lookin' at us."

And when the Dutch governor had formalised the surrender, and the British had marched into the town to take possession of it and the seaward fortress, Popham, in the vanguard of the parade, looking as if he would wave to expected cheers from the conquered, barely had more than a dis-believing glance at Lewrie, who had stubbornly stayed in his shabby condition.

"Clean hands and fingernails, Jessop," Lewrie said, coming back from that rather sweet reverie.

"Right, sir . . . if I must," the lad answered.

"Must and shall, you scamp," Lewrie shot back, grinning. "For now, I think I'll take a wee nap in a soft bed, for a change."

"It does make a nice change, sir," Pettus agreed. "Same as I'm looking forward to my hammock tonight, after all that hard ground, and all the bugs."

"Sorry I put you through that," Lewrie apologised, yawning.

"Oh *no*, sir!" his cabin steward exclaimed. "Why, I wouldn't have missed it for anything, and I'm glad you took me along, for it was a grand adventure, and a rare thing to see! The beasts, the scenery, and the battle? Even if we didn't see any elephants."

"Well, I'm glad someone liked it," Lewrie said with a laugh. "And, do we spend much time anchored in Table Bay, you may see your elephants yet. Wake me one hour before the supper. Here, Chalky! I need pesterin'!"

He rolled into his swaying bed-cot, plumped up the damp and mildew-smelling pillows, and was out to the world within a minute, oblivious to his cat's wee *mew*s for more attention. Chalky tried pawing, to no avail. Finally, he padded up to the pillows and lay down nose-to-nose and employed the intent, concentrated stare that made humans uncomfortable enough to wake. But no, even that did not work this time. Chalky gave up and slinked round to cuddle against his master's chest, closed his eyes, and waited for later.

CHAPTER THIRTY-TWO

*P*ettus, and the rest of *Reliant*'s crew, got to see their elephants, and a great many other beasts, on their shore liberties, and got a few hours of perfect ease in Cape Town's public houses, eateries, and brothels. As important as Cape Town was as a mid-way stop-over point for the rich China and East Indies trade, though, it was not all that large a place, so liberty had to be rationed. At least half of General Baird's five thousand soldiers garrisoned the fortresses with the rest out scouting and mapping at any given time, so they placed a heavy burden on the taverns, eateries, and whores, so shore liberty had to be given to only one watch of each ship in turn, to the two-decker warships first, which ate up several days before the frigates were allowed to send only half their crews ashore in rotation on any given day.

Officers were another matter, of course, since they did not stand Harbour Watches in port, and they were allowed ashore by their captains as often as they wished, barring demands of the service. It was safe enough to allow shore leave, even in what had been a hostile foreign harbour, for Cape Town and its environs were well-patrolled by the Army, and the terms of surrender offered to the Dutch were of so mild a nature that most locals simply shrugged their shoulders and submitted to new masters with little ill will.

The Dutch army of around five thousand men had lost seven hundred in killed and wounded, and perhaps two or three hundred more who had just ridden off and disappeared before the formal surrender; local militia men who would not leave their families and lands. What uniforms they had worn they had shed, and had melted back into the back country, some to hitch their waggons, gather their cattle, their horses, and their Hottentot slaves, and trek off for the wild frontiers of Cape Colony. The bulk of them, though, were offered return to Holland in British transports, at British expense, after giving their parole not to take arms against Great Britain 'til properly exchanged for British prisoners of equal rank. And, since the British Army and the Dutch Army had not faced each other in the field since the disastrous expedition into the Low Countries in 1798, those returnees would be twiddling their thumbs on parole for a long time to come!

Lewrie and his officers enjoyed their jaunts ashore, as well. There were hunting parties with proper tents and camp equipment, this time, and lots of game meat wolfed down round blazing campfires, with selected seamen accompanying them. They organised sports competitions, watch against watch, and ship against ship, in open fields out past Fort Knocke. Lt. Westcott sketched and painted everything in sight—when he wasn't chasing quim—and Lt. Spendlove satisfied his curiosity about Africa's exotic *flora* and *fauna,* whilst Lt. Merriman and Marine Lt. Simcock revelled in galloping rented horses 'til they and their mounts were worn quite out and soaked in sweat, returning to the ship still whooping their triumphs at races against the officers of the 34th or the 20th Light Dragoons, or the local equivalent of steeplechasing.

For a time, Lewrie hoped that he would be assigned to escort the Dutch back to Europe; in point of fact he was sure that *Reliant* would be given the task by the odd way that Commodore Popham looked at him whenever they met face-to-face. Popham was "hail fellow, well met" with almost everyone he dealt with, but Lewrie sensed a faint distaste towards him. The odd, lifted brow, the tongue-in-cheek comments anent his shore adventures, and the way Popham would cock his head and leer in his direction amongst the meetings and supper parties made Lewrie certain that Popham almost *resented* him for his favourable mentions in General Baird's despatches to London!

Is he jealous, *by God?* Lewrie was forced to wonder; *Did I shine too bright for his liking? Steal some of his lustre from his victory?* Which made Lewrie recall Popham's early comment about how *someone* in the Navy would, *must,* become as famous as the late Admiral Nelson—was Popham aspiring to that title, and worried that others might beat him to the punch? Whatever the reason, Lewrie got the impression that Popham would be happy to see him and *Reliant* gone.

It didn't happen, though. The Dutch prisoners of war were put aboard the transports and sent off with hardly any escorts, leaving HMS *Reliant* swinging to her anchors, a condition which turned boresome after a fortnight or so. By the end of February, Lewrie was itching to get back to sea before his crew got too bored, sullen, and out of practice. All the competitions he could stage aboard, all the rowing races and sailing races he could arrange with the ship's boats, had lost their appeal. Personally, he had re-read all his novels, and a few new to him borrowed from the wardroom, had written so many letters to Lydia, his sons, his in-laws, his daughter, his father, old friends from the Navy, fellow lodgers at the Madeira Club in London—even Peter Rushton and Clotworthy Chute—that he had nothing more to *say*!

When he asked Popham's permission to patrol round Cape Agulhas and points East into the Indian Ocean, Popham had been more than eager to allow him, telling a gathering of his officers, "But, of course you may. After all, sirs, we know by now that we must keep Captain Lewrie amused, and spared anything humdrum, what? Haw haw!"

"Thank you, sir," Lewrie had said, though thinking, *Eat shit and die!*

He took a month away from Cape Town and its delights, working his crew back to well-drilled competence at striking and re-erecting topmasts, at tacking or wearing about on a sudden whim, at taking in sail by reefing or striking or ugly and baggy "Spanish Reefs" to spill wind from courses and tops'ls by clewing them up into bats' wings with their centres drawn against the yards and the outer corners resembling flabby sacks. And, of course there was arms drill almost every morning, with boarding pikes, cutlasses, and musketry fired at towed kegs well astern of a barge under sail. Even if the Ordnance Board didn't care for the expense, *Reliant* went to Quarters at least four days a week to practice live-firing with the great guns, from quarterdeck 9-pounders to bow chasers, carronades, and her battery of 18-pounders, expending kegs of gunpowder and hundreds of flannel cartridge bags.

In his early, confused, and miserable days as a Midshipman in old HMS *Ariadne*, back in 1780, the one redeeming feature of his term of servitude had been when the ship had gone to Quarters and the lashings had been cast off the guns. The crashes, the leaping recoils, the thunderous rumble of carriage trucks as they were hauled back to be loaded, then run up to the ports once more, and the thick, rotten-egg stink of spent powder that be-fogged the decks had put him in heaven! The blasts which fluttered his innards always put him in mind of shuddery raptures! And to get off three rounds per gun in two minutes and hammer a patch of sea with concentrated broadsides, well!

By the time Lewrie was satisfied with his crew's gunnery, even Bisquit the dog had taken to running below on his own whenever the Marine drummer and fifer started the Long Roll, with no one to lead him by the collar, and Chalky learned that his wicker travelling cage was a safe and snug place to run to!

Off the Southern tip of Madagascar, near the mouth of the Mozambique Channel, Lewrie decided to return to Cape Town. After he had breakfasted on oatmeal and coffee, he went to the quarterdeck to give that order. Bisquit was playing fetch with some of the ship's boys, but broke off and began to slink towards the hatchway, wary of his presence which might presage another morning of dread thunders, but Lewrie took time to whistle him up and give him some petting before mounting the ladderway.

"Good morning, sir," Lt. Westcott, who had the watch, said.

"Good morning to you, Mister Westcott," Lewrie said back with a grin. "Put the ship about, if you please, and shape course back to Cape Town."

"Very good, sir!" Westcott replied, perking up and baring his signature brief smile. "Bosun, pipe all hands! Stations to wear!"

Once about and steady on a course of Sou'west by West, Lewrie summoned Westcott to join him at the windward rails.

"Aye, sir?" Westcott asked.

"I've been ponderin' something, Mister Westcott," Lewrie said. "The complete absence of any Dutch warships in the area."

"Well, one would think the Dutch are too busy protecting their East Indies colonies, sir . . . Java and such," Westcott said after a moment of musing. "Or, they're preying on our India and China trades, alongside their allies, the French. What they now call Holland, the Batavian Republic, is occupied by, and subordinate to, the French. If any Dutch warships are around, one'd most-like find them at the isles of Réunion and Mauritius . . . under overall French command."

"It still makes no sense to me that they just abandoned and set fire to that sixty-eight gunner anchored in False Bay," Lewrie told him.

"The *Bato,* sir," Westcott supplied.

"Aye. We were so busy landing troops, we didn't have a rowing boat t'spare," Lewrie continued. "They could've sailed her out to sea and run to Réunion and we wouldn't have known a thing about it. And, if the Cape Colony was so important to the Dutch, and the French, why was she the only one there? We've seen one of our East India Company trades, a couple of Swedish ships, an American whaler or two, but not hide nor hair of the Dutch or the French. I don't like it. I have a . . . fey feeling that once they get word that we've taken Cape Town, the French and the Dutch together could put together a decent-sized squadron t'take it all *back*."

"Well, a squadron of ships, perhaps, sir, but with five thousand of our soldiers ashore and in control of the forts, they wouldn't stand much of a chance at counter-invasion," Westcott dismissed with a shake of his head.

"There is that, granted, Mister Westcott," Lewrie allowed as he turned to gaze aft as if searching for a hostile sail on the horizon . . . *any* hostile sail. "We beat the stuffings out of the Dutch Navy at Camperdown, but they'd have a long time since t'rebuild it, even if Napoleon's used their yards t'build all those thousands of invasion craft so he could land in England. They could send at least *one* two-decker sixty-eight to defend Cape Town, so . . . why not *more*, t'protect their East Indies colonies? Or, d'ye think I'm jumpin' at shadows?" he asked, turning back to his First Officer to pull a face in self-deprecation.

"More . . . planning against the worst, sir," Westcott replied with a hint of a grin. In his three years' service under Lewrie, he had yet to see him take himself seriously, or become pompous. "Fore-warned is forearmed, what? But, it may be, sir, that it's half what you might *wish*, more than what the Dutch have, or might do. God, we have been so busy and active for so long that this idling in harbour, and so-far fruitless cruising, is . . . nettlesome. Making us sit up late at night, waiting for the shoe to drop, and listening for the odd creaking."

"We?" Lewrie scoffed. "*Me*, ye mean. Frankly, it'd be better did *all* our ships spend more time at sea, 'stead of holdin' victory suppers, and pattin' ourselves on the back. Roam farther afield than Cape Agulhas and Lamberts Bay to the North o' Cape Town. Bring every crew beyond 'river discipline' competence again."

"You're thinking more like a Commdore, again, sir, not just another subordinate Captain," Westcott dared to comment, "serving at another man's whims."

"Well, I will allow that my brief time in that position was . . . habit-forming," Lewrie said with a self-mocking shrug. "All that *vast* power and authority was intoxicatin'!"

Westcott laughed along with him.

"How to suggest such to Commodore Popham, though, sir," Westcott said in a lower voice, "and express your suspicions of a Dutch and French combined riposte, hmm?"

"That is the rub, aye," Lewrie replied, scowling, "without him thinkin' me an old lady, or unwilling t' hear anything from anyone that goes against his set thinkin'. Or, takin' any suggestion from the likes of *me*, at all! I think he's a 'down' on me, ever since we went off on our own with the Army. Oh, well."

"Commodore Popham is a very active sort, though, sir, just full of schemes and ideas," Westcott noted. "With the Navy's part in the conquest done, and the Cape Colony in General Baird's total control, might he be looking for other fish to fry, by now? Who knows, sir. The tiniest flea planted in his ear, and we could all be out to sea and having a go at raiding Fort-de-France!"

"Hmm, now that sounds . . . interesting," Lewrie mused. "Just bung-full o' prospects for fresh laurels. Once back at Table Bay, we will see."

CHAPTER THIRTY-THREE

*E*ven before the *Reliant* frigate could complete her gun salute to the Commodore, put down her bower anchors, or take in all sail, a signal appeared on HMS *Diadem*'s halliards: *Reliant*'s number and "Captain Repair On Board".

"Well, damme," Lewrie muttered. "Impatient about something . . . ain't he?"

"Away, the Captain's boat crew!" Lt. Westcott took time to yell, amid all the other necessary commands which would bring their ship to safe and secure anchorage. Table Bay was not the snuggest harbour in the world, and when the winds came Westerly, they blew directly onto shore and raised choppy surges that put all anchored ships on a lee shore. "Afterguard! Haul the first cutter up from towing and lay it abeam the starboard entry-port!"

"Look presentable, do I, Mister Spendlove?" Lewrie asked their Second Officer in jest, tugging at his shirt cuffs and his neck-stock. He was in slop-trousers, scuffed boots, and his oldest and shabbiest uniform coat and hat.

"Oh, fit for the King, sir," Spendlove replied with un-characteristic puckish humour.

"We will see to making the ship all tiddly, sir," Westcott promised. "No worries. And, no need to keep the Commodore waiting."

"Very well, sirs," Lewrie said, bound for the entry-port for his rushed departure.

"Once aboard the flagship, sir," Lt. Spendlove called after him, "might you ask where yonder French frigate came from?"

"Indeed, I shall," Lewrie told him, for he was as curious as the rest as to the why and the how that a large French frigate sat at anchor with a large Union Jack flying over the enemy Tricolour from her stern staff.

What lucky bastard made her prize, and when? Lewrie pondered as he took the hastily-gathered side-party's salute, doffed his hat, and scrambled down to the waiting cutter; *We spent a month prowlin' and saw nothing, and one of the others had a good, brisk fight? Damn!*

"Ah, Captain Lewrie!" Commodore Popham cried in apparent good humour as he entered the flag officer's great-cabins. "Have a pleasant cruise, did you . . . all fair winds and claret?"

"Good weather for the most part, sir," Lewrie replied, warily. He was waiting for the criticism to come. "Nought t'show for it, unfortunately. Quite unlike the fortunate fellow who nabbed that Frog frigate."

"Come, have a glass of wine with us, and the tale will be told, sir!" Popham hooted with delight, waving Lewrie to take a seat with the others at his long, gleaming dining table.

Captain Josiah Rowley of *Raisonnable* was there, Commander Joseph Edmonds of *Diomede*, her Acting-Captain; beside him was Captain Robert Honyman of the *Leda* frigate and Captain Ross Donnelly of the 32-gun *Narcissus* frigate. At the foot of the table, "below the salt", sat Lieutenant James Talbot of the 14-gun *Encounter*.

"It is everyone's prize, and it is no one's prize," Popham said with a playful air of mystery, as if telling ghost stories to a pack of children, "for she came into Table Bay, the fourth of March, just a few days after you sailed, Lewrie, with no idea that we had taken the place."

"There were enough Dutch flags flying on the shipping in the harbour to mis-lead her," Captain Rowley said with a snicker.

"Aye, and I quickly ordered all our warships to hoist false colours 'til she had let go her best bower and taken in most of her sails," Popham said, beaming with glee, "then hoisted our true colours and ordered her to strike. She's the *Volontaire,* of fourty guns, and was part of their Admiral Willaumez's squadron, bound for Mauritius and Fort-de-France. The sweetest part is that she and other ships of her squadron had captured two of our troop transports somewhere in the Bay of Biscay, and had over two hundred soldiers from the Queens' Regiment and the Fifty-fourth Foot aboard, whom we liberated, ha ha!"

"Who may prove useful to General Baird's garrison force, once re-armed and re-equipped," Captain Donnelly suggested. "What does the Army call such a rag-tag and motley gathering, sir?"

"A Battalion of Detachments," Popham quickly supplied, He had a reputation of getting on with the Army better than most Royal Navy officers. "They might make four companies . . . hardly a full battalion, really, but, as you say, Donnelly, they may be useful to Sir David . . . or at other endeavours." And there was the enigmatic smile, again.

He's goin' cryptic, again, Lewrie thought with a silent groan; *At least his wine's good, even if it is local.*

"You said you saw nothing of enemy activity on your cruise, Lewrie?" Popham asked him. "How far did you go?"

"As far as the longitude of Madagascar's Southern tip, sir, makin' long boards to either tack, then zig-zagged North to sight of Madagascar and the Mozambique Channel," Lewrie summarised. "We saw a 'John Company' trade, some Yankee Doodle whalers, and some neutral merchantmen, but no French or Dutch warships. I was wondering why the Dutch didn't have more than one warship here at the Cape when we arrived, sir, and, given how important the Cape Colony is to both the French *and* the Dutch—"

"So, except for one or two French frigates and several large French privateers working out of Réunion and Mauritius, our new possession is in no danger from that quarter. Good!" the Commodore said energetically, all but clapping his hands together in delight. "Now, before we sailed here, the last time I was up to London and had the honour of dining with the Prime Minister, we did discuss this operation, and other . . . possibilities for future action once the Cape was successfully carried."

No one rolled their eyes exactly, but all had heard, perhaps once too often, of Captain Sir Home Riggs Popham being all but cater-cousins and a close confidant to William Pitt, the Younger. He *did* trot out his excellent connexions, the way some wealthy wives would tell one just how expensive was everything in their parlours, at the drop of a hat!

"Whilst I was in London, I was introduced to a Spanish gentle-man, one Colonel Miranda," Popham continued, "most un-officially, of course . . . all back-channel and *sub rosa,* do you see, so no firm promises could be made to the man by anyone in the Prime Minister's administra-tion, nor by anyone in His Majesty's Government. This Colonel Miranda declared himself to be a representative of a nationalist movement in Span-ish South America, from Buenos Aires in the Argentine, in point of fact. He came seeking aid to bolster his cause, which would be a local, popular rising to throw off Spanish rule and gain the Argentine total autonomy and independence!"

"God, another bloody revolution," Captain Rowley said with a grim little laugh. "But, will it be like the Americans', or more like the one in France?"

"Aye, out come the guillotines, and chop chop!" Captain Honyman sneered. "The Americans, now . . . at least they were of British stock, and British common sense. Once they won, they didn't go to massacres and reprisals like the French. They spent their bile writing their Constitution. Rule of law, what? But, what may one expect of fiery-hot *Spaniards,* I ask you? Hey-ho, and huzzah the Inquisition for anyone on the losing side!"

"The possibilities, though, gentlemen!" Popham interrupted in some heat. "Great Britain, by her very position, commands the approaches to the Baltic trade, and the Channel. Our presence at Gibraltar controls ac-cess to the Mediterranean, as will our holding the isle of Malta. Now, we have taken the Cape of Good Hope, and may deny any other world power the India and China trade.

"Just think what the taking of Buenos Aires and Montevideo and the Plate Estuary would *mean,* sirs! There would in time of war be *no* trade round Cape Horn but for neutrals and our, and allied, shipping! Port Stanley and the Falkland Islands could never support a squadron of ships sufficient to dominate the Cape Horn passages, but the Plate could," Popham insisted, half-cajoling, half-battering down any argument to the contrary; smiling wide but talking loud and quickly as he bestowed beam-ing good will.

"Aye, but how would we go about that, sir?" *Diomede*'s captain asked, frowning. "Other than that Colonel Miranda you met, what are the odds that he represented a *real* rebel movement, and not just some pack of mal-contents meeting in some coffee house? Is there *really* a sizable portion of the population all *that* eager to throw off Spanish rule, and welcome us?"

"We *are* godless Protestant heretics, don't ye know," Lewrie had to say, with a snicker. "Good Papists, rebel or no, would rather cut *our* throats. Hated us for *ages!*"

"When in London, Colonel Miranda gave firm and believable assurances that his nationalist movement is widespread, and popular with all classes in the Argentine," Commodore Popham countered. "He came to *Protestant* England to ask for our aid, and was authorised to grant us basing rights, in exchange for local rule, and civil autonomy, sirs." Popham paused and brought out a stack of newspapers from a drawer in his sideboard. "I obtained these quite recently from a Captain Waine, of the American merchantman *Elizabeth*, just come to anchor in Table Bay. They are in Spanish, of course, but my clerks and some of Captain Downman's officers read and speak Spanish, and they are in full consensus that these papers speak of civil unrest, complaints about Spain taking hands with *godless*, heretical Jacobin France, the rules by which the Argentine trade is crippled by far-off decrees limiting shipping to Spanish ships only, with no inter-colonial trade allowed, and *et cetera* and *et cetera*. No local merchantmen may trade with America, with Portuguese Brazil, for one instance.

"And, there is *rich* potential in the Argentine, sirs," Popham enthusiastically drilled on. "Cattle, hides, tallows, and lards, and mineral wealth, along with vast *seas* of grain crops, and the bark of the *cinchona* tree, which is a specific against Malaria. And, Buenos Aires is one terminus of the Spanish Philippines trade, with all the spices, gold, and silver that that means, annually. Our Drake, in his time, would have given his right arm for the chance to take one of the 'golden galleons'. Who knows what untold wealth now lies in the warehouses and counting houses of Buenos Aires, gentlemen? Do we appear in the Río de la Plata to augment and light the match to the nationalist uprising, we will outnumber, and overawe, those Spaniards who still cling to the old regime in Madrid, and they are a distinct minority, all our intelligence, and Captain Waine's personal observations, assure me!"

He's mad as a hatter! Lewrie gawped to himself; *As daft as a March hare!*

"Won't this require an army at least as large as the one that we brought to the Cape, though, sir?" Captain Rowley hesitantly asked, sounding tempted, but wary. "And, do we sail for Buenos Aires, and leave Cape Town un-defended, might we run the risk of losing it to an expeditionary force from the French bases in the Indian Ocean, once they learn of its loss?"

"The French have barely enough troops to garrison Réunion and Mauritius," Popham was quick to dismiss, "so General Baird will be as safe as houses so long as he holds both fortresses, and can field one brigade of his present strength. A naval presence to defend the Cape is of secondary importance, leaving us free to undertake the invasion of the Argentine.

"I have already spoken with Sir David, and he assures me that he may spare us the Seventy-first Foot, and some dis-mounted dragoons, along with field artillery. . . . Perhaps we may arm and equip these rescued soldiers from the Queens' and Fifty-fourth Regiments with surrendered Dutch arms and accoutrements, or trade them for a half-battalion more of Sir David's troops. General Beresford will command our landing force. And," Popham paused to give them an reassuring smile, "since the passage to South America requires us to take a great circle route Nor'west with the Sou'east Trades and currents, then over towards neutral Portuguese Brazil, I intend to break our passage at Saint Helena for more water and firewood, and prevail upon the island's governor to lend me some more troops. A force of two thousand, all told, should be more than sufficient for the initial landings, after which the nationalists come to us. Both Colonel Miranda, and Captain Waine, assure me that there are no more than two thousand Spaniards under arms round Buenos Aires."

"And here I thought we'd be goin' East, not West," Lewrie gaped to fill the uneasy, thoughtful silence. "Have a shot at Réunion, and clean out one privateers' nest. Have a chance to engage a French squadron, broadside-to-broadside? We'll be back at convoyin'."

"Well, in this instance, Lewrie," Popham said with a pleased simper, "we will most assuredly muster all our Marines and as many sailors as may be spared for shore duty. You may have a chance for even more action ashore . . . and more mud and dirt on your boots!"

"It *could* be . . . glorious," Lieutenant Talbot of the little *Encounter* brig spoke up for the first time.

"As glorious as Lord Clive of India, sirs!" Popham exclaimed, seizing upon that word. "One man, with a laughably small force of sturdy British for the backbone, leading native armies in rebellion against the great Moghuls and their tyranny, won not just a province, but the entire Indian sub-continent, and came home with honour, and the untold wealth of emperors! And, might I add, un-dying renown, hey?"

"I fully intend," Popham said, turning more business-like, as if his case was won, "to depart round the middle of April, if not earlier, so see to your victualling and readiness, gentlemen. We shall be having future conferences anent our preparations, and meetings with General Beresford and his staff officers. It would be good for all our Sailing Masters to meet, as well, to share what knowledge they possess of the Plate Estuary, their pertinent charts, along with what charts may be available from the chandlers here in Cape Town. . . ."

Lewrie looked round the table at his fellow captains, wondering if he should say something along the lines of *Have ye lost yer bloody mind?* or *This is all a load of moonshine!* and would speaking up make a groat's worth of difference. There were several hooded expressions of worry, but in the main, his compatriots looked as if they would go along with Popham's orders, "muddle through", and hope to make the best of it. Deference to the authority of one's commanding officer was sacrosanct in the Royal Navy; men had been court-martialled for *mute* insubordination for obeying but doing so in a surly manner, or for questioning a superior's order too strongly.

He ain't askin' *for our suggestions*, Lewrie thought; *His mind's made up and he's Hell-bent on his little . . . crusade, and nothing anyone can say'd dissuade him! This* ain't *goin' t'end well!*

". . . may appear wide, but it is rather shallow, so we may have to put off the selection of our landing beaches until we enter the estuary," Popham had been going on, just bubbling over with enthusiasm, and waving his cabin stewards to come forward with newly-opened wine bottles. "A glass with you all, sirs!" Popham cried as their glasses were filled. "To victory and glory in the Argentine!" he proposed, and they had no choice but to echo that toast and toss back their wines.

"Well, that was . . . breath-taking," Captain Donnelly of the *Narcissus* frigate muttered to Lewrie as they stood near HMS *Diadem*'s entry-port to make their departures in order of seniority.

"Aye, *breath-takin*'s a *mild* way t'put it," Lewrie agreed in a low voice. "Never been there, mind, but it does strike me that there is a lot more to the Argentine than Buenos Aires. God only knows how many people there are, in a long-settled country nigh the size of *all* Southern Africa. And we're t'take it with only one infantry regiment? Sounds daft t'me!"

"We *might* get a second regiment, or a battalion at the least, at Saint Helena," Donnelly speculated. "With three hundred and fifty of our Marines and sailors . . . strip our ships to the bare bones . . . we *might* suc-

ceed. *If* we find allies in the rebels, and the Spanish garrison is weak."
Donnelly didn't sound hopeful.

"If there's no opposition from the Spanish navy," Lewrie had to point
out, scowling. "If that Colonel Miranda is to be believed. It is just *too* . . .
iffy."

"The Dons don't have much of their navy overseas, and we will have
two sixty-fours, a fifty-gunner, and three frigates, so we have little to
fear on that head," Donnelly said.

"Only *two* sixty-fours?" Lewrie asked.

"*Belliqueux* is to escort the East India Company ships to Madras, now
their part in the invasion's done," Donnelly told him.

Captain Honyman of the *Leda* frigate emerged from Popham's cabins,
looking as if he was in a pet, his fingers drumming on his sword hilt.

"I am to stay here at Cape Town," Honyman announced, growling.
"Don't know whether to feel cheated, or mightily relieved."

"Protect it all by yourself, sir?" Lewrie asked, amazed.

"I will have the *Protector* gunboat," Honyman sneered, "and the *sight*
of that French fourty-gunner, *Volontaire*, anchored between the shore
fortresses. She hasn't a full Harbour Watch aboard, but anyone who sails
in for a look *should* take her at face value for a ship in full commission."

"Who got her?" Captain Donnelly asked.

"Commander Josceline Percy," Honyman said with a snort. "Left England too late with orders to have *Espoir*, and had to beg a passage in
Protector. Lucky fellow."

"Lucky, indeed!" Lewrie said, chuckling. "Lose a brig, get a frigate,
and be sure t'be made 'Post'! Ehm . . . even with your ship here, sir, isn't
the Commodore takin' a huge risk? Admiralty might have a very dim
view of it, success at Buenos Aires be-damned."

"Ah, but he has so *many* friends in high places, Lewrie!" Captain
Honyman said more loudly, his sneers more pronounced. "He's the ear of
the Prime Minister, a doting patron at Admiralty in Lord Melville, an
host of 'petti-coat' allies in every salon through his wife's excellent connexions . . . perhaps cater-cousins in the Privy Council, I shouldn't wonder! As he had told us . . . so very, *very* often, what? 'When last I played
at bowls with the Prince of Wales' . . . 'When Noah and I compared
notes on tides and currents'? God, *spare* us!" Honyman gravelled. "But,
in the end, I expect he'll be excused for abandoning his post . . . it's the
way of things."

"But, only if we're successful," Lewrie cautioned.

By God, we'd better, or it's the ruin of us all, he thought.

"Well, there is that!" Captain Honyman hooted with a snicker, as if failure was no skin off his own nose. "Gentlemen, I wish you both the very best of good fortune over there in South America. Just so long as I'm not part of it, no matter which way it goes. Take joy of the Commodore's success. Are you lucky, he might even share a bit of the gloss with you, haw!"

BOOK FOUR

Where is Montjoy the herald? Speed him hence;
Let him greet England with our sharp defiance.
Up, princes! and with spirit of honour edged,
More sharper than your swords, hie to the field.

-WILLIAM SHAKESPEARE
*THE LIFE OF KING
HENRY THE FIFTH,*
ACT III, SCENE V, 36-39

CHAPTER THIRTY-FOUR

*S*ignal from *Diadem*, sir," Midshipman Rossyngton called out from the taffrails. "It is . . . 'Report . . . Provisions'."

"Lovely way t'start the day," Lewrie said, scoffing. "What's the tally today, Mister Westcott?"

"The Purser's inventory says we still have seven days' water and five days' of bisquit remaining, at full issue, sir," Lt. Westcott replied, referring to the morning's tally which Mr. Cadbury had given him after breakfast.

"Pass those to Rossyngton, then," Lewrie told him, "and pray that this voyage doesn't last much longer. We're almost to the Plate Estuary, but how we're to victual from a hostile shore is anyone's guess."

When Commodore Popham had announced that they would break their passage at St. Helena, lengthening the duration of the voyage, Lewrie and his officers had determined to buy or have built extra water butts to stow below. Cape Town had the facilities to bake bisquit in great quantities to service the needs of the merchant trade which put in to victual, so HMS *Reliant* had left the Cape with a goodly extra supply as well.

The problem had arisen after leaving St. Helena, for the expedition had had to sail further North, riding the Sou'east African Trade winds and the Agulhas Current, to the latitude of the Cape Verde Isles to catch the Nor'east Trades that would carry them across the Atlantic to South America, and the ships of the squadron had wallowed in the variable zone between those two great wind and current routes, some days barely making steerage way, before resuming adequate progress. The requests for reports on how much basic provisions remained lately had become a daily fret.

"We *could* have put in somewhere in the Vice-Royalty of Brazil, sir," Westcott commented after returning forward from relaying their figures to Midshipman Rossyngton. "Portugal is neutral, after all. It would not have had to be Rio de Janeiro, or another major port. Any fishing port would have served."

"Hah!" was Lewrie's sour reply. "After the blow Popham got from Governor Patten at Saint Helena, I don't think he wants anyone in authority t'know where we *are*!"

News had come from London that the Prime Minister, and Popham's "dear friend" and supporter, William Pitt, had died on the 22nd of January. The new Prime Minister, Lord Grenville, had quickly assembled his new administration, "The Ministry of All Talents" due to the many new and younger men who, on paper at least, possessed such great potential and brilliance. William, Lord Grenville, was *not* a fan of Popham's.

And, to make things even worse for the Commodore, the Right Honourable Charles Grey, M.P., was the new First Lord of the Admiralty, and no one knew what he might think of any expedition to South America, especially one dreamt up on the fly, without official leave. Lewrie strongly suspected that their little squadron was now *slinking* to Buenos Aires, hoping to achieve victory before anyone could recall them, staying a days' sail ahead of any orders from London, and out for a very quick *fait accompli*!

How that would be achieved was worrying, too. General Baird had given Popham and Brigadier Beresford only seven hundred men of the 71st Highlanders, along with six pieces of field artillery and two troops of dis-mounted Light Dragoons from the 20th. Popham's hope for enthusiastic support from Governor-General Patten at St. Helena had been dashed; he had contributed only two companies of infantry, all that he might spare from the defence of such a vital mid-ocean post.

To make up the lack of soldiers, Popham had invented the "Royal Blues", stripping all his warships of most of their Marines and as many sailors as could be spared, to add another 340 men who would be landed ashore when the time came. After witnessing the size and power of General Baird's army of five thousand in combat at Cape Town, though, Lewrie had his doubts what a force of around sixteen hundred could accomplish. It was seeming dafter and dafter!

"How much longer, Mister Caldwell?" Lewrie asked the Sailing Master, who had been scribbling on a chalk slate and humming happily to himself, with a now-and-again reference to one of his charts pinned to the traverse board by the compass binnacle cabinet.

"Hey, sir?" Caldwell responded, as if roused from a nap. "Oh, well I dare say that, should this wind continue in its present slant, and at its current strength, we should be entering the Río de la Plata Estuary around tomorrow's dawn . . . with the sun astern of us once we alter course Westward, which will make any reefs or shoals easier to espy ahead of us, sir. Of which the Plate Estuary has an ominous plenty, that is."

"You would feel much better did we reduce sail and post leadsmen in the fore chains, and lookouts at the fore top, sir?" Lewrie asked.

"Oh, very much better, sir!" Mr. Caldwell agreed quickly, with a broad, relieved smile plastered on his phyz.

"Well, so would I, frankly," Lewrie told him, grinning. "I've not run aground in ages, and may be more than due. Though from what I gather from my charts, the Plate's shoals are more sand and silt than rocks?" He knocked wood for luck on the starboard bulwark's cap-rails.

"That is true, sir . . . in the main," Caldwell replied, doing the same on the top of the binnacle cabinet.

Lewrie turned away and rocked on the balls of his feet, hands clasped in the small of his back and his head tilted up to savour the morning. It was a beautiful day, bright, glittering, and fresh-washed by light rain the evening before. They had left the oppressive heat of the Equator behind after falling South of Recife in Brazil, and the days had cooled to the low eighties since. In promise of their landfall, sea birds and shore birds seen close to shore swirled overhead in small flocks, some flitting or gliding between the masts and sails to delight the ship's dog, Bisquit, and make Chalky, who was perched atop the cross-deck hammock racks, sit up and swivel his head skywards, with his whiskers standing out and his mouth making eager chitterings and longing trills.

Lewrie petted his cat, then paced forward up the starboard sail-tending gangway to the forecastle, idly thumping and tugging at the stays to determine their tautness. He made several circuits of the gangways, stepping up his pace on the later laps. Once back aboard from their African adventure, he made it a point to exercise as much as shipboard life allowed, cramped and constrained as that was. None of them had really been fit for long marches, or all the trotting and running that fighting alongside the Army had demanded. Sometime during the hands' spell of cutlass drill, he would pair off against one or more of his officers on the quarterdeck with his hanger and practice swordplay 'til his tongue lolled out and his shirt turned damp. That was the most demanding exercise he could think of, and a fine precaution against getting too rusty to defend himself should they board an enemy and have to fight for their lives.

Bisquit came trotting up with his tail wagging as Lewrie made a last circuit, hopping and whining playfully. Lewrie allowed the dog to rise and place his paws on his chest to give him a good rubbing, before reaching into his coat pocket for what Lewrie suspected was Bisquit's real purpose . . . he gave the dog a strip of *biltong,* a good, long, and thick-ish piece of salted, spiced eland.

"Permission to come to the quarterdeck, sir?" the Purser, Mr. Cadbury, requested at the foot of the larboard ladderway as Bisquit went off to chew his way to bliss.

"Aye, come up, sir," Lewrie agreed as he went back to his proper post at the windward bulwarks.

"I was wondering what to do with these, sir?" Cadbury began as he drew an ornate rolled-up document from his coat.

"I thought we'd share 'em 'twixt my cabins and the officers' quarter-galleries, Mister Cadbury," Lewrie said. "That's what we decided."

"Aye, sir, but they're not exactly suitable for such uses, are they, sir?" Cadbury told him, rolling the document out to its full length. "Too stiff a paper stock, and one would have to peel all the seals off, first. Even quartered, they are too stiff."

"Aye, nothing like a good, used newspaper for wipin' one's bum," Lewrie said with a laugh. "They might even scratch one's arse."

HMS *Narcissus* had spotted a strange sail and had dashed off in pursuit several days before, returning with a small Spanish merchant brig as prize, and the envy of every bored officer and sailor in the expedition. She had been bound from Cartagena to Buenos Aires with a cargo of general goods from the Vice-Royalty of New Granada, in defiance of Spanish absolutism which forbade inter-colonial trade. Among her cargo were several dozen large chests sent out from Spain containing Papal Dispensations, hundreds upon hundreds of them, bearing the seals and signatures of various Romish cardinals and the Pope himself in far-off Rome. Captain Donnelly had sent several chests aboard each ship in the expedition, as a jape, with notes explaining that the florid documents were "Get Out of Hell Passes for The South American Sin Trade", which local archbishops and bishops would sell, and parcel out to the many rural churches, were there any left, to forgive the mortal sins of wealthy country people. What sins they committed later would be their own lookout.

"It's not just their stiffness, sir," Mr. Cadbury suggested in a softer voice. "It's our Irish lads, and our Catholic hands. Some of them came to me . . . your Cox'n Desmond among them . . . on the sly like, to wonder if they would be . . . put to a use that was dis-respectful. Mean to say, sir, with their Pope's seal and signature upon them?"

"They ain't Hindoos forced t'eat pork, Mister Cadbury, or one o' their sacred cows," Lewrie said, scowling.

So much for decent bum-fodder, he thought; *And the Mids are runnin' out o' foolscap for their paperwork, too.*

"Might any use upset them, though, sir," Cadbury muttered on. "We can't use them to light the galley fires, make up fresh cartridge for muskets and pistols . . . even tossing them overside might be deemed insulting."

"Mean t'say we're stuck with 'em?" Lewrie frowned.

"Very possibly, sir," the Purser said with a grimace. "Though . . . some of the hands did express the desire to be *issued* one."

"And very well they might," Lewrie replied, chuckling. Tars of any religion, or no religion, were always in need of forgiveness for something. "Think we could sell 'em off? No, most of our lads don't have two pence t'rub together. And we don't have a chaplain aboard with the authority to sign 'em."

"Well, perhaps a Protestant Church of England official doing the signing might not go down all that well, either, sir," Cadbury said with a snicker of his own. "But, a Post-Captain could."

"One *without* sin, sir?" Lewrie scoffed. "That's a rare commodity hereabouts. Like the Devil baptisin' new-borns!"

"I gather they would appreciate it, sir," Cadbury prompted.

"Oh, very well," Lewrie relented. "They're useless to our purposes, and not worth a groat in prize-money, so I suppose no one'd miss a few.

Get me a list of those desirin' one and I'll write down his name on 'em, no more. No sense in temptin' Fate, tryin' to act like a prelate."

"Aye, sir," Cadbury said, smiling to have the matter settled. "Though, once ashore in Buenos Aires, they *might* prove valuable. The local bishop would be glad to obtain them and sell to support him and his church. We might gain six pence to a shilling each, and God only knows how much they go for when *he* sells them."

"Really? Hmm," Lewrie exclaimed in surprise, beginning to scheme. "They'd go dear in the local market, hey? Hmm," he pondered.

Admiralty'd have my hide, he thought; *Breakin' bulk, stealin' from a prize's value for private gain 'fore submission to the Prize Court? How many of the Articles of War does* that *violate?*

So far, this year of 1806, *Reliant* had had no opportunity to earn a single penny in prize-money, and what captures they had made in the Bahamas and off the coast of Spanish Florida in the previous year were still in the hands of the Admiralty Court in Nassau. When their judgements would be announced, and in what amounts, might not come 'til 1810! And, as was the case with the takings of enemy privateers, the net sums after all those deliberations might not cover the Proctor's fees, once all was said and done.

I s'pose I'll just have t'hope that the Argentine produces a few decent wines, Lewrie consoled himself; *A ten-gallon anker for instant salvation for the vintner and his family, perhaps? Maybe the dispensations'd serve for* paper *money!*

CHAPTER THIRTY-FIVE

*T*hey entered the outer-most reaches of the Plate Estuary on the 27th of May, arriving in a thick and dense fog that took half the day to burn off, groping their way slowly West under greatly reduced sail and sounding with the short leads, already in shoal water. It was, to Lewrie's lights, an ignominious beginning to the invasion of an enemy country. If the look-outs aboard Commodore Popham's flagship, *Diadem,* had been able to *see* a signal, Lewrie would have hoisted the suggestion that they come to anchor for a time before they all took the ground far short of the actual mouth of the Plate. They sailed on nothing but Dead Reckoning, already encountering shoal waters, with the leadsmen in the fore chains calling out soundings that ranged from ten fathoms to a mere six, at times. The deck lookouts in the eyes of the bow could barely see their hands in front of their faces, much less a disturbance in the waters ahead, or a change of colour that might indicate peril. The lookouts high aloft at the cross-trees could only now and then make out the top-most trucks and commission-ing pendants of the other ships, either.

It ain't as if the Spanish know we're comin', or can even see *us if they* knew *t'look out for us,* Lewrie groused to himself, pacing the deck and wincing at each leadsman's call; *so what's his bloody urgency? It's like Popham's runnin' from his creditors!*

Poor Mr. Caldwell, the Sailing Master, looked as if he would fret himself to an early grave, breaking out in a fine sweat despite the coolness of early morning as he was reduced to tracing his index finger round his much-pawed charts each time a new sounding was called out, as if to divine their exact position by the procession of indicated fathom markers. Lewrie noted that that index finger shook at times, and that Caldwell was actually mouthing silent words; curses or prayers, no one could say.

The fogs did burn off by mid-morning, relieving one and all. As soon as it did, though, the flagship was hoisting a flurry of signals. The first was a "General" to all ships, announcing that the Commodore would shift his flag to the *Narcissus* frigate and proceed up the Plate Estuary to gather the latest local information. In his absence, his Flag-Captain, Downman, would command the squadron and the troop transports. They should look for him off Flores Island on the North shore of the estuary, near Montevideo. The second hoist summoned *Narcissus* alongside *Diadem*, so the Commodore and his entourage could be barged over to her to arrive in state, break out his broad pendant, and scamper away at a rate of knots, leaving the rest of the ships to wallow along as best they could.

"Wants t'beat us to the loot, does he?" Lewrie speculated to Lt. Westcott in a low voice. "Ah, Mister Caldwell! My congratulations on seein' us through. I am sending down for a pot of cold tea. Might I offer you a glass?"

"Thankee, but no, sir," Caldwell said, mopping his face with a red calico handkerchief after he had gathered up his personal navigation aids and rolled up the large scale chart. "If I may have your leave to go below for a bit, I had something stronger in mind. This morning has taken its toll upon me, I do confess."

"Nice enough, now, though," Lewrie made note, pausing for a moment to hear one of the leadsmen call out, "Eighteen fathom! Eighteen fathom t'this line!"

"A pretty morning, aye, sir," Caldwell agreed, looking out and up at the skies and clouds and the state of the glittering seas as if seeing them for the first time in his life, blinking in amazement.

"Do you reckon that the ship is in no danger for the moment, sir, you have leave to go below," Lewrie allowed.

"Thank you, sir, and I shall return shortly," Caldwell vowed.

"After all this fog and uncertainty, I feel in need of a stiff 'Nor'wester' myself, sir," Lt. Westcott stated.

"Should I send down for rum, instead?" Lewrie teased.

"Cold tea's fine, sir," Westcott said with a twinkle.

Lewrie left the windward bulwarks and went to the binnacle cabinet to look over the other chart that Caldwell had left behind for their use, the one which showed the Plate Estuary all the way beyond Buenos Aires to the mangrove swamps and jungles on the North bank of the estuary, where the great river spilled out from the interior. He found Flores Island, still hundreds of miles away, and heaved a sigh.

"Pass word for the Purser if you will, Mister Westcott," he reluctantly said. "It'll be days 'til we come to anchor off Flores, and we'll have to wait for the Commodore's return. In the meantime, it will be necessary to reduce the bread and water rations to three in four, unless God grants us a deluge. Perhaps we can make up the lack with small beer, or try to bake fresh bread, if the wind and sea state allows."

"Just slipped his mind, did it, sir?" Westcott whispered with a savage, knowing look on his face.

"Perhaps he'll find a fresh-water stream far out of the way of any watchers," Lewrie sneered. "Or, meet up with some Spanish bum-boat traders."

"Lashings of water, wine, and charming *señoritas*," Westcott wistfully said. "Ah, the possibilities!"

"You quite forgot the chance they'd have fresh fruit," Lewrie reminded him.

"Hmm . . . mangoes . . . coconuts . . . or even . . . *melons*!" Westcott japed, raising cupped hands to his chest as if weighing the mentioned delights, widening his palms at each in lustful anticipation for the young women of the Argentine.

"You're bloody hopeless, ye know that," Lewrie told him.

It was the 13th of June before all ships were together, again, off Flores, where they did find fresh water, and dead-calm waters which allowed them to bake bread. Commodore Popham was off again almost at once, shifting his flag to the *Encounter* brig, which drew even less water than *Narcissus*. Before departing, though, he took the time to hold a quick conference aboard *Diadem*.

"My initial reconnaissance went well, sirs," Popham energetically told them with a smile. "In *Encounter*, I intend to scout as far as Buenos Aires. Colonel Miranda, when I met him in London, told me that Buenos Aires has never felt the need for defensive walls, or any fortifications beyond some harbourside batteries. The fortified town is Montevideo, much closer to the open ocean, and is garrisoned more strongly to protect Buenos Aires from invasion . . . hah! We shall deal with Montevideo last.

"In the meantime, Captain Downman, and Acting-Captain King, I wish you place *Diadem* so as to keep a close eye upon Montevideo," Popham continued, "and prevent any of its garrison from crossing over to the South bank of the estuary to re-enforce Buenos Aires before we may pluck it, ha ha!"

"Very good, sir," Captain Downman agreed.

"Now, someone must keep watch on the back door whilst we make our preparations and choose a good landing spot," Popham said with a cheerful clap of his hands. "To that end, Captain Lewrie, Captain Rowley, and Commander Edmonds, I wish for your ships to fall back down to the mouth of the estuary and cruise to keep a lookout for any impudent intruders who might turn up and interfere . . . as well as taking any Spanish merchantmen bound into the Plate."

Ye brought us all this way, Lewrie thought, fuming up at once; *and we're not t'take part? Christ!*

He could only nod in obedience.

"Now, upon my return, and the determination is made as to where the army is to be landed," Popham went on with a merry grin, "we shall transfer our 'Royal Blues' aboard *Encounter* and *Narcissus*. That will give us the equivalent of a half-battalion of infantry. Each ship will give up around twenty armed seamen, making one hundred, and all of our Marines—that would be three hundred fourty all told, is my reckoning right, and no one falls overboard and drowns whilst I'm away, what?—together that gives us four hundred fourty extra men to assist Brigadier Beresford. With the army troops, we may field one thousand six hundred and thirty."

"About that, yes, Sir Home," Beresford said, nodding.

"As we saw at Blaauwberg Bay, gentlemen," Popham went on and drawing them to gather round his dining table where a copy of a very old Spanish chart was laid out, "it is vital that we land everyone as close to Buenos Aires as possible, giving the Dons little time to react . . . assuming they can, ha! I will be taking a rowboat inshore after dark to look at Point Quilmes, which is only twelve miles from our goal. Above Point Quilmes, the depths are too shallow for any of our ships to swim. Do you concur, sir?" he asked General Beresford,

Beresford blinked his eyes and peered nigh myopically at the chart for a long moment before responding. "If we can get our ships no higher up the coast, then Point Quilmes has much to recommend it, Sir Home . . . though there is this river, the Chuelo or the Cuello . . . three miles from Buenos Aires, where the Spanish could make a stand. How dearly I feel myself in need of a squadron of cavalry."

"General Baird had none to spare," Popham said with a dismissive wave of a hand, "and the horse transports had to be released for return to England immediately following the landing at Blaauwberg Bay. We *do* have those dis-mounted troopers of the Twentieth Light Dragoons . . . perhaps they could dash ahead on 'shank's ponies', what?"

He got his expected laugh.

"With a swift landing, I have complete trust in your ability to brush aside what meagre opposition we may face, General. Now!" Popham declared, then clapped his hands once more and began to sketch out details of the landings.

Lewrie had a look at Beresford, and gathered that that worthy was not quite as sanguine as Popham was. For his part, he wasn't as confident in Brigadier Beresford, either.

He's a pleasant old stick, but what's he done in the past, and against whom? Lewrie wondered; *Our Army officers* buy *their ranks,* buy *their way* up, *and make Colonel or General by* seniority, *not experience! Belong to the right clubs, patrons an' friends at Horse Guards, in Parliament? And, Beresford looks so mild a fellow, God help us.*

General Baird had done a fine job at Cape Town, but he had had equal numbers against the Dutch, all the time in the world to get his troops ashore with no opposition, and had had to fight only one brisk skirmish to clear the Blaauwberg, and one sharp set-piece battle, with everything all "tiddly", and superiority in artillery and infantry. Baird even *looked* like a soldier who knew what he was about!

A quick landing, a quick march to Buenos Aires, against how *many?* Lewrie speculated; *Un-opposed? That might be askin' a lot this time! From what I've seen of our Army, they don't have "quick" in their field manuals!*

He had been rapt in his own thoughts, with only half an ear for Popham, who had been carrying on with zest and enthusiasm, most-like formulating ideas for crossing the Andes to seize Chile, next, set up cattle ranches the size of France for every participant, or have a city named for himself, for all he knew.

Don't matter, really, Lewrie sourly thought; *Popham's his own best audience.*

". . . once the mid-day meal is piped, we shall begin transferring Marines and sailors to *Encounter* and *Narcissus,*" Popham said, as if he was summing up, at last. "Captain Lewrie, not only shall we need your fourty-odd Marines and twenty armed sailors, I fear that I must requisition your barges and cutters, to speed the landings when they begin. You'll get them all back, once the landings are done."

"Of course, sir," Lewrie answered.

"Can't let you have all the fun ashore, this time, hey? This time, Acting-Captain King of *Diadem* will command the 'Royal Blues'," Popham said. "Your *Reliant* draws too much water, in any event, to accompany us further up the estuary."

"I understand, sir," Lewrie said by rote, reminding himself to plaster a wee smile on his phyz.

"That should be all for now, gentlemen," Popham concluded. "On the morrow, we shall set off for Point Quilmes, land the Army and our naval contribution, and win ourselves a splendid victory!"

"Hear hear!" the others shouted, pounding and drumming their fists on the table top. "Toast, toast! To victory!"

CHAPTER THIRTY-SIX

*R*eliant's sailors and Marines returned back aboard to a hearty welcome, loud cheers, and good-natured teasing, boasting of their experiences alongside the army, and crowing over their easy victory. A soon as Marine Lieutenant Simcock, and the Second and Third Officers, Lts. Spendlove and Merriman, gained the deck, Lewrie and Lt. Westcott were all over them, demanding news.

"It came off as easy as 'kiss my hand', sir!" Lt. Merriman crowed. "We waded ashore on the twenty-fifth and the morning of the twenty-sixth, set off up the coast road, met the Dons, and had a battle—"

"Not much of one, sir," Lt. Simcock interrupted, bubbling over with good cheer. "They were all cavalry, about fifteen hundred or so, and we saw them off after a few volleys and some sharp practice with our artillery. They scampered, and we marched again to catch them up, but they melted away."

"They did cut the bridge over the Cuello, but they didn't stay to deny us crossing, sir," Lt. Spendlove boasted. "Captain King had all the landing boats come up the river, we used bridge timbers to make rafts, and were in the city's outskirts by the twenty-eighth. After that, the Spanish had no choice but to surrender the place to us."

"God, the *loot*, sir!" Simcock hooted. "We took nigh a million silver Spanish dollars from the treasury, and a company of Highlanders caught up with their viceroy's coaches on his way to the back country, and took over six hundred thousand more! What we seized by way of goods in the warehouses might be worth *double* of all that!"

"A rather peaceful and un-eventful occupation after that, sir," Lt. Spendlove said with a shrug. "A lot of angry looks were all that we got. The Commodore ordered that private property was respected."

"That, and some harsh wines, and high prices in the taverns and eateries," Lt. Merriman stuck in. "Beef steaks the size of serving platters with almost every meal, though. The Argentines are simply awash in cattle. They roast steaks over hot coals on almost every streetcorner."

"So the independence movement is now in charge?" Lewrie asked.

"Pshaw, sir!" Lt. Simcock spat. "As far as any of us could determine, there *is* no independence movement, save for a few top-lofty scribblers and rich intellectuals. The whole idea seems more an idle salon exercise than a real revolutionary movement."

"Not one?" Lt. Westcott asked with an amazed brow up.

"Let us just say that no one *we* encountered came up to congratulate us, or thank us, sir," Lt. Spendlove told him in his usual serious mien.

"Were the ladies at least pretty?" Westcott pressed.

"Oh, sir," Lt. Merriman said in mock sympathy, "had you been with us, you would have been mightily dashed. Anyone with a fetching young miss, and a *tad* of common sense, would keep them locked behind iron-barred windows and doors from *los heréticos ingleses* such as us."

"Our sailors and private Marines might have seen one or two somewhat fetching doxies in the brothels," Lt. Simcock teased, "but surely, one cannot expect gentlemen officers to stoop to entering establishments like that. Right, sir?"

Westcott delivered Simcock a very bleak expression. Westcott had proved himself such an ardent chaser of quim that he *might've*!

"Any of our people killed or wounded, Mister Spendlove? Any 'run'?" Lewrie asked.

"Not a one, sir, and all are now safely back aboard," the Second Officer reported in a brisker tone.

"Good," Lewrie said, "for we may have need of them."

"Sir?" Spendlove asked.

"Since you all set off on the sixteenth, there's been hints of *something* on the horizon, out seawards," Lewrie explained. "I spoke *Diomede* and *Raisonnable* now and again on our patrols off the mouth of the estuary, and we've all spotted a single set o' t'gallants or royals lurkin' out t'sea. Round dawn, round sunset, and whatever sorta ship it is, it scuttles off soon as we stand out to 'smoak' her. She may be a Spanish merchantman, fearful of enterin', some neutral afraid of what we are . . . an American worried we might press some of her hands off her? Or, it could be a warship. She stands aloof, either way, and if she is a warship, there might be a fight in the offing."

"Hmm, I see, sir," Lt. Spendlove commented, turning even more sober. "It may be deemed unlikely that she is French. This side of the South Atlantic is too far from their usual haunts. Spanish? We saw none at Buenos Aires, and there was only one little four-gunned cutter in the port of Ensenada, further up the coast."

"One can only hope," Lewrie told him. "Very well, gentlemen. Congratulations on the victory, and I trust you enjoyed yourselves on detached duties. Welcome back aboard, and see to getting the hands settled back in. I will be below. Mister Westcott? See that those boats are led aft for towing, then get us under way, course Nor'east."

"Aye, sir," a dispirited Westcott glumly replied.

"We will not be getting any steers on the hoof, sir?" Yeovill asked Lewrie as he laid the mid-day meal an hour or so later. "From what I heard from the shore party, grilled beef steaks are available for a song at Buenos Aires. Mister Cooke and I were hoping."

"No one's offered us any, Yeovill, sorry t'say," Lewrie told him as a roasted quail was put before him, accompanied with potato hash and boiled beans. Quail and rabbit appeared so often that he was growing heartily sick of them, and the very mention of those huge steaks almost made his stomach sit up and beg. "Perhaps Commodore Popham will take pity on the rest of us, his flagship at the least, and send a few down to us."

"Your Cox'n and your boat crew told me they had quite a spree, sir," Yeovill revealed.

"Aye, they were first to volunteer, weren't they?" Lewrie recalled.

"Even returned with some money in their pockets, sir," Lewrie's cook commented as he presented the bread barge which held a few weevily and hard portions of ship's bisquit.

"Loot, d'ye mean, Yeovill?" Lewrie snapped.

"Oh no, sir!" Yeovill said, snickering. "They said that they'd crammed their haversacks with some of those Papal Dispensations, and sold them to a couple of the churches near where they were barracked, temporarily . . . traded them in the taverns for wine and their meals." With a wink and a leer, he further imparted, "They found them to be very useful with the Spanish doxies, too. Pleasures exchanged for written proof of salvation from past sins, sir? What poor whore *wouldn't* be eager to make such a trade. A Spanish silver dollar apiece, I think was the going rate."

"Why, the clever buggers!" Lewrie exclaimed.

"Desmond and Furfy said that even our Church of England sailors and Marines claimed to be good Catholics, so they could sign the names of the recipients, and make their, ah . . . exchanges, sir," Yeovill said.

"Who would've thought they were that enterprising," Lewrie marvelled with a shake of his head, and a brief chuckle.

O' course, I'll have t'take 'em down a peg, he told himself.

Filching those dispensations was a court-martial offence, worthy of at least a dozen lashes; profiting off the proceeds of their illegal sale might earn every sailor involved another dozen. He would have to take Desmond and Furfy aside and give them a good talking-to, warning them that they had best not try to work that sort of "fiddle" in the future, or they *would* stand before him at Captain's Mast at the least, or be given over to a proper court at the worst.

Warn 'em t'pass word to their fellow profiteers, too, he thought; *Before all hands turn so corrupted, they'll be sellin' whatever they can lay hands on, or treat ship's stores, and spirits, like their own to take whenever they like!*

After a bite or two of his dinner, though, Lewrie came to the sad realisation that discipline would demand a more public response, and a harsh warning to the ship's crew . . . perhaps even some few of them flogged as examples? *Reliant* had become a fairly happy ship in the three years of her active commission, and it was a rare thing for Bosun Sprague and his Mate to "take the cat out of the bag" to administer a flogging on a malefactor. The sentence of a week's reduction to bread and water, denied the twice-daily rum rations and tobacco, in most instances was thought more of a punishment belowdecks.

He took a sip of wine and looked down at his plate, the conundrum of how to maintain discipline making his meagre meal seem even more disappointing.

"A celebratory supper tonight, Yeovill," Lewrie decided. "All officers, and the Mids who went ashore with the Army, Eldridge and Grainger, and I will ask the Sailing Master to take the watch during the meal. Any ideas? Besides quail or rabbit, that is?"

"We've a promising piglet, sir, and a sea-pie always goes down well," Yeovill said after a long pause with his head laid over. "And, if I'm fortunate enough to catch a decent-sized fish, so long as we don't go dashing at any great speed, I could bread and grill one . . . no promises on that head, though, sir. A good fish is 'catch as catch can'."

"I know that you will do your best," Lewrie said, to cheer him up. "You always rise to the occasion."

I'll lay the problem of discipline, and punishment, if any, on them, and see what the best solution'll be, he thought.

CHAPTER THIRTY-SEVEN

*Y*eovill's "promising piglet" did not provide as large a roast as to feed seven diners sufficiently, nor was the sea-pie all that big, either, but Yeovill and Jessop had managed to land not one but two red snappers, which made for a supper bountiful enough to sate even the Midshipmen, who were perpetually hungry. For dessert, Yeovill had even conjured up heavily-vanillaed pound cake, with dollops of cherry preserves.

"One *could* say, sir, that it was not our men who committed the first violation, but the *Narcissus*, for taking chests of dispensations out of her prize and sharing them round the squadron," Lt. Spendlove speculated in a grave manner, "thus abusing Article the Eighth."

"I don't think that'd cover it, though," Lewrie said, shaking his head. "They have no value to us, so I doubt they'd be counted as goods worth a groat to a Prize-Court. No, it's the principle of the thing."

"Article Thirty-six, sir," Westcott offered, "the 'Captain's Cloak' . . . 'all other crimes not capital, committed by any Person or Persons in the Fleet, which are not mentioned in this act' and all that?"

"Article Seven, sir," their waggish Lt. Merriman said with a snicker, "about not sending in all papers found aboard prize ships? The dispensations *were* paper, after all."

"Now, that's just silly," Lewrie gravelled.

"Oh, even worse, sir!" Marine Lieutenant Simcock added, in an even more jovial manner. "Since the dispensations relieved enemy civilians of their sins, might we have violated Article the Sixth . . . 'no person in the Fleet shall relieve an enemy or Rebel with Money, Victuals, Powder, Shot, Ammunition, or any other supplies whatsoever'? Do we ease their *minds,* would that count against us?"

"I wonder if *officers* could be flogged for quarrelling, under the Twenty-third Article?" Lewrie mused aloud with an evil grin. "I don't want t'flog anyone. I start that, I might as well have half the sailors and Marines on detached duty at the gratings. Starting with Desmond, Furfy, and half my own boat crew."

"Well, sir," Midshipman Eldridge piped up from the far end of the dining table, "it's not as if any of our people *profited* from it. What they made, they spent. I doubt if any man came back aboard with a single pence . . . or Spanish *centavo* . . . to show for it."

"Poxed to their eyebrows by the Spanish whores, I expect," Lt. Merriman said. "*That's* what they have to show for it, and they'll be out fifteen shillings each for Mister Mainwaring's Mercury Cure. That may be punishment enough . . . the loss from their pay, and the agonies of the Cure, both."

"Summon 'All Hands' at this Sunday Divisions, sir, and lay the law upon them," Lt. Westcott sensibly suggested, pausing to pour himself a glass as the port bottle was passed to him. "Just come out and say that you know what they did, after reading them only the Seventh and the Eighth Articles of War, throw in the 'Captain's Cloak', and warn them that they'd best not be doing anything like that, again, or there *will* be some bloody backs among them."

"Pretty much a harmless lark, sir," Lt. Spendlove said with a rare grin, "nothing that would undermine the ship's discipline in the long run. You would not appear to be a 'Popularity Dick'. They know you, by now, sir. They also know that they got away with a very rare prank, and know that it is best a one-time thing. A show of your dis-approval, without punishment, would more than suit."

"Then that is what I'll do," Lewrie agreed after a moment to mull that over. "With your able assistance, of course, gentlemen. It would aid in that direction did you, in the course of your duties and interactions with the men, caution them that my sense of humour, and my toleration, is not boundless, hey?"

Captaining by committee? Lewrie scoffed to himself; *Damme, just how bone-idle lazy do I appear? But, there's no helping it, this time.*

"Your cook, sir, did us very well this evening," Lt. Westcott said, "but I still envy the tales I've heard of those massive steaks to be had at Buenos Aires. And these greedy gentlemen made no effort to fetch a few back aboard, in a spirit of companionship!"

"Oh, but we *would* have, sir!" Merriman laughed, "had we any way to preserve them that long."

"Stuff them in a crock of lard?" Spendlove wondered aloud. "In a cask of local brandy? Roll them in salt and brine them, as our salt-meats are preserved? I doubt any method would avail, and by the time we fetched them aboard, they would be no better than the casked meats on the orlop."

"Now, the submersion in the local brandy sounds divine!" Lt. Westcott shot back, laughing. "How marvellous that would be, and the brandy could make up for any loss of freshness.

"But," he grumbled, "I suppose our Army, and all their prisoners, grabbed most of the beef for themselves."

"What prisoners?" Merriman sneered, his eyes drawn to the last slice of cake on the sideboard. "The Spanish sloped off inland."

"Mean t'say, General Beresford didn't capture any of them?" Lewrie asked, a tad uneasy at the news.

"Well, once we repulsed their cavalry a few miles above where we landed at Quilmes Point, we saw very little of them, sir. No one did," Lt. Spendlove answered. "They'd departed before we got to the bridge over the Cuello, and then we sat on our hands from the twenty-fifth of June 'til the formal surrender of the city was signed on the second of July, and we could march in and take the town."

"Well then, how many of them got away?" Lewrie pressed.

"I heard an Army officer say that we'd been up against about fifteen hundred at the skirmish, sir," Spendlove told him.

"Aye, and I heard later that General Beresford thought that he had fought two thousand," Merriman gravelled, looking round the table to see if anyone else had a wish for cake, before summoning Pettus to fetch him that last slice. "Mind now, the Commodore boasted that we'd engaged *four* thousand!"

That would *sound better in the London papers, aye!* Lewrie told himself, recalling a time or two that he had inflated the odds, too.

"They were allowed to just ride off inland?" Lewrie asked.

"Well, we had no cavalry of our own, and with such a small force, I suppose that General Beresford and the Commodore thought that securing the town, and gathering up the treasure and all, was more important, sir," Lt. Spendlove told them all.

"Like Henry Morgan sacking Panama, sir?" Midshipman Grainger said with a snicker, very tongue-in-cheek.

"No more port for the youngsters," Westcott teased.

"Oh, sir!" Grainger pretended to cringe.

"Then it sounds as if Beresford has no idea where they've gone, or how far they retreated," Lewrie surmised, "nor how many Spanish troops are still in the field! *That* don't sound healthy. How many has Beresford left? Less the four hundred and fourty the Navy lended him, that from sixteen hundred thirty is . . . less than twelve hundred men! That few, to patrol the town, scout the environs for the return of the enemy, and mount defences? *Very* un-healthy!"

"More patrolling and policing of the town than anything else, really, sir," Lt. Spendlove said with a worry-furrowed brow. "None of the local watchmen were co-operating with us when we were there, and if the Spanish had any police force in the city before, we didn't see a one of them."

"Nothing but dirty looks from the locals, too, those that took note we were present," Lt. Merriman commented between bites of cake. "There was a lot of shunning and 'cuts sublime', casting their noses high and sniffing . . . mumbled curses and such. None of our lads went out after dark unless they were in groups, and well-armed, to boot."

"Or snug for the night in a tavern or brothel," Lt. Spendlove added. "In their temporary quarters, rather, for those were what was chosen for their lodgings."

"How *entertainin'*," Lewrie drawled. "And, no sign of any who'd rise up and cheer for their independence from Spain, I take it."

"The Commodore's Colonel Miranda was spinning moonbeams, sir," Merriman groused. "I don't think any of his nationalist rebels even *exist*! Not among the Argentines *we* saw."

"They'd cut our throats as soon as look at us, sir," Midshipman Eldridge spoke up.

"And that's not the port talking, sir," Grainger joshed, and shared a grin with Eldridge, who was much older, risen from Quartermaster's Mate, and not possessed of the usual Midshipman's cheek.

"God help our soldiers, then, if the Argentines decide to rise up against *us*," Lewrie gloomily said, slowly turning his port glass by the stem. "Hard as it was t'get 'em ashore in the first place, does it prove necessary to evacuate 'em, it could turn into a real mess. I think the charts show less than three fathoms of depth right along the town piers, is that right? Beresford might have t'retreat down to the Cuello River, again, set himself up on the South bank, make sure that the bridge is completely destroyed, and hope that all our boats can get them off."

"And, except for *Encounter,* sir, none of our ships could get within gun-range to support them during the evacuation," Westcott pointed out.

"How long would it take for orders to that effect to reach us to send the boats inshore, too, sir?" Merriman said, sucking the last few crumbs which adhered to his fork. "At short notice, there would be only *Encounter*'s, *Narcissus*'s, and the five transports' boats to do the work, and it would take too long to get them *all* off before the Spanish find a way across the river up-stream, where it might be a tad shallower and narrower."

"Even worse, if there's another bridge up-stream, or a ferry," Lewrie fretted. "We've no maps of inland Argentina, so we just don't *know*! Christ, I hope that Popham . . . the Commodore, mean t'say . . . wrote Admiralty for re-enforcements before we left Cape Town, or Saint Helena."

Slim chance o' that, Lewrie thought; *He wanted his marvellous coup t'be a grand surprise! Maybe Governor Patten sent a report home, after giving us those extra men and guns.*

"Then, we must hope that General Beresford can hold out 'til we do get re-enforcements, sir," Westcott said, grimacing, and his savage face looking even harsher. "Assuming the government even knows where we are, and how long it would take to get word to London that we are even *here*, and in *need*! Good Lord above."

"Unless that Army officer's estimate of enemy forces was right, sir," Lt. Merriman said with a hopeful expression. "If they only had fifteen hundred or so to begin with, suffered some casualties when we skirmished with them, they may have run so far that they are no threat any longer, and our twelve hundred or so can stand on the defensive in the town. We may be borrowing trouble."

"Then let us pray that that is so, Mister Merriman," Lewrie intoned. "Else, we have a debacle on our hands."

Well . . . Popham'll *have a debacle on his hands,* Lewrie thought; *And we're safely out of it!*

CHAPTER THIRTY-EIGHT

A day later, manna figuratively fell from Heaven. A dowdy brig-rigged vessel, captured in the small port of Ensenada, came down from Buenos Aires laden with beef, pork, and bread, some of the meat fresh-slaughtered and newly salted and casked in brine, and some of it still on the hoof. As if in answer to Lt. Westcott's prayer, some smaller kegs contained choicer slabs of steaks and roasts, not a week off the cow, and, when the salt was rinsed off in the steep-tubs, were as fresh and juicy as any that could be ordered in a London chop house.

Reliant received two live bullocks and four hefty pigs, guaranteeing fresh meat for all hands for several days, and at least a week's worth of much fresher salt-meat in casks. All of it was welcomed aboard as enthusiastically as chests of prize-money.

Equally welcome were the fresh vegetables and fruit. The Argentine had been settled for centuries, time enough for orchards and market gardens to provide a year-round cornucopia of European staples and the more exotic crops native to the Indios. Yeovill scrambled from one case or keg to the next, gathering all manner of peppers and raw spices or herbs, snagging hands of green bananas, mangoes, guavas, and Spanish fruits for Lewrie's table, trailed by the Purser, Mister Cadbury, and his

Jack-in-the-Breadroom who were trying to inventory the lot before it could be pilfered.

Cadbury was pleased, as well, for with all the victuals, there were sacks of coffee beans, bundles of leaf tobacco, and many kegs of local red wine suitable for issue in lieu of the Navy's "Blackstrap", and for once it would not cost him a single pence, for it was all for free, taken as booty from a conquered foe!

"A steak for your supper tonight, sir!" Yeovill promised with glee. "Along with these wee white potatoes, broad beans, and baked rolls. Medium rare, as you like it, the potatoes roasted in wedges with garlic, onion, and rosemary, the beans in oil . . . as good as any shore supper you ever tasted! Will you be having guests in, sir?"

"Not tonight, Yeovill," Lewrie told him, "for I fully intend t'be a pig and feast upon this bounty all by myself. I will even try the local red wine."

And so will Pettus, Jessop, and yourself, Lewrie assured himself, for a captain's servants in essence ate from the same dishes as the man they served, even if it was only the left-overs. But, it was the wise captain who did not question how much was prepared for him alone! Even his clerk, Faulkes, usually shared in the bounty, at least the tastier bits, though he was officially fed alongside the sailors.

"Hoy, there!" Lewrie called over to the older Midshipman from the *Narcissus* frigate, who was in charge of the victualling vessel as another net-sling load of goods was swayed up from her holds by the main course yardarm. "Any orders for us?"

"None, sir!" the Mid called back.

"How do things go in town?" Lewrie asked.

"*Mostly* quiet, sir, in the main," the Midshipman answered, "though there have been some . . . scuffles with the locals. They are not happy with our being there, and some trouble-makers have become bold enough to shake their fists and shout, but the Army patrols daunt them . . . so far. That is the last due you, sir," he said, pointing to the sling-load. "I will be off to victual *Diadem*. Is she still anchored off Montevideo, or does she cruise?"

"No matter, sir, she's the only vessel swimming off there," Lewrie assured him, "and thankee kindly for all the goodies!"

"As the French say, sir, *bon appétit!*" the Midshipman cried as he began to get his little ship back under way.

Lewrie turned his attention back to *Reliant*'s forward weather decks, where their burly Black Ship's Cook, idle sailors, and ship's boys were herding the hogs into the forecastle manger and barring them in, and hobbling the two bullocks, preparatory to one of them being slaughtered.

"Thank God today is not a Banyan Day, sir," the Sailing Master, Mr. Caldwell, jovially said from nearby on the quarterdeck. "It'd be hard on the people to see all that juicy meat on the hoof, and still be fed on porridge, bisquit, and cheese!"

"And the officers' mess is so looking forward to a hefty beef roast, hey?" Lewrie teased.

"Individual steaks, sir, at least a pound apiece I was told," Caldwell chortled. "Grilled, not boiled, praise the Lord! It appears that if there will be no prize-money doled out for taking the Argentine, there are at least *some* compensations."

"Even if there were prize-money awarded, we weren't 'In Sight' at the moment of capture, and are unable to share," Lewrie said with a sigh. "Come to think on it, neither were *Encounter* and *Narcissus* . . . where they lay at anchor off Point Quilmes was twelve miles or more from the city."

"It was all seized by the Army, sir," Mr. Caldwell countered as he patted his belly. "Mark my words, it will all be deemed to be Droits of The Crown, not Droits of The Admiralty, and be whisked to England, soon as dammit."

"One may only hope, then, t'be the ship that whisks it," Lewrie said with a snicker. "There's a wee percentage allowed the 'whiskee', at least."

"Then it is just too bad that we draw too much water to be able to go and fetch it, sir," Caldwell said with a disappointed grimace.

"Captain Donnelly, and *Narcissus*," Lewrie supposed, grimacing along with the Sailing Master. "The lucky . . . fellow!"

"Sure to be, sir," Caldwell gloomily agreed. "Sure to be."

Up forward, a wash-deck pump was being rigged and manned before Mr. Cooke, who had so aptly named himself after fleeing slavery on Jamaica, began the killing. He had a middle maul with which to stun the beast, his sharpest and longest knife with which to cut its throat and bleed it—helpers stood by with buckets to catch as much blood as they could for other uses—and then a boarding axe and stouter, shorter knives with which to skin it and butcher it into eight-pound chunks. Bisquit was prancing about in anticipation, and in mock hunting growls and barks; it was quite possible he'd never seen a bullock, certainly not aboard ship, and didn't know what it was. Idle crewmen stood about on gangways and the foredeck hatch cover, cheering, jeering, and ready to whoop in glee over the bullock's impending demise.

"Shall we get under way, again, after the steer's been dealt with, sir?" Lt. Westcott asked after he'd joined them.

"Hmm, no," Lewrie decided. "We'll stay at anchor the rest of the day and night. We've ten fathoms of depth, and a decent holding ground, for a change. Small arms practice, and an hour of cutlass drill after the hands have eat their fresh victuals."

"Aye, sir," Westcott said. "Your cook has lent ours a bottle of Worcestershire sauce for this evening's steaks. Might you express our thanks to him, sir?"

"Of course, Mister Westcott," Lewrie allowed, grinning. "Anything else that would please the wardroom?"

"Shore liberty, sir," Westcott puckishly said, "a noon-to-noon, with 'All Night In'."

"All night in what?" Mr. Caldwell whispered with glee.

"Huzzah! Whoo! Done 'im wif one blow!" sailors were cheering and hooting as the bullock's thick skull was crushed and it sprawled dead on the deck. Its compatriot bellowed and thrashed in terror of the deed, and ship's boys leapt and capered over the carcass in glee.

"You might also ask Yeovill for some of his vinegary pepper sauce, Mister Westcott," Lewrie suggested as he made his way to the ladderway. "If I can spare it, that is."

The next evening, as *Reliant* cruised along under reduced sail in deep waters South of Maldonado and Lobos Island, the *Narcissus* frigate came calling, free of the banks and shoals of the Plate Estuary at long last, and laden with gold and silver. Her captain, Ross Donnelly, sounded jubilant as he brought his ship within easy hailing distance.

"Captain Donnelly, I hear that you are to be congratulated!" Lewrie shouted over with a brass speaking-trumpet. "Will you allow me to dine you in? If you are not sick of beef steak, by now, that is?"

"I will accept your offer most happily, Captain Lewrie!" Captain

Donnelly shouted back. "I shall fetch you the wine! I discovered an anker of French Bordeaux in a warehouse, and your kind invitation is cause to broach it!"

"Come aboard, sir, come aboard!" Lewrie cried, then turned to Midshipman Shannon, who stood watch on the quarterdeck. "Pass word to my cook, Mister Shannon. He's to cut my supper steak into two shares, and lay on a second course of roast rabbit, or quail, quick as he can."

"Aye, sir!"

"A brandy before supper, sir, or would a Rhenish suit?" Lewrie offered, once Captain Donnelly was seated at his ease on the starboard-side settee.

"Rhenish would be delightful, thank you, sir," Donnelly responded.

"Bound for England, I assume," Lewrie commented.

"With but two brief breaks in passage," Donnelly replied, "one at Cape Town, to drop a letter to General Sir David Baird, requesting more troops, and a second at Saint Helena to speak with the island's governor, Patten, to do the same. Then, weather permitting, it will be 'all to the royals' for Portsmouth."

"I envy you," Lewrie baldly admitted as their wine arrived, "for doing something other than pace back and forth 'cross the mouth of the Plate. You'll be bearing the loot, I take it?"

"Aye, over one million six hundred thousand dollars' worth!" Donnelly exclaimed, more than happy to boast. "The most of it in silver, of course, but some gold coins as well. Droits of The Crown," he added with a wince, "but, if the traditional customs are followed, and even if the Treasury is parsimonious, I could end up with a mere one percent of the total sum . . . and my family and estate and heirs set for life, ha ha!"

Ha ha, mine arse! Lewrie thought, appalled but striving not to show it; *The fortunate turd!*

"My *word*, how marvellous for you!" he said instead. "You could afford a whole *county*, or your *own* frigate!"

"There's at least another million dollars' worth of goods in the warehouses we seized, as well, but it would take an armada to haul it all away, and flog on the London markets," Donnelly further crowed.

"You'll be carrying the Commodore's report to Admiralty, and a revelation of where he's got to, as well? I wonder how that'll go down," Lewrie speculated.

"Well, he *did* send word that he was quitting the Cape, and what he was intending," Donnelly told him, more than happy to accept a top-up of his wine glass. "Now that we've succeeded, I expect that we'll see the Crown back his play to the hilt, and accept it all as a *fait accompli*. Commodore Popham also entrusted me with an open letter to the merchants of London, adverting them to the commercial possibilities in the Argentine."

"Would that not be forcing the Government's hand?" Lewrie had to ask. "Rather . . . *high*-handedly? Runnin' rough-shod over Parliament and the new Prime Minister?"

"The success, and the prospects of new sources of wealth, *may* gain him so many allies that he might be spared a court-martial. All the huzzahs and acclaim?"

"Well, as he's told us so often, I'd think he already has more than *enough* allies," Lewrie said with a smirk. "Most-like Popham has won over the local Argentines, to boot."

"Not so one would notice, no," Donnelly countered with a wink. "Oh, he's tried dining in as many prominent people as he can, taking shore lodgings and laying on lavish feasts, but . . . they'll drink his wines, eat his meals, and promise nothing. In point of fact, I am more than glad to depart. Does one go ashore for a few hours, one comes away with an uneasy feeling that the mood of the Argentines is going from a low simmer to half a boil."

"Some trouble in the streets, I heard from the victualling vessel's Midshipman?" Lewrie prompted, taking another glass of wine when Pettus offered. "Unrest?"

"It hasn't gotten *too* bad . . . yet," Captain Donnelly told him, leaning forward to speak in a lower voice. "General Beresford's put more men in the streets, in larger parties, to keep the lid on, but the reason it hasn't boiled over yet is the departure of the young men who would be causing trouble, were they still in Buenos Aires."

"And with too few troops t'keep 'em in—?" Lewrie said.

"And no city walls, or gates to seal, aye, Lewrie," Donnelly completed for him. "The soldiers can inspect any waggon or mule load coming in, or going out, but many Argentines possessed arms before we arrived, and without house-to-house searches to confiscate them, due to the lack of troops, God only knows whether weapons are being smuggled in, or carried out, in the dark of night by Spaniards trying to join up with armed bands beyond our reach. The terms of surrender put private property off-limits, so . . . ," he said with a hapless shrug. "There are rumours of a *criollo* by name of Puerdin or something like that who's forming a patriot band, somewhere out in the hinterlands, and where the original Spanish troops that Beresford beat at Quilmes have gone is anyone's guess."

"Are defences being prepared, just in case?" Lewrie asked.

"Frankly, I haven't a clue," Donnelly admitted with a deprecating laugh. "After your adventure with the Army ashore at Cape Town, I expect you know bags more than I do of soldierly doings. The Commodore still *seems* confident, though."

"But he would, wouldn't he?" Lewrie said with an open sneer. "Commodore Popham is confidence personified. It's a pity that his considerable charm is wasted on the Argentines."

"Matter of fact," Donnelly confided, "he told me that, had he but two more regiments, he'd have a go at Montevideo and make a clean sweep of the Plate Estuary's last defences."

"I'd think a brigade of three regiments, *with* a regiment of cavalry added, *might* be barely sufficient to hold Buenos Aires, alone," Lewrie scoffed.

"Well, there you are, then," Donnelly replied, laughing again. "Military problem solved! As I just said, you understand the ways of our redcoats better than I . . . all that square-bashing of theirs?"

"Addles the brains, eventually," Lewrie japed. "Will you stand off-and-on with me 'til morning?"

"Yes, I thought I might," Donnelly said, "then, with a decent slant of wind, I can fall down near the Fourtieth Latitude and catch the Westerlies, straight on to Cape Town."

"Did the Commodore advise you on our mysterious sightings of a visitor offshore?" Lewrie asked.

Hard as it was to get a despatch boat up to Buenos Aires, all three ships posted to cruise the mouth of the estuary had sent reports of those strange sails on the horizon, but this was the first that Captain Donnelly had heard of them. Lewrie quickly filled him in.

"Hmm, in that case, it might be best did we cut our supper short," Donnelly pondered, looking concerned, "and I make my offing in the dark . . . lights extinguished. From nine P.M., say, 'til dawn tomorrow, does this stern wind hold, I could be seventy miles out to sea by six A.M."

"The last sighting was late this afternoon, twenty miles or more off

Cape Saint Mary, up to the Nor'east," Lewrie advised. "We don't know what she is, but she is persistent. With any luck, she'll pop up round mid-channel, leagues from where you intend to be."

"Excuse me, sirs, but supper is ready to be laid," Pettus announced, and Yeovill came bustling in with his metal food barge.

"You've broached my anker of Bordeaux, have you?" Donnelly asked Pettus. "Good ho, then! Let's sup, for I am famished!"

CHAPTER THIRTY-NINE

S ighted her again, sir," Lt. Merriman reported as Lewrie came to the quarterdeck, spurred by the lookouts' cries of "Sail Ho!" days after *Narcissus* had departed with her precious cargo. "Her royals or t'gallants only. Can't spot her from the deck, so she's over fifteen miles seawards."

Lewrie extended his telescope anyway, looking not towards their mysterious stalker, but at HMS *Diomede,* the old 50-gunner, several miles to the North.

"I'm growing tired o' that bastard," Lewrie spat. "What does her captain think he's playin' at? If she's a Spanish warship, there is nothing t'be gained by hangin' about this long after we conquered the bloody place. She should be scuttlin' off t'warn the other Spanish colonies . . . go find other men o' war and come back t'take us on."

"Unless she's been left to keep an eye on us whilst the other ships are preparing to come to the Plate, sir," Lt. Merriman speculated. "Perhaps the word has already been passed?"

"Where are we this morning, Mister Caldwell?" Lewrie asked the Sailing Master, going over to peer at his charts.

"About ten sea miles East of Lobos Island, sir," Caldwell offered, "and our lurker would be about fifteen miles further seawards of that, is Mister Merriman's estimate correct."

Lewrie concentrated on the much-thumbed and pencil-marked sea-chart, looking for inspiration, or a single clue, for long moments. From the port of Maldonado and Cape St. Mary to Cape Norte on the South, the Plate Estuary was over 120 miles wide, narrowing between Montevideo and Point Piedras. It was an impossible distance to cover with three warships, even sailing independently of each other, and their stranger could pop up just temptingly out of reach each dawn and dusk wherever she willed along that line, coming up as near as Point Piedras sometimes, without any risk of interception. Did *Diomede, Raisonnable,* or *Reliant* attempt to beat up to her, she would go about and run over the horizon, but, a day or two later, there she would be again, sniffing round the mouth of the estuary.

"Here," Lewrie muttered, jabbing a finger at the chart, "off Cape Saint Mary, then . . . here, round mid-entrance, then the next day or so later, she pops up down to the South, like she's standing on sentry-go, same as us. North, in the middle, in the South . . . hmm. Not always, though. Her captain must have a pattern to his madness, but I don't see it. Clues, any-one?" he asked his officers.

"Well, sir, there have been times when she appears in the South at dawn, then comes back within sight not too far away from there at sun-down," Lt. Westcott pointed out. "The next dawn she might be near the middle of the estuary's mouth, and appear in the North by dusk. At other times, she will make her probes off Cape Saint Mary at dawn *and* dusk, then pop up to the South. I'm not all that sure that there *is* a discernible pattern."

"Perhaps her captain is trying to avoid showing us a pattern, sir," Lt. Merriman said with a shrug, "but, he seems to have but three places where he closes the coast for a look-see . . . Cape Saint Mary, Cape Norte, and the middle of the estuary mouth."

"She was off the middle yesterday?" Lewrie asked. "Then, it may be good odds she'll either be off Cape Saint Mary just before sundown to-night, or round the middle. Hah!" he barked. "Let's gamble! We will stay near Cape Saint Mary and Lobos Island the rest of the day, standin' off-and-on, but slowly make our way seaward a few more miles. Not enough t'frighten her off. Whether she appears off the Cape, or further down towards the middle of the estuary mouth, I intend that we dash out once it's full dark. . . ." He paused, looking aft at the taffrail lanthorns either side of the stern. "We won't light the lanthorns but replace 'em with small hand-held lamps. That'll make us look as if we're further off from her. Once she's had her evening look-see, we'll douse 'em, one at a time, as she makes her way back seaward for the night, then douse the last 'un, show no lights at all, and chase after her, get seaward of her, and catch her on a lee shore! Pin her 'twixt us and the other ships!"

"Even if we don't bring her to action, we might give her such a scare that her captain tosses in his cards and sails away," Lieutenant Westcott chortled.

"Mister Merriman, I'd be much obliged did you alter course to seaward, nothing too drastic . . . perhaps no more than two points. We have all day," Lewrie ordered. "*Diomede* is bound South, the same as us, and I wish t'stay within signalling distance of her, perhaps no more than six or seven miles off 'til sundown."

"Very good, sir! Bosun! Pipe all hands to the braces, and be ready to alter course!" Lt. Merriman shouted down to the waist of the ship.

"Hah!" Lewrie exulted, clapping his hands together. "I will be below, Mister Merriman, finishin' my breakfast. Carry on. Drill on the great-guns in the Forenoon, finishin' with live fire."

"Aye, sir."

Damme, I feel like a feagued horse! he thought as he trotted down the ladderway to the waist, stopping to pet Bisquit and let him stand on his hind legs with his paws on his chest, ruffling fur and telling him what a good dog he was.

Days on end of boredom and frustration, with very little news of what was transpiring round Buenos Aires, denied any part in the landings at Point Quilmes, left to cruise fruitlessly . . . now, all of that was swept away by the prospect of discovering just who, or what, had been lurking just out of reach, by the possibility of a sea-fight, broadside-to-broadside . . . or the imagined shock they might cause when they appeared to *seaward* of their mysterious lurker, and cutting off her escape!

Very much like an aged horse, dosed by shrewd traders with a plug of ginger up the rump to appear young and lively, Lewrie felt as if he'd suddenly shed ten years and could prance in circles!

"A warm-up of your coffee, sir?" Pettus offered as Lewrie swept the tails of his coat back and sat himself down at the dining table once more, tucking his napkin into his shirt collar, then rubbing his hands in delight.

"I'd much admire it, thankee kindly, Pettus!" Lewrie happily replied, so loud that Chalky, at the other end of the table, started and crouched behind his food bowl. "Oh, don't be such a scaredy-cat, puss. It's only me, in high takings for once."

"High takings, sir?" Pettus asked as he poured the coffee.

"Our spook is back, but tonight we're goin' t'have a go at 'smoaking' her out," Lewrie explained, beaming in glee. "Once I've eat, Pettus, we'll see to my weapons. There's a good chance I'll have need of 'em on the morrow. Oil, brushes, rags, and flints. And, do see that I've a clean silk shirt and stockings, and a fresh-washed pair o' breeches, just in case.

"Damme!" he cried. "With any luck at all, I'm going t'catch that bastard ghost ship out yonder if it kills me!"

CHAPTER FORTY

"Sir? Sir?"

"Uhmph?"

"Seven Bells of the Middle Watch, sir," Pettus prompted by the edge of Lewrie's hanging bed-cot, with a small candle lanthorn in his hand. "You said to wake you half an hour before the change of watch."

"Um, aye," Lewrie agreed with a curt nod. "I'm awake."

Don't want *t'be,* Lewrie thought, for he had been having one of the grandest dreams of a neck-or-nothing steeplechase, soaring like a falcon over hedgerows, stone walls, and stiles in company with boisterous old friends; even stout Clotworthy Chute, his old school chum who'd been expelled with him from Harrow, could keep up and keep his saddle like a born horseman—which he most certainly was not! There had been naked ladies, full tits bouncing most wondrously, too, all of them handsome. No one he'd *known,* but it had felt *damned* promising!

"Cold tea, sir," Pettus offered.

"Cold, and scant, comfort," Lewrie muttered, whisking back the covers and rolling out of the bed-cot barefoot, clad in nothing but his underdrawers. As he sipped the tea he looked round his cabins to assure himself that all the sash-windows in the stern, and both the windows in the quarter-galleries, were covered with jute sacking, and would show no light out-board. It was stuffy, humid, and almost cool to the shivering point belowdecks, in those hours before sunrise.

With the pewter mug of tea in hand, he went to the larboard quarter-gallery, had a long pee, swished and gargled with tea, then spat into the "necessary" to clear his mouth.

"Let's shove me into order, Pettus," he bade, stripping off the under-drawers and donning a fresh-washed set. He sat in his desk chair to pull on silk stockings and bind them behind his knees, stood to pull on clean breeches, then his Hessian boots. Pettus offered him a silk shirt, then helped tie the neck-stock. With the addition of a waist-coat, uniform coat, and cocked hat, he was ready to go on deck, just a quarter hour before Eight Bells and the change of watch, and the call for all hands to "wakey-wakey, lash up and stow".

"Cap'm's on deck!" the Master's Mate of the watch alerted the the others on the quarterdeck as Lewrie made his way up from the waist.

"Good morning, sir," Lt. Spendlove said in a soft voice.

"Good morning, Mister Spendlove," Lewrie replied, tapping his fingers to the brim of his hat. "Now, where away is our spook? And what is our heading?"

"As at midnight, when you went below, sir," Spendlove answered. "Course Sou'west by South, making six knots by the last cast of the log, and about fourty miles seaward of the estuary, by Dead Reckoning. The lookout at the main cross-trees reports that he has our stranger's taffrail lanthorns in sight, just barely . . . *inshore* of us, sir! Not twelve miles off! Three points off the starboard bows, at the last hailing."

"So she *is* makin' for the middle of the estuary mouth!" Lewrie exclaimed, clapping his hands together in satisfaction, a sound much too loud for the wee hours, and the tense anticipation of the entire on-watch crew. "Any idea of her course?" Lewrie asked, going to the starboard, lee, bulwarks to peer out, even if nothing could be seen in the deep darkness from the deck.

"She seems to be plodding along on roughly the same course as ours, sir," Lt. Spendlove said as he followed Lewrie to the rails, "though if she intends to close the coast to visual range of *Diomede* or us . . . were we there, of course . . . she may haul her wind at any time."

"Uhm, aye," Lewrie agreed. "We're fourty miles offshore, and she's twelve miles closer . . . twenty-eight miles off. Even at a plod under reduced sail, she could get within twelve miles of the middle of the estuary mouth just before dawn . . . if she goes about soon. Is she a warship, she surely stands the same watches as us. At Eight Bells . . ."

He pulled out his pocket watch, but couldn't read its face in the darkness. The wee lanthorn at the forecastle belfry was shrouded, as was the light from the compass binnacle, with just enough of a slit in the cloth covering for the helmsmen to steer by. He gave the idea up and shoved it back into his pocket.

"Ye know, Mister Spendlove, I think this is goin' t'work!" he said in a low voice, though one tinged with humour.

He hadn't been all that sure and confident at sundown the evening before, wasn't even sure that their mysterious ghost would appear near Lobos Island, or had in the meantime made off South nearer the mouth of the Plate Estuary. When within signalling distance of HMS *Diomede*, he had spelled out his intentions to her captain, requesting that *Diomede* play the anvil whilst *Reliant* would be the hammer, or the beater. The frigate had slowly made her way a few miles further offshore, waiting.

Lewrie had felt *real* hope when the stranger's uppermost sails had arisen over the horizon, six leagues to the Sou'east of Lobos Island, her royals or t'gallants lit amber by the last rays of the descending sun. *Reliant* lay to her West with her sham taffrail lanthorns already lit, making her easy to spot, but not so far out to sea near her to give their ghost alarm. Playing the peek-a-boo game too long, their stranger had lulled herself into complacency . . . or so Lewrie prayed. One last look before supper, and a turn out to sea to wallow along South to the mid-point of the estuary entrances, out of sight for the night, and she would be safe as houses 'til the morrow, when she closed the coast and came in sight once more, still too far aloof and seaward to risk any real danger.

Or so her captain would think!

Once night had fallen, the sea had turned to ink, and the only light came from a myriad of stars, the Southern Cross most prominent, their stranger was below the horizon and out of sight, and Lewrie had ordered a change of course to stand out Sou'-Sou'east, and the reefs shaken from her courses and tops'ls, and the hand-lanthorns at the stern extinguished.

He'd gone below just long enough to shave and take a sponge-bath, then had returned to the quarterdeck, to pace and fret 'til one of the lookouts had called out that he espied their stranger's stern lights on the horizon, down to the South, and two points off the starboard bows. An hour and a half later, and the report was that their ghost was abeam, and Lewrie had gone below again for a light supper, sure that they would be to seaward of her when the dawn came. They'd altered course at 9 P.M., had cracked on sail for a time, and Lewrie had finally gone below at midnight for a few hours' rest.

Eight Bells chimed at the belfry up forward in four twin taps, the last stroke lingering, as the Middle Watch ended and the Morning began. Lt. George Merriman relieved Spendlove, and groggy-sleepy men turned out from the gun deck below to replace the night watchstanders. Bosuns' calls trilled orders, and the frigate rumbled to hundreds of feet as sailors rolled out of their hammocks to thud onto the planks, grumbled, and lashed up their bedding and hammocks into long sausages narrow enough to pass through the ring measures. Off-watch sailors went below to fetch their rolled-up bedding and bring them on deck to stow in the metal stanchions down both sail-tending gangways and the bulwarks of the quarterdeck, and the cross-deck stanchions at the front of the quarterdeck. Other hands were breaking out and rigging the wash-deck pumps for the usual morning's cleaning with brooms and mops, and holystone "bibles" to scrub the decks snowy-clean.

"Deck there!" a lookout tried to shout down over the din. "Do ye hear, there? Chase is goin' about! She's stern-on!"

"Mister Spendlove . . . before we start swabbin', I'll have the ship put about to West-Nor'west," Lewrie ordered.

"Aye, sir," Spendlove replied, pausing to grin and ask, "So she really is inshore of us?"

"Aye, she is, and we may soon have her," Lewrie told him. "Do be quick about it."

"Aye, sir!"

The Third Officer, Mr. Merriman, had gone below for a brief nap after standing the Middle Watch, and perhaps a bite or two before returning to the deck prepared for possible action. Lt. Westcott, the First Officer, came up after four hours of sleep, along with Marine Lieutenant Simcock. The both of them were armed already, sporting their swords and braces of pistols. Simcock looked the freshest, for with no watchstanding duties to perform, he always had "all night in".

"Where is she? Can we see her yet?" Simcock eagerly asked, all but bouncing on his toes to gain an inch or more of view to the West.

"Still hull-down to us from the deck, and only the lookouts can see her," Lewrie told him. "She's there, rest assured she is." He had to speak loudly over the dins as the braces and sheets were manned and eased, as the helm was put over, and their frigate swung her bows onto the new course in pursuit of their stranger.

"Deck, there!" a lookout yelled down. "Chase is one point off the starb'd bows!"

"We *are* chasing her, now," Lewrie told them with a laugh, "even if she doesn't know it, yet. We can now call her a 'Chase'. Once she spots us and tries to run . . . what will she be then, Mister Munsell?" he asked the nearest Midshipman of the Watch, who had been listening.

"An 'Enemy Then Flying', sir!" Munsell quickly piped up.

"Well, I for one wish she takes no notice of us 'til after the galley fires have been lit, and I can have a cup of strong coffee, or two," Lt. Westcott said with a groan and a long, wide yawn.

"I fear we'll be silhouetted against the dawn, perhaps even by the false dawn, long before that," Lewrie commented as he looked up at the sails, almost lost in the darkness. "Today's a Banyan Day, at any rate. The best we may expect'll be small beer, cheese, and bisquit. Hot porridge'll be out of the question."

"Well, damme," Westscott said, yawning again.

"Have a bad night of it, did you?" Lewrie asked in jest.

"Tossed and turned, even after a stiff brandy," Westcott said with a shrug.

"That's more due the Sailing Master's snores," Lt. Simcock told Lewrie. "I compare them to a beach full of sea lions, but Merriman's of the opinion he sounds more like a whole warehouse full of rolling casks. Back and forth, rumble, rumble, rumble!"

"He's the loudest in the Middle Watch," Westcott said with a grimace, "right in the middle of my most vivid dreams!"

"Hmm, the lookouts aloft are most-like seeing our ghost by her taffrail lanthorns," Lewrie speculated, looking up again at the masts. "It's still too dark to see her sails. That puts her hull-up above the night horizon from them. That'd be . . . inside twelve miles of visibility, perhaps about eight.

"Mister Spendlove?" Lewrie said, turning to the Officer of the Watch. "What is the last cast of the log?"

"Six knots, sir," Spendlove answered.

"Very well. Let's take one reef in the main course to slow us down a bit," Lewrie ordered. "I'd like our stranger to only see our t'gallants by false dawn, which'll be about an hour and a half from now. She just *might* think we're a transport fetching re-enforcements, and come out to us."

"Or, she might spook and run, sir," Westcott cautioned.

"Aye, but run to where, sir?" Lewrie posed, grinning. "South, I think. The winds are fair for Mar del Plata down the coast, or to Bahía Blanca, if she needs a hidey-hole. Perhaps that's where she's come from in the first place, and got word of our invasion overland. We knew almost nothing but rumours and fantasies about the Argentine before we invaded it, and the Plate Estuary's a bad place to maintain warships, what with all the shoals and banks, as we've discovered."

"Main mast captain and crew!" Spendlove was bellowing through a brass speaking-trumpet. "Trice up, lay out, and take one reef in the main course!"

Westcott and Simcock began to pace to kill the time, even if they were strictly not on watch, and could have gone below once the wash-deck pumps were stowed away. Westcott's yawning had infected Lewrie, and, after a few more minutes standing stern and stoic by the forward windward corner of the quarterdeck, he felt his eyelids lowering and his head nodding. He shook himself several times to try and stay awake, but when he caught himself leaning on the bulwarks, with an arm threaded through the shrouds to stay upright, he surrendered to the moment. He called for his collapsible wood-and-canvas deck chair and had himself a sit-down, and allowed himself a little nap before the sun came up, and the game would be afoot.

"Think we're in for a scrape this mornin'?" one of the Quartermasters on the helm, Baldock, asked Master's Mate Hook.

"Sounds like it," Hook whispered back.

"Cap'm don't look worried," Baldock said as he eased a spoke or two. "Might come out aright, then."

"Wager ya he's schemin' on how t'beat 'em, this very minute," Hook assured him with a grin. "Cap'm knows how t'win, and fight. Seen it before, when I was in the old *Proteus* with him, and God help Frogs, Dons, and Dutchies . . . any o' the King's enemies."

Up forward, and un-heard by Baldock and Hook on the helm, the "fighting" Captain Alan Lewrie, RN, snorted as his chin drooped onto his chest.

Ting-Ting! Ting!

"Umph."

The striking of Three Bells of the Morning Watch pulled Lewrie from his nap with a grunt. He raised his head a few degrees and saw that the false dawn had crept up on *Reliant* from the East, astern of her, while he had drowsed. His ship was once more a solid thing from the bulwark beside him to the out-thrust tip of the jib-boom, though still an indefinite greyness.

He stood, and looked forward in search of the strange intruder, but she was still below the horizon from his vantage on the quarterdeck, as was the Plate Estuary and the Argentine coast. Far enough to sea beyond the jungles and the estuary, there was no hint of the daily fogs, either; what he could see of the sea's horizon was as flat and sharp-edged as a table top. Closer to, the sea was not the ink-black of night, but had lightened to a slate grey, flecked here and there with lighter grey foaming wave crests, like dirty wash suds.

Aloft, the intricate maze of both standing and running rigging was a spider web done in charcoal, and the sails still colourless, almost indistinguishable from a rainy-day overcast. Even the bright red-white-blue commissioning pendant that streamed off towards the larboard bows might just as well been a long hank of rope.

"I miss anything?" Lewrie asked after he paced over to the iron hammock stanchions at the forward break of the quarterdeck to speak to Lt. Spendlove.

"No, sir," Spendlove replied, "we're standing on as before at about five knots. The lookouts report that the Chase is still burning her taffrail lanthorns, and that they can now make out her t'gallants."

"Very good, carry on, sir," Lewrie said, turning to note that Mr. Caldwell, the Sailing Master, was now on deck. "Dawn, sir?"

"Full dawn at fifteen minutes after six, sir," Caldwell said. "It is now half past five, and a bit."

The decks had been washed, scoured, and were now almost dry. The wash-deck pumps had been stowed away, and only the duty watch was on deck. Lewrie caught the scent of burning firewood from the galley funnel.

"Larbowlines at their breakfast?" he asked.

"Hot porridge, sir," Lt. Spendlove said.

"Let's make sure the starboard watch division has their breakfast before we shut the galley down," Lewrie said. "I suppose Mister Westcott has got his coffee, at last? Hah, good! Pass word for my steward. I could use a bowl of porridge, and a mug of coffee, too."

Four Bells were struck at 6 A.M., as the skies astern lightened even more, and the indefinite greyness of the sails, the ship, and the sea took on vivid "early-early" colour, as if this day would come fresh-laundered after the worn drabness of the day before. The airs were cool and refreshing, the nippiness of night quickly forgotten as a breeze scented with deep-sea iodine and salt freshened. Inshore, in the estuary, there would be fogs and overcasts, but this far out to sea, the skies promised lots of sunshine and few clouds.

"Deck, there!" a lookout called down. "Th' Chase'z doused 'er lights! One point orf th' starb'd bows!"

Lewrie paced down to the helm, and the chart pinned to the traverse board. He picked up one of the Sailing Master's brass dividers to measure off distances, then looked astern at the dawn. Mr. Caldwell shared a look with him, gazed sternward himself for a moment, and drew out his own pocket watch.

"Seven minutes 'til dawn proper, sir," Caldwell adjudged.

"By the casts of the log, we've made up fifteen miles of Westing, and should be about twelve miles astern of our spook," Lewrie determined. "She should be spottin' us soon, now, if our top-masts are above the horizon . . . unless they're blind as bats, o' course."

"There is a chance, sir, that they're so used to peering shoreward that they may not take too many glances over their shoulders, and we could get very close before they spot us," Caldwell offered.

"Well, that'll never do," Lewrie jovially objected. "I *want* us t'be seen, and draw her too far out for her to run for Mar del Plata or Bahía Blanca and get away."

"Deck, there!" the mainmast lookout in the cross-trees yelled. "Th' Chase'z goin' about! 'Er bows'z pointin' South, beam-onta us! She's fine on th' starb'd bow!"

"Should we alter course more Sutherly to cut her off, sir?" Lt. Spend-love asked. "Make more sail, perhaps?"

"Hold course for a bit more, sir," Lewrie told him. "Let's see if she runs, or she comes about towards us. We're loafin' along like a transport, under reduced sail for the night, and on a rough course for enterin' the Plate. Let's see if she bites."

"Deck, there! Chase'z *wearin'* about!" came a call from aloft. "Turnin' Easterly!"

"Well, now!" Lewrie said, beaming with delight. "If the people have finished their breakfast, I'll have the galley fires cast overboard, Mister Spendlove. Stand on for a bit more, like *we're* blind as bats, 'til we can spot her sails above the horizon from the deck, *then* we can sham panic, and go about. Mister Westcott? I will fetch you the keys to the arms lockers, now. We'll wait, though, to 'Beat To Quarters' 'til she's much closer. Once I'm back on deck, you *can* begin to strip down the ship for action."

"Aye aye, sir," Westcott crisply replied with a feral gleam in his eyes, eager for the fight to start.

Lewrie went to his cabins, unlocked his desk, and fetched out the keys to the arms lockers and crammed them into a side pocket of his coat. He went to his own weapons rack and strapped on his plain hanger sword, primed his pre-loaded double-barrelled Manton pistols, and stuck them down into his coat pockets, too.

"Is it beginning, sir?" Pettus asked.

"It appears t'be, Pettus," Lewrie told his steward. "You and Jessop box up the last of my things, and see everything to the orlop, Chalky and the dog, too."

"I been drillin' with the other lads, sir," Jessop piped up. "I can run powder cartridges from the magazines, good as any, now."

Lewrie paused and cocked his head to look Jessop over; he had come aboard a twelve-year-old waif, and was now almost sixteen, and nigh a grown lad as much like the teenaged topmen who served aloft.

"Very well, Jessop," Lewrie said with a stern nod. "You wish to do a man's part, you have my leave t'do so."

"Thank ye, sir!" Jessop cried, looking so happy that he could turn St. Catherine's Wheels in delight.

"Luck to the both of you," Lewrie bade them, stopping to give Chalky a parting petting. The cat was crouched atop his desk, curled up into a wary meat loaf shape, as if he sensed something ominous in Lewrie's weapons, or the sight of the domed wicker cage that was used to bear him below and out of harm.

Lewrie got back to the quarterdeck and handed Lt. Westcott the arms locker keys. Westcott grimly nodded, then bellowed for word to be passed for the Master-At-Arms and the Ship's Corporals to come to fetch them. With another nod to Bosun Sprague and his Mate, Wheeler, he gave permission for Quarters to be piped. Lt. Simcock's Marine drummer and fifer began the Long Roll, then a gay martial air that drew off-watch hands back on deck. One of the ship's boats was hauled from towing astern and filled with chickens, ducks, rabbits, and quail from the manger, with the nanny goat and her kid, and several squealing piglets. HMS *Reliant* thundered and drummed to the sounds of deal-and-canvas partitions being struck down and carried to the orlop, of officers' and seamens' chests stowed below to turn all of her decks to long, empty spaces from bow to stern, filled only with guns.

Half an hour later, and the frigate was ready for combat, and the only step left was to load, prime, and run out. Lewrie called for everyone to stand easy. He went to the lee bulwarks to larboard and raised a telescope to peer at their stranger past the wind-curved jibs.

"I can make out her t'gallants and tops'ls, now, from the deck," he said to Lt. Westcott as he crossed back to amidships. "She'll be hull-up in the next half hour. Time t'shake our lazy night reefs out, Mister Westcott, like our idle merchantmen do, and make more sail . . . except for the main course, which we'll have to brail up before fire is opened, anyway. Chain slings on the yards whilst you're at it, and rig the boarding nettings inboard of the bulwarks, out of sight 'til needed."

"Aye, sir. Colours?" Lt. Westcott asked, peeking aft at the bare gaff and spanker boom line.

"Not 'til she breaks out hers," Lewrie decided, pausing, then grinning impishly. "We've Spanish Colours in the flag lockers? Damme, I wonder what our stranger'd make o' *that*! Or, do we have a British merchant ensign . . . I wonder which'd tempt him more!"

I'm pretty *sure she's Spanish,* Lewrie mulled over to himself as his First Officer tended to making more sail, and the rigging of the slings and anti-boarding nets; *I don't think there's a Dutch warship in the entire South Atlantic, and God only knows what'd draw a French ship this far afield. A*

British merchant flag t'lure her on, or show them a Spanish flag, and bring her out to warn a fellow countryman to the British invasion? God, that'd be rich! And she'd be put off her guard, her gun crews stood down.

"Deck there!" a lookout called down. "Th' Chase'z hoistin' *British* Colours!"

"The Devil ye say!" Lewrie barked, going back to the bulwarks to lift his telescope once more. Sure enough, even from the deck, he could make out the merest hint of bright bunting, an imitation of the Union Flag.

"Mine arse on a band-box!" Lewrie hooted. "I'll wager ye that her captain thinks he's a clever 'sly boots', Mister Westcott! Hoist the Red Ensign, if ye please. Show him we're a fat, dumb merchantman. And everyone look *relieved*, haw!" he called to the officers and men on the quarterdeck. He looked aft to watch Midshipman Shannon and the hands of the Afterguard bending on and hoisting the Red Ensign on the spanker's boom peak. "When we've fetched her fully hull-up, we'll put up our number in this month's code book, and see what the Dons make of that."

We can fight her under the Red Ensign, Lewrie thought, tautly smiling; *It's the Navy's Red Squadron flag, too. Nobody'll fault me for opening fire under false colours, not this time!*

In 1794, when he'd first had command of the old *Jester* sloop, he hadn't had false French colours lowered and Navy colours run up before delivering one broadside, and he'd been criticized for it in enemy newspapers, and Nelson himself had torn a strip off his arse.

"Sir!" Midshipman Rossyngton cried from his perch halfway up the larboard mizen mast shrouds. "She's almost hull-up!"

Lewrie gave him a wave in recognition, then went to the forward edge of the quarterdeck and the cross-deck hammock stanchions. "Mister Spendlove?" he called to the Second Officer, whose post when at Quarters was between the two batteries of guns. "Run in the guns and load, but do not prime . . . both batteries."

"Load, but do not prime, aye, sir!" Spendlove called back.

He tried to peer at the enemy warship—for that was what she had revealed herself to be by hoisting false colours—from the larboard corner of the quarterdeck, but the fore course and billowing jibs were in the way. He crossed over to his proper place to windward, and got a better view. She was almost bows-on to *Reliant,* all of her sail plan now visible above the horizon, and perhaps only nine miles off. She seemed to be hardening up to the wind a point or so, trying to sneak up and steal the wind gage, intending to pass close aboard and deliver her first broadside from her starboard guns into *Reliant*'s starboard side.

Lewrie collapsed the tubes of his telescope, hunched into his coat, and pondered, frowning in concentration. How *would* he fight her? The slant of wind limited how far to starboard he could turn and surprise her by wheeling "full and by". That morning wind was fresh enough at the moment, but could weaken before both ships got within gun-range. Serving her a broadside from his larboard guns and bow-raking her would be too chancy.

It was a given for Royal Navy captains to gain the weather gage, upwind of a foe where one's ship could steal wind from the foe's sails, and command when one fell down alee to musket-shot or pistol-shot. Sometimes, though, the leeward ship, heeled over to larboard in this instance, could elevate her guns higher, whilst the enemy's guns were depressed, even with the elevating quoins fully out.

It'll be a passin' engagement, Lewrie stewed, pursing his lips and gnawing on the lining of his mouth; *one, maybe two broadsides if we're quick about it, and then we're past each other, and swingin' about t're-engage. Once she's past us, it might be best t'haul wind and wear alee, with the larboard battery ready for 'em that instant. The Spaniard will, too. It'd make no sense for them to turn up into the wind.*

Lewrie used both forefingers to sketch out the manoeuvring on the wood of the cap-rails, supposing that the Spaniard would want to stay close enough for his further broadsides to be fired at a range of less than one hundred yards, giving his gunners surer chances of hits.

Christ, we'll end up spirallin' round each other like "country dancers", Lewrie thought; *but, I'll have the pre-loaded larboard guns, and he'll be re-loadin' his starboard battery . . . and the Dons ain't all that well drilled, in the main, at gunnery or ship-handlin', both!*

At least the Spanish were slower and clumsier back in Europe, he had to caution himself. With the Royal Navy's incessant blockades of enemy harbours, it was rare for French, Dutch, or Spanish warships to get much sea time, or chances to practice live firing. This Spaniard, though, based out of the Argentine, or some other Spanish possession the other side of Cape Horn, *might* have been free to drill his crew to deadly competence.

He raised his telescope for yet another look at the approaching enemy warship, and made a decision.

"A point to windward, Mister Westcott," Lewrie ordered. "We are stupid, weak, and civilian . . . or so the Dons imagine. It's only natural for us t'get to speakin' distance and say hallo to another British ship, hey? I want us to pass starboard-to-starboard, damned close, so our first broadside's a blow to the heart."

"Aye, sir," Lt. Westcott replied.

Might he haul his wind before *then, cross our bows and rake us with his larboard guns?* Lewrie had to consider; *Or recognise us as a frigate, and decide t'bugger off South?*

He shrugged that off, deeming that the Spaniard's move could be spotted soon enough, and even at longer range, he still had time to turn up higher into the wind and present his larboard battery. Once the Spanish captain did that, he'd surrender the wind gage, and who in his right mind would give that advantage up, once seized?

Well, I have, Lewrie confessed to himself with a wry grimace; *Hell's Bells, I'm plannin' on givin' it up, this minute!*

Another decision made; he would hold course.

"Mister Spendlove, my apologies to your gunners," Lewrie called down to the weather deck and the waist, "but, I wish for roundshot to be drawn from the starboard great-guns, and replaced with chain, star, and bar shot, and double-loaded with grape canisters atop those. The twelve-pounder bow chaser, carronades, and quarterdeck nine-pounders will retain solid shot. We will pass close, and I want her rigging cut t'pieces, and her quarterdeck pummeled!"

"My, sir," Lt. Westcott said in a whisper near his shoulder, "but how very un-British."

"He'll be expectin' our usual 'twixt wind and water broadside, t'punch holes in his hull and dis-mount his guns," Lewrie said with a wee snicker, "and, he may be plannin' t'fire high and cripple us with his first broadside, but, I s'pose now and then we can emulate the customs of the French Navy, and his. And, there's the biter, bit."

"Deck, there!" a lookout sang out. "Chase is a . . . *frigate!*"

"Hull-up, sir!" Midshipman Rossyngton yelled, now standing on the starboard sail-tending gangway, having left his former perch on the shrouds.

Lewrie and Westcott could see the enemy as clear as day, by then, too, bows-on to *Reliant* with her entire hull in plain sight; not a now-and-then thing which depended upon the rise and scend from an active sea to shove her higher for a time. The seas were fairly calm with few cat's paws, and any apparent waves no higher than one foot or so. The fully-risen early morning sun had brightened those waters to a brilliant dark blue, too, with no more sign of the muddy coloured outflow from the Plate River and its estuary.

Atop that brilliant blue sea, the Spanish frigate stood out starkly, a dark brown hull with a faint band of pale yellow paint, and her sails the colour of weathered parchment, Lewrie could take note after a long look with his telescope. The enemy looked a bit worse for wear, as if she had been at sea for months on end, which made him feel a touch of uneasiness that she might be that rare Spaniard who had had time to make herself hellishly efficient, and would be quicker off the mark than he had hoped, or expected.

Devil take it, he grimly thought; *we're committed.*

He lowered his glass and looked aloft to the streaming commissioning pendant. "Another point to windward, Mister Westcott."

"A point more to windward, aye, sir," Westcott replied.

"Once our first broadside is delivered, we will haul our wind as quick as dammit, take the wind fine on the quarter, even wear if we have to, t'keep her in close gun-range. Be ready for it."

"Aye, sir," Westcott said, nodding and smiling. "Chomp down on her, and hang on like a bulldog."

"That's my good fellow!" Lewrie congratulated him.

He raised his glass once more to watch the enemy ship close the distance between them. She was altering her course slightly, hardening about one more point to windward, and baring a bit more to see of her starboard side.

Dogged, and implacable, Lewrie thought.

"Spanish frigates, Mister Westcott," Lewrie mused aloud. "How many guns do they mount? I can't make a count of her ports, yet."

"Uhm, anywhere from twenty-eight to fourty, I read somewhere, sir," Westcott told him, after a long moment to dredge that information up. "We haven't had much dealings with them, as we have had with the French. Anything from nine- to eighteen-pounders, or their equivalents. This one doesn't appear all *that* large, so . . . ," he said with a shrug.

Lewrie judged the range to the Spaniard at about five miles or less, by then, and wondered just how much longer their enemy might be mis-led as to their nature, or whether the Spanish captain would stand on, thinking he would soon seize a British merchantman.

Surely, he must *realise we're a frigate,* sooner *or later!* he thought, worried that the Spaniard would haul off and begin to flee long before they came into decent gun-range, and all his preparations would be for nought.

Why, why *do I trust to my cleverness!* Lewrie bemoaned; *Every time, I come a cropper! Clever,* me? *What a sour joke* that *is!*

"Last cast of the log?" Lewrie asked.

"Just under eight knots, sir," Westcott reported.

"Let's run up the main top-mast, middle, and main t'gallant stays'ls," Lewrie ordered of a sudden. "Do we have to wheel round at short notice, we'll need that extra canvas aloft."

"Aye, sir," Westcott said, raising his brass speaking-trumpet to bellow the order forward.

"Mister Simcock?" Lewrie called to the Marine officer, who was idly pacing the starboard sail-tending gangway behind his men posted at the bulwarks and hammock stanchions. "That Don yonder still thinks we're a merchantman, so it'd be best were your Marines not visible to him 'til the last moment. Have 'em squat down, if you will."

"*Squat,* sir?" Simcock asked, aghast.

"You, too, sir! Kneel, or hunch . . . or, as the Yankee Doodles say, *hunker* down, 'til we spring our surprise," Lewrie ordered with a laugh. "Your men in the fighting tops should lie down out of sight, as well. I don't wish your splendid red coats t'give 'em the squits!"

The gun crews and powder monkeys, who had been sitting or standing idle, and the portion of the crew assigned at Quarters to tend to the braces, sheets, and fighting tops and yards, had themselves a good, tension-relieving laugh at the "lobster back's" expense.

"We're closing rather fast, sir," Lt. Westcott reported to him. "About three miles off now, she is. Both of us making the same rate of knots. The next ten minutes will tell."

"I expect you're right," Lewrie said, nodding soberly. "He is either still gulled, or he's recognised us for a frigate and doesn't give a damn. Either way, it's of no matter."

He raised his telescope again to study the Spanish frigate, to try to count gun-ports down her starboard side. Closer to, she gave the impression that she *had* been at sea longer than most. That pale yellow hull stripe was bleached by sun and time to almost white, but her gun-ports were still closed, and the same outer colour as the hull stripe.

Lewrie crossed to the helm, and stowed his telescope away; it was no longer necessary. The Spaniard was close enough to trust his own eyes. He paced back to the weather side of the quarterdeck, and planted his feet, clasped his hands in the small of his back to seem stoic and confident, and waited.

One mile of separation, and the Spaniard began to brail up his main course against the risk of catching fire from the discharges from his own guns.

Half a mile between them, and it appeared that both warships would pass each other, starboard-to-starboard, at about two or three hundred yards' distance. Lewrie looked to his guns, drawn up to the port sills and ready to be run out as soon as the gun-ports opened, their elevating quoins drawn back from underneath the breeches for a high angle. Could they elevate high enough to savage the Spaniard's sails and cripple her?

"A point free, Mister Westcott," Lewrie said, his mouth as dry as dust, of a sudden.

"Point free, aye, sir."

"Just before we open upon her . . . ," Lewrie further said, having a last-minute inspiration, "haul in the lee braces and flat the sails to the wind. That'll lay us over t'loo'rd a few degrees more."

"Aye, sir," Westcott replied, sounding mystified.

"Once the last gun fires, ease 'em again."

"Ah! I see. Aye, sir!" Lt. Westcott answered.

A quarter-mile apart, and the Spanish frigate at last began to swing up her gun-ports. Lewrie counted twelve of them down her starboard side, rapidly calculating. Twenty-four great-guns on her main deck, two bow chasers, perhaps two stern chasers, and at least six lesser guns on her quarterdeck . . . *She's a thirty-four?* he thought.

"Mister Spendlove!" Lewrie roared to *Reliant*'s waist. "Open yer ports and run out! Stand by to fire as you bear, at the highest elevation! Mister Simcock? You can stand up, now!"

She won't *wheel cross our bows, not now, she's left it too late!* Lewrie thought; And, *the Dons don't have carronades!*

CHAPTER FORTY-ONE

*W*e will be haulin' our wind, as soon as the last gun is fired, Mister Spendlove!" Lewrie cautioned. "Serve the larboard battery, and have spare hands re-load the starboard guns with solid shot!"

"Aye, sir!" Spendlove shouted back, and Lt. Merriman raised his hat in sign that he had also heard the order and would comply.

"It looks like we'll pass within a cable's range, sir," Lt. Westcott pointed out, his voice gruff. "Perhaps *less* than two hundred yards. Any moment, now."

"Stand ready!" Lewrie shouted to his gun crews, and the brace-tenders on the gangways.

He's a proper little Spaniard, at least. He'll do things the honourable way, Lewrie thought; *Religious, too!*

That false British flag the enemy frigate had flown was struck down, and the horizontally-striped red-gold-red flag of Spain with the royal coat of arms in the centre of the middle gold stripe was soaring up in its place. At the same time, a large wooden crucifix was being hauled up to rest against the front face of the frigate's fore course.

"Haul taut, the lee braces, Mister Westcott," he barked.

"Haul taut, lee braces . . . ease weather braces!" Lt. Westcott yelled forward with a speaking-trumpet. and the yardarms of all three masts, linked together on each mast, were swung more fore-and-aft to point their larboard tips toward the larboard stern quarter, flattening the courses, tops'ls, and t'gallants against the wind. The deck heeled over to leeward, only a few degrees, but . . .

Maybe just enough! Lewrie thought.

"As you *bear . . . Fire!"* he roared, and the world exploded.

The 12-pounder bow chaser barked, then the 18-pounders down the starboard side went off with louder roars, each about a second after the first, thundering back from the gun-ports with their carriage trucks squealing, followed mere seconds later by the deep booms from the 32-pounder carronades and the sharper cracks from the quarterdeck 9-pounders, amid an instant bank of sour-reeking powder smoke, almost so thick that it was hard to make out the bulwark next to him. The frigate juddered and trembled under his feet, not just to the recoil of her own guns, but to the slamming impacts of Spanish roundshot in reply. *Reliant* was punctured! He could hear the scream of wood!

"*Wear,* Mister Westcott!" Lewrie yelled, finally spotting his First Lieutenant as the clouds of powder smoke thinned a bit.

"Hard up your helm!" Westcott told the helmsmen. "Stations to wear ship! Ease lee braces, haul taut weather braces, and get some drive back on her as we fall off!"

Lewrie looked out-board for the Spanish frigate, but she, too, was all but invisible in her own drifting cloud of spent powder, and that was wafting down-wind toward *Reliant.* At least he could see his own decks, noting that Spendlove had shifted the bulk of his gunners to larboard, leaving a few men from each gun under Lt. Merriman to see to re-loading the starboard battery. A stream of ship's boys dashed past Lewrie, bearing the fire-proof leather cartridge cylinders to feed the muzzles of the quarterdeck guns. Jessop was among them, saddled as a "new-come" with the heavier charge for a 32-pounder carronade, his feet bare for greater traction on the sanded decks and ladderways, and a neckerchief bound over his ears to save his hearing. He gave Lewrie a brief grin as he whisked by.

Reliant was coming round, pointing her stern to the smoke bank from her own guns, and the Spaniard's, the wooden balls strung together in the parrels crying out as the yards were swung round. With a loud whoosh, the spanker over the quarterdeck swung over to starboard as the frigate completed her wear.

"Starboard battery re-loaded and ready, sir!" Lt. Merriman reported from the waist. "Spare hands, tail onto the run-out tackle for the larboard guns!"

"Prime your guns!" Spendlove insisted. "Open the ports, and run out!"

"There she is, sir!" Westcott cried, pointing off the larboard quarter, coughing a bit on the rotten-egg fumes that still lingered from the guns' discharges.

The Spanish frigate had run on for a time after her broadside, slower to begin her turn off the wind. To re-engage, though, she did not have to wear but merely alter course Sou'easterly. That put both ships twice as far apart, with *Reliant* on a course almost the reciprocal of her original heading, now bound almost Due East. They would converge again in another minute or so.

"I think we chewed her rigging up a fair bit," Lewrie said after a quick look, going to the binnacle cabinet for his telescope.

"I see pieces missing, sir," Mr. Caldwell, the Sailing Master, said with a chortle. "Her fore t'gallant's gone, her main tops'l's shot to ribbons, and her main top-mast shrouds appear half-shot through."

"Good Lord, we've be-headed Jesus!" Westcott exclaimed.

A piece of grape shot or some other bit of ironmongery which they had fired had decapitated the figure on the crucifix hung aloft in her rigging! The rest of it was still swinging like a pendulum.

"Half her stays'ls are gone by the board, too," Lewrie said, lowering his telescope. "She's about three hundred yards off, now? Almost too far for the carronades, but . . . we'll make things hot for them." He went forward to look down into the waist. "The larboard guns, Mister Spendlove! Serve her a broadside, 'twixt wind and water!"

"Cock your locks! By broadside . . . Fire!" Spendlove roared.

Every larboard gun lit off in a spectacular bellowing, rattling the air in Lewrie's lungs and making his heart flutter, and causing a ringing in his ears despite the plugs of wax he'd inserted. Once more, the enemy frigate was blotted out by a fresh fog bank of reeking greyish-yellow powder smoke.

Three shots every two minutes, Lewrie grimly thought, sure of his gunners' proficiency, gained through un-ceasing drill and live-fire practice. He'd loved the guns, from his first exposure to them as a raw Midshipman, loved the thunder, the power, and the very stink of them! As harsh as the sour reek was that wafted back on him, he could almost think it as bewitching as a lover's cologne!

More guns slammed, and his ship trembled and shook as Spanish roundshot struck home. The anti-boarding nets hoisted on the larboard side twitched and thrashed, a section of bulwark and hammocks stored in the stanchions were flung apart, and two Marines were shot from their posts on the gangway to land like tossed-aside dolls on the planking in the waist. There was a *Rawrk!* of rivened wood as one ball struck between two 18-pounders, flinging a cloud of splinters at sailors re-loading their pieces. Something heavy hummed over the quarterdeck like a gigantic bumblebee, thankfully missing high. The cloud of smoke from the Spanish frigate was punctured by quick amber and red flashes as her guns fired, now as blind as Lewrie's.

"Loblolly men, here!" Spendlove was yelling. "Clear those men away! Run out! Prime! Cock your locks! Wait for the smoke to clear, and . . . on the up-roll . . . *Fire!*"

Before his view was blotted out, again, Lewrie got a quick impression of their foe's condition which allowed him a brief twitch of a smile. The Spanish frigate's weakened top-mast stays had given way, and her brailed-up main royal and her main t'gallant sails had swung over like a felled pine tree onto her starboard tops'l and yard, fouling her lee braces and the work of the men in her main mast fighting top, in a jumble of spars, canvas, and rigging.

They'll have t'chop all that away, Lewrie thought, pleased at how that would slow her down. In his head, he sketched their convergence—*Reliant* going East and the Spaniard going Sou'east—anticipating that his own ship could be at least one hundred yards ahead of the enemy when they closed. Could he be faster, he could contemplate bow-raking her by turning up-wind a few points.

Or, she could haul her wind near Due South and rake us right up the arse! he realised with a shock; This *Spanish captain is eager enough for a fight, more so than most of 'em!*

The early morning wind was cause for fretting, too. It hadn't been all that fresh a breeze to start with, and after a few minutes of gunfire, it could be reduced by half, or so his experience told him. He could feel the change on his face and cheeks, and up from below his feet; *Reliant* was wallowing much less livelier than before.

"Cast of the log!" he shouted aft.

"Aye, sir!" Midshipman Shannon replied, taking his own fumbling time to cast the triangular drag and line over the stern, time it with his pocket watch, then nip it at the one-minute mark. "Five and one half knots, sir!" he finally reported.

Reliant had gotten another broadside off, by then, and her labouring gun crews were running out for another by that time, the hands streaked with sweat and powder smut, and the powder monkeys scampering like panting hounds to keep the supply of propellants timely. Idlers who assisted the Surgeon and his Mates down below in the orlop cockpit were scurrying with a mess table for a carrying board which bore a savagely wounded man, bound for a hatchway. Fresh sand was being scattered onto pools of spilled blood where the Spanish roundshot had penetrated the ship's side between two guns.

There came a stuttering series of booms from within the smoke cloud, and more flashes of red and amber as the Spanish ship fired a ragged broadside.

"Gun-captains!" Lt. Spendlove ordered. "Aim for the flashes! On the up-roll . . . by broadside . . . *Fire!*"

It was utter cacophony; their guns erupting, the Spanish guns roaring, with shot splashes close aboard and rising in feathers of spray and foam, balls thudding into the hull, followed by distant thuds and parroty *Rawrk*s of punctured planking and shattered timbers as their own shot struck home! *Reliant*'s guns were hot, now, leaping back in recoil, even the 18-pounders leaving the decks six inches or more, and staggering down to slue almost sideways before being snagged by their stout breeching ropes, making their gun crews hop for their lives. One 18-pounder, the anchoring ring-bolt of her breeching rope weakened by the earlier hull puncture, swung completely round to face fore-and-aft, and rolled amidships, crushing its loader!

"Secure that gun! Chock it, lash it to the foremast trunk!"

"Loblolly men, here! Quickly!" Lt. Merriman called.

Bosun's Mate Wheeler knelt by the loader, gave him a shake or two, slapped his face, then shook his head. He waved another sailor from the idle starboard battery to come help, then together they bore him to an open gun-port and put him over the side. It was bad for the crew's morale to leave dead men strewn on the decks, or piled up like a day's rabbit hunt round the foot of a mast. It was best to dispose of them quickly, if the surgeons could do them no good, to be mourned by their mess-mates later. If wounded so badly but still awake, it was a mercy to knock them out with a maul before disposal.

Lewrie jerked his attention away from that scene, and looked outboard, searching for a clear view of their foe. The thick smoke thinned a little as their own bank wafted alee, and the smoke from the Spanish frigate that was blown down on them didn't seem quite as thick as before.

There she was, still half-indistinct, no more than two hundred yards off, a bit ahead of *Reliant*'s beam!

"How the Devil's she out-footin' us?" he spat. "Half her sails are shot away! Give us a point free, helmsmen!"

"Carpenter's sent a runner, sir," Lt. Westcott said, "he says there's nigh a foot of water in the bilges, and we've taken some hits on the waterline. He asks for spare hands to plug them."

"Aye, give him four, if ye can spare 'em," Lewrie agreed. "I wish t'God I'd served that bastard a *second* broadside in his rigging, just t'slow him down a bit more."

"By broadside . . . on the up-roll . . . *Fire!*" Lt. Spendlove was screeching, his voice gone harsh and raspy, and the guns erupted with a roar, leaping back from the ports once more. Thuds and *Rawrk*s were heard distinctly from the Spanish frigate, and ragged star-shaped holes blossomed down her starboard side before powder smoke made her disappear.

"She's flying her fore and middle stays'ls again, sir!" Caldwell exclaimed. "They've re-roved. And, she's bared her main course!"

"You sure, Mister Caldwell?" Lewrie asked, turning to face him.

"Sure, sir!" the Sailing Master insisted.

"Well, no wonder she's out-footin' us!" Lewrie groused, trying to peer out to confirm that with his own eyes. "If she gets far out ahead of us, that bastard Don could bow-rake us. Or—!"

If we can fall back far enough t'harden up t'windward, we can just *squeak the jib-boom and bowsprit short of her stern and shoot* her *up the arse,* Lewrie schemed. He looked aloft at the commissioning pendant, which was streaming towards the starboard side, a point or two abaft of abeam.

No, that won't work, he sadly told himself.

Their course was still Due East, or a point off to East by South. The pendant showed that the wind was from the Nor'-Nor'east, and they would end up in-irons if they turned up to windward much further. He would have to continue slugging it out on this heading, with the foe slowly creeping further and further ahead towards the larboard bows.

"Mister Westcott! Soon as the next broadside is fired, haul our wind and come to Sou'east," Lewrie ordered. "That'll place her back abeam of us, and open the range a bit."

And just keep poundin' her, hopin' that something aboard her will give way, sooner or later, Lewrie thought with a groan.

There were stabbing flames of discharge in the smoke as their enemy fired again, a very ragged and stuttering broadside. Feathers and shot pillars shot skyward, mostly ahead of *Reliant*'s bows, with very few shot actually striking her, for once.

"She can't be sure of where to aim, with all this smoke, sir!" Lt. Westcott rasped out. "They think we're still abeam of her!"

"Aim for the gun flashes! By broadside . . . *Fire!*" Spendlove cried from the waist.

"Helm up, Quartermasters!" Lewrie snapped. "Come about to the Sou'east! Hands to the braces, Mister Westcott!"

Reliant wheeled away Sutherly, wreathed in her own fresh fog bank of powder smoke, and sailing into the clouds of smoke from previous broadsides, which by now were taller than the mast-head trucks.

"Been at it for a full hour, now, sir," Caldwell commented. "I do believe by the sound of it that the Dons are *very* slow to fire and load."

"And our lads are just as tired as theirs, Mister Caldwell," Lewrie told him, gesturing toward the ship's waist, and *Reliant*'s gun crews who were streaming sweat despite the coolness of the morning, who were taking the short time between running out the guns and their firing to dash to the scuttle-butts for a sip of a water, or dip up handfuls of water from the swabbing tubs between the guns, now foul with the black nitres from spent gunpowder. "That's not three rounds every two minutes any longer."

"At least we haven't taken much damage aloft, sir," Westcott said, looking up at the masts and sails. "Our Spaniard's playing the game fair, unlike the French."

"And we've cheated, by tryin' t'cripple his yards?" Lewrie asked with a brow up. "*All's* fair, so long as we win."

"*Hold* fire, hold fire, there!" Lt. Spendlove shouted.

"What's the problem, Mister Spendlove?" Lewrie demanded from the forward edge of the quarterdeck nettings.

"Can't *see* him, sir, for all this smoke," Spendlove replied. "It's so thick, I'm firing at his gun flashes, and I don't wish to waste a broadside on thin air. Sorry."

The sudden lack of ear-splitting thunder was eerie. Combined with the thickness of the masking powder smoke, it was eerier still, so when Midshipman Shannon called out a fresh cast of the log at the taffrails, everyone could make out his thin young voice. "Only five knots, now! Five knots even!"

"Ah, we've shot the wind to nothing," Mr. Caldwell spat, "and whipped a fog of our own making. The air must be very humid, today."

Boom-Boom . . . Boom, from out to larboard, more off the bows now, than abeam, as Lewrie had hoped his turn-away might place the Spanish frigate. It was yet another ragged, stuttering broadside, as if the Dons could see a target to engage as they bore, rather than the full weight of a co-ordinated broadside.

"I only count ten, not twelve," Lewrie said, feeling a bit of hope. "We may have silenced two of his great-guns."

"Speak of firing into thin air," the Sailing Master scoffed.

All could hear the moaning of solid shot as it passed ahead of the bows, could hear the splashes as heavy iron balls slapped the sea and skipped off into the distance. *Reliant* wasn't even touched!

"Mister Caldwell, the last clear sight you had of our enemy," Lewrie posed, "you said they'd sheeted home their main course? Was it reefed, or drawn fully down?"

"Un-reefed, sir," was the Sailing Master's firm assurance.

"I'd hoped, by hauling our wind, t'keep her abeam, but it seems she's sailin' faster than our own five knots," Lewrie plotted aloud. "She now lies more-like only three points off the larboard bows. Do you believe we have enough wind t'go back up to Due East, or East by North?"

"Aye, sir, but no higher, else we'll almost be in-irons," Mr. Caldwell allowed.

"Mister Spendlove!" Lewrie yelled down. "A water break for all your gunners, then man the *starboard* battery!"

"Aye, sir," Spendlove replied, both weary and mystified.

"Put yer helm down, Mister Westcott, and lay us on the wind, East by North. Hands to the braces and sheets!"

If I can find *you in all this, you Spanish bastard, I'll* bugger *you, yet!* he thought.

CHAPTER FORTY-TWO

*T*he decks tilted a bit, first coming upright and level from the slight heel to starboard as HMS *Reliant* swung back towards her original course. Her hull slightly groaned at the easing, the myriad pulley-block sheaves squeaked and chattered, and the yard parrels squealed as braces and sheets were tailed on to swing the yards to angle the sails for a close reach, more up-wind. Once the yards were trimmed, and the fore-and-aft jibs and stays'ls were drawn tauter to cup that scant wind, the decks took on a slightly greater heel to starboard, but nothing as dramatic as they would be when going close-hauled on a stronger wind.

"Five and *three-quarter* knots, sir!" Midshipman Shannon cried from the stern, as if thrilled by the improvement. Casting the log was a minor chore, one that Shannon's limited experience at sea rated him, so he would perform it as best he could 'til given a better one.

"*Tastes* a bit healthier, anyway, sir," Lt. Westcott commented after a deep sniff, then flashed one of his brief grins. "It hardly smells like rotten eggs any longer. We'll be in clear air any second now."

"The enemy's ceased fire," Lewrie fretted, going to the break of the quarterdeck by the starboard ladderway to peer out.

"Saving shot and powder 'til he can see, again, most-like, sir," West-cott said with a shrug, after following him over. "Same as us."

"Aye, but did he haul off more Sutherly t'find us, or hope to work ahead of us and wheel round t'bow-rake us?" Lewrie wondered out loud. "Or, did he come back on the wind, and sail clear of all this on the same tack as ours?"

I'll either see his stern, open for the raking, or his larboard guns, which are fresh and un-damaged, Lewrie thought; *and the range greater than before. We now have the wind gage, and can fall down on him, at the very least. Which, dammit? Show yourself!*

He was too impatient to pretend to be implacable, or properly stoic; he left the quarterdeck and went forward up the starboard gangway to the main mast stays for a better view, shouldering two Marines out of the way. "Mornin', sir," one of them whispered.

"Ah, good mornin', Private Dodd," Lewrie replied without looking at him. "Enjoyin' sea life, are ye?"

"Aye, sir!" Dodd said with a twinkle. "Most exciting!"

"Speak only when spoken to, Dodd," Lt. Simcock warned.

"Thought I did, sir!" Dodd answered, stiffening his posture.

"Leg up," Lewrie demanded, taking hold of the thick and tarry stays to scramble to the top of the bulwarks and the filled hammock stanchions. He swung out-board and began to climb the rat-lines for an even better view, 'til he was half-way to the cat-harpings.

He *was* in clearer air! Swivelling his head round, Lewrie saw sparkling sea to windward, ahead, and astern. They had sailed above the pall of battle, into bright blue morning skies and innocently white clouds. The only blotches of sour yellow and dirty grey smoke were to leeward, to the South, and with the suspension of fire from either frigate, that bank of smoke was thinning, and slowly scudding away.

"Mastheads!" the main mast lookout in the cross-trees shouted. "Deck, there! Mastheads, one point ahead o' th' starb'd beam!"

There she is, by God! Lewrie silently exulted; *Her mizen and spanker . . . her main, and main course? She's almost stern-on!*

He quickly scrambled down to the top of the bulwarks, pointing to leeward. "*There* she is, Mister Spendlove! Almost abeam, and her stern open to us! There she is, lads! See her? A bit more than one cable off, but she's there! See her?"

Gun captains, officers, and Midshipmen ducked down to peer out the gun-ports, then stood back up, shouting fierce "Ayes!" of comfirmation, growling lusty eagerness.

"Aim small, then, fire as you bear, Mister Spendlove, you lads, and tear her heart out!" Lewrie urged them, clinging to the stays with one hand and jutting his other like a pointer at the foe.

"*Cock* your *locks!*" Spendlove shrilled. "Aim for her stern . . . crow levers, there! *As* you *bear* . . . slow and steady does it, now! *As* you *bear* . . . *Fire!*"

Oh, sweet Jesus, yes! Lewrie thought as the enemy frigate came swimming from the thinning haze, becoming almost substantial, as the 18-pounders crashed and thundered below his feet, as a fresh, thick pall of smoke, bright amber stabs of explosions, left those cruel iron muzzles, and firefly sparks swirled in the new smoke. In the scant seconds between discharge and the masking of their target, he could see the Spanish frigate's spanker boom shatter, her proud ensign go flying free of its halliards, and great holes and showers of broken stern windows be smashed into her transom!

"Pound her! Go, my bully lads, and *murder* the bastards!" he yelled over the last echoes of his guns. A loud cheer from his men rewarded his urgings. With help, he jumped down to the gangway and quickly made his way back to the quarterdeck, beaming fit to bust.

"We've got them now, sir!" Lt. Westcott chortled.

"Damned right we do! We *stern-raked* her, by God, and I think ev'ry shot went home!" Lewrie crowed with glee. "That's a *killing* blow! Let's see what *Señor* Spaniard does, now! Mister Spendlove?" he shouted to the waist. "Hold fire 'til you can see her, again!"

"Aye, sir!" came a disappointed reply. Spendlove's, and everyone's, blood-lust was up, now "gun-drunk" enough to want to continue battering the foe 'til they could see chunks flying off her and bodies hurled aloft.

"There she is, again!" Lt. Merriman urgently pointed out to the gunners. "Her mizen's gone by the board! Huzzah!"

The Spanish frigate was well and truly stricken, with her mizen mast damaged belowdecks, perhaps half-severed by the weight of metal shot up her wide-open stern. It lay over to starboard at a drunken angle, leaned forward onto her main mast. Gallantly, someone was on his way up her main mast with a fresh Spanish flag, perhaps to nail it to the top-masts in defiance.

She had swung up onto the wind, or was trying to, making barely a ripple of wake, in an attempt to expose her larboard guns and continue the fight, but it was a slow, crippled manoeuvre.

"*As* you *bear . . . Fire!*" Spendlove was ordering again.

"Two points free, Mister Westcott," Lewrie snapped. "Let us close the range and hammer her t'kindling."

"Two points free, sir, aye!" Lt. Westcott echoed. "Helmsmen, up helm, and steer East by South."

"She's not gotten her larboard gun-ports open, yet!" Caldwell exclaimed, a second before sight of their foe was blotted out, again.

"Fine with me!" Lewrie said with a laugh.

When a ship was brought to Quarters, all interior partitions were struck, all mess-tables hinged to the overheads, leaving a long alley on her gun-deck. When she was stern-raked, there was nothing to prevent solid iron shot from ravening from her transom planking to her forecastle galley and livestock manger, snapping carline posts and dis-mounting guns, and massacring her sailors, wholesale. There was a very good chance that that stern-rake had killed and wounded so many of her crew that those still on their feet were too stunned for a proper response!

"There's her larboard quarters!" Lt. Westcott shouted as the smoke thinnèd again, wafting down past the Spanish frigate. "Two, three . . . she's opening her larboard gun-ports, now. About one hundred and fifty yards off?"

"*As* you *bear . . . Fire!*"

The Spanish frigate's crippled mizen mast split, its top-masts splintering free from the thicker trunk of the lower mast, and tearing her main course and main tops'l apart like a butcher's carving knife! The gallant fellow with the fresh flag was ripped free of her upper stays and was flung into the sea to her dis-engaged side!

"Does that constitute her striking, I wonder, sir?" Mr. Caldwell hooted.

Fresh gun flashes erupted down the enemy's larboard side, and round-shot howled over *Reliant*'s decks, one or two slamming into the side with shuddering thuds.

"Beg pardon, sirs, but the Carpenter, Mister Mallard, says the water-line shot holes in the larboard side 're mostly plugged," a sailor reported, knuckling his brow. "When we come about, they didn't suck water no more, but they's still a foot and a half o' water in the bilges, and he says t'tell ya the pumps'll be needed t'be rigged and manned, soon."

"Very well, but tell him it may be a while yet before we can," Lewrie told the man. "Tell him I know he's doin' his best."

"Aye, sir," the sailor said again, knuckling his brow before he dashed back to the waist, and the main hatchway which was guarded by a Marine.

"Ah, there's yet another fresh flag," Lt. Westcott announced. "It appears that *Señor* is a game one." There was a new bright splash of colour exposed on the enemy's foremast, near where the decapitated crucifix still swung wildly.

"*As* you *bear . . . Fire!* Slow and steady, brave lads!"

Bow chaser, 18-pounders, carronades, and quarterdeck 9-pounders crashed and boomed down *Reliant's* side, as steady and regular as the ticks of a metronome. The range was close enough to marvel at planking and bits of bulwark being smashed in and sent flying in swirling clouds of paint chips and long-engrained dust and dirt. They could almost hear—or imagine that they could hear—the thuds, and the parrot-like *Screech-Rawrk*s of stout oak being smashed in, as if the Spanish frigate was crying out in fresh agonies.

"Beam-on to us, at last," Lewrie noted aloud. "No! Damn my eyes, but is she comin' up hard on the wind?"

"Her rudder may be gone, sir!" Lt. Westcott whooped. "She's not under control!"

"Now, she *must* strike her colours," Lewrie insisted.

"As you bear . . . *Fire!*" Lt. Spendlove shouted, delivering yet one more crushing salvo, at a range of only one hundred yards.

"In the tops, there! Swivel guns!" Marine Lieutenant Simcock shouted to his Marines in the fighting tops with a speaking-trumpet, and both sailors and Marines opened fire with muskets and swivel guns to clear the enemy's decks.

"Musket-fire . . . that's iffy," Westcott said with a wee laugh. "One can't hit anything much beyond sixty yards, unless one fires a whole battalion volley."

"Clear their tops!" Simcock yelled, spotting Spaniards aloft in the enemy frigate's fore top, and what was not draped with ruin in her main top. The Marines along the starboard gangway took up the task, aiming upward and discharging their muskets.

"She's falling off, again!" Mr. Caldwell shouted. "What sails they have left will carry her dead down-wind. We've got her, sure!"

"Now, she *must* strike!" Lewrie snarled. "Ow!"

Something smashed into his right leg, turning it dead-numb in a twinkling, with so much force that it was swept out from under him, spilling him on the quarterdeck on his face, and wondering how he'd got there.

"Oh Christ! Loblolly men to the quarterdeck!" someone cried.

He'd fallen so hard that the wind was temporarily knocked from him, had landed on his cheek and bitten his tongue, and his nose hurt like the very Devil.

Can't hit shit over sixty yards, mine arse! he thought, before a sudden wave of pain came in such a rush that he couldn't think!

"Smartly, now! Roll him over! A length of small line, now!" several voices were insisting.

Lewrie's senses were swimming, and he felt faint, even before his head lolled over towards his injury, and he could see the spreading stains of blood on his breeches, at which he could but gaze, amazed, and suddenly frightened.

Someone was jerking something very tight round the top of his thigh. Someone else was feeling him over like a pickpocket in a great hurry. "Just that'un . . . must've broken his nose, or something," he heard, sounding very far away and echo-y.

"Pass word to the Surgeon!"

Very roughly, and most un-dignified, Lewrie was shoved atop a mess-table carrying board, and bound up with ropes. He felt himself rising from the deck, fearing that his soul was fleeing his body for a second, before the urgent trot began . . . down the starboard ladderway to the waist, down the main hatchway to the gun-deck, down below to the orlop, and aft to the Midshipman's cockpit, with each jogging and thump making his pains multiply, as if someone was jabbing his wound with hot, sharp pokers.

Won't be a one-leg! his mind jabbered; *Won't be made a cook! Oh God, I think I'm killed!*

Hands were stripping off his coat, waist-coat, sword belt, and tearing at his neck-stock and breeches buttons. His boots were jerked off, making him cry out. And there was the Ship's Surgeon, Mister Mainwaring, looming over him, with his leather apron liberally spattered with gore, blood to the elbows and his rolled-up shirtsleeves, looking like a demon straight from the bowels of Hell.

"Bite on this, sir," Mainwaring said from very far away, and a saliva-slick twine-wrapped piece of wood was shoved into his mouth.

There were ripping sounds as his breeches and underdrawers got slitted away, then came a cool, wet splash of something on his leg, firm hands holding it, then a piercing, tearing, burning agony that he could not imagine.

Lewrie arched his back and bit down on the gag, roaring at the intensity of the pain . . . before he swooned, felt like he was falling down and down a deep, dark shaft, and he knew no more about it.

CHAPTER FORTY-THREE

*I*t could not be Heaven, so he could surely think it Hell.

He was vaguely aware of a raging thirst, but could not seem to get any-one to pay attention to his want of water, for all he *thought* he saw were un-caring wraiths that floated round him. He felt as hot as if he was im-mersed in a boiling pot, hot and feverish, and forever tipping forward head-over-heels as if hellish imps tilted his bed up to spill him on his face.

He thought he sweated, ravaged by something like Malaria or the Yel-low Jack, or some other disease far much worse.

And there was the pain, sometimes a mere ache, sometimes so bad that he could imagine that wolves were devouring him alive, and he had to scream, but could not.

And, then, he felt cold, clammily cold, and very weak, but he could open his eyes, though fearing to, in dread of seeing a canvas shroud over his face. *Something* was up against his face, something . . . cold, wet, and furry?

"Chalky?" he croaked.

His cat squatted on his chest, his nose a mere inch from his.

"Ah, you're awake, sir!" Pettus exclaimed. "Parched, I should not won-der. Cold tea, sir, brewed fresh this morning. Help me prop the Captain up, Jessop. Extra pillow from the transom settee, here."

How'd they get so tall? Lewrie wondered as his damp pillow was plumped up and turned over, and two more from the settee were placed under his head. He reckoned that he was in his cabins, and slung in his hanging bed-cot, but the overhead looked very far away, and all his furnishings appeared gigantic in scale.

When the tea came, he finished a whole tumbler in seconds, and belched with contentment, though still thirsty. At least the litter-box taste and dryness in his mouth were gone. With that out of the way, he felt himself over, very gingerly, expecting the worst. There was his thigh, a great blob of batting where he'd been shot, and lots of bindings. Further down . . . *all* of his leg was still there! But . . . what was his groin doing with bandages? Had he been shot in the testicles, or lost his manhood?

"What . . . what's this for?" he croaked in dread.

"Ehm . . . you've been quite out of it for several days, sir, so instead of trying to move you to your quarter-gallery, we had to put you in swaddles," Pettus shyly explained. "Mister Mainwaring said we should re-sling your bed-cot lower to the deck, too, for when you can manage to get in and out of it. Be a while, yet, he said."

"Sponge-bathed ya, too, sir," Jessop told him, " 'specially when ya were sweatin' so bad. A hard fever, ya come down with."

"I'll not have it, I can manage . . . ," Lewrie said, flinging the covers off and attempting to rise, but lifting his wounded leg caused a fresh wave of pain that made him gasp and fall back limply and weak.

"We'll get your strength back, sir," Pettus assured him, "soon as you can sit up and take solid food."

Lewrie suddenly realised that he was ravenously hungry, as if his body had gone out like an un-tended fireplace, and was coming to life again in fits and starts. While taking a second glass of cool tea, Pettus babbled on about the broths he'd been given, the eggs in wine, the heavily sugared brandy laced with laudanum for the worst of the pain, and the hot teas with powdered willow tree bark for when he didn't sound as if he was suffering *too* badly.

"That's one of Mister Mainwaring's grandmother's folk remedies, sir, but it certainly eased you," Pettus said. "You don't remember any of that?"

"Not a bit," Lewrie replied, shaking his head.

"Good for breaking fevers, Mister Mainwaring said, and you had a bad'un . . . it only broke last night, and you slept deep, at last," Pettus said. "He'll look in on you, soon as he finishes the morning sick call, and tends to the other wounded lads."

"How long?" Lewrie managed to ask.

"Soon, sir," Pettus assured him with a grin.

"No . . . how long have I been like this?" Lewrie insisted.

"Why, nigh on a *week,* sir," Pettus told him.

Boots stamped and a musket butt slammed the deck outside of the cabin doors as the Marine sentry announced, "First Off'cer an' th' Captain's cook, SAH!"

"Enter," Pettus granted for Lewrie, and Lt. Westcott and Yeovill came breezing in, peering aft at the bed-cot, looking anxious.

"Ah, you're awake at last, sir!" Westcott exclaimed, breaking out in a broad grin of relief as he came to the bed-cot. "We've been quite worried about you."

"We won, didn't we, Mister Westcott? We've a prize?" Lewrie demanded, suddenly noting that *Reliant* was at sea and under way, with the hull gently groaning and the overhead lanthorns gently swaying.

"Well, of course we *won,* sir," Westcott said with a surprised laugh. "She struck her colours not five minutes after you were borne below to the Surgeon. A prize? Well, not exactly."

"What?" Lewrie managed to ask.

"Recall, she was flying her main course, instead of brailing it up against the risk of fire?" Westcott explained with a grimace. "Our stern-rake must have dis-mounted a loaded gun or two, or there were some powder cartridges lying loose; something sparked off and flashed her main course alight, all that mess of her torn main tops'l and the tangle of her mizen top-masts that had fallen forward on her main top? Damned near the blink of your eye, and she's ablaze, with no hope of saving her.

"Her captain ordered her abandoned, and her colours struck, but they couldn't haul their boats up from towing astern quickly enough, so there were few survivors," Westcott went on. "We picked up some who could swim to us, and a few more when we got our boats over to her.

"Her captain . . . ," Westcott mused for a moment before continuing. "The poor bastard stayed on his quarterdeck to the end, then he put a pistol to his head and blew his brains out, can you imagine?"

"Mad as a March Hare," Lewrie said with a grunt.

"She was the *San Fermin* . . . one of their minor saints . . . and had been over on the Pacific side for about three years," Lt. Westcott said.

"She finally was recalled to Spain, put into Bahía Blanca after rounding the Horn, for supplies, and heard of our invasion, one of her surviving officers told me. She really needed a major re-fit, but her captain, *Don* Francisco Montoya-Uribe, felt his highest duty would be to stay and attack any transports that came in, or engage one of our warships, to whittle down the odds before a relieving squadron turned up, after he learned how few we were.

"The poor sods didn't even know about Trafalgar 'til we told them, sir," Westcott marvelled, "and they still can't quite believe it!"

"Honourable . . . for a Don," Lewrie commented. "Very proud lot."

"It's a wonder they put up as good a fight as they did, sir," Westcott said, shaking his head in awe. "Half her original crew had taken 'leg-bail' to seek their fortunes, looking for silver and copper, and got replaced with local *criollos* or starving *Indios*. Her captain had hardly any funds for her up-keep, or his crew's pay half the time, and their Ministry of Marine sent money out only when they remembered to, so she wasn't much of a happy ship. I gather that her Captain Montoya kept them together with *kindness*."

"*That's* a new'un," Lewrie said with a scowl.

"The survivors gave the impression that they *liked* him, sir, even if he was dull, scholarly, a tad shy, and soft-spoken," Westcott told him. "An *hidalgo* from an ancient family, but poor as church-mice. Honourable to the end, they said. They pitied him, I think."

"All this way," Lewrie sadly bemoaned, "all this time, and not a *groat* t'show for it. Our own losses, our damage?"

"Dis-mounted guns back on their carriages, the shot holes along the waterline plugged, scantlings re-planked, painted, and tarred over," Westcott ticked off, more business-like. "We've still rope and canvas fotherings over them, but there is a slow seepage the Carpenter still can't find, but an hour on the pumps twice a day keeps around six or seven inches of water in the bilges. We've used up all our stores of lumber, and had to borrow from *Diadem*. Left the prisoners with them, too, so Captain Downman is less than pleased with us."

"Casualties?" Lewrie asked.

"Seven dead, right off, and two more who died of wounds, sir," Westcott told him. "I'll bring you the muster book when you're up to it. Eighteen wounded, counting yourself, but there are only two who are really bad off, Surgeon Mainwaring says. Your stroke-oar, Furfy, got quilled with wood splinters, and a knock on the head, so he's laid up in the foc's'le sick-berth for a week, with another week on light duties."

"He'll relish *that*, I'd wager," Lewrie said, chuckling. "Bed-rest, no chores, and he still gets his rum and beer rations. God, my manners, Mister Westcott! Drag up a chair and sit!"

Pettus had already fetched one from the dining coach. "Thank you, sir. That close to the galley heat, Furfy and the others will be as snug as bugs as we drop down to pick up the cold, hard Westerlies round the Fourties."

"*Good* morning, Captain, sir!" Lewrie's cook, Yeovill, cheerily intruded, "You will be taking breakfast today, some solid food?"

"God, yes!" Lewrie enthused.

"Thick, sweet cocoa to start, sir," Yeovill said, handing him a large china mug, "scrambled eggs, a rice pudding for later, and I whipped up a batch of hot water-drop cornmeal fritters. The Surgeon is of a mind that your victuals had best be soft and bland for a few days, sorry."

"Damn his eyes," Lewrie groused. "Aye, bring it on, even if it is pap. We're fallin' down to the Fourties, Mister Westcott?"

"Already about two hundred miles Sou'east of the Plate Estuary, sir, and I expect Noon Sights will place us near the Fourty-third Latitude. We're bounding along quite nicely, bound for Cape Town. Then England," Westcott added, looking pleased.

"God, at last!" Lewrie said with a gladsome sigh. "Commodore Popham released us?"

"With urgent despatches to General Baird at the Cape, requesting immediate re-enforcements, and his latest reports to Admiralty," Westcott said, still grinning almost impishly as he added, "I *might* have given the Commodore the impression in my report that we had taken more damage than was the case, along with how long *Reliant* has been in commission, and was overdue paying off?"

"Happens even in the best of families," Lewrie said, grinning in turn. "Even Nelson was prone to exaggeration."

Pettus was fussing about, tucking a napkin into Lewrie's shirt collar, and fluffing the pillows again. Lewrie tried to use his hands and elbows to scoot up higher in the bed to a half-way sitting position, but he could manage only an inch or so, and the leg wound awoke in fresh pain, making him suck air and wince.

"God, I'm weak as a kitten," Lewrie said through gritted teeth, freezing in place to let the pain subside. Westcott, Pettus, and young Jessop took him by the armpits and dragged him up, making things even worse, bad enough for Lewrie to growl at them.

"Your cocoa, sir," Yeovill announced, "a refill?"

"Aye," Lewrie agreed, once his leg quit screaming and merely ached. "Whew! The Commodore wants more troops, instanter, does he? Any idea what's happening up at Buenos Aires?"

"Only what Captain Downman told me, sir, and it doesn't sound all that good," Westcott said, frowning as he sat back down. "Troops from the Montevideo garrison and local volunteers are getting over to Buenos Aires at night in fishing boats, in the shallows where Popham can't get at them. He's only *Encounter* and her boats and crew, and she can't swim that high up the estuary. They're joining up with volunteers under Sobremonte, the Viceroy of La Plata, and a man by name of Pueyrredón. There's a Frenchman, Liniers, commanding them, too, and the Commodore's sure that it's all a nasty Napoleonic plot. General Beresford beat about fifteen hundred of them, but that was on the defensive, and he's unable to chase them down and drive them off.

"The city isn't safe at night, so all Beresford can do is to *patrol*," Westcott growled, "maybe dig some entrenchments, and wait for the shoe to drop. It sounds rather grim, in all."

"Popham still has five transports," Lewrie said, frowning at that news. "If it's *that* bad, he should pull Beresford's men out, fall down to Point Quilmes, take 'em off the Cuello's banks, and sail back to Montevideo, before he loses the whole lot."

"And admit defeat, sir?" Westcott snickered. "Fail, and admit rashness and bad judgement, more to the point? After his glowing reports, and that open letter to the London merchants, I can't see him withdrawing."

"Here's breakfast, sir!" Yeovill sang out, placing a plank over Lewrie's lap to span the bed-cot, upon which was a plate of eggs and a basket of fritters. "You'll be happy to know, sir, that Mister Mainwaring said you could take as much red wine as you wished, as it's grand for building up the blood and your strength."

"Whisky?" Lewrie hopefully asked.

"With sugar and raw eggs, and medicine, only at bed-time, he said, sir," Yeovill informed him.

"Damn his eyes a second time," Lewrie grumbled, taking a first, delicious bite of eggs and a fritter that dripped fairly fresh butter.

"He saved the bullet for you, sir. Interested?" Yeovill asked.

"Christ, *no*!" Lewrie barked. "That's . . . ghoulish!"

"Nothing to be done for your breeches. sir," Pettus told him, "but, if you don't mind that the tail of your silk shirt is shorter, it's quite serviceable."

"It'll be a while before I'll need either, but thankee kindly, Pettus," Lewrie said with a smile.

"We've still some of those fresh-casked Argentine beef steaks, sir," Yeovill happily babbled on. "You'll be ready for some of them in a week or so."

"And, once we anchor at Cape Town, there'll be all manner of fresh wild game meat," Westcott added, sounding wistful.

"I hope I'm able t'totter, by then," Lewrie said, "and not end up a gimp."

"Well, time heals all wounds, sir," Westcott teased, "both the physical and the wounds of the heart. Mister Mainwaring is sure that you'll recover fully. He took great care, he said, to extract every thread of cloth, and a few wee slivers that the bullet nicked off your thigh bone. You just rest easy and take your time, sir, and we'll have you *dancing* by the time we get to Table Bay!"

"Well, if Mister Mainwaring *insists* on bed-rest!" Lewrie said with another wide grin. "After all, the ship is in the best of hands."

"Thank you for saying that, sir," Westcott said, bowing his head for a moment. "Long naps, catch up on your reading, amuse your cat, and enjoy a sea voyage, sir, with nought to do but plan what you will do when we get back to England. At any rate, our part in Commodore Popham's fiasco is over and done, and we're well shot of all that."

Lewrie's jaw dropped as he peered owlishly at Westcott.

"Geoffrey . . . did you *have* t'say 'well shot'?" he asked.

"Oh Lord, my pardons, sir, I—!"

Lewrie could keep his stern expression for only so long, then began to laugh out loud. "Well shot, mine arse! Hah!" which set Westcott to relieved nervous laughter, and amused the others, too.

Damme, but it hurts *t'laugh so hard!* Lewrie thought, wincing and yet unable to stop or calm his cackling.

"Yeovill, ye say I'm *allowed* red wine?" he asked. "Well, pour me a mug. I have it on the best authority that I'm well-shot, and prescribed it! I might even have *earned* it. Well-shot, my God!"

AFTERWORD

*I*f there had been shrinks around in 1805–1806, they could have diagnosed the British people as schizophrenic, swinging from elation to despair in mere months, with nary a bottle of Valium in sight.

Since the end of the brief Peace of Amiens in the spring of 1803, they had lived in dread of a gigantic army which Napoleon Bonaparte, now the self-crowned Emperor of France, had assembled along the Channel coast, and the thousands of landing craft and gunboats he had ordered built to carry it the seemingly short distance across the "Narrow Sea" and invade England, bringing down Napoleon's principal opposition to his ruling of all Europe, and perhaps a goodly chunk of the world. He did dream big!

When Lewrie is still in the Bahamas, he had no way of knowing that the presence of Admiral Villeneuve's massive fleet was not there to conquer anything in the Caribbean, but to lure off the Royal Navy so that that massive army and invasion fleet would meet little opposition during that "six hours of mastery of the English Channel, and I will be master of the world" boast. Nelson, of the "Immortal Memory", of course, put paid to that scheme by defeating the combined French and Spanish fleets at the Battle of Trafalgar, dying in the process.

There was great elation at first, followed by woe that Nelson was gone, and there were no other senior naval officers of his fame and stature in the wings to take his place.

Since that climactic defeat, Napoleon Bonaparte might have been in need of some Xanax or Valium, too, after spending so much money on his invasion forces, and seeing his grand scheme dashed to pieces. It was rumoured that Bonaparte groused that Villeneuve had lost because "I cannot be expected to be everywhere", as if had *he* been at Trafalgar, the result would have been a different kettle of fish! At one time, before he had attended a military academy in France and had become an artillery officer, Bonaparte had expressed a notion to go into the French Navy; it may be an apocryphal tale, something that he dreamed up in his less-than-truthful, self-serving memoirs.

At any rate, what is a tyrant and conqueror to do after such a setback? Why, go bash his enemies in Europe, on the ground!

Austria was still a threat, itching to avenge itself upon the French for earlier embarrassments in the field since 1792, and could not abide that Napoleon had gone down to Italy and crowned himself the king of that patchwork land, where the Austrians thought that *they* ruled the roost. The young Alexander, Tsar of All the Russias, despised Napoleon, feared his ambitions, and personally wished Napoleon punished for the murder of the Duc de Angoulême, and when the British offered lashings of silver for every hundred thousand troops, he took the deal eagerly. Along with Austria and Russia, the Prussians—well, they *were* Prussians, of the same sort that brought the delights of World Wars One and Two, almost as militaristic and despotic as the French had become, and the money sounded sweet to them, too.

When it appeared that a fresh grand coalition of European powers had arisen against poor little much-put-upon "Boney", encouraged by Nelson's victory, and Prime Minister William Pitt's cash stash, he had to act, and was surely more than happy to go bash the stuffings out of *somebody* to make up for it, and make him feel better.

The Austrians had improved their army and its tactics since the last time they'd been slobber-knockered by the French, but they *still* weren't quite up to snuff, and they just got reamed at the battles of Ulm, then the joint battle with their new Russian allies which happened at Austerlitz, Napoleon's most complete and crushing victories of his long career. To add insult to injury, he later went on to rip the Prussians a new one at Jena and Auerstädt, and add Prussia as part of Metropolitan France!

It's possible that the news of all those defeats were the cause of William Pitt's demise, which so stunned Commodore Popham when he learned of it. The people of Great Britain took all that bad news, and Pitt's death, pretty hard, too, and a great war-weariness set in once more. ("Doc, I just feel so *depressed*!")

The quick and easy conquest of the Cape Colony early in 1806 really didn't do much to lift their spirits, either, though the news that Popham sent back to London made it sound a lot grander than it really was.

No wonder, then, that in the middle of gloom and doom, news of Popham's conquest of Buenos Aires, and all the money appropriated in the process, set the London papers and the government aflame with praise. Patriotic Funds ordered presentation swords and complete sets of silver plate in his honour, and grand resolutions were announced in Parliament. When Popham's open letter to the merchants of London, in which he boasted of the immense profits that could be made there, was published, Commodore Popham was acclaimed as the New Nelson, which I suspect was his aim all along.

Admiralty, though, even with Popham's friend Earl Grey in charge as First Lord, was appalled that the Commodore had abandoned his post at the Cape and gone gallivanting off on a "Mad As A Hatter" escapade, profits be damned. Cape Town was left almost defenceless. There was talk of court-martial, despite the loud public accolades and fresh joy.

Commodore Sir Home Riggs Popham, inventor of the flag signals code, an endless font of ideas for aggressive action against the King's enemies (and his own advancement!), found that he had bitten off a bit more than he could chew when he took Buenos Aires. He'd been sold a thrilling bill of goods by that Colonel Miranda, a lecherous gad-fly who'd traipsed the Continent promoting his grand vision of a South America free of Spanish rule, united into a great republic of native peoples—meaning Spanish-descended *criollos*, not the real indigenous natives or the slaves—which could take its place on the world stage, in emulation of the American Revolution, and the relatively new United States. In the process, Miranda's assurances of people yearning to breathe free, and revolutionaries just champing at the bit to arise and open their markets to anyone who'd aid them, had grown grander and bigger over the years. In truth, though, except for some idle talkers in intellectual circles and wealthy salon society, it was all a fraud.

Resistance arose quickly, under the leadership of Sobremonte and Pueyrredón, as mentioned. In addition, there was a former French naval officer under the old Bourbon regime, Liniers, in Spanish service, who styled himself *Don* Santiago de Liniers, who took part; his name and presence utterly convinced Popham that it was all a French plot!

Liniers rode into Buenos Aires, claiming that he wanted to see to his family's needs, then was allowed to ride out, again, after he had scouted Brigadier Beresford's positions, the strength of patrols, and how few British troops were actually present. Liniers also had no trouble crossing the estuary to Montevideo and meeting with his fellow rebels, and the *reconquista* was on!

Barely a month after taking the place, by mid-July Brigadier Beresford knew that he was "in the quag" right up to his neck. Enemy forces were gathering rapidly from the ranches in the hinterland, and from the garrison and volunteers from Montevideo. Popham had very few boats to row guard to prevent the movement of troops, and his only warship, *Encounter,* could not sail up into the shallows where enemy fishing boats were ferrying men over in the night. *Diadem, Diomede,* and *Reliant* drew too much water to even get close to helping. Indeed, Captain Donnelly's *Narcissus* had spent her first day in the Plate Estuary aground on the Chico Bank, *far* from Buenos Aires!

It was not for nothing that in later years, once the nations of Argentina, Uruguay, and Paraguay had been carved out of the larger Spanish possessions, that the deep-water Canal Punta Indio was dug out from the docks of Buenos Aires to deeper water South of Montevideo!

Popham could give the unfortunate Beresford no help, and the weather did not cooperate, either. There were heavy rains, gusty gales, and heavy fogs. Popham could not even manage to get his ships to the wee port of Ensenada to take off Beresford's wounded, or evacuate the army. They might have saved themselves by marching down to Point Quilmes, where they'd landed, and been taken off by boats from the five transports that remained in the Estuary, from the mouth of the Cuello River, but Beresford stood his ground, and on the night of August 11th, 1806, his troops stood to-arms all night. On the morning of August 12th, he was attacked by overwhelming numbers, and, after suffering 48 dead, 107 wounded, and 10 missing, he was forced to surrender. The terms were fairly generous, but Brigadier Beresford and his remaining men were marched inland.

By now, Lewrie's part in the Buenos Aires fiasco was long done, but if you thought that Commodore Popham would tuck his tail beneath his legs and slink off like a frustrated fox, you've another think coming; the comedy of errors was only just starting!

Even though there were no Spanish merchant ships or warships in a thousand miles of the Estuary, Popham used his remaining squadron to "blockade" Buenos Aires (I'm sure *that* looked good in reports!) until he received a few re-enforcements from General Baird at the Cape of Good Hope. By this time, Admiralty had sent orders for his recall to London, and a replacement had been sent out.

With his re-enforcements, Popham tried to make a silk purse out of a sow's ear (perhaps to salvage his arse!) by making a stab at taking Montevideo! His few ships couldn't get close enough for their guns to make an impression, so he settled for going up the coast and taking the port of Maldonado and the island of Gorrete, where his troops could set up winter camps, on the 30th of October.

This defeat was considered an insult to the honour of British arms. Popham's replacement, Rear-Admiral Charles Stirling, arrived with a fresh army, and hopes expressed in London that not only would Buenos Aires and Montevideo be re-taken, but an expedition would also sail round the Horn and take the city of Valparaiso in Chile, then build a string of fortresses right cross the entire continent! London would make a virtue of necessity.

Stirling and his army commanders, General Samuel Auchmuty and Lieutenant-General John Whitelocke, had a second go at Montevideo in February of 1807, and took the place, being "gallantly carried".

From there, another go at Buenos Aires was launched, an army of twelve thousand men to do the job proper, this time.

Unfortunately, it was entrusted to Lieutenant-General Whitelocke, who was no brighter than Beresford had been. He led them cross the swampy lands near Quilmes and cross the Cuello, and right into utter disaster! Nearly 2,500 British soldiers were killed and Whitelocke's army was also forced to surrender, with Whitelocke meekly agreeing that all British forces would evacuate the Plate within two months.

Whitelocke was subsequently court-martialled, cashiered, and deemed "totally unfit and unworthy to serve His Majesty in any military capacity whatsoever."

"Wasn't the Navy's fault, Yer Honour, sir! Wasn't any of *our* doing!"

When Popham got back to England, he was also called before a court-martial board aboard HMS *Gladiator* at Portsmouth from March 6th to the 11th, and the sentence was as follows:

The court has agreed that the charges have been proved against the said Captain Sir Home Popham; that the withdrawing, without orders so to do, the whole of any naval force from where it is directed to be employed, and the employing it in distant operations against the enemy, more especially if the success of such operations should be likely to prevent its speedy return, may be attended with the most serious inconvenience to the public service, as the success of any plan formed by His Majesty's ministers for operations against the enemy, in which such naval force might be included, may by such removal, be entirely prevented. And the court has further agreed that the conduct of the said Captain Sir Home Popham, in the withdrawing the whole of the naval force under his command from the Cape of Good Hope, and the proceeding with it to Rio de la Plata, is highly censurable; but, in consideration of circumstances, doth adjudge him to be only severely reprimanded; and he is hereby severely reprimanded accordingly.

Good looks, good connexions, the "Petti-coat influence" of a good-looking wife, and all the smarm of a used-car salesman pulled Popham through, with only the slightest blot on his escutcheon. He went on to serve, again, zestfully babbling up schemes like former Speaker of the House Newt Gingrich, and enjoyed a long career . . . though when he served under "The Gallant Pellew" in 1813–1815, a man rightly famed as one of the finest and boldest frigate captains in the Royal Navy, it was said that Pellew couldn't stand the sight of him!

Ironically, after this British humiliation, there was one bright spot. The subjects of the Viceroyalty de la Plata, in uniting to defeat and oust the British, turned into revolutionaries intent on winning their independence! On May 25th, 1810, the *Primera Junta* was formed at Buenos Aires to throw off slothful and ineffective Spanish rule, and establish home rule in the new nation-states of Argentina, Paraguay across the Plate, and

Uruguay. News of the *Junta* caused the beginning of a series of uprisings throughout South and Latin America, culminating in the ultimate military and political victories of Simón Bolívar. Let's just caution, though, that winning independence didn't *exactly* result in Jeffersonian Democracy, as Colonel Mendoza wished to emulate!

A late friend of mine, Bob Enrione, was in Argentina during the Falklands War with a CBS Network news crew, and, due to extremely strict control and censorship by the military *junta*, had a lot of time on his hands, lounging round the hotel, sampling the famed local wines, and dining very cheaply on incredibly large, fine steak dinners. In the course of his rambles, he did, however, manage to talk with many Argentinans, and got the distinct impression that they thought that they might have been a *tad* too hasty in kicking the British out! Had they accepted British help in winning independence, they might have had a stable Parliamentary system, fair taxation, the best of older Spanish law and English Common Law combined, as it was in India under the East India Company and the later *Raj*, they imagined, and their country would have been spared all the "aggro" and "agita" of wars with their neighbours in the 1880s, and a sad parade of *juntas, el jefes*, and *generalissimos* that crushed every democracy that they set up. Who *knows* how it would have turned out? We'll never know, unless someone wishes to write an alternate-history sci-fi novel. Are there any takers out there?

So, there's the gallant Alan Lewrie, flat on his back and for a time in swaddles, *forced* to indulge his lazy streak, for a rare once, 'til he's strong enough to get back on his feet and make it as far as his quarter-gallery . . . and his wine-cabinet. The pity of it; all that time abed, and nary a woman in sight! It will be weeks before *Reliant* will anchor in Table Bay at Cape Town, and he can expect letters from home. Remember, no one told the post packets that he'd sailed off for the Plate Estuary!

When *Reliant* reaches England, she will surely be paid off, her officers and crew, except for the Standing Officers, scattered to the four winds, and the needs of the Fleet, and she might prove to be his *last* frigate. Lewrie is senior-enough, and experienced-enough, to be given an active commission into a larger ship. Might she be an older 64-gunner that could still prove useful on foreign stations, or will he be shoved aboard a Third Rate two-decker 74 and end up on gruelling blockade duty, for years on end?

In the back of Lewrie's mind, there are some dreads, too. As a part of

Commodore Popham's failed expedition, might some of the blame end up harming his career? Will Admiralty even *offer* him a new commission? Will he heal up sufficiently to *accept* one? He's in his fourties, now, and not as spry or as quick to heal as he was in his early years. If his wound cripples or lames him, how dreadful would life be, on half-pay, ashore for good, with no further part to play in ridding the world of Napoleon Bonaparte and his armies of "Frogs"? He's *had* his bucolic, peaceful years 'tween the wars, and hated every day of that time! Two or three months of rest would be more than welcome, but the rest of his *life*? The Navy, and war, are the only things he's *good* at!

Idling round his father's estate at Anglesgreen, smack-dab in the middle of his former in-laws' spite, his daughter's bile . . . *Pah!* And, would Lydia Stangbourne still think him dashing, assuming that she *ever* makes up her mind to trust him enough to re-marry? Would Lydia, and no one else, be enough for Lewrie's libidinous nature? He *knows* what happens when he's idle, and his eyes roam.

And, when *Reliant* pays off, what will become of Biscuit?

I fear you'll simply have to wait awhile longer to discover the answers to all those posers, but, here's a wee hint . . .

> *Farewell, and adieu, to you* Spanish *ladies,*
> *Farewell, and adieu, to you ladies of* Spain,
> *For we've received orders to sail for old England,*
> *but, we hope very shortly to see you, again!*